BOOK ONE
THE VALORIAN CHRONICLES

BEYOND
THE
MURAL

RYAN MCNEILL

SILVERSMITH
PRESS

Published by Silversmith Press–Houston, Texas
www.silversmithpress.com

ISBN 978-1-967386-35-2 (Softcover Book)
ISBN 978-1-967386-36-9 (eBook)

For Ashlyn—
who once picked up a paintbrush
and unknowingly opened a portal.
Your wonder lit the first spark
that became Sara's light.

CONTENTS

PREFACE

Seven long years of searching for answers had taken its toll. Special Agent Jack Sweeney, of the FBI, believed he had finally found the truth about what had happened to his wife, Lily. Instead of relief, he felt sick to his stomach. Losing his wife had been hard enough, but finding proof her death was more than a random murder twisted the knife deeper.

The files spread out before him on the dimly lit desk told a story he could hardly believe. Classified reports, encrypted communications, and a diary written in a hand he knew so well—Lily's hand—revealed a hidden world he had never imagined. His training told him he was crazy, yet the proof was right in front of him. On top of that, Jack had almost lost Sara too.

Jack stared down at the spread of documents in front of him. How could he have been so blind? Seven years . . . the truth sat right in front of him, wrapped in lies and buried in redacted reports. The memory of telling eight-year-old Jolene her mother was gone flashed in his mind, and something inside him snapped. His hand shot out, sweeping the papers off the desk, sending them scattering to the floor.

He slammed his fist into the desk, the sound echoing through the quiet room. It wasn't enough to release the fury boiling inside him.

"I should've seen it . . ."

Jack stood abruptly from his chair, taking a deep breath.

Bending down, he began gathering the scattered papers.

Then Jack slowly stood back up. He carefully placed the diary into a large envelope, including his personal notes and a video he'd compiled on an encrypted flash drive. He sealed it up. As he fixed the FedEx label to the package, addressed to the initials J.F., he couldn't help but feel like he was running out of time.

After the FedEx truck picked up his package, he went into his bedroom, packed his duffle bag with clothes, grabbed his passport and three extra clips for his Glock. He picked up his cell and dialed. Someone on the other end picked up.

"Meet me in thirty minutes," said Jack.

"Got it," the man on the other end replied.

"Have you taken care of the arrangements for my girls?" Jack asked.

"It's all taken care of. Don't worry. We'll see you soon."

Jack hung up the phone, grabbed his bag, and headed out. He sped as fast as he could to get to the interstate. The thirty-minute drive to the rendezvous point felt like it took forever. His eyes darted to the rearview mirror every few minutes.

"Nobody saw me . . . right?" He tried to convince himself, gripping the steering wheel tighter. His heart pounded in his chest, a dull throb refusing to settle. The feeling had gnawed at him ever since he had sent the package, a creeping sensation of being watched.

He took a breath. "Just get there, Jack. It's almost over." He checked his watch. Fifteen minutes.

By the time Jack pulled up to the secluded warehouse downtown, his nerves were frayed. There was nobody there. The parking lot was eerily empty. Jack glanced at his watch again. He had arrived about three minutes early. He parked the car and cut the engine but left the keys in the ignition—just in case.

His hand instinctively rested on the Glock at his side as he scanned the area through the window. The hairs on the back of his neck stood up.

Everything's fine. It's just your nerves, he thought, trying to calm the rising tension in his chest.

But that nagging voice in the back of his mind whispered otherwise.

He scanned the upper floors of the warehouse through his windshield, his trained eyes sweeping for any signs of movement. A flicker of doubt crossed his mind. Maybe sending the package had tipped them off. Maybe they knew.

Jack took a deep breath, trying to shake off the paranoia, though the cold pit in his stomach remained. His contact should have been there by now. He glanced at his watch once more. Two minutes.

"Come on. Just be on time," Jack muttered to himself.

His heart rate slowed, though his hand never left his sidearm.

Then it happened.

The crack of the rifle echoed across the warehouse lot, but Jack never heard it. His body slumped forward, lifeless before his mind could register what happened.

From the shadows, two black vans roared into view, their headlights cutting through the darkness as they screeched to a halt near Jack's car. The doors flew open, and men in dark clothing spilled out, moving with military precision. One of them, a heavyset figure with a commanding presence, barked orders as they surrounded the vehicle.

"Move! No traces," the leader growled.

Two men carefully lifted Jack's body from the car, wrapping it tightly in a dark tarp before carrying it to the back of one of the vans. Another team fanned out around the vehicle, wiping down every surface. The faint smell of cleaning solvents filled the air as they worked, removing fingerprints, blood, and any trace of glass or debris.

"Check his bag," the leader snapped, his voice low but sharp. "Anything on Lily—documents, drives, anything."

One of the men rifled through Jack's belongings, pulling out a worn leather bag. He unzipped it quickly, sorting through its contents with gloved hands. "Got something," he muttered, holding up a folder and a small black device.

"Good. Bring it," the leader replied, his tone clipped. He turned to the others. "Let's move."

Within minutes, the scene was cleared. The men climbed back into the vans, and the vehicles disappeared into the night, their engines fading into the distance.

The lot fell silent once more.

Five minutes later, the faint hum of an approaching car broke the stillness. Headlights pierced the darkness as the vehicle slowed and pulled alongside Jack's abandoned car.

Inside, the driver cursed under his breath, gripping the steering wheel tightly. "Oh God," he muttered. "Someone got here before we did."

The passenger, a woman with a tense expression, leaned forward, her sharp eyes scanning the empty lot. "We're too late," she said, her voice low but urgent. "We need to move. Get the girls to the garage immediately. They can't be left exposed."

The driver exhaled sharply, a mixture of frustration and dread in his voice. "We can't lose hope yet . . . but we'd better prepare ourselves. This isn't looking good."

CHAPTER 1

"Too much red," twelve-year-old Sara mused. Her brush hovered delicately over the canvas while studying an old photograph with worn edges propped on the easel. The photo was all muted browns and faded light—like time itself had tried to wash it clean but hadn't quite succeeded.

Outside, the rain pattered rhythmically against the windowpane, a soothing backdrop to the dim, cozy interior of her room. A cool breeze slipped through the slightly ajar window, carrying the scent of wet earth and the gentle murmurs of distant thunder. The pale, silvery light filtered in, like someone had taken a watercolor brush and washed out the sun. A dreary day in Muxley, the soft, ambient sound was a welcome companion, blending seamlessly with the scratch of her brush against the canvas.

"It needs a touch more green." As she leaned closer to the canvas, the faintest sigh escaped her lips. Her hand hovered above the painting, brush poised delicately.

The artwork depicted a tranquil spring morning in a forest, with a cozy log cabin nestled among the trees. Wisps of smoke curled from the chimney, carrying the illusion of warmth and life. A crystalline lake shimmered like glass in the background, framed by the cascading majesty of a distant waterfall.

1

Sara's lips pressed into a thin line as her brush touched the canvas again. She adjusted the green in the leaves, deepening their vibrancy, trying to capture the exact shade she saw in her memory.

As Sara looked at the photo once more, her eyes glazed over, and for a moment, the room seemed to fade. The edges of the photograph blurred in her vision as her mind filled with fragmented feelings—warmth, laughter, and the sense of safety only family could bring. She didn't remember their mother—not truly—but Jo's stories painted her in rich, tender tones.

Those summers lived in her memory like unfinished sketches—rough bark under her fingertips, the muddy smell of the lake, Jo's grin when their father got overly dramatic telling a story. Sara hadn't understood half the words, but she remembered the warmth in Jo's eyes. That had been enough.

Her chest tightened as she traced the photo's worn edges.

A sharp clap of thunder cracked across the sky, shaking the windowpanes like they might rattle off the frame. Sara blinked rapidly, her gaze snapping back to the photo.

Sara let out a shaky breath and wiped her free hand across her eyes. "Stay focused," she muttered, gripping the paintbrush a little tighter.

The sharp ring of her cell phone startled her. She glanced at it on the table, the screen glowing with Jo's name. Sara hesitated for half a second before picking it up.

"Hey," she answered, her voice soft but steady.

"Hey, kiddo," Jo's familiar voice crackled through

the line, carrying the faint background hum of traffic. "I'm about five minutes from home. You need anything? Art supplies, snacks, whatever? I'm making a quick stop."

Sara smiled faintly. "No, I'm good," she replied, forcing her tone to stay casual. "I think we're pretty stocked up."

"You sure? No last-minute requests? Don't make me come back out later," Jo teased lightly.

"Yeah, I'm sure," Sara said smiling. "Thanks, though."

"All right. Be there soon," Jo said.

As the line went dead, Sara set the phone down and turned back to the easel, her fingers curling around the brush once more. Her heart fluttered with a mix of excitement and nerves.

"Five minutes," she whispered to herself, glancing at the clock. Determination lit her eyes as she added the final touches, her brush gliding with precision and care.

The storm outside rumbled faintly, but Sara barely noticed. She was now lost in the colors, in the strokes capturing a piece of their past, her heart set on surprising Jo the moment she stepped through the door.

CHAPTER 2

The dim light of the library cast an amber glow across the worn wood floors, the gentle creak of Smith's chair punctuating the stillness as he hunched over the desk. The air was thick with the scent of old paper and salt, the latter carried by the sea breeze slipping in through the cracked window. The steady, rhythmic crash of waves against the rocky shore, mingled with the soft rustling of palm leaves outside, for a fleeting moment, was comforting.

Smith's pen scratched across the parchment with urgency. His usually steady hand faltered as he wrote, *"The darkness stirs once more,"* the ink smudging. He paused, the pen hovering, as he took a ragged breath. His gaze lifted to the portrait above the fireplace—a young girl, eyes serene and haunting.

The clock on the wall struck twelve, each chime reverberating through the quiet room like a judge's gavel. Smith set the pen down and rubbed the bridge of his nose, eyes squeezed shut against the memory that gnawed at him.

"Not again," he whispered, the words swallowed by the gentle hiss of the wind.

He folded the letter, slipping it into a wooden box carved with an intricate leaf symbol—now dulled with age and forgotten meaning. His thumb lingered over the carving, tracing its grooves. As his touch pressed into the symbol, a subtle warmth spread through the wood.

Smith pushed back from the desk, the chair scraping against the floor as he stood. He moved to the coat rack, slipping into his well-worn trench coat and adjusting the brim of his flat cap. A glance back at the library was all he allowed himself before descending the spiral staircase to the living room below.

Through the large windows below, Muxley's rain-slicked streets glistened under the pale glow of streetlamps. Raindrops drummed a steady, melancholy tune against the glass. Smith paused at the door, his eyes narrowing as he took in the quiet chaos of the city.

"I liked the library better," he muttered. He stepped out onto the front stoop and, with deliberate care, locked the bright-red door with a skeleton key. The key's metallic coldness pressed against his palm. As he slipped it back into his pocket, it seemed to dissolve into an intangible weight, hidden from the world.

Sara finished her last brush stroke as she heard the key in the door.

"Hey, Sara!" Jo called out as she stepped into their cozy two-bedroom apartment, shaking off droplets of rain as she dropped her bag on the floor. She hung her raincoat and umbrella on the coat rack. The rhythmic patter of rain outside continued.

"Hey, Jo," Sara said, glancing up from her painting with a small smile.

Jo kicked off her shoes and let out an exaggerated sigh. "What a day! Professor Farley was in full drill sergeant mode during anatomy class. I swear, my brain's fried," she said, running her fingers through her long brunette hair, still damp from the rain.

Sara watched as Jo moved through their small living space, the lines of exhaustion evident in her sister's posture. Jo's life had become a whirlwind of school, shifts at The Crowley's Coffee Shop, and responsibilities that weighed heavier than anyone their age should bear.

"Are you hungry?" Jo asked, peering into the tiny kitchenette with its mismatched dishes and the faint scent of last night's soup still lingering.

Sara nodded, putting down her brush. "Starved."

Jo chuckled softly as she opened the fridge. "Chicken salad okay?" she asked, glancing over her shoulder.

"Perfect," Sara replied, her eyes darting to the nearly finished painting propped on the easel. She felt a nervous flutter in her stomach.

"Great," Jo said, grabbing ingredients from the fridge. "I'll whip it up for you, then I need to get ready for my shift."

Sara's face fell. "Your shift? I thought you had the night off."

Jo hesitated, hearing the change in Sara's tone. She turned around, her eyes meeting her sister's. "I'm sorry, Sara," she said. "They're down two people tonight, and they called me in. We could use the extra money."

Sara tried to hide her disappointment.

Jo's expression softened as she walked over and rested a hand on Sara's shoulder. "I'll be back before you know it," she promised. "And when I get home, you can tell me all about your day."

"Okay," Sara said, forcing a smile. But as Jo turned back to the kitchen, Sara's gaze drifted to the painting.

Her fingers fidgeting with the hem of her shirt. The anticipation was building to an unbearable level, and she couldn't hold back any longer. "Hey, Jo . . . I was going to save this for later, but . . . I have something to show you," she said, her voice wavering with excitement and nerves.

Jo turned, a tired but affectionate smile on her face. "Something to show me, huh? All right, let's see it," she said, wiping her hands on a kitchen towel as she walked over.

Sara hesitated for just a moment before stepping aside to reveal the painting. Jo's eyes widened as they settled on the canvas. Jo's gaze moved over the small details. For a moment, the room fell silent, the rain outside the only sound filling the space.

But then, the warmth in Jo's expression shifted. Her eyes clouded over, and her jaw tensed.

"Jo?" Sara's hopeful voice barely reached her. Without a word, Jo stepped back, her hands trembling as she tried to steady herself. The kitchen towel slipped from her grasp, forgotten as her vision blurred with tears.

"I . . . I need a minute," Jo choked out, turning on her heel and rushing out of the room before Sara could react. The door to her bedroom clicked shut, followed by the muffled sound of a sob piercing through Sara's heart like a blade.

Sara stood frozen, the excitement bubbling inside her now replaced with a sinking feeling of shame. Her eyes dropped to the painting. She reached out, tracing the edge of the canvas with trembling fingers.

"I'm sorry," she whispered to the empty room.

The sound of muffled sobs eventually faded. Sara stood in the living room, staring at the closed bedroom door, wishing she could take back the moment that had triggered Jo's pain. She hugged her arms around herself.

The door creaked open. Jo emerged, her eyes red-rimmed but her expression composed. She avoided Sara's gaze as she moved to the hallway closet and pulled out her work apron and the familiar worn-out shoes she kept by the door.

"I'm heading out now," Jo said, her voice strained, barely above a whisper. She turned her back as she slipped on her raincoat and reached for her umbrella.

Sara swallowed hard, wanting to say something, anything, to make it right. "Jo, I . . ." she began, her voice cracking.

Jo paused, her hand resting on the doorknob. Jo let out a breath. "We'll talk later, okay?" she said, her tone neutral, carefully controlled. Without waiting for a response, she stepped out into the rain and closed the door behind her, leaving Sara in the dim glow of the living room.

The rain's rhythmic patter the only companion to her swirling thoughts. Sara sank onto the couch. She grabbed her blanket, pulled her knees up to her chest, and hugged them tightly, her gaze locked on the painting. The vibrant colors blurred as tears welled in her eyes, but she blinked them away, refusing to let them fall.

CHAPTER 3

Stepping into the rain, Smith opened his umbrella. The streets bustled even in the downpour—people rushing under awnings, taxis honking, the city alive and unaware. Smith moved through the throng, his tall frame cutting a determined path.

A man in a gray coat, a newspaper held up against the rain but peeking ever so slightly, stood across the street. Another figure leaned against a lamppost, seemingly casual but with too rigid a stance. Smith had a wry smile flickering across his lips. They were good, but not good enough.

"And I haven't even eaten yet," he muttered, humorless, as he approached Winker's Tavern. The black Mercedes idling nearby didn't escape his notice either. It reeked of surveillance.

Inside, the warmth of the tavern wrapped around him, the scent of ale and roasted meat mingling with the low hum of conversation. He spotted Mr. Mason in the far corner, his rugged face shadowed by the dim light.

Sliding into the booth without a word, Smith met Mr. Mason's gaze. "Been a long time," he said.

"Aye, Smith," Mr. Mason said, his Scottish lilt unmistakable, his tone low but edged with urgency. "Got yer message loud an' clear. The darkness stirs again, does it no'?"

Smith's expression tightened, a flicker of pain crossing his features. "Yes," he said. "I'm not sure how though."

Smith leaned in, voice low. "We need to be quick. We're being watched."

Mr. Mason's eyes darted to the windows and back. "Watched? I took every precaution tae keep us off the grid, did I no'?"

"It doesn't matter. They're here," Smith interrupted, his tone clipped, eyes scanning the room.

Mr. Mason reached into his coat, pulled out a small parcel wrapped in plain brown paper and, slid it across the table. "Here it is, just as ye asked. What's the plan now, then?"

Smith's fingers brushed against the package, a subtle nod of understanding passing between them. Before more could be said, a server approached, tray balanced on one hand, eyes too inquisitive for comfort. She set down two ales with a polite smile, lingering just long enough for Smith's attention to shift.

Smith leaned back. He picked up the glass. Mr. Mason did the same, their eyes meeting in a brief, knowing exchange. With a clink of glasses, they shared a drink.

Setting his glass down, Smith stood, his expression serious. "We'll rendezvous elsewhere. Watch your back," he said, voice low and resolute.

With a final nod to Mason, Smith navigated through the kitchen, the chef giving a knowing glance as he provided cover. The back exit led him into a narrow alley, the rain drumming steadily against the cobblestones, soaking through his coat and chilling him to the bone. The parcel felt heavier in his pocket than he remembered, but Smith, nevertheless, moved swiftly into the night, making sure he was not followed.

Sara lay curled up on the couch, the open pages of a sketchbook resting against her chest. She had fallen asleep.

The sound of the key turning in the lock jolted her awake. She blinked, disoriented for a moment. As the door creaked open, Jo stepped inside, shaking the light drizzle off her coat before hanging it on the hook by the door. Their eyes met, and Jo paused, taking in the sleepy, startled look on Sara's face.

"Hey," Jo said softly, her voice carrying the fatigue of a long shift.

Sara pushed herself up, rubbing the sleep from her eyes. "Hey," she echoed.

Jo walked over to the couch, her footsteps soft against the worn floorboards. "I didn't mean to wake you," she said.

Sara shook her head, a small yawn escaping. "It's okay. I wasn't really sleeping," she said.

A beat of silence stretched between them. Jo looked down, fingers fidgeting with the hem of her shirt. "I'm sorry about earlier. About everything, really," she said.

Sara sat up straighter, the sketchbook slipping from her lap onto the couch. "Jo, it's okay," she said.

Jo's eyes turned to the painting propped up on Sara's easel.

"No, it's not okay," Jo said, meeting Sara's eyes. "You put so much into that painting, into trying to bring some of that happiness back for me, for us. And I pushed it away because I couldn't handle how it made me feel. Honestly, it just caught me off guard. It wasn't your fault."

Sara's eyes softened, the sting of their earlier exchange fading as she reached out to take Jo's hand. "I just wanted to share something good with you, Jo. I didn't mean to make you sad."

Jo smiled as she squeezed Sara's hand. "I know. And it was beautiful, Sara. I see that now." She let out a breath she hadn't realized she'd been holding. "So how about we do something fun tomorrow? Just us. We could go to Savor Street Market, get those pastries you love, and maybe even look for a frame for your painting?"

Sara's face lit up, the fatigue forgotten as excitement sparkled in her eyes. "Really? You're not working?"

"Nope," Jo said.

A smile broke across Sara's face. "Deal."

CHAPTER 4

Eli Whitaker glanced up from his computer monitor as Smith entered the room, his face shadowed by the dim glow of Lucy's interface. The faint hum of the AI system was the only sound filling the air with an electric tension.

"I've found something," Eli said. He gestured toward the screen where a paused video feed flickered faintly. "Lucy flagged this from a surveillance camera near Muxley. It's . . . strange."

Smith stepped closer, his eyes narrowing as he glanced at the interface. "How's Lucy coming along?" he asked.

Eli's fingers flew over the keyboard, the faint glow of the monitor reflecting off his glasses. "Better than expected," he replied. "She's learning to process anomalies faster, even those outside her initial parameters. This—" he gestured to the video feed, "—is her latest catch. The distortion, the spikes in energy—it's all flagged in real time now."

Smith nodded, his gaze briefly shifting to the sleek hardware rig surrounding Eli's workstation. Cables snaked across the desk, connecting custom-built processors and a translucent server tower pulsing with faint, rhythmic light. Lucy's logo—a stylized *L* encased in a hexagon—hovered faintly on the screen, its soft blue glow complementing the endless streams of cascading code.

"She's a bit . . . temperamental, though," Eli added wistfully as he tapped a command. The screen momentarily froze, then recalibrated itself with precision. "I've had to rewrite half her adaptive learning scripts this week just to keep her from overloading. But she's getting there."

"Good," Smith said.

Eli hit play on the feed. The scene depicted a wide, empty field under a setting sun, the grass overgrown and wild. For a moment, it seemed innocuous, just another forgotten stretch of land. Then Eli paused it again, zooming in with practiced precision.

"See this?" he said, pointing to the faint shimmer on the edge of the frame. "Lucy caught it immediately—energy distortion. It's subtle, but it shouldn't be there."

Smith leaned closer as Eli resumed the video. A boy, maybe twelve years of age, wandered into the frame, his figure small against the vast expanse of the field. He moved with curiosity, his head swiveling as though searching for something. In his hand, he carried a flashlight, its beam jittering over the uneven terrain. The footage jumped slightly, and the boy crouched, his flashlight apparently illuminating something half-buried in the grass—a metallic object glinting faintly in the fading light.

Smith's expression hardened as the object began to glow faintly on the screen. "The Abyssal Key," he murmured.

Eli glanced up sharply. "You're sure?"

Smith nodded.

Eli hesitated, his fingers pausing mid-command. "What's it doing here? And why now?"

Smith didn't answer immediately, his eyes fixed on the screen as the glow intensified. The boy froze, staring as the light grew brighter, his face illuminated in crimson. Then—a figure. Tall, shrouded in shadow, emerged, its form barely distinguishable through the distortion of the feed. The boy stumbled back, his face pale with fear as the figure loomed closer. The footage cut to static.

Smith straightened. "That's all?"

Eli nodded grimly. "The feed ends there. Whatever happened next . . . it wasn't captured."

Smith's gaze lingered on the blank screen. "How long ago?"

"Two weeks," Eli replied. "Lucy cross-referenced the coordinates. It's the same field where those agents disappeared years ago." Eli hesitated. "If that's the Abyssal Key, then . . ."

Smith exhaled. "It's him."

Eli rubbed his temples, leaning back in his chair. "So its confirmed . . ."

Smith shook his head. "It doesn't matter. Focus on what we can control. We know where this is heading—what his ultimate target might be."

Eli didn't press further. Instead, he leaned forward, his fingers flying over the keyboard as Lucy's interface responded with cascading streams of data. "I'll reroute Lucy's surveillance grids, extend the net. If there's more activity, we'll find it. But Smith . . . this changes everything."

Smith nodded curtly. "We adjust the focus. But the plan remains. Be ready to go dark."

Eli leaned back, his eyes narrowing. "And the boy?"

Smith paused, his hand resting lightly on the back

of Eli's chair. "If he's still alive, . . . then he's already part of the game."

The lively hum of Savor Street Market surrounded Jo and Sara, a symphony of chatter, clinking teacups, and the occasional burst of laughter from nearby vendors. Sara crouched near a street corner, her pencil moving in quick, precise strokes across her sketchpad as the guitarist strummed an upbeat tune. The man's fingers danced over the strings, his hat tipped low to shade his face. A soft smile tugged at Sara's lips as she captured the play of sunlight on his instrument.

Jo leaned against a lamppost nearby, watching her sister. "You could do this all day, couldn't you?" she teased.

Sara glanced up, tucking a loose strand of hair behind her ear. "If he keeps playing like that, maybe."

When the guitarist finished and tipped his hat to the small crowd, Jo nudged Sara with her elbow. "Come on, Picasso, there's more market to explore."

The two strolled through the market, weaving between stalls overflowing with ripe fruit, handwoven scarves, and sparkling jewelry. A cheese vendor called out, offering samples, and Sara hesitated before plucking a morsel from the tray. The sharp tang lingered on her tongue as Jo sipped a steaming cup of chai from the tea stall across the way. At the fish market, Sara couldn't help but laugh as a vendor launched a silver-scaled fish through the air to a grinning customer, cheers erupting from the crowd.

But for Sara, as the hours stretched on, the laughter and noise, once pleasant, now seemed to echo too loudly in her ears. Her hands fidgeted with the strap of her bag as her steps faltered.

When they stepped out of a quaint tea shop, Jo turned toward a nearby stall, her attention caught by a display of hand-painted pottery. Sara lingered behind. A group of children dashed past, nearly knocking her into a man carrying a tray of pastries. She stumbled, muttering a soft apology, and when she looked up, Jo was gone.

"Jo!" Sara called out. Determined, she pushed through the bustling throng, careful not to jostle the other patrons.

Jo's going to be worried sick, she thought anxiously. She won't know where I am. She won't be able to—

Sara turned her head for a moment.

"*Oomph!*" Sara collided with a man. The impact sent Sara stumbling backward, her breath knocked out of her. She landed on the cobblestone ground, momentarily disoriented as her vision blurred and a high-pitched ringing filled her ears.

Blinking to clear her vision, Sara sat up, looked upward—and froze. The man she had collided with was watching her. His gaze was piercing, as though he could see straight through her. He didn't say a word.

As Sara tried to steady herself, her hand brushed against something. Looking down, she realized a small, brown-wrapped package had fallen next to her. Without thinking, she picked it up. The rough paper felt warm to the touch, almost alive.

The man's eyes turned to the package in her hands, and for the briefest moment, his expression shifted—something between alarm and urgency. Before Sara could react, a strange blue glow began to emanate from the package, spreading quickly to engulf her entirely.

A surge of energy coursed through Sara's body, and the world around her seemed to slow to a crawl. Every detail of the bustling market sharpened in her mind—the laughter of children, the distant clang of a cash register, even the faint buzz of a fly nearby. She could see and hear everything with unnerving clarity, as though her senses had suddenly expanded beyond their limits.

Sara's gaze darted back to the man, who now stood perfectly still, his figure partially obscured by the glow. He seemed to be watching her even more intently, as though waiting for something.

The man extended a hand to help her up. As she reached for his hand, he tilted his head. "So . . . it's you," he murmured.

Just as quickly as it had begun, the moment ended. Sara blinked, and the blue glow dissipated. She glanced around in confusion, but the man was gone. It was as if he had vanished into thin air.

"Sara?!" Jo's frantic voice pulled her back to reality. Sara opened her eyes to see Jo kneeling beside her.

"Jo?" Sara's voice trembled. "Wh-What happened? Where . . . where did he go?"

"Who?" Jo asked. "I backtracked as soon as I realized we got separated. I was only a few feet ahead." A crowd began to gather near them. "I found you lying on the ground. Are you okay?"

Sara blinked, her mind racing. "The man," she said quickly, her voice rising. "There was a man. He tried to help me up. I saw him. He was right here."

Jo's frown deepened. "Sara, no one was here when I got to you. Just me."

Sara shook her head, the image of the man vivid in her memory. "No . . . no, he was real. He . . . he had dark eyes and this calm voice. He told me—" She stopped, looking to her side where the package had been.

Jo's grip on her arm tightened slightly. "Sara," she said gently, "there was no man. When I got here, you were lying on the ground. Are you sure you didn't just faint? Maybe you got too much sun?"

Sara opened her mouth to argue but hesitated. Her head still felt foggy. She glanced around, her gaze darting through the crowd. No sign of the man—just unfamiliar faces milling about, none of them even remotely familiar.

"I . . ." Sara's shoulders slumped. "Maybe you're right. Maybe I just . . . imagined him. I don't know. I feel so light-headed." She let Jo help her to her feet, wobbling slightly before regaining her balance.

"Maybe we should head home. You look pale.", said Jo.

"Yeah," Sara agreed. "I think I've had enough sun for one day."

As they made their way home, Sara didn't bring up the strange encounter with the man. Yet the memory of the blue glow and his cryptic words lingered. As she thought more about it, if she were to tell Jo about it, what would she even say? I ran into a man who was glowing blue and zapped me with blue electricity while uttering cryptic words? The thought alone made Sara question her own sanity, let alone trying to explain it to Jo.

Later that evening, as they settled in to watch TV, Sara's mind remained elsewhere. They both sat on the couch, but Sara barely registered the Syfy show on the screen.

"Hey, Jo?" Sara yawned. "I'm tired. I think I'm going to turn in for the night."

"Okay. Rest well," said Jo as she leaned over and gave her sister a hug.

Sara got up and walked to her room. Her thoughts returned to the man in the market—his intense gaze, the blue glow, and his words, "So . . . it's you."

CHAPTER 5

That night Sara had a dream.

She wandered through Muxley's streets, though something felt wrong. The buildings leaned at odd angles, stretched taller than they should be, their windows dark and hollow. She didn't remember how she got here. The sky above was a color she couldn't name.

The pavement shimmered as though slick with rain, yet when she stepped forward, her shoes left no sound. The air was thick—too thick—as though pressing in on her from all sides.

The people . . . They weren't right either.

Trench-coated figures brushed past her, their faces blurred, hollowed out as if someone had erased their features. They moved without hesitation, without breath, without being.

Muxley was never silent.

But here, there was nothing. No cars, no distant voices, not even the whisper of wind. The silence pressed against her ears, heavy and unnatural.

Sara turned a corner, and ahead of her stood a gnarled oak tree with scorched, blackened bark, its branches brittle and bare. Acorns dropped from above, striking the pavement with a sharp crack—but instead of rolling, they shattered like glass.

She reached down, but before her fingers touched one, there was suddenly . . . a howling wind.

In the wind . . . something stirred—not sound, not

21

exactly. More like a thought slipping into her mind. A whisper not spoken but placed.

And then—the weight in her hand.

She looked down. A paintbrush.

She hadn't picked it up. Hadn't even seen it before now. But it was there, its handle warm and smooth, pulsing with a faint glow.

The glow spread, seeping into her skin like liquid light, weaving through her veins in streaks of vibrant blue. It hummed inside her, awakening something she didn't understand.

Before she could process it, she wasn't standing anymore.

Her feet left the ground.

Sara let out a breathless gasp as gravity lost meaning. She floated upward, the wind curling around her like unseen hands guiding her toward the side of a looming building.

She wasn't afraid.

She reached the wall. Something deep inside her—something instinctual—told her what to do.

Her hand lifted, bristles sweeping across the surface.

The bristles touched the wall.

And the world erupted.

Deep greens. Bursts of gold. Electric purple. Streaks of light danced beneath her touch, unfurling like roots and sky all at once. She moved through the air from one end of the wall to the next. The city of Muxley seemed to vanish.

Sara had no concept of time. The experience seemed to last for hours, yet maybe it was just a few minutes. Then the mural twisted and reshaped.

In its place—a landscape unlike anything she had seen before.

Towering mountains. Rivers of light. Fields of golden flowers stretched endlessly. And beneath a gnarled tree stood a figure.

Tall. Shadowed. Waiting.

A sudden light burst from the wall.

Sara reeled backward. A cry caught in her throat as she crashed onto the pavement.

And then—it stepped out of the mural.

Wings.

They unfurled in an instant, their edges rippling with iridescent hues gleaming against the void.

Eyes—silver, piercing, knowing.

The figure moved toward her, its presence both beautiful and terrifying.

Sara couldn't move.

Her lips parted to scream—

But no sound came . . . .

Then . . . the vision shattered.

Sara jerked awake, her chest heaving, her sheets tangled around her legs.

For a moment, the dream still clung to her. The room swayed—or maybe she did.

The moonlight coming through the curtains painted silver lines along the walls, casting shadows.

She dragged in a breath, pressing her palms to her face. "It was just a dream," Sara said aloud.

Except—her hands glowed.

Sara froze.

She stared down at her fingers.

Blue. Gold. Purple. The same colors from the mural.

The same streaks of light flowing through her veins in the dream.

Sara shook her hands "No . . ." she whispered. The colors did not go away.

She scrambled out of bed, her heart hammering, racing to the kitchen. She turned the light on, turned on the faucet at the sink and thrust her hands under the water. To her amazement, the water ran clear. "What the . . .?" Sara whispered.

She pulled her hands back, staring.

After a few minutes, the colors faded, but deep down, she swore she could still feel the glow beneath her skin.

"What's happening to me?"

For a moment, she considered waking Jo. But what would she say? That she had a dream—no, a vision— where she painted something impossible, where something stepped out of her art? That the paint had followed her back?

Sara stood there for a long time lost in thought. With a sigh, she turned off the light and made her way back to bed, exhaustion weighing her down.

She slipped beneath the covers, closing her eyes and willing herself to calm, though the echoes of wings and the soft blue glow haunted her mind.

Sara no longer knew if the dream had been *just* a dream.

The Mountain Citadel loomed over the jagged peaks like a specter, its stone spires rising defiantly against the darkened sky. Inside, the towering halls whispered with unseen forces, their dark crown moldings casting jagged shapes against the marble floors. Tinted windows framed a sky heavy with storm clouds, but within these walls, the true storm resided in the chamber at the heart of the citadel.

Azazel Blackthorn's sanctuary.

The chamber was as much a throne as it was a prison. Vast bookshelves lined the walls, filled with ancient tomes, each crackling with forbidden knowledge. Silver candelabras burned with a soft, flickering glow, illuminating the massive desk at the center. Resting upon its polished surface was a small metal box, its surface etched with arcane markings. The faint red glow emanating from its seams pulsed like a heartbeat, slow and deliberate.

Azazel stood at the desk, his posture both commanding and composed. His short black hair framed a face carved in pale angles, his eyes hollow pools of darkness catching the dim candlelight. A ring embedded with a crimson stone pulsed faintly on his hand, casting shifting patterns along the veins of his long, slender fingers.

His gaze lingered on the box for a moment longer, and for an instant, something stirred in him—a memory, unwanted but persistent of a grand hall bathed in golden light. Banners hung from the vaulted ceiling. Voices raised in unity.

The illusion fractured at the sharp knock on the heavy doors.

Azazel's fingers brushed over the box before sliding it into a hidden compartment in the desk.

"Enter."

The doors creaked open. Sykes, Azazel's most trusted operative, entered first, moving with the careful confidence of a man who had long learned how to measure his steps in this place. Two more figures followed, their postures rigid, their eyes downcast.

"The boy is ready to begin, sir," Sykes reported.

Azazel's smile deepened. "Good. Transfer him to the underground and inform me once he's there."

Sykes inclined his head. "Sir, there's also been a . . . development."

Azazel's expression did not change, but something in the room shifted.

Sykes continued. "A surge of blue energy was detected in Muxley. It was faint but unmistakable."

Azazel's fingers stilled against the desk.

The second operative, a thin, sharp-featured woman, took a careful step forward. "It was registered yesterday. We dismissed it at first—an anomaly, perhaps a malfunction—but then, late last night, another incident occurred."

Azazel's eyes darkened. "Go on."

She swallowed. "A mural appeared overnight. It was unlike anything we've encountered for some time."

Sykes picked up where she left off. "The operatives who saw it described it as unnatural. It hummed with the old magic, a signature that matches Valoria before its fall." He exhaled. "And word is spreading through town about it."

Azazel remained motionless.

"That is not all," the woman added carefully. "One of our men at the Savor Street Market claims to have witnessed something unusual."

Azazel turned fully to face her, his presence a storm on the cusp of breaking. "Explain."

Sykes answered. "A girl. Young. She collided with an older man. The operative reported that, for a moment, her energy shifted. He swears he saw blue light around her hands before it faded."

Azazel's ring pulsed in response as his grip on the desk tightened ever so slightly, though his face remained impassive.

For a long moment, the room was silent, save for the faint flicker of candle flames. Then Azazel moved—not rushed, but with an eerie, calculated stillness, stepping toward the tall windows overlooking the chasm below.

"And tell me," he said, his voice smooth but razor-edged, "what else have these watchful operatives of yours failed to retrieve?"

The second operative hesitated. "We thought we had all the blue orbs . . . sir . . . We must have missed one . . ."

Azazel's fingers twitched.

A reddish shimmer pulsed through the air, threads of it slithering toward the operative. The moment it touched his skin, he jerked upright—lifted by some unseen force—and yanked him skyward. His throat seized. He clawed at it, legs kicking, but no force was visible, only the unnatural stillness of the room and the wet, ragged sound of his breath failing him.

Azazel's voice remained soft. Too soft. "I have waited centuries for this moment."

The operative's feet kicked uselessly in the air. His face darkened, his lips parting in a choking, soundless plea.

The sharp-featured woman stepped forward, breaking Azazel from the memory. "We only wish to ensure the success of your plan, sir. If you believe handling the situation yourself is best, we stand by your judgment."

Azazel tilted his head. His fingers flicked, and the suffocating operative crumpled to the floor, gasping for air.

His hollow eyes lingered on the others. "Find the girl."

Sykes stepped forward again, adjusting the cuffs of his coat. "Sir, what of Smith? Should we prepare for his interference?"

At the mention of the name, Azazel's gaze darkened. The glow of his ring intensified.

Smith.

The name was a blend of disdain and anticipation.

"He seems to still be clinging to the past." Azazel turned back toward the window, watching the mist curl along the jagged peaks. "But soon, he will see there is no room for relics like him in my new world. Leave him to me."

Sykes nodded. The other two recovered themselves, retreating toward the doors.

The heavy wood creaked closed behind them with a resounding thud.

Silence.

Azazel stood motionless before the glass, watching the storm gather over the mountains.

He thought of the blue light. The girl.

He reached for the glass of crimson wine on the table beside him, swirling the liquid slowly before raising it to his lips.

The bitter taste grounded him, but for the first time in years, he felt it—the whisper of something beyond his grasp.

He exhaled through his nose, slow and measured.

"This complication will be dealt with," he murmured.

His grip tightened around the glass, and with a sharp crack, the stem snapped in his hand.

Deep red spilled over his fingers.

Azazel barely glanced at the broken shards before setting them aside.

His eyes burned with new determination.

"We'll find her . . . And Smith."

A gust of wind rattled the glass windows as the storm roared to life.

CHAPTER 6

"Hey, Sara," Jolene glanced up briefly from the news article she read on her cell phone. "Sleep well?"

Sara managed a small smile. "Yeah, pretty well," she replied, her words belying the strange night she had endured. She hesitated, glancing at Jo already absorbed in what she was reading. "Actually, Jo, I . . ."

Jo didn't look up, her attention focused on the screen in front of her. Sara hesitated. "I had this really vivid dream last night," she finally said.

"Hmm?" Jo muttered distractedly, scrolling to the next page. She took a bite of her oatmeal and squinted at something on the screen. "Weird," she said.

Sara blinked as Jo's focus remained firmly on her phone. The moment passed, and Sara forced a small laugh and reached for her own bowl of oatmeal.

Jo tapped her phone. "It's that field again," she said, half to herself. "Out past Mulligan Road . . . You know, the one people always talk about—the so-called 'haunted' one."

"The one with all the conspiracy theories?" Sara asked, raising an eyebrow. "That field?"

"Yeah," Jo replied, her voice tinged with skepticism. "You know, the same field where those two FBI agents disappeared years ago. Now there's a report about a boy going missing out there. He was supposedly out exploring with some friends, and they said he wandered off and never came back. They've got search teams combing the place."

Sara frowned, a faint unease creeping over her. "What was he doing out there?"

Jo shrugged, scrolling the page to skim the article further. "Same thing most kids do when they hear all those stories, I guess. It's practically a rite of passage for anyone looking to prove they're brave or whatever. But this time, the kid didn't come home."

"Hmm. That is weird," said Sara. ". . . And the FBI's back on it?"

"Looks like it," Jo said, shaking her head. "But who knows if they'll find anything. That place is infamous for leading people in circles. Some of those conspiracy sites say it's a vortex or something." Jo rolled her eyes. "People always need a reason to make a creepy place even creepier."

Jo scrolled back up on her screen, her gaze catching on another link. "Hey, Sara, look at this," she said, holding her phone up for Sara to see the article.

Sara's eyes widened as she took the phone from Jo's hand. The headline and accompanying image read: "Citizens Perplexed by Large Mural." The words seemed to leap off the screen. She read on, absorbing the details of the mural painted on the brick wall behind Walter's General Store on 5th Avenue—a fixture of their community.

Her heart raced as she studied the image. The mural depicted a sprawling landscape bathed in the soft hues of twilight, with majestic mountains towering in the distance. The colors were vibrant and rich. But it was the central figure in the mural giving Sara pause—a mysterious woman with flowing robes, her face obscured by shadow, standing beneath an ancient, gnarled tree. Two large figures loomed in the distance behind her.

A sense of déjà vu washed over her, mingling with a growing sense of unease. Could it be . . . ?

But Sara pushed aside her doubts, unwilling to entertain the notion the mural could be connected to her own strange dream. She forced a casual tone as she handed the phone back to Jo.

"Yeah, it's pretty impressive," she remarked, her voice carefully neutral.

"Well, it's definitely got people talking," said Jo, her tone light as she got up to clear her dishes.

Sara nodded absently, her gaze lingering on Jo's phone still sitting on the table.

Jo wiped her hands on a dish towel and turned back to Sara. "Hey, now that I think about it—what were you trying to tell me earlier? Before I interrupted you with the stuff about the missing boy?"

Sara blinked, startled by the question. "Oh . . . nothing," she said quickly, forcing a smile. "It's nothing important."

Jo gave her a curious look, tilting her head. But then she shrugged, walked to the table, grabbed her phone, and picked up her school bag. "Okay, if you're sure. I've got to head out. Don't forget to lock up before you leave, all right?"

"Yeah, sure," Sara replied, her voice distant as Jo bustled out the door. The front door clicked shut behind her, and Sara sat alone at the table, staring at the empty space where Jo's phone had been.

Her fingers brushed against the tabletop as her thoughts churned. The dream, the glowing paint on her hands, the mural—it was too much to ignore. And yet . . . she couldn't bring herself to say it out loud. Not to Jo. Not yet.

Sara grabbed her bag to head out for school. "It's just a coincidence," she said to herself, though the words felt hollow. "It has to be."

The lair hummed with an eerie stillness, its cavernous walls lit by the crimson glow of Azazel's ring. Shadows stretched long and jagged, twisting with the faint, rhythmic flicker of the boy's brush on the mural.

Azazel stood at a distance, his arms crossed, watching. Each stroke brought the image closer to life: a towering structure of jagged spires encased in shadow and flame. But the process itself was far from ordinary.

The boy, no older than twelve, hovered inches above the ground, suspended by an unseen force. Streaks of light—red, gold, and a sickly green—traced each movement of his brush, the colors bleeding into the air before fusing into the mural. The glowing veins running up his arm pulsed in time with each stroke.

Azazel's expression darkened as he observed the boy's trembling form. The scene rippled faintly on the mural's surface, the painted flames flickering like real fire. The jagged spires seemed to stretch, reaching toward the edges of the wall as if yearning to break free.

For a moment, the hum of the lair faded, replaced by a memory clawing its way to the forefront of Azazel's mind.

He stood atop a ridge, his voice ringing out over a battlefield bathed in twilight. Below, warriors in shimmering black armor awaited his command. Their leader—a towering figure with a helm gleaming like obsidian—hesitated, his blade poised between loyalty and doubt.

"Your King sends you to die for the illusion of preserving unity between the realms." Azazel's voice was sharp. "He clings to fragile ideals while you are left to fight his wars. But with me . . . you can transcend such petty causes. With me, you can become gods."

The air had tasted of ash and blood. Azazel remembered the way the leader's hand had tightened on his hilt, the faint flicker of hope in his eyes giving way to something darker.

The memory fractured, splintering as the boy's brush reached the mural's final stroke.

"Good," Azazel said, voice low but commanding.

The boy swallowed hard and nodded, his focus unwavering despite the strain. As he applied the final stroke, a crackling sound filled the chamber, like distant thunder. The mural pulsed, its surface rippling as though alive.

Azazel stepped forward. From within his dark robes, he withdrew a red orb, its crimson core swirling with energy like liquid fire. The orb's glow intensified as it neared the mural, casting sharp shadows across Azazel's face.

"Now," Azazel said, voice soft but laden with power.

He held the orb aloft, and the energy within it surged outward, a tendril of red light snaking through the air and latching onto the mural. The painted surface erupted with life, the jagged spires vibrating as though shaken by an unseen wind. The flames on the mural roared to life, flickering with intensity lighting up the entire chamber.

The boy collapsed to the ground with a gasp, his brush clattering to the floor. His wide eyes remained fixed on the glowing portal now pulsating before him.

Azazel lowered the orb, the tendrils of light retracting into its core. The mural had transformed, no longer just a painting but now a shimmering window, its surface undulating like liquid fire.

"Perfect," Azazel murmured.

Sykes stepped forward cautiously. "The team is ready, sir," he said.

Azazel didn't respond immediately. His attention remained fixed on the mural. "Send them," he said finally, his tone sharp. "When they retrieve the armor, have them return it here to be transported to the warehouse."

Sykes nodded.

He motioned to four of his operatives who moved toward the portal, their forms outlined by the crimson glow. As they stepped up to the mural, the surface rippled like water, swallowing them whole.

Azazel turned his gaze to the boy. "Rest. Your work is not done."

The boy nodded weakly, collapsing back onto the cold stone floor. The glowing veins on his arm dimmed but never fading entirely.

Azazel stepped closer to the painted wall. His ring pulsed faintly as he reached out, his fingers brushing the edge of the mural. The painted flames seemed to hiss under his touch.

"This," he whispered, more to himself than anyone else, "is only the beginning."

CHAPTER 7

After school, Sara went and sat alone in the park, her easel set up beneath the shade of an old oak tree. The smell of fresh-cut grass and the hum of the distant crowd blended into the background as she tried to focus on her painting. Across the field, a group of boys played a loud, energetic game of football. Sara recognized Devin Thompson, with his usual confident swagger unmistakable even at a distance. Devin was the star college quarterback for the Muxley Wildcats. Everybody knew Devin.

Sara dipped her brush into a streak of blue, forcing herself to concentrate on the canvas. She came here to forget about the dream, to ignore the glow on her hands that morning and the strange man at the market haunting her thoughts. She thought it would be a good escape. Sara had intended to go to Walter's General Store to see if the mural there was the one from her dream, but she wasn't ready for that.

"Set . . . hut, hut!" Devin's voice carried across the park, drawing Sara's attention. She glanced up just in time to see him launch a perfect spiral through the air, the football cutting cleanly across the field.

"Nice throw, Dev!" Demetri, Devin's best friend, called, clapping him on the back after the catch.

Devin grinned, brushing imaginary dust off his shoulder. "Yeah, what can I say? Your pass rush looked like it came out of kindergarten recess."

Laughter rippled through the group, and Devin flashed

his trademark grin. He was the picture of effortless confidence—a leader on the field.

Sara let out a small sigh and turned back to her painting, determined to shut out the noise. But the colors on her canvas blurred, overtaken by the unwelcome thoughts forcing their way in—the dream too vivid to forget, the shadowed figure watching, and that glow curling around her fingers. None of it made sense. And part of her didn't want it to.

But something made her pause.

The shadow stretched across her easel.

"Sara Sweeney?"

The smooth, deliberate voice made her heart stop. She looked up sharply, paintbrush slipping from her fingers as her eyes met the four men standing in front of her. Four of them—black suits, blank faces, and eyes that seemed to see too much.

"Don't be alarmed," the leader said, his voice calm but unsettling. "We're here as friends."

Sara instinctively leaned back, her pulse quickening. "I—I don't know who you are."

The man crouched down, picking up her fallen paintbrush with almost too much care. "We know about what happened at the market the other day," he said, holding out the brush. "Our friend was worried about you. He asked us to check in."

Sara's paused. How do they know about the market, she thought. Her skin prickled with unease, and she stood quickly, gathering her supplies. "I need to get home. My parents are waiting for me."

A cruel expression passed across the man's face. He smiled. "Sara, we know your parents aren't home."

The words hit her like a blow. How could he know that?

"Please, let me go!" Her voice broke as she stumbled back a step, her belongings clattering to the ground.

Across the field, Devin turned at the sound of her cry. He frowned, motioning to his friends. "Hey, what's going on over there?"

Demetri glanced up. "Some guys hassling her, maybe?"

"Doesn't look right," Devin muttered, already jogging toward the scene. "Come on."

The four men in suits turned at the sound of Devin's voice. "Hey!" he called, his tone sharp. "What's going on here?"

"This is not your concern, boy," the lead man replied.

Devin scoffed, stepping closer with Demetri and a couple of others at his back. "Who are you calling a boy, pencil neck? Why don't you leave her alone?"

Sara glanced up, relief flashing across her face as Devin stood between her and the men. But the lead man's expression remained blank, unbothered.

"You don't want trouble," the man said, a warning buried in his tone. "Take your friends and go."

"Not happening." Devin's eyes narrowed. "Back off."

Without thinking, Devin snatched up the football from Demetri and hurled it at the nearest man. The man barely moved. He just lifted one hand and casually swatted the ball aside, like brushing away a fly. It hit the ground with a dull thud.

"What the . . . ?" Devin's voice faltered, his brain struggling to process what he just saw.

The men moved then—fast. Too fast. Devin's friends

barely had time to react before the suited figures disarmed them, knocking them aside with impossible ease. Devin staggered back as the lead man grabbed him, an ice-cold blade—no, a *hand*—morphing into a dagger and pressing against his throat.

"You should have listened," the man hissed.

"Please, man . . . please." Devin's voice cracked. The fearless quarterback was gone, replaced by a boy who didn't understand the rules of the game he was in.

A second man turned sharply, looking around. "She's gone."

"What?" The lead man released Devin roughly, his focus snapping to where Sara had been moments ago. She was nowhere to be seen.

Devin stumbled to the ground as the men vanished in a blink, leaving nothing but scattered paint supplies and a ruined canvas.

Devin collapsed onto his back. Confusion clouded his thoughts. "What the hell was that?" he muttered, tears welling in his eyes. Slowly, he rose to his feet. His friends began to stir, their confusion mirroring his own. "What happened, Dev?" Demetri asked. "You okay, man?"

Devin struggled to find an answer. After a moment's pause, he said, "Yeah, I'll be fine. I don't know what happened either. Let's just go . . . and guys, let's keep this to ourselves."

"Wait—what? We should tell someone, right? Like the cops or—" Demetri started.

Devin cut him off. "Yeah, sure, let's tell them we saw Wolverine's evil cousin. Who's gonna believe that? They'll think we're messing around or losing it."

Demetri opened his mouth to argue, then closed it again. The others exchanged uneasy glances, but eventually they all nodded.

As they started to leave, Devin gathered his things. He picked up one of his course textbooks: *Greek Mythology*. He glanced at the cover, at the images of mythical creatures. Dismissing it with a shake of his head, he muttered, "Nah . . ."

Sara sprinted as fast as her legs could carry her, but her frantic pace proved too much as she stumbled over her own feet, crashing to the ground with a thud. Her knee smarted from the rough impact, and her glasses flew from her face, landing just out of reach.

"No, no, no," she muttered, her voice shaking as she scrambled on all fours, patting the ground blindly.

A shadow fell over her. She froze.

"Here," said a calm voice, low and steady. A hand extended into her blurry vision, holding her glasses.

Sara hesitated, her fingers trembling as she reached for them. Sliding the frames onto her face, she blinked, her vision sharpening to reveal the man standing before her. It was him—the man from the market.

"How . . . ?" she stammered.

"Don't be afraid," he said, his tone calm. "You need to come with me, Sara."

Sara's eyes widened. "How do you know my name?" she asked.

The man took a small step forward, his hands raised in a gesture of reassurance. "I will answer your question in time, but you're not safe here. The men in the park will be back. And they won't stop until they find you."

"How do you know that?" she demanded. "Who were those men? What do they want from me? How do *you* know anything about this?"

"I'll explain everything," the man said, "but not here. We don't have time."

"I'm not going anywhere with you!" she shouted. How do I even know you're not with *them*?"

The man's expression softened. "You know I'm not," he said gently. "If I were with them, I wouldn't be trying to protect you."

Sara recoiled slightly, tears welling in her eyes. "Please, I just want to be alone. I want to go home," she pleaded.

"I promise I won't hurt you," the man assured her. "You can call me Smith," said the man. "Do you remember seeing me in the market?"

She nodded reluctantly, the tears spilling over now. "I don't understand any of this," she whispered.

"It's because of what happened in the market," Smith said. "It's awakened something in you. Have the dreams started?"

"The dreams?" she echoed. Sara nodded again.

Smith stepped closer, his movements deliberate and non-threatening. "Don't be afraid to remember," he said softly.

But Sara couldn't shake her doubts. She shook her head violently. "No!" she cried. "I don't want to remember. I don't want any of this! I want everything to stop."

"Sara, I understand this is hard, but . . . we'll need

to tell Jo too," Smith added. "She'll need to know what's happening."

Her stomach dropped. "Jo?" she murmured. The thought of dragging her sister into this nightmare made her feel sick. "How am I supposed to explain this to Jo?"

Smith didn't answer.

Sara stiffened. "Wait . . . how do you know about Jo?" she asked, her voice trembling. "Who *are* you? Really?"

Smith opened his mouth to respond, but Sara didn't wait. Her body moved before her mind could catch up. Her feet pounded against the ground as she darted into the shadows.

"Sara—" Smith's voice followed her, but he made no move to follow.

Sara didn't look back.

CHAPTER 8

Devin sat slumped in his apartment chair, his gaze locked on the streaks of amber and gray in the evening sky. His fingers drummed absently against the arms. The events at the park replayed endlessly in his mind.

The men in suits, the girl with the easel—Sara, they'd called her. The way those men had moved, faster than humanly possible. And that dagger. His throat tightened at the memory of the blade pressing against his skin.

He couldn't make sense of it.

From the kitchen came the rhythmic clatter of pans, accompanied by Stacy's soft hum. Devin glanced toward her. She moved with easy confidence, as if she hadn't a care in the world.

They'd been together since high school. The golden couple, everyone had called them—Stacy the cheerleader with an infectious laugh, Devin the star quarterback destined for greatness. Their parents had latched onto that image, their futures planned in glossy detail. Devin in the NFL. Stacy on the sidelines, radiant in her support.

Stacy glanced over her shoulder as she caught sight of him. "Hey," she said softly, setting down the pan. "You okay?"

Devin blinked. "Huh? Yeah, sorry. Long day."

Her lips twitched into a small smile as she crossed the room, holding out a plate. "Made your favorite. Thought it might cheer you up."

The scent of garlic and melted cheese wafted to him, but Devin's stomach churned at the thought of eating. "Uh . . . thanks, Stace . . . but I'm not really hungry," he said, shifting uncomfortably in his chair. "I just need to sit for a bit."

Stacy's smile faded. She set the plate down on the coffee table and perched on the edge of the couch. "You sure? You've been weird all evening. It's like . . . It's like you've seen a ghost or something."

Devin forced a laugh, though it came out hollow. "Yeah, that's funny. No, I'm fine. Just tired, that's all."

Stacy leaned back, her gaze lingering on him for a moment longer. "All right," she said, reaching for the remote. "How about we watch something? Sci-fi night?"

Devin winced. His mind flashed to the men in suits, their inhuman speed, and the way reality itself had seemed to warp in the park. He couldn't stomach the thought of anything remotely otherworldly. "Uh . . . maybe comedy instead?" he suggested, his voice a little too quick.

Stacy raised an eyebrow, clearly puzzled. "Comedy? Really? You?" She gestured to him dramatically. "Because you look like a ball of laughs right now."

Despite himself, Devin chuckled. "Sorry, Stace. It's just . . ." He rubbed the back of his neck, searching for the right words. "It's been a weird day."

Something softened in her expression, her teasing replaced with quiet understanding. "Okay," she said gently, flipping through the channels. "Comedy it is."

Devin leaned back in his chair, letting the hum of the TV fill the silence. Stacy's laughter at a corny joke on the screen echoed faintly, but Devin barely registered it. Stacy, the girl who had stood by him through every triumph, every injury, every bad play. The girl who believed in him more than he believed in himself. Her presence should have been comforting, but it only added to the gnawing unease in his gut. He couldn't tell her what had happened in the park. He didn't even know how to explain it to himself.

"Hey," Stacy said, her voice pulling him back. She was smiling now, her legs curled up on the couch, the plate of food untouched beside her. "Remember when you used to do that impression of Coach yelling at Demetri? God, it was so bad it was hilarious."

Devin gave her a faint smile. "Yeah," he said, his voice quiet. "Good times."

His gaze drifted to the window again, the scene outside darkening as night fell.

The apartment door closed behind Sara with a thud. She stood there for a moment leaning against the door, catching her breath. The events of the past few hours replayed in her head like a disjointed movie reel.

Why was this happening to her? Ever since that chance meeting with that man who called himself "Smith" at the market, her life had spiraled into a whirlwind of inexplicable events.

She turned toward the small living room, where Jo's neatly folded blanket lay draped over the arm of the couch. For a fleeting moment, Sara thought about wrapping herself in it, curling up on the couch, and shutting out the world.

But her gaze drifted to her easel, the blank canvas beckoning her. She crossed the room and reached for a brush. The cool wood felt solid in her hand, grounding her for the first time since she'd fled the park.

She dipped the brush into some paint, the pigment spreading across the canvas in uneven strokes. The motion of her hand, usually so sure and steady, felt jerky and uncertain. Still, she kept going, layering colors over each other—blue, gold, soft grays—until the chaos in her mind began to spill out onto the canvas.

But the colors weren't enough to quiet the questions.

How did the men in the park and Smith know my name?

How does he know Jo?

Why does he feel so . . . familiar?

She exhaled sharply.

Her hand moved instinctively, the brush gliding across the surface in long, fluid strokes. The colors began to blend in ways she hadn't planned, deep blues and shimmering golds weaving together like threads of light. Her grip tightened on the brush as a faint warmth spread through her fingers.

Then she saw it.

A soft, blue glow began to pulse from her hand, radiating outward in delicate waves. It wasn't harsh or blinding, but mesmerizing, like moonlight on water. Her breath caught as a surge of energy coursed through her arm, each stroke of the brush bringing the canvas to life.

The sensation was exhilarating and terrifying all at once. Her heart raced as she stared at her glowing hand, the familiar warmth from her dream wrapping around her like an embrace. Is this really happening, she thought.

But just as quickly as it started, the glow faded, disappearing as though it had never been there. The energy ebbed, leaving her hands steady but cold.

The apartment door creaked open.

"Hey, Sara! How was your day?"

Sara blinked and her hand dropped limply to her side. Her mind scrambled to switch gears.

"Umm . . ." Sara started. Jo picked up on her hesitation immediately.

"You okay?" Jo asked. "Did something happen? Are those boys picking on you at lunch again? Because I swear, I'll kick their—"

"No, Jo," Sara interrupted. "Nothing like that."

Jo crossed her arms, one eyebrow raised. "Then what? Tell me."

Sara hesitated, gripping the brush like a lifeline. Her mouth opened, the truth trembling on the edge of her tongue: the men in suits, the terror, Smith's cryptic words. Instead, she heard herself say, "I was at the park today . . . painting."

Jo tilted her head, waiting.

"And there were some football players playing nearby," Sara continued, the lie forming before she could stop it. "One of the guys threw a ball, and it hit my canvas. Wrecked my painting. But it's fine—I came home and started a new one." She gestured weakly to the half-finished piece in front of her, hating the words even as they left her mouth, but at the same time wondered, What if the brush glows again? What if Jo sees?

Jo leaned in, her eyes widening. "Whoa," she said,

pointing at the canvas. "That looks amazing so far. Did you do something different? The colors look so . . . alive."

Sara's heart jumped, her mind scrambling for a response, but before she could say anything, Jo waved her hand dismissively and turned back to her usual soapbox.

"Anyway, those football players. Total jerks. They think they own the park, like they're God's gift to—" She launched into one of her familiar tirades, pacing as she spoke, her gestures animated. Sara nodded absently, her gaze fixed on the brush in her hand, half-expecting the faint glow to return at any moment.

The lie sat heavy in Sara's chest, but she couldn't bring herself to interrupt Jo's rant.

After dinner, Jo retreated to her room to study, leaving Sara alone with the quiet hum of the apartment. She stared at the canvas, her brush hovering over it but unmoving. Sara sighed and set the brush down. I can't keep this from her. Jo deserves to know.

No matter how strange, how unbelievable, she would tell Jo. She had to.

But not tonight. Not yet.

CHAPTER 9

Sara sat at the kitchen table, her fork slowly dragging lines through a pile of scrambled eggs she had no intention of eating. Jo had already left for work. Normally, the silence would've been comforting—an open door to drift into painting or lose herself in a daydream. But today, it just made her thoughts louder.

Her mind kept circling back to the men from the park—and then the man she ran into after she fled—Smith. He'd known her name. Jo's too. And for a moment, something about him had felt . . . safe. Familiar, even. But she'd bolted, instincts overruling reason.

Now, in the stillness of the apartment, she wondered if she'd made a mistake.

Should she have trusted him?

And then there was the image of the mural from the article Jo read the other morning. It was just a dream, she had told herself repeatedly.

But what if the mural was connected to her dream? What if it held answers to the strange energy coursing through her, the glow in her hands, the men in suits, and even Smith?

Her gaze drifted to her schoolbag by the door. It was time to leave for school. Sara's fingers tightened around her mug, the ceramic warm against her trembling hands. What if those men are still out there? What if going to the mural puts me in danger again?

49

She could stay home, fake sick, and wait for Jo to come back. Jo would make tea, throw on one of their favorite shows, and everything would feel normal again. Safe.

But the thought of sitting in the apartment all day, stewing in unanswered questions, made her stomach churn. I have to know. The words bubbled up from somewhere deep inside her, surprising even herself.

Sara sighed. She grabbed her bag, tucking a sketchpad and a pencil inside, and stepped out the door.

The morning air was cool, the sunlight filtering through the trees casting shadows on the pavement. Sara kept her head down as she walked. The streets were quiet, save for the occasional hum of a car passing by. She kept looking nervously over her shoulder.

By the time Walter's General Store came into view, Sara's pace slowed. A crowd had already gathered around the mural, larger than she had anticipated. Why are there so many people here, she thought.

She had expected to find the place quiet, to be alone with her questions and the painting. Instead, it seemed the mural had become the town's newest fascination.

Everyday citizens stood in clusters, chatting animatedly, their voices overlapping in an almost festive hum. College students sat cross-legged on the pavement, sketchpads balanced on their knees as they attempted to replicate the mural's intricate details.

But it wasn't just the artists and onlookers unsettling her. Sara's eyes drifted to a small group of men and women standing a bit apart from the crowd. Their tailored suits and polished shoes set them apart from the casual spectators. She recognized some of them—city council members, local business leaders—faces she'd seen in newspaper articles and community events. They weren't admiring the mural like everyone else. Instead, they whispered to one another in low, urgent tones, their uneasy glances darting between the mural and the crowd.

Sara's brow furrowed. Why are they here? And why do they look so . . . nervous?

Shaking off the thought, Sara forced herself to step closer. Her gaze locked onto the mural, and the rest of the world seemed to blur around her. The colors were even more vivid in person, the brush strokes impossibly precise.

The woman in the flowing robes seemed to glow with an inner light, her expression serene yet commanding.

Sara took another step closer. Her fingers twitched at her sides, an inexplicable urge to touch the mural tugging at her. The longer she stared, the stronger the pull became, as though the painted woman reached out to her, beckoning her forward.

Her hand lifted, trembling, toward the brick wall.

"Sara," a voice said softly.

The spell broke. Sara turned to find Smith standing beside her, his expression calm.

A wave of jitters ran through her.

"Smith?" she whispered. "What are you doing here?"

"There are things we need to discuss," he said, his voice low. "But not here, not in the midst of all these people."

She studied his face. There was no threat in his eyes. Just patience.

Sara relaxed some and turned her gaze back to the mural. "Why not?" she asked.

Smith leaned closer. "Look around," he said, subtly gesturing with a tilt of his head toward the group of well-dressed individuals standing apart from the crowd.

Sara followed his gaze as she noticed the city leaders again.

"They're watching," Smith continued. "Not just the mural—they're watching the people who are drawn to it. Including you."

"How do you know that?" she asked.

"I know more than you think," Smith replied. "But this isn't the place to explain. Come with me, Sara. We need to talk somewhere private—somewhere safe."

Before Sara could respond, the sudden wail of a police siren shattered the low hum of the crowd. Her heart jumped at the sound, and she instinctively took a step closer to Smith.

A patrol car pulled up to the curb, its lights flashing red and blue. Two uniformed officers stepped out, their expressions stern as they addressed the onlookers.

"All right, folks," one of them called out. "We need you to disperse. You're blocking access to the store. Let's move it along."

The crowd hesitated, reluctant to abandon the mesmerizing mural. The officer's partner stepped forward, more forceful. "You heard him. Let's go. Take your pictures and move out."

Reluctantly, the people began to scatter, some muttering under their breath while others continued snapping photos as they walked away.

Sara watched the commotion. The uneasy knot in her stomach tightened when her gaze caught one of the city council members. He wasn't leaving with the crowd.

Instead, he lingered, his sharp eyes scanning the dispersing onlookers—until they landed on her.

She turned back toward Smith. "Okay, Smith. Where do we go?"

He nodded. "Follow me."

Sara didn't hesitate this time. She followed Smith, casting one last glance over her shoulder. The councilman still watched her. Sara quickened her pace, her hands trembling as they turned the corner and disappeared from view.

The sharp whistle cut through the air, jolting Devin back to reality. He crouched behind the line of scrimmage, his hands hovering over the ball. The center glanced back at him, waiting for the snap. But Devin's mind was elsewhere.

The memory of the park replayed in his head like a bad dream. The men in suits, the effortless way they overpowered him and his friends—it didn't make sense. And the girl—Sara, wasn't it? Had she gotten away? Was she okay?

"Devin! Snap the ball!" Demetri's sharp bark broke through the haze.

Devin flinched, realizing he held up the play. He called the cadence, his voice lacking its usual confidence. "Set . . . hut, hut!"

The ball hit his hands, and he dropped back into the pocket. His eyes scanned the field, but the movement felt robotic. He hesitated for a beat too long, and the defense crashed through. The whistle blew, cutting the play dead.

"Come on, Dev!" Demetri groaned, jogging past him. "That's, like, the third time today. Where's your head, man?"

Devin didn't respond. Each missed read, every delayed pass chipped away at him. He could feel the frustration of his teammates mounting.

Across the field, the cheerleaders practiced their routines. Stacy's familiar laugh floated over the din of the field, usually enough to make him crack a smile. But not today.

"All right, take a knee!" Coach Conner's voice cut through the growing tension. Devin dropped to the turf, his hands resting on his thighs as he avoided his coach's eyes.

Coach Mike Conner strode over, clipboard in hand, his whistle bouncing against his chest. To Devin, he wasn't just a coach—he was a mentor, the kind of guy who had been around since Devin's Pop Warner days. He'd seen Devin at his best and worst.

"Devin," Coach said, crouching beside him, his voice low enough for only him to hear. "You're not yourself today. What's going on?"

Devin exhaled sharply. "I'm fine, Coach. Just . . . a lot on my mind."

Coach Connor squinted, and he glanced toward the sideline. "Son, I've known you long enough to know when something's eating at you. You're not doing anyone any favors by keeping it bottled up."

Devin knew his coach was right, but how could he explain what had happened without sounding like a lunatic? "I'm just off today. It won't happen again," he said.

Coach sighed, standing to his full height and clapping a hand on Devin's shoulder. "All right, but you know where to find me. My office is open anytime."

Devin nodded. "Thanks, Coach. I'll . . . I'll think about it."

"Good. Now let's get back to work," Coach said.

As Devin rose, a football whizzed past his shoulder, hitting the ground with a dull thud. "Hey, Dork!" Demetri called out, a grin splitting his face. "You good now, or should we all just hit the showers?"

Devin smirked faintly, shaking his head. "Let's run it again," he said, jogging back to the huddle.

From the corner of his eye, he caught Stacy glancing his way. Her auburn hair caught the sunlight as she whispered something to one of her teammates, her gaze lingering on him. Devin couldn't tell if she was concerned or just curious.

As the team lined up for the next play, Devin gripped the ball, the leather cool and familiar in his hands. For now, he had to push everything aside. Football was the one thing he was supposed to have control over—if only it still felt that way.

The cobblestone street wound through downtown Muxley, flanked by rows of historic buildings whose brick facades bore the charm of decades gone by. Amid the quaint storefronts and urban hum stood a row of townhouses, their uniformity broken by one striking feature—a bold red door that seemed to pulse faintly against the muted tones of its neighbors.

Smith led Sara up to the red door. She hesitated, her

eyes going back and forth between the door and Smith. The key in his hand caught her attention—a peculiar, antiquated skeleton key, its intricate leaf pattern glinting faintly in the sunlight.

"Do you always carry keys like that?" Sara asked.

Smith glanced at her, a flicker of amusement crossing his face. "Yes," he said simply, inserting the key into the lock. The mechanism turned with a satisfying click, the door swinging open to reveal the world within.

Sara stepped cautiously inside. Warmth greeted her first. The living room was cozy yet understated, with plush armchairs arranged around a central coffee table. Sunlight poured through large windows, its beams catching on the polished hardwood floors and illuminating the faint scent of sandalwood lingering in the air.

"It's . . . nice," Sara murmured.

Smith smiled but said nothing, motioning her toward a staircase tucked against the wall. Its spiral form rose elegantly. As they ascended, Sara's hand brushed the cool metal, grounding her as her curiosity and unease wrestled within her.

The second floor opened into a library that seemed plucked from another time. Shelves stretched from floor to ceiling, crammed with books whose spines bore titles in languages Sara didn't recognize. A faint golden light emanated from no discernible source, wrapping the room in an almost ethereal glow. The air smelled faintly of sea salt, an inexplicable contrast to the scent of leather and old paper.

Sara's gaze fell on a portrait above the fireplace. The girl depicted looked no older than twelve, her delicate features serene, her eyes . . . knowing.

"Who is she?" Sara asked.

Smith paused, his eyes following hers. For a moment, he seemed to weigh his answer. "A story for another time," he said. "Come."

He guided her toward a set of double doors on the far wall, their frosted glass panels catching and refracting the golden light. Smith pushed them open, and Sara froze mid-step.

Beyond the threshold, a vast expanse of tropical beauty unfolded. Palm trees swayed gently in the breeze, their fronds whispering against the sky. The ocean stretched endlessly, its waves lapping at a shoreline. The air carried the tang of salt and the faint sweetness of hibiscus, each breath filling her with both wonder and disbelief.

"What is this?" she whispered, stepping closer to the door. Her fingers brushed the frame as though testing its solidity, her wide eyes fixed on the scene beyond.

Smith leaned against the doorway, watching her reaction. "What do you think it is?"

"I—" Sara faltered, her words caught somewhere between awe and confusion. "This can't be real. We're not near any coast. How . . . How is this possible?"

Sara tore her gaze from the vista to look at him, searching his face for answers he wasn't giving. "Am I dreaming?" she asked, though the faint tick of the library clock and the solid warmth beneath her feet told her otherwise.

"Not at all," Smith replied.

She turned reluctantly away from the view, her mind a storm of questions she couldn't yet form.

Smith gestured toward a worn leather chair positioned

beside a small writing desk, its surface scattered with papers and an old globe. "Sit," he said gently. "There are things you need to know, but first, I need you to trust me."

Sara hesitated but complied, sinking into the chair as her eyes darted back toward the door and the impossible ocean.

Smith pulled another chair closer and sat across from her. For the first time, his expression softened, the sharpness of his gaze easing into something gentler.

"Sara," he began, his voice low but firm. "What's happening to you is only the beginning."

CHAPTER 10

The hum of old fluorescent lights buzzed overhead, but the only true illumination came from Eli's portable terminal—its pale-blue glow casting shadows across the dark, makeshift room. Eli hunched forward, fingers dancing across the keyboard with relentless urgency. Lines of code blurred across the screen.

Mr. Mason stood nearby, arms folded, leaning against the desk. His rugged face, half-shrouded in shadow, was carved in stone.

"Lucy," Eli said, not looking up. "Pull energy signatures from The Veilstone Caverns. Prioritize dimensional shifts and artifact resonance anomalies."

The AI responded instantly, her voice smooth but laced with synthetic tension. "Analyzing now, Eli. One moment . . . Energy surge detected—twenty-four hours ago. Intensity: high. Origin: corrupted orb resonance. Classification: red."

Mr. Mason's eyes narrowed, and his voice dropped low with a Scottish bite. "Red orbs again. Azazel is truly back. That madman's stirrin' the pot again, and I'd wager me soul he's now got dat boy he's keepin' down there."

Eli's fingers flew across the terminal. A topographical map blinked to life on the screen, layered with glowing red veins of energy bleeding outward like a spider's web.

"There's something else," Eli muttered. "The energy

spike isn't isolated. It's leaking—seeping into surrounding zones like a toxin."

Mason leaned in. "Bleedin'? That ain't natural. You think he opened a portal?"

"Either that," Eli said grimly, "or something *came through*. Lucy—track the spread vector. Overlay it with known hotspots and activity clusters from the last week."

A pause. Then Lucy's voice returned.

"Overlay complete. Convergence zone detected: thirty-five miles southeast of Muxley. Coordinates place it at . . . Brackenridge Hollow."

Mason let out a slow breath. "Brackenridge? Hidin' in the woods?

Eli's jaw tightened. "If the red orb energy's converging there, it's not by accident. He must have some sort of facility there. The caverns were just the ignition point."

Mason pushed off the desk, pacing now. "Then we don't wait. We get tae Brackenridge and find out what he's cookin'."

Eli hesitated. "And then what? Say we do find red orb artifacts. Say we catch a glimpse of Azazel's blueprint—his next mural, his weaponized pawn—what can we *do* about it? We're not exactly the cavalry anymore."

Mason stopped. Turned. His eyes burned with the weight of old wars.

"We might not be the cavalry," he said, voice gravel-thick, "but we've faced worse. We always find a way."

Eli let out a breath and allowed a small, reluctant smile. "You really think stubbornness is a strategy?"

"Aye," Mason said with a half-smirk. "When it's all you've got, it best be enough."

Eli shut the terminal with a decisive snap. He stood, tall now, resolved. "Then let's not waste time. We scout Brackenridge. Quietly. If Azazel's made a move, we move faster."

Mason clapped him on the back with a grin. "There's the Eli I know. Let's rattle his cage."

Just as they turned to go, Lucy's voice chimed in one last time—

"Eli . . . I'll continue monitoring energy patterns. Be careful."

Eli paused, hand on the door. "Thanks, Lucy. Keep the lights on. We'll be back—with answers."

Sara felt herself relaxing more with each passing minute in Smith's presence. Still, questions buzzed in her mind. She glanced at the tropical paradise just beyond the glass doors of the upstairs library, still struggling to believe it was real. Just moments ago, they'd been in Muxley. Or . . . were they still in Muxley? She couldn't be sure.

Smith, sensing her restlessness, leaned forward. "I know I said we needed to talk," he said gently, "but I also know you have questions. I can answer some now—and others when the time is right."

Sara hesitated, then blurted out, "At the market, when we ran into each other . . . you said, 'So it's you.' What did you mean by that?"

"I figured you'd ask," he admitted. "It wasn't meant to sound cryptic, but I imagine it felt that way."

Her voice trembled slightly. "And how do you know me and Jo? We've never met you before."

Smith gave a small, reflective smile. "Those are exactly the things I wanted to talk to you about." He leaned in, his expression soft but serious. "What happened at the market wasn't an accident. When I said those words, it was me recognizing something I've been wondering about for a long time—wondering who would carry your mother's mantle."

Sara tilted her head. "Wait—our mother? You knew her too?"

Smith leaned back, his tone thoughtful. "I did. Lily was a dear friend. When she died, you were practically a newborn. We weren't sure how we would keep you and Jo safe from . . . our enemies."

"Enemies?" Sara asked, her brow furrowed. "No one ever told us our mother had enemies."

"Do you remember the men in the park?"

"How could I forget?" she said. "Scariest moment of my life." She paused. "They . . . They seemed to know my mom."

Smith nodded, almost reading her thoughts. "Yes, Sara. They know all about you and your family."

"Then why are they after us?"

"Because your mother left behind . . . very special . . . things. Things that, she believed, in the right place and time, would find their way to you and Jo. Our enemies want to make sure that doesn't happen."

He hesitated for a beat. "They want to prevent you from accessing what's yours."

Sara's mind spun. "I don't understand. What things?" Then, as the realization began to click:

"Wait . . . the dreams, the blue glow, the mural—is that what you mean?"

Smith nodded. "Yes."

"My mom could do these things too?" Sara asked, her tone skeptical.

"Yes," Smith said without hesitation.

"But how? Was she some kind of magician or something?"

Smith chuckled. "Not quite. I know this is a lot to take in. But stick with me. I won't give you every detail tonight—not until Jo can hear it too."

Sara's voice softened. "Did my dad know any of this?"

Smith nodded again. "He did . . . . eventually. Jack was brave, loyal, and utterly devoted to protecting you both. He and I worked together for a time. When he realized the threats Lily feared might one day come true, he asked me and a friend—Mr. Mason—to keep watch from a distance."

Sara frowned. "If you were supposed to protect us, why stay hidden?"

"It was safer that way. There are things you'll understand soon, but the less you knew growing up, the more protected you were."

Sara pressed on. "After Dad died, Jo and I lived with Aunt Janice for several years. She never mentioned you. Never said anything about someone watching over us."

Smith's expression softened. "Your Aunt Janice was part of the plan. Your father trusted her completely. She agreed to care for you both while keeping the unusual things hidden. She honored that promise—even when it wasn't easy."

Sara's grip tightened on the armrest. "So all this time . . . she knew? She knew there was more going on?"

Smith nodded. "Yes. She did the best she could with the weight she carried."

Sara's throat tightened. "And now? What's changed?"

Smith exhaled slowly. "Things have . . . shifted. What happened at the market wasn't just chance. When the orb reacted to you—"

"Orb?" Sara cut in. "What do you mean?"

Smith reached into his bag and carefully unwrapped a cloth. Inside was a glowing blue orb. Its light pulsed gently, casting a soft glow around the room.

"That's the light I saw at the market . . . and in my dreams," she whispered.

Smith nodded. "It's the same. This orb holds a power unlike anything else. It enhances certain abilities—abilities that awaken in those it chooses."

"Chooses?" she repeated. "Why would it choose me?"

"Like I said," Smith replied gently, "some answers now, some later."

Sara's thoughts spiraled. "But why not Jo? She's stronger, smarter, braver—"

"Jo has her own path," Smith interrupted. "And when the time comes, she'll play her part. But this one . . . this one is yours."

The words settled between them.

Sara's voice was barely above a whisper. "The mural at Walter's Market . . . it felt like it was pulling me. Why?"

Smith's gaze shifted. "Because it's not just an ordinary mural. It's a portal."

"A portal?" she echoed.

"Yes. What you painted connects your world to mine. It's a gateway. A bridge for my people to cross when they're needed."

Sara stared at him, stunned. "Wait—your world? You're not from Earth?"

Smith tilted his head, amused by her reaction. "That's right."

Her mind scrambled. "So . . . what, you're an alien?"

Smith laughed softly. "Not quite. I come from a place called Valoria. Think of Valoria as a parallel realm—a world beside your own. Different, but connected."

Sara leaned forward. "So I painted a magical portal . . . to another world. And you're from that world?"

Smith nodded.

"This is weird," she muttered. "I mean, you look . . . normal."

"Normal?" he said with a playful eyebrow raise.

"You know what I mean! You don't look like some interdimensional being."

"Well," he said with a shrug, "I try to blend in."

Her mind reeled. "How did I even create it? I was just dreaming . . ."

"The orb amplifies your gift," Smith explained. "In your dream, you saw a broken future—a place in need of hope. You resisted it the only way you knew how: through your art. In that moment, you were in two places at once."

Sara's eyes widened. "That's why I had glowing paint on my hands when I woke up . . ."

"Exactly. The orb gave life to what you saw—and what you felt."

Her next question came fast. "The men in the park—who were they?"

Smith's expression darkened. "One of them was a being named Azazel Blackthorn, a being intent on severing the connection between our worlds. He wants to control your world, and the murals you create are a threat to his plans. He wants to silence the hope that our murals represent."

"But how did he get here?"

Smith shook his head. "That answer will come. For now, what matters is this: the murals you paint are not just portals. They're shields. As long as Valorian light burns through them, he cannot realize his ambitions."

Sara paused for a moment. Then after a minute or so, she asked, "So . . . how long have you been here?"

Smith answered, "I have been overseeing—well, watching over your world—for a while now."

"How long?" asked Sara.

"Eh . . . a long while," said Smith, trying to avoid the question.

Sara looked at him with a direct stare. "How long?"

Smith sighed. "Well, in your terms, maybe . . . . 350-400 years, give or take."

Sara's jaw dropped. "What? You're four hundred years old?"

"Well, not exactly," said Smith. "Look, Sara—"

"You don't look four hundred years old," Sara interrupted.

"Sara . . . please," he said, growing solemn again, "I need you to understand something important. The murals you create—"

"Wait," she interrupted, "did you say murals? Plural?"

"Yes," Smith said. "There will be more. And they'll be vital. But there's something else—something important. The creator of a mural cannot step into it."

"Why not?"

He paused, meeting her gaze. "Because the murals are powered by the spirit of Valoria inside you. If you cross through, that connection becomes unstable. You'd become . . . untethered."

Sara went still.

"You'll feel the pull," he added gently. "But you must resist it. Do you understand?"

She hesitated, then nodded slowly. "Okay . . . but you still don't look four hundred years old."

Smith laughed, the sound like a warm breeze. "I'll take that as a compliment."

A smile tugged at her lips.

"Come on," Smith said, rising. "Let's take a walk. There's nothing like ocean air to help you breathe again."

Sara followed him through the door and onto the sunlit beach. The salty wind tousled her hair, and the crashing waves seemed to echo the rhythm of her thoughts.

"So," she said, glancing back toward the townhome, "how are we at a beach when Muxley is . . . downstairs?"

Smith's grin widened. "Great question," he said, evasive but teasing. "Another time."

Sara narrowed her eyes but let it go—for now. "All right. But what about Jo? How are we going to explain this to her? I mean . . . your age alone is going to be a hurdle."

Smith smirked. "My age? That's what worries you?"

"Well, yeah," Sara replied. "You're ancient."

He laughed again, shaking his head. "Jo's tougher than you think. And as for everything else . . ." He gave her a knowing glance. "One step at a time."

As they walked farther down the shore, the sound of the waves filled the quiet. And for the first time in a long time, Sara didn't feel so alone.

Jo was nodding off in the school library. All the hours of working, her studies, and taking care of Sara had caught up with her. Exhausted, her head nodded, and she woke herself up. "Wow, I need some coffee," Jo muttered to herself. She got up and went to the little coffee stand just outside the study area where she had curled up trying to review her notes for her exam. She grabbed a cup, paid the cashier, and went to fill it with some half and half. That's when she noticed a couple sitting in the café area, engaged in an intense conversation. She recognized the guy as Devin Thompson, the quarterback for the Muxley Wildcats. She didn't know the girl with him but assumed it was his girlfriend. The girl had an expression on her face that seemed like she couldn't believe what she was hearing.

Jo shrugged it off and thought to herself, "Not for me . . ." She turned to go back to her studies.

"Devin, you sound crazy," the girl said, her voice tinged with frustration.

Devin responded, "Look, I know I sound crazy, but this girl was painting in the park where me and the guys were playing."

Jo did a double take. A girl painting in the park? Were these the guys that threw the ball and wrecked Sara's painting? Typical, she thought. But why was he telling his girlfriend this? Something to laugh about? But he didn't look like he was laughing. Jo didn't care. She was going to stick up for her sister and give the football "god" a piece of her mind.

"Excuse me," Jo said, clearly edgy as she approached their table. "I couldn't help but overhear your conversation. Did you say you saw a girl in Scrimsky Park painting yesterday? Young, like, maybe twelve years old?"

"Uh, yeah," said Devin, looking up at her in surprise. "Who are you?"

"I'm her sister," Jo said, her voice rising. "She told me how you guys threw your little ball around and demolished her piece of art."

"What?" said Devin, looking genuinely puzzled. "That's not what happened."

"You know what," said Jo, her anger mounting. "Save it. You guys think you can walk around high and mighty and damage a girl's work who is almost half your age and get away with it."

Stacy, Devin's girlfriend, stood up, trying to defuse the situation. "Hey, calm down. Dev didn't do anything to your little sister's stuff."

Jo glared at Stacy, then turned her attention back to Devin. "You think you can just ruin someone's hard work and then act like it's nothing? My sister put her heart and soul into that painting!"

"Hey, why don't you back off!" said Stacy. Jo's brow furrowed, and she was about to retort when Devin stepped in.

"Wait a minute," Devin said, standing up as well.

People in the café and surrounding area started to turn their heads toward the intense conversation brewing.

Devin lowered his voice and looked intently at Jo. "Look, that's not what happened. Honest." Jo began to calm down. His sincerity caught her off guard. "If I tried to explain to you what actually happened, like I tried here with Stacy, you wouldn't believe me. But I promise, we didn't wreck anything. We were trying to protect your sister."

"Protect her? From who?" asked Jo.

"I don't know who they were, but they were . . . creepy."

"But she told me some football guys threw a ball and wrecked her canvas. Why would she tell me that if what you are saying is true?" asked Jo.

"I don't know," said Devin pensively. "Maybe because she doesn't understand what she saw either and doesn't know how to tell you. Here, sit down and I will tell you exactly what happened."

CHAPTER 11

Jo sat in stunned silence, her mind reeling from what Devin had just told her about the park incident with Sara and the mysterious visitors. It sounded genuine, but it was so farfetched she didn't know how to process it.

"What do you mean they moved through the air?" Jo asked, her voice tinged with disbelief.

"I know it sounds crazy, but they moved so fast. They knocked my teammates out like they were flies, and then the guy held a dagger that was . . . um . . . his arm?" Devin struggled to explain.

"You mean like a prosthetic arm?" Jo asked, trying to make sense of it.

"No," said Devin, shaking his head. "Like his arm became a dagger." Devin sighed heavily. "I know I sound crazy, but I'm telling you what I saw."

Devin glanced at Stacy, who took a deep breath. "I know it's a lot to take in," Stacy said softly. "Honestly, I don't know how to process it either."

Jo's determination grew. "I have to find her. She's my sister. I can't just sit here and do nothing."

Stacy and Devin nodded. "Look," said Devin, "like I said, we wanted to protect her . . . um . . . maybe if we come too, we can talk with her together. She should remember me. I'm sure she is scared and doesn't know what to say to you either. I mean, I didn't want to tell you. I think about checking myself into a mental hospital every time I think about this."

Jo looked at Devin, then Stacy, and back to Devin. "I need to find Sara and make sure she is safe. But what about these other people lurking about? Should we go to the police?"

Devin thought for a moment. "Look, what about your parents? I'm sure they are taking care of her right now, right? I'm sure she is safe."

Jo paused, a somber expression crossing her face. "No, our parents . . . passed away a while ago. I am Sara's guardian."

Devin and Stacy paused, taken aback. "Wow. I'm so sorry," said Devin, not knowing what to say. After a moment of silence, Devin spoke, "Look, normally I would call the police, but in this situation, would they even believe us?" Devin paused. "I think we might be on our own here, as weird as that is. Stacy and I will come with you. Let's go find Sara and talk this out."

Jo felt a wave of gratitude. "Thank you. Let's go."

Thick woods flanked the dirt road leading to the Brackenridge Hollow warehouse, the trees casting eerie shadows under the pale moonlight. Eli and Mr. Mason parked their vehicle well out of sight, hidden beneath the canopy of towering oaks. Mr. Mason killed the engine, and the sudden silence was almost deafening. "This'll do," he muttered.

Eli adjusted the straps of his satchel. "How far to the warehouse from here?"

"Couple hundred yards," Mason replied, peering through the binoculars at the warehouse. "Looks quiet, but dinnae trust appearances." His warning was as strong as his accent.

72

Eli nodded. Mr. Mason and Eli stepped out of the vehicle and quietly shut their doors. The cold night air nipped at their face. They moved silently on foot, their boots crunching lightly against the gravel path.

As they neared the warehouse, they both crouched low behind some bushes. Eli's eyes narrowing on the faint glow emanating from one of the warehouse windows. "That's red light . . . It's gotta be the orb."

"Aye," Mason agreed, his tone grim. "All right, then. Ye go in, grab the orb, and get out. No dawdlin', Eli."

"Got it," Eli said, his voice steady. He pulled his earpiece snugly into place, linking it to Lucy. "Lucy, patch me in. Let's get a read on the energy signatures."

"Connection established," Lucy's calm, synthetic voice replied in his ear. "Energy spikes consistent with red orb emissions detected inside the warehouse."

"Good enough for me," Eli muttered, pulling up the hood of his jacket and moving toward the warehouse. He kept low, weaving through the underbrush and taking cover behind stacks of old, rusted shipping containers that littered the property.

"What about Azazel's men?" he whispered. "Can you give me a layout?"

"Scanning thermal signatures now," Lucy replied. A brief pause followed before her voice returned. "Two guards stationed outside near the east and south exits. Inside the warehouse: six operatives. Four in the main loading area, one near the cart containing the orb, and one patrolling the catwalk above."

Eli's brow furrowed as he considered the information. "And the best path to avoid them?"

"Recommendation: enter through the side door

73

closest to your position," Lucy said. "It leads to an empty corridor that bypasses the main loading area. You'll need to move quickly past the open walkway to reach the cart. Timing is critical to avoid the patrolling operative on the catwalk."

Eli glanced at the side entrance Lucy mentioned, mentally tracing the route she outlined. "Got it. What about cameras?"

"Minimal surveillance detected," Lucy replied. "Three static cameras monitoring the loading area. Their coverage does not extend to the corridor or the orb's current location."

"Perfect," Eli muttered. "Mason, you copy all that?"

"Aye," Mason's voice crackled softly in his earpiece. "Two outside, six inside. Stay sharp, lad. I'm watchin' yer back."

Eli smirked faintly, his breath steadying as he prepared to move. "Don't worry, Mason. I'll be back before you miss me."

Eli slipped from his hiding spot, moving low and fast across the gravel yard. Reaching the side door, he eased it open just enough to slip inside, the hinges letting out a faint groan. He froze, listening for any sign his entry had been detected.

Nothing.

He crept into the corridor, the dim light casting long shadows on the cold concrete walls. The air was thick with the scent of oil and metal, the hum of machinery a faint backdrop. Eli's muscles tensed as he neared the walkway Lucy had warned him about. Through the slatted opening, he could see the patrolling operative's shadow moving above.

"Patrol's at the far end," Lucy's voice guided him. "You have approximately twenty seconds before he turns back."

"Plenty of time," Eli whispered, slipping across the walkway and pressing himself against the wall on the other side. The red glow of the orb was now visible, pulsing faintly from a box on the cart ahead.

Eli exhaled quietly, his grip tightening on the satchel's strap. He had made it this far. Now came the hard part.

Lucy's voice, again, guided him through his earpiece. "Two guards near the main bay, three unloading crates from the truck in the rear," Lucy reported.

Eli nodded to himself, slipping past a stack of crates as he approached the glowing cart. The red light grew brighter, illuminating the area around him. The three operatives nearby were preoccupied, their muffled voices drifting from inside the truck.

Perfect, Eli thought.

He reached the cart and paused, taking a moment to assess the surroundings. The orb sat within an open crate, its crimson glow pulsating like a heartbeat. Eli slipped a box from his satchel, the intricate symbols on its surface flickering faintly in response to the orb's energy.

With quick, precise movements, Eli donned his gloves and carefully lifted the orb from the crate. The energy emanating from it was almost palpable, sending a faint vibration through his hands. He placed it into the box, the lid sealing shut with a series of mechanical clicks. The glow dimmed instantly, the orb contained within the box's protective layers.

"Item secured," Eli whispered, his voice calm despite the adrenaline coursing through him. He turned toward the exit, ready to slip back into the shadows.

But as he stepped away, his eyes drifted to the other crates surrounding the cart. They were marked with unfamiliar symbols, their surfaces scratched and battered as though they had endured a long journey. A nagging feeling tugged at Eli's mind.

What else is Azazel moving, he wondered.

He hesitated, glancing back at the sealed box in his hand. Logic screamed at him to leave, but his instincts urged him to look. Just one, he told himself. One look.

"Eli, where are ya?" Mason's voice crackled in his earpiece, sharp and insistent. "You've got the orb—get out now."

Eli froze, his hand hovering above the nearest crate. He knew Mason was right. He should leave. But the unease gnawed at him, refusing to let go.

"Lucy," Eli whispered, "what's in these crates? Can you scan them?"

"Energy signatures detected," Lucy replied. "Composition suggests materials originating from Draegora."

Eli's blood ran cold. He swallowed hard, steeling himself as he lifted the lid of the crate. Inside, dark, gleaming pieces of armor reflected the faint light from the room. The designs were intricate, almost other-worldly, and pulsed faintly with an eerie, malevolent energy.

"Oh my God," Eli muttered, his voice barely audible. "Lucy . . . is this what I think it is?"

CHAPTER 12

As Jo, Devin, and Stacy headed toward Jo and Sara's apartment, the evening sky darkened, the streetlights casting a soft glow over the cobblestone street lined with neatly kept townhouses. The chill in the air mirrored Jo's growing unease.

Is she safe, she worried. Why didn't she trust me enough to tell me what happened? Did I do something wrong?

The closer they got, the faster Jo's heart pounded. What if something's happened to her? What if she needs my help?

Jo suddenly froze mid-step, her eyes narrowing. "Wait. That's Sara." She pointed ahead, her voice tinged with disbelief. Devin and Stacy followed her gaze.

Sara walked briskly alongside an unfamiliar man, their figures illuminated briefly under a streetlamp as they walked away from a red-doored townhouse. Jo's stomach churned.

"Who is she with? Who is that guy?" Jo demanded, her voice rising.

Devin squinted. "That's not one of the guys from the park. I don't know him."

As Sara and the man walked away from townhouse, Sara gestured back to the door, speaking quickly, though her words were too faint to hear. The man nodded, pulling a key from his pocket, walking back to unlock the red door. Sara glanced over her shoulder briefly before they both disappeared inside.

Jo's confusion turned to urgency. "What is she doing here? She's supposed to be at the apartment."

Devin shrugged, his brow furrowed. Stacy instinctively moved closer to Devin, her unease evident. "I don't like this," she murmured. "Something feels off."

Jo had already made up her mind. Without another word, she broke into a sprint toward the townhouse, her boots clattering against the cobblestones. Devin and Stacy exchanged a look before chasing after her.

By the time they reached the door, Jo's hand was already on the knob. She twisted it without hesitation and pushed the door open.

"Okay, you psycho," Jo yelled as she stormed inside, "where is my sis—"

Her words died in her throat as she froze, taking in the sight before her. The townhouse was empty. Completely empty. No furniture, no decor, nothing but bare walls and floors, as if no one had ever lived there.

Devin and Stacy stepped in behind her, their eyes wide with confusion. "What is this?" Devin asked, his voice echoing in the hollow space. "Where's the furniture? Where's anything?"

"This doesn't make any sense," Stacy whispered, her arms wrapped tightly around herself. "We just saw them walk in here."

Jo felt her stomach twist. "They couldn't have just disappeared," she said, her voice trembling.

Devin moved toward the walls, rapping on them with his knuckles. "Maybe there's a secret passage or something," he suggested, though his tone betrayed his skepticism.

Stacy crouched by the corners, checking the floor-boards. "I'll look over here," she said.

Jo stood in the middle of the room. The tears she had been holding back finally broke free, her shoulders shaking with each sob. "What if something's happened to her?" she whispered.

Devin walked over and placed a hand on her shoulder. "Hey, we'll figure this out," he said softly. "We'll find her."

Stacy nodded, her voice steadier. "Yeah, Jo. We're not leaving without answers."

Before Jo could respond, faint voices reached their ears. All three froze, their eyes darting toward the sound. It was unmistakable—Sara's voice, along with the man's.

The air shimmered faintly, and a spiral staircase seemed to materialize out of nowhere, descending from what appeared to be thin air. Jo's eyes widened as Sara and the man stepped into view, their expressions a mix of tension and surprise.

"Jo?" Sara's voice trembled as her gaze locked onto her sister's. "What are you doing here?"

"What are *we* doing here?" Jo shot back, her arms already folding tight across her chest. "I don't know, maybe chasing my little sister across town because she decided to vanish with some trench-coat-wearing stranger? Ring any bells?"

Her relief was buried under a layer of anger—and fear she'd never admit out loud.

The man stepped forward. "Name's Smith," he said plainly.

Devin moved in, eyes sharp. "You're going to have to give us more than a name."

79

Smith didn't flinch. Instead, he reached into his coat and tapped a small, circular device. A soft pulse of blue light blinked once. His face darkened.

"That was a silent code from one of my partners," he said, voice low and clipped. "Something's gone wrong at a site we've been monitoring. I'm needed elsewhere. We need to move. We can talk there."

"I'm sorry, what?" Jo said, incredulously. "Did I accidentally stumble into an episode of *Paranoid and Mysterious?*"

Devin took a half-step in front of her, his shoulders squaring. "You better start explaining. Now."

Smith raised a hand in a gesture of peace. "I understand your concern and your need for answers," he said, his tone calm yet firm. "Sara is safe with me, and I promise you'll have the answers you're looking for. But first, we need to move."

Jo arched a brow and let out a dry laugh. "So now we're supposed to just hop into the mystery van with this guy who's apparently receiving silent distress signals?" She stepped protectively in front of Sara. "Without even knowing what we're walking into?"

Sara stepped from behind Jo, eyes steady. "Jo, I know how this looks. I do. But I trust him."

Jo stared at her, stunned. "Based on *what* exactly?" she snapped. "And since when do we keep things from each other? Because I'm guessing this has something to do with what happened at the park, doesn't it?"

Sara opened her mouth, but words failed.

Smith's eyes turned to Devin, his gaze sharp. "The men you encountered at the park are connected to the same threat we're dealing with now. They're not finished, and if we linger here, we'll be putting everyone at risk."

Devin considered Smith's words. He turned to Sara, watching her closely. Her posture was tense, but there was no fear in her eyes—just resolve.

After a beat, Devin turned. "Look," he said to Jo and Stacy, "I don't know everything that's going on, but Sara seems to trust him. If he was like those guys from the park, she wouldn't. We need to hear him out—and if he says we have to move, we should listen."

Jo crossed her arms, her weight shifting from one foot to the other. "I don't like this," she admitted, her voice trembling. Then she exhaled and jabbed a finger toward Smith. "Fine. We'll go. But if you turn out to be some creeper with a badge and a God complex—" she narrowed her eyes, "—I swear, I'll make you regret it."

A flicker of dry amusement crossed Smith's face. "Noted."

They left the townhouse, tension trailing behind them like fog, and moved quickly down the street.

Jo cast a sideways glance at Devin, then at Sara. "You still should've told me." Her voice was quieter now.

Sara nodded, guilt painting faint shadows under her eyes. "I know."

Devin and Stacy exchanged a brief look, then fell into step behind Jo as the group pushed forward into the cold, quiet neighborhood. The night seemed to hold its breath, as if it knew what was coming better than they did.

CHAPTER 13

Eli's pulse quickened as Mr. Mason's voice crackled through his earpiece. "Eli, get outta there. Now."

Eli hesitated, his gaze locked on the crates surrounding him. His breath caught in his throat as he ran his fingers over the jagged markings etched into the wood. The sigils were now unmistakable.

"Not yet," Eli muttered under his breath. "Mason, these crates . . . they're holding . . . Voidwalker armor." Silence hung heavy for a moment before Mr. Mason's voice came through again, sharp and urgent. "Aye, I ken what that means, lad. That's why I'm tellin' ye tae leave."

Eli shook his head.

"Mason," Eli whispered, his voice strained, "if this armor is here, it means . . . ."

Mason's tone grew darker. "Aye, I know what it means. An' that's why ye need tae get out now, before yer caught up in it."

Eli's gaze dropped to the sealed box in his hands, the faint glow of the intricate symbols a small comfort. A spark of hope flared in his chest, cutting through the fear. "But I have the red orb," he murmured. "Without it, the boy can paint all the murals Azazel wants, and they'll still be useless."

Mason was quiet for a beat before his voice softened. "Aye."

Eli clung to the thought. "We've bought ourselves

82

time," he insisted. "If the Voidwalkers can't emerge, we might actually have a chance."

But before the hope could fully settle, a faint clatter echoed from the far end of the warehouse. Eli's head snapped up, his body tensing as the sound of footsteps broke the fragile stillness.

Eli crouched low behind the stack of crates, his gloved hand gripping the sealed box containing the red orb. "Lucy," he whispered, his voice barely audible over the faint hum of the warehouse machinery. "Update on the patrols?"

"Patrolling operative on the catwalk is heading toward your position," Lucy replied calmly. "Main loading area movement detected. Estimated time to safe passage: unclear."

"Mason," he murmured into his earpiece. "I'm boxed in. Patrols are tightening. I'll need a minute."

Mr. Mason's voice crackled back, laced with urgency. "Don't wait, lad. Get yerself out now!"

"I can't," Eli hissed, glancing toward the walkway. The shadows of two operatives moved closer, their boots clanging against the metal grating above. "They'll see me."

Mason let out a low curse. "Fine. Hold tight. I'm movin' closer. See if I can draw their attention away."

Eli bit back a retort, focusing instead on staying perfectly still. He slowed his breathing, his eyes scanning for the slightest opening. Above, the patrolling operative's shadow stopped, lingering just above his position.

Meanwhile, Mr. Mason crept closer to the warehouse, his large frame somehow moving silently through the underbrush. His binoculars hung loosely around his neck as he reached a stack of abandoned pallets near the side of the building. He pressed himself against the cold metal, peering cautiously through a crack between the boards.

Inside, the scene unfolded like a dark tableau. Azazel stood at the far end of the main loading area, his imposing form commanding attention even from a distance, the crimson glow of his ring illuminating his pale face. Nearby, the boy painted, suspended a few inches above the ground, streaks of unnatural light emanating from his brush.

Mr. Mason's gaze shifted to another figure—a well-dressed man in a tailored suit standing near Azazel. "Councilman Haldine," he muttered under his breath. "What in the blazes are ye doin' here?"

"Mason?" Eli's voice came softly through the earpiece. "What's happening?"

"Haldine," Mason whispered back. "The bloody councilman's here. Chatting with Azazel like old pals."

"What?" Eli hissed, barely containing his shock. "Why would he—?"

"Shh," Mason hissed. "They're talkin'. Let me listen."

Eli remained crouched behind the crates, the faint glow of the red orb inside his sealed box still emanating a residual warmth against his gloves. His heart pounded as he monitored the shadows of the guards on the catwalk. One lingered for a moment, scanning the room below, before turning and continuing his patrol.

"Lucy," Eli whispered. "Status on the guards?"

"Patrolling operative on the catwalk is now moving toward the north end. Two guards near the loading area are stationary, but motion detected toward the east wing," Lucy reported.

Eli exhaled quietly, tension easing slightly. He leaned into his earpiece. "Mason, patrols are shifting. I might have a window."

"Good," Mason replied in a low whisper. "But stay low, lad. Haldine is still gabbin' with Azazel. An' the boy's still paintin'."

Eli's stomach churned at the mention of the boy. What kind of grip did Azazel have on him? Pushing the thought aside, Eli moved carefully along the edge of the room.

As he reached a narrow opening leading into the main room, Eli froze.

The boy hovered midair, suspended by an invisible force, his small frame illuminated by streaks of unnatural light emanating from his brush. Each stroke on the mural brought the image closer to completion: a jagged, hellish chasm, its depths glowing with a faint, ominous red. The energy rippling from the mural made the hairs on Eli's arm stand on end.

Azazel stood nearby, his hands clasped behind his back.

"Nearly there," Azazel said, his voice smooth yet commanding. He turned slightly toward the well-dressed man at his side. "Councilman Haldine, I must say, your efforts to suppress the spread of blue energy in this realm have been . . . less than satisfactory."

Haldine stiffened, his polished exterior faltering for a moment. "Lord Azazel, we've done all we can. The orbs—"

"All but eradicated, yes?" Azazel interrupted, his tone icy. "And yet, here we are. A vessel of Valoria's power has emerged in plain sight. How . . . inconvenient."

Haldine faltered, glancing toward the boy as though seeking a distraction. "We didn't anticipate—"

"You failed," Azazel snapped, his ring flaring briefly.

Eli squinted as he absorbed the conversation. Haldine, a councilman of Muxley, working for Azazel?

"Mason," Eli whispered into his earpiece. "He's got Haldine in his pocket. You think this ties back to . . . ?"

Before Eli could finish, the boy's voice broke through the tension. "It's . . . done," he said, lowering the brush.

Azazel turned to the mural, his lips curling into a predatory smile. "Excellent."

Azazel stepped closer, his movements deliberate, and withdrew an object from within his robe.

Eli's momentary hope shattered. "He's got another orb," he murmured.

"Aye, lad. I see it," Mr. Mason replied.

Azazel held the orb aloft, the energy within it surging outward like tendrils of fire. To everyone's surprise and with a sudden, deliberate motion, Azazel hurled it against the mural. The impact sent a shockwave through the room, the glowing chasm erupting into life as a swirling vortex formed within the painting.

The operatives in the room stepped back, their eyes wide as the portal stabilized. From within the vortex, dark shapes began to emerge—figures cloaked in shadow, their forms wreathed in ethereal mist.

"Voidwalkers," whispered Eli.

"I see 'em," Mason growled through the earpiece. "Get yerself out, Eli. Now."

Eli's gaze flickered between the mural and the crates behind him. His instincts screamed at him to run, but he couldn't tear his eyes away from the unfolding nightmare.

Before Azazel could speak, one of his operatives rushed to his side, breathless and tense. "Sir, we've got a breach. Someone tripped the silent alarm near the west entrance. There's no sign of forced entry, but they're inside."

Azazel's eyes narrowed, his expression darkening. "Get the armor from the back for our new arrivals," he said coldly. "Seal every exit. No one leaves this warehouse until the intruder is found."

Eli's heart sank. He was trapped.

Eli crouched low behind the crates, every muscle in his body tense as the sound of Azazel's men echoed through the warehouse. Orders were being barked, boots clanged against metal walkways, and the air buzzed with a menacing energy.

"Secure the perimeter!" one of the operatives shouted. "No one leaves."

Eli's breath came in shallow bursts. His heart thundered in his chest as he clutched the sealed box containing the red orb. Trapped. The word rattled around his mind like a death sentence.

"Mason," he whispered, his voice barely audible over the chaos. "They're locking it down. I'm stuck."

"Hell's bells," Mason hissed through the earpiece. "Stay low, lad. I'll try tae draw 'em away if I can."

Eli risked a glance around the corner of the crate

stack, his stomach knotting as he saw operatives across the way, sweeping the area with sharp, practiced precision. He knew it was only a matter of time before they reached him.

"Mason," he said, his voice edged with desperation, "they're closing in."

Before Mason could respond, a soft buzz in Eli's earpiece interrupted him. "Eli," Lucy's calm, synthetic voice broke through. "There is a trap door located three feet to your left. Tunnel routes located below."

"A trap door?" Eli whispered, glancing toward the indicated area. His eyes landed on a section of the floor covered by a rusted steel panel, almost invisible in the dim light.

"Yes," Lucy confirmed. "The operatives will reach your location in approximately twenty seconds."

Eli clenched his jaw, steeling himself. "Mason, I've got a way out," he said quickly. "Trap door in the floor. I'm going for it."

"Aye," Mason replied, his voice tight. "Do it, but keep yer head down. I'll meet ye at the car. Send me yer location!"

Eli took a deep breath and moved. Keeping his steps silent, he slid across the cold concrete, reaching the trap door just as the beam of a flashlight swept dangerously close to his position. He lifted the panel, its hinges creaking faintly, and slipped through, pulling it shut over him.

The air in the tunnel pressed against Eli's skin like a damp cloth, the faint emergency lighting casting flickering, ghostly shadows across the rough walls. Eli adjusted his satchel, clutching the sealed box tightly as he began to move forward.

Above him, muffled voices reached his ears. He paused, straining to hear.

"Nothing yet, sir!" a man shouted, his tone panicked.

"Keep looking," another voice, colder and sharper, snapped. "Secure the warehouse. No one leaves until they're found."

Eli's blood ran cold, and he quickened his pace.

"Lucy," he whispered, his voice low and urgent. "Guide me out. Fast."

Meanwhile, outside the warehouse, Mr. Mason had his own problems. Azazel's operatives were expanding their patrol, their flashlights slicing through the night as they swept the perimeter. Mason pressed himself against a stack of pallets, waiting for a break in their pattern.

When the moment came, he bolted, his heavy boots pounding against the gravel as he made for the cover of the tree line. "Eli," he said into the earpiece, his breath labored. "I'm out. Headin' tae the car. Get yerself clear."

The static was his only reply.

"Proceed straight for fifty meters," Lucy replied. "Then take the right fork. It will lead to an exterior drainage outlet."

Eli pushed forward, the sound of his footsteps echoing in the confined space. Mr. Mason's voice cut through the growing static, "Eli—out—car—clear—"

Eli tapped his earpiece trying to make out Mr. Mason's words. "Lucy, send my location to Mason."

"Coordi . . . sent," Lucy's voice crackled through the

earpiece. Then suddenly it came in clear again. "Proceed to the drainage outlet."

Eli emerged minutes later, stumbling into a drainage ditch just beyond Brackenridge Hollow. The cold night air hit his face like a slap. He paused to catch his breath, his gaze darting back toward the warehouse in the distance.

His earpiece crackled faintly. "Eli? Yae out?"

"I'm clear," Eli replied, his voice steady despite the adrenaline coursing through him. "Waiting on you."

"Stay put," Mason ordered. "I'm comin' tae get ye. Hold tight."

Eli adjusted his grip on the sealed box and crouched low in the ditch, his eyes scanning the woods for any sign of movement. Every sound set his nerves on edge as he waited for Mr. Mason, the weight of the red orb feeling heavier than ever.

CHAPTER 14

The warehouse loomed heavy with shadows, the faint red glow from the mural casting jagged, flickering patterns across the walls. Azazel stood at the center of the room. The Voidwalkers hovered silently nearby, their wraithlike forms pulsing and shifting, the faint runes on their bodies glowing dimly in the gloom.

Standing off to the side, Councilman Haldine adjusted his tailored suit, his expression carefully neutral as he watched the scene unfold. Though his outward appearance was one of calm composure, a bead of sweat slid down his temple, betraying his unease.

A sharp series of hurried footsteps broke the oppressive silence. A group of Azazel's agents entered, their faces pale and drawn.

"Master," one of them began, swallowing hard, "the red orb. It's gone. Taken."

Azazel's back remained turned, his silhouette rigid against the mural's shifting light. He let the silence stretch. The agent shifted nervously, glancing at his companions. Councilman Haldine, still standing near the edge of the room, crossed his arms tightly, pursing his lips as he watched Azazel.

Azazel's voice was quiet, yet razor-sharp. "And the intruder?"

The agent hesitated, his throat bobbing as he swallowed. "We—We can't find anyone, Master. It's as if they vanished."

Azazel's fingers twitched at his sides. "Vanished?" His tone sent a shiver through the room.

The agent stammered. "We—We believe it was Smith, Master. His people . . . They—"

Before he could finish, Azazel raised a hand, fingers curling. The air rippled, shimmering like heat off pavement, and then the agent's body jerked violently. His limbs snapped straight, his feet lifting an inch off the ground before an unseen force slammed into his chest. With a brutal crack, the man flew backward, his body crumpling into a heap against the cold concrete floor.

Azazel barely spared him a glance. Instead, with a lazy flick of his wrist, he gestured toward two Voidwalkers lurking near the edge of the mural. They glided forward, their forms half-solid, half-shadow.

They knelt beside the unconscious agent, and with hands more bone than flesh, they reached for him—fingers sinking just beneath his skin, as though his body were no more solid than water.

A soft, crackling hiss filled the air as the agent's skin turned sallow and grey. His chest rose once, sharply, then fell. His eyes snapped open, wide and glassy, pupils shrinking to pinpricks. The Voidwalkers drank him in, pulling at something deeper than breath, deeper than blood—siphoning his very life force until all that remained was an empty husk.

The agent's body twitched once more, then went still, his face locked in an expression of vacant horror.

Haldine closed his eyes, jaw tightening as he turned slightly away, pretending to adjust his cufflink.

"Smith has stolen from me?" Azazel's voice broke

the silence, a cold thread of fury woven through each word. "A grave mistake."

Councilman Haldine took a cautious step forward. "Lord Azazel," he said carefully, his voice striving for steadiness, "perhaps there is a way to turn this setback to our advantage."

Azazel turned slowly, his red-ringed eyes locking onto Haldine. "Oh?" he drawled. "And what brilliant scheme do you propose, Councilman?" The question dripped with mockery.

Haldine swallowed, choosing each word like a man defusing a bomb. "Smith's interference may indicate . . . he's becoming desperate. We know his power is diminished—fragmented, even. If we can anticipate his next move, perhaps we can set a trap. Use his predictability against him."

Azazel's gaze bore into him. The silence stretched a beat too long before Azazel spoke. "Your political maneuvering might serve some purpose after all," he mused. "Very well. Continue."

Emboldened, Haldine gave a small nod. "I can leverage my connections within the city to monitor for unusual activity. I'll assign Councilman Graeves to the task—and we'll have him deploy the Riftstone Beacon. Its reach extends beyond this realm, into the thin spaces where realm walkers pass. If Smith or his allies slip between, the beacon will pulse and mark the breach."

A sly smile spread across Azazel's face. "You assume I have forgotten what the risks are for using that device."

Haldine stiffened slightly. "Of course not, my lord, I only meant—"

Azazel cut him off with a slow raise of his hand.

"Every pulse from that device tears at the veil, Councilman. Every pulse not only allows us to track them, but risks revealing us and our position also. Timing is everything."

He stepped closer, his presence towering over Haldine. "But . . . .perhaps now is the time? Let Smith see. Let him feel us closing in. Let him know that wherever he runs, the Riftstone will follow."

Azazel's lip curled faintly. "Loyalty without results is meaningless, Councilman. Find him—and the rest of his team—or you'll find your own life force feeding my Voidwalkers."

Councilman Haldine's nod was slower this time, his throat tight. "Of course, my lord," he murmured, lowering his gaze.

One of the remaining agents found the courage to speak, his voice barely steady. "Master, we will recover the orb. We'll—"

"You will do nothing," Azazel interrupted, his voice a sharp edge. His crimson gaze turned toward the Voidwalkers, standing silently at the edges of the mural's glow. "They will handle it. Once the councilman locates Smith and his team, we will send these soldiers to retrieve the orb and the girl."

Haldine's brow furrowed. "The girl?"

Azazel's jaw tensed, his fingers flexing unconsciously. "The one wielding Valorian power. The blue energy now flows through her—because of your failure, Councilman."

Haldine stiffened. "My failure?"

Azazel turned fully toward him, his red-ringed eyes narrowing. "The blue orbs. You assured me they had all been accounted for. But your people missed one—and now that power has awakened in the girl." His voice dipped into something colder, almost reflective. "She doesn't yet understand what she carries . . ."

A flicker of something rare passed through Azazel's expression—not fear exactly, but the memory of an old threat. "If the girl learns to wield what's inside her, she could become the same threat Lilianna once was—or worse."

Interrupting Azazel's train of thought, a second group of operatives entered from the side corridor, struggling under the weight of dark, twisted armor laid across their arms. The metal—if it could even be called metal—shimmered in the dim light, not polished, but as if it were perpetually slick with some dark, viscous substance.

The operatives laid the armor at the feet of the Voidwalkers, then stepped back quickly, as if afraid to linger too close. The Voidwalkers stirred for the first time, their forms shifting unnaturally, caught between this world and the next. Long, wraithlike fingers reached down, caressing the armor almost reverently before the pieces began to affix themselves—moving as if alive, snapping into place with sharp, organic clicks.

Their violet eyes burned brighter, the armor somehow amplifying their presence.

"Once they have the orb and the girl, our plans can proceed without hindrance," Haldine offered, his voice thinner than before.

Azazel nodded slowly. "Indeed." He glanced at Haldine, a hint of amusement curling the corner of his mouth. "And you, Councilman, will ensure the city's authorities remain . . . oblivious?"

Haldine forced a tight smile. "Of course. My influence guarantees that any anomalies will be dismissed or overlooked. I have others perfectly placed in the city government who are loyal. And the populace . . . trusts me."

"Trust," Azazel echoed softly, stepping closer. "A fragile thing." He leaned in, his voice barely above a whisper. "Remember your place, Haldine. Do not mistake convenience for necessity."

A subtle shudder rippled through Haldine, but he held his ground. "I serve at your pleasure, Lord Azazel. My only aim is to see our objectives fulfilled."

Azazel held his gaze a moment longer before turning away. "See that you do."

He faced the Voidwalkers again, their new armor gleaming darkly, almost as if the pieces drank in the dim light around them. "Smith believes he can hide. Let him believe it a little longer."

One of the Voidwalkers stepped forward, the motion rippling the air around it like disturbed water. Azazel's eyes gleamed with satisfaction. "Await my command."

Without sound or ceremony, the Voidwalkers moved as one, dissolving into shadow—the dark vapor of their bodies seeping into the floor, the walls, the very bones of the warehouse itself.

Azazel glanced back at Haldine. "Do not make me question your usefulness again."

"Yes, Lord Azazel," Haldine said quickly, bowing his head before turning and retreating toward the exit. The heavy metal door groaned shut behind him, the sound echoing in the stillness.

Azazel stood, the faint glow of the mural casting

a twisted, otherworldly light upon him. Slowly, he extended his hand, fingers trailing across the mural's shifting surface. The patterns rippled beneath his touch, alive beneath his fingertips.

"Soon," Azazel murmured. "This world will see true power."

The heavy warehouse door groaned shut behind Councilman Haldine, sealing Azazel inside. Haldine exhaled sharply, the night air cool against the sweat beading at his hairline. He tugged at his collar, fingers trembling as he reached into his coat pocket and withdrew a slim, dark comm device.

The line crackled to life. "Greaves," Haldine said, his voice low and urgent. "Activate the Riftstone Beacon. Now."

There was a beat of hesitation on the other end. "The Riftstone? Sir, that's—"

"Spare me the lecture," Haldine snapped. "Smith breached the warehouse. The orb is gone. Azazel wants every possible crack between realms lit up like a bonfire. Use it to track any realm disturbances tied to Smith's signature—and prepare a sweep for the girl."

"The girl?" Greaves' voice dipped into confusion. "What girl?"

"The one . . ." Haldine paused. "Apparently we missed one of the blue orbs in our collecting of them, and . . . now there is a girl carrying Valorian power," Haldine hissed. "Just track it. And Greaves—if you feel the Beacon pulse even once, do not speak of it to anyone outside the council. Understood?"

". . . Understood, sir."

The line went dead, leaving Haldine alone under the pale moonlight. For a long moment, he stared at his reflection in a puddle at his feet—a man caught somewhere between his ambition and his fear.

CHAPTER 15

The dimly lit streets were eerily quiet as Smith led the group through the winding alleyways of the city. The night air carried a faint chill, amplifying the tension in the group.

"Where exactly are we going?" Jo asked. She quickened her pace to catch up with Smith. "You've dragged us halfway across the city, and we still have no idea what's going on."

Smith glanced over his shoulder, his expression calm but unreadable. "We're almost there. Not much longer."

Jo scoffed, her patience wearing thin. "You appear out of nowhere, you take my sister, and now we're wandering the streets without any explanation. How exactly is this supposed to inspire trust?"

Devin touched Jo's shoulder lightly. "Jo, maybe we should give him a chance. Sara doesn't look like she's in danger."

Jo turned to look at Sara, who walked beside Smith. Her younger sister's face was tense but resolute. Jo's frustration softened.

Stacy stayed close to Devin, her unease evident. "Devin, I really don't like this either. We're walking blind into . . . who knows what."

Devin gave her hand a reassuring squeeze. "I know, but if there's even a chance this leads us to answers, we have to follow through. I've got you."

After what felt like an eternity of twists and turns

through shadowed streets and narrow alleys, Smith finally stopped in front of a large, nondescript building. The industrial structure loomed over them, its weathered exterior blending into the dim surroundings.

Jo frowned, folding her arms. "This . . . is where you're taking us?" she asked incredulously. "What is this place?"

Smith didn't answer immediately. Instead, he turned to the heavy red door at the center of the building's facade. The bright crimson stood out starkly against the worn gray walls, almost glowing in the faint moonlight. Reaching into his coat, Smith retrieved a ring of ornate skeleton keys.

Jo exchanged a wary glance with Devin and Stacy. "You've got to be kidding me," she muttered. "This doesn't exactly scream safe."

Devin placed a steadying hand on her arm. "Let's just see where this goes."

Sara, standing quietly beside Smith, finally spoke. "Jo, please."

Jo looked at her sister and nodded reluctantly.

Smith flipped through the keys with practiced precision, his expression unreadable as he selected one etched with intricate patterns. He slid it into the lock, and the door clicked open. Pushing the door inward, he gestured for them to follow.

They hesitated briefly before stepping inside, their eyes widening at the sight before them. The interior was nothing like they expected. Instead of an abandoned industrial space, they found themselves in what could only be described as a sanctuary of ancient relics and advanced technology.

Holographic maps floated above a central table, glowing softly. Along the walls, weapons and artifacts shimmered with an otherworldly light. Charts, maps, and star charts lined another wall, while a small armory gleamed with meticulously polished tools. The air carried a faint hum, as though the space itself was alive with unseen energy.

"This . . . this is incredible," Sara whispered, her eyes darting around the room. She glanced back at Smith. "I kind of liked the library better though," she said, smiling.

Smith chuckled. "I know what you mean."

Devin, Jo, and Stacy glanced at each other wondering what Sara was referring too. Jo also was taken by how relaxed Sara seemed with Smith.

Devin and Stacy stood in stunned silence as they continued to look around the room, while Jo's skepticism wavered. "What is this place?" she asked quietly.

Smith secured the door behind them. "This is one of our safe houses," he explained. "It's where we plan, monitor, and secure items of importance. No one can find us here unless we want them to."

Jo narrowed her eyes. "Unless you want them to? That's not exactly comforting."

Smith gave her a small, knowing smile. "Fair point. But trust me, this place is off-grid. No signals in or out unless we allow it. The entrance is shielded, and the building itself . . . let's just say it's layered between this world and yours."

"That's supposed to make us feel better?" Stacy muttered, inching closer to Devin.

Sara took a slow step further into the room, her

fingers brushing the edge of the holographic map. The soft blue glow reflected in her eyes.

Before Jo could press further, the sound of approaching footsteps echoed from a side room. Two men emerged, their expressions serious as they stepped into view. One was tall and broad-shouldered, his sharp eyes immediately scanning the group with an appraising glance. The other was leaner, carrying a small, intricately locked box pulsing faintly with a dim red glow.

Smith stepped forward to greet them, his tone lightening. "I suppose introductions are in order," he said, gesturing to the newcomers. "This is Mr. Mason and Eli Whitaker. Trusted allies and friends. They've been working with me for a long time."

Mr. Mason gave a curt nod. Eli remained silent, his expression serious but not unkind, his eyes lingering on Sara for a moment longer than the others.

Sara hesitated for a moment before moving away from the holographic map and turned toward the newcomers. "I'm Sara," she said. "This is my sister, Jo, and our friends, Devin and Stacy."

Eli inclined his head, while Mr. Mason's gaze remained sharp. "Aye, we know who ye are," Mason said, his tone even.

Jo blinked, her brow furrowing. "You . . . You do?"

Mr. Mason exchanged a brief glance with Eli before responding. "We've known about you for some time."

Before the tension could escalate, Smith raised a hand. "We'll get to all of that soon. For now, there's something more pressing we need to address first."

He nodded toward the table, where Eli carefully placed the box he carried. As the lid opened with a series of mechanical clicks, the red orb inside was revealed. Its malevolent energy pulsed through the room, casting a sinister glow on their faces.

Smith nodded curtly, his focus shifting to the glowing orb on the table. Its pulsing light seemed to reflect in his eyes, pulling him into a memory before he could stop it—

The air in the room around him faded, replaced by a different darkness. He stood again in a shadowed chamber, his arms bound by an invisible force, his strength bleeding out with every breath.

Two figures loomed before him, their forms wreathed in flickering shadows, their faces obscured by shifting veils of smoke and sorcery.

"Did you think this unity would last forever?" one figure asked, its voice smooth and cruel. "It was always a lie—a fragile illusion built on borrowed power."

The second figure stepped closer, the glow of a red orb illuminating their silhouette. "You saw it, didn't you?" he said softly. "You saw the weaknesses in the King's plans long before anyone else. And yet you still chose loyalty."

Smith strained against the unseen bonds, pain lancing through him as the ring that once adorned his hand—began to be removed.

The first figure laughed, low and hollow, a sound that echoed through the chamber. "Only now do you understand true power. And soon, the rest of the realms will too."

The memory shattered as quickly as it had come, the safe house rushing back into focus. The red orb sat on the table. Smith blinked as he forced himself back to the present.

Jo's arms were crossed. "I'm asking you a question. What is that thing on the table?"

Smith turned to face her, his expression carefully composed. "A red orb," Smith said gravely. "One of our enemy's tools. One of the reasons we're all here."

Before Jo could press further, the conversation shifted—all attention drawn to Devin, who stood unnaturally still, his eyes locked on the orb.

The orb pulsed again, its sickly light seeming to reach for him. A magnetic pull coursed through him, like a hidden wire inside his chest suddenly tugged taut. The rhythm of the pulse . . . it matched his heartbeat.

His fingers twitched involuntarily, aching to reach out—like an itch beneath his skin, impossible to scratch.

"Devin?" Sara's voice broke through the haze, her concern pulling him back just enough to breathe. "Are you okay?"

Devin clenched his fists, forcing his hands to his sides. "Yeah," he said quickly, his voice tight, almost too quick. "I'm fine."

Jo's gaze sharpened. "You don't look fine. Maybe that thing is messing with you."

Stacy stepped closer, resting her hand on his arm. "Devin, what's wrong?"

He shook his head, pasting on a weak smile. "It's nothing. Just . . . tired."

The words felt hollow even to him, but no one pushed—except Eli, whose eyes lingered on Devin just a heartbeat too long, his brow furrowed with something halfway between suspicion and understanding.

Without a word, Eli reached for the orb's case. "Good idea," he muttered to no one in particular, lifting the orb and carefully placing it back inside. The case hissed softly as the seals activated, gears whirring and ancient runes flaring briefly before the lock slid into place. The moment the orb was fully sealed, Devin's chest eased. The invisible pull lessened, the buzzing under his skin quieting. He took a slow breath, trying not to make the relief obvious, but inside, it felt like surfacing from underwater.

Mr. Mason looked at Eli, his brow furrowed. "We need tae secure that orb, lad. Keep it well off Azazel's radar."

"Who's Azazel?" Devin asked, stepping forward—his tone a little too casual, as if changing the subject might anchor him back to solid ground.

Eli, Mr. Mason, and Smith exchanged another glance.

"You'll want to sit down for that answer," Smith said quietly.

CHAPTER 16

Smith took a measured breath. "It all began centuries ago," he said, his voice steady, "in a realm known as Valoria. A land of vast beauty, unmatched power, and magic interwoven into the very fabric of existence. It was ruled by King Thalion, a wise and just leader who brought peace and prosperity to his people."

Jo rolled her eyes and let out a sharp exhale. She crossed her arms, as she stared at Smith like he'd just recited a bedtime story. "Are we seriously supposed to buy into this?! *Valoria? Magical realms?*" She scoffed. "What's next, dragons?" She shot him a pointed look. "You expect us to just nod along like this isn't completely insane?"

Smith didn't flinch. His gaze remained steady, unreadable. "No dragons," he replied, his tone calm. "But I understand how this sounds."

Jo threw up her hands. "We've been dragged into— *whatever this is*—and you're expecting us to just *believe* in ancient kings and magic realms?" She turned to Sara, her voice edged with disbelief. "Sara, you can't seriously be okay with this."

Sara met Jo's eyes. "Jo . . . what if it's true?" Her voice was softer and made Jo hesitate. "I mean . . . with *everything* I've seen lately."

Jo didn't know what to say.

Devin, who had been silent, finally spoke up. "Look, Jo, I get it," he said. "This all sounds like something out of a movie. But the park? Those . . . things that came after us? Now the orb?" He gestured toward the now-empty platform where the red orb had rested just moments before. "Are we just going to pretend none of that happened?"

Before Jo could fire back, Eli, who had been standing near the central table, interjected. "Speaking of the orb . . ." He turned toward them, his posture tense. "We need to make sure it stays hidden."

The group turned in time to see Eli stride toward the south wall carrying the secured case. Jo, Devin, Stacy, and Sara exchanged uneasy glances as they followed him, their gazes locking onto the imposing vault door embedded into the steel-reinforced wall.

Eli moved with purpose, his fingers flying over the keypad as he entered a combination. A faint metallic *click* echoed through the space as the vault door hissed open, revealing a dark interior lined with intricate, rune-like etchings.

Carefully, Eli stepped inside and placed the case on a raised pedestal in the center. As soon as he withdrew his hands, thin metallic arms emerged from the vault walls, locking onto the case with precise, mechanical efficiency. The moment Eli stepped back, the vault's mechanics groaned to life, and the massive door swung shut with a slow, ominous thud.

Then, to their complete disbelief, the entire vault *shimmered*—its frame rippling like water before fading entirely from view.

Stacy sucked in a sharp breath. "What . . . just happened?"

"The vault moved," Eli said simply, as if that explained everything.

Devin blinked. "It . . . *moved?*" He ran a hand over the spot where the vault had been, feeling only cool, solid wall.

Mr. Mason folded his arms. "Aye. It's no' just hidden," he added. "It's beyond Azazel's reach now."

Jo, still standing, gestured wildly at the now-empty space. "So let me get this straight. You've got *disappearing vaults, magic realms,* and now . . . what? *Bad guys from another dimension?*"

Smith's expression darkened. "In a manner of speaking, yes." He took a step closer. "Azazel—what you might call a man turned monster—is not just from another realm. He's from Valoria. He was once a man of great influence, but his hunger for power led him to betray everything Thalion built. He was exiled, but now, he's returned."

Jo opened her mouth to argue, but Smith lifted a hand, silencing her. "I'm not asking for blind faith," he said. "I know this is a lot to take in. But whether you believe me or not, *Azazel is here.* His reach has already spread into your world. Now. And if we don't act, there won't be anything left to question."

The weight of his words settled over the room. Jo swallowed hard, her mind racing. Devin and Stacy exchanged uneasy glances, while Sara shifted uncomfortably.

Devin finally broke the silence. "What exactly does this Azazel want with . . . all of this? The orb? Us?"

Smith exchanged a look with Mr. Mason and Eli before answering. "Azazel doesn't just want power. He wants to tear down the barriers between realms. He wants control—over every world connected to this one.

And the red orbs? They're one of the tools he's using to do it."

He let the words sink in for a moment before adding, "That's why we had to steal this one. If we didn't, it would've been one step closer to completing his mission."

Jo's head snapped up. "Okay, but what does that have to do with us?"

Mr. Mason exhaled slowly. "Because, lass . . . whether ye realize it or not, you three are connected to what he's after—especially you and Sara."

Jo's brow furrowed. "What does that even mean?"

Smith stepped in. "Sara and I ran into each other the other day at Savor Street Market."

Jo's eyes widened slightly. "The market? Wait—" Her memory jolted into place. "Sara passed out that day, muttering something about looking for a man. She was talking about you?"

Sara's face reddened slightly, but she nodded.

Smith gave a tight smile. "That wasn't just a random fainting spell. Sara was filled—overwhelmed, actually—with the power from an orb. Not a red one, but a blue orb. Valorian energy."

"Valoria?" Stacy asked, confused.

"The realm of light," Eli supplied. "Its power was thought to be lost after the Overseers fell. But Sara . . . she's a carrier of that power now."

Jo shook her head in disbelief. "Okay, hold on. That's insane. You're saying my sister somehow has magical realm power inside her? How?"

"That's part of what we need to explain," Smith said. "But what matters right now is that Azazel knows.

He'll see her as a threat—because Valorian power is one of the few things capable of stopping him."

Sara swallowed hard, her mind racing. "But why me?"

Mr. Mason's expression softened slightly. "Because of who your mother was, lass."

Both sisters froze.

Jo's voice was low, almost a whisper. "What do you mean . . . who our mother was?"

Smith started to answer, but before the words could leave his mouth, Lucy's voice cut through the room like a blade.

"Alert: Unauthorized tracking signal detected. Temporal signature identified. Source—Riftstone Beacon."

Smith's head snapped toward the console. "Damn it."

Jo's arms flew up. "What now?!"

Lucy's voice continued, crisp and unforgiving. "Tracking pulse first detected upon entry to the warehouse. Signature lock—Smith and Valorian carrier."

"Me," Sara whispered, her voice barely audible.

"And me," Smith said grimly.

Eli's expression darkened. "They're tracking her already."

"Aye! And now they know we're here," Mr. Mason finished.

CHAPTER 17

Jack sat at his desk, staring at the grainy, black-and-white crime-scene photos spread out before him. His hands trembled slightly as he shuffled through the images, each one more disturbing than the last. One photo showed the living room in complete disarray—furniture overturned, some oddly missing. Picture frames shattered, and deep gouges in the walls, as if some monstrous force had torn through the room. His breath hitched every time he glanced at the one photo that showed Lily, his wife, lying motionless in the hallway of their once peaceful home.

But Sara, their infant daughter, had been hidden away, untouched, in a small closet. Jack's heart ached at the thought of her tiny cries muffled behind that door. And Jolene, his older daughter, was at school when it happened. Safe but shaken ever since.

The investigation had hit a dead end weeks ago. Six months. Six months of staring at crime-scene photos, sifting through inconclusive police reports, and fielding questions from both colleagues and his own relentless mind. Six months since his world had been shattered.

Jack stood abruptly, the legs of his chair scraping harshly against the hardwood floor. He ran a hand through his hair, pacing the small home office. The photographs, the reports, the coroner's notes—they were all spread across the desk, mocking him with their silence. Every official document read the same: no sign of forced entry, stab wounds in shoulder and side—not fatal, suspicious but inconclusive. "Cause of death: undetermined."

But Jack knew better.

He knew it wasn't just some random break-in gone wrong. It was too . . . controlled, too targeted. There had been no signs of forced entry, nothing stolen. This was something more. Something darker.

"What am I missing?!"

With a sudden burst of anger, Jack reached for the nearest object on his desk—a paperweight—and hurled it across the room. It smashed into the bookshelf on the far side, knocking over a set of decorative items, books, and a small wooden box that clattered to the floor.

"Damn it," Jack muttered under his breath, feeling a slight twinge of guilt at the mess he'd just made.

But then he saw it.

Amidst the clutter of fallen items, one thing stood out.

As the dust settled, Jack's eyes caught a small, almost imperceptible glint on the back wall of the bookshelf. His brows furrowed in confusion as he stepped closer. A few decorative trinkets had tumbled from their place on the shelf, and among them was a . . . keyhole—a keyhole Jack had never noticed before.

His heart skipped a beat.

He crouched down, moving aside the books and shattered items to get a better look. There, embedded in the back of the bookshelf, was an old, intricately designed keyhole.

"What the hell is this?" he muttered.

But before he could process further, his gaze fell on something else—a small wooden box that had fallen open in the chaos. He recognized the box immediately. It was a gift Lily had kept for years, something she always cherished but never explained.

Now, the box lay open, its contents spilled across the floor.

Jack reached for it and froze.

Among the fallen objects, a key glinted in the dim light of the room. It wasn't just any key. It was small, ornate, and adorned with a beautifully carved leaf symbol on its handle.

He hesitated for a moment before picking it up.

As he held it, the key seemed to hum with some sort of energy.

Jack stood, heart pounding, and turned toward the bookshelf. Without thinking, he walked over to the hidden keyhole and gingerly inserted the key.

For a moment, nothing happened.

Then, with a faint click, the bookshelf shuddered slightly.

A hidden compartment slid open from behind the shelves, revealing a small space about eighteen inches wide and eight inches high tucked into the back of the third shelf of the bookcase. Jack reached inside and pulled out a faded, leather-bound journal that had been tucked away, hidden from view.

Jack stood there, frozen, staring down at the book in his hands. The leather was worn, the edges frayed, and his wife's handwriting was scrawled across the cover in faint ink. Lilianna.

His heart hammered in his chest as he ran his fingers across her name. He swallowed hard, steeling himself to open the journal. But as he tried to lift the cover, it wouldn't budge.

Confused, Jack turned the journal over in his hands and noticed a small, intricate keyhole embedded into the leather strap that bound the book shut.

"What the heck?" he muttered under his breath. He glanced at the ornate key he had just used to open the hidden compartment in the bookshelf.

With a flicker of hope, he tried the key in the journal's lock, but it didn't fit. Frustration flared in his chest. He gave the journal one last attempt before setting it down on the desk, its secrets still locked away.

"What were you hiding, Lily?" he whispered to the empty room.

Before he could go further with that question, a sharp knock on the door shattered the stillness of the moment. Jack flinched, the abrupt sound jerking him out of his spiraling thoughts.

Quickly, he tucked the journal into the desk drawer, shutting it with a quiet click. His hand reached behind the doorframe, fingers wrapping around the cold steel of his gun as he moved cautiously toward the front door.

He peered through the curtain. Standing on the porch, wearing his usual politician's smile, was Councilman Greaves.

Jack's brow furrowed. What the hell was he doing here?

Reluctantly, Jack opened the door just wide enough. "Councilman."

"Jack," Greaves said smoothly, his smile wide and

sympathetic. "I was just in the area and thought I'd stop by. I've been meaning to check in. See how you're holding up."

Jack's grip on the doorframe tightened. "I'm fine. Please, come in"

Greaves nodded slowly as he entered the doorframe. "I understand. It's . . . a lot to carry, losing a wife like that. And with no clear answers? That would eat at any man."

Jack said nothing.

"I know you're still digging," Greaves added softly. "I'd do the same in your shoes. Hell, I admire it. You know, there are some channels I could lean on. Maybe help reopen the case, get fresh eyes on it."

Jack's gut twisted. The offer sounded good—but something about Greaves' eagerness felt off, perhaps contrived. Too rehearsed.

"Appreciate it," Jack said flatly. "But I'm managing."

Greaves' smile didn't falter. "Of course. Of course." His gaze wandered—past Jack, down the hall—and into the office, where the bookshelf still sat ajar, its hidden compartment partially exposed.

Jack stepped sideways, subtly blocking Greaves' line of sight.

"That's quite the shelf you've got there," Greaves said, trying to get a better look. "Don't suppose you found anything . . . interesting?"

Jack forced a thin smile. "Old storage spot of Lily's. She liked her secrets." He gave a hollow chuckle. "Nothing useful, though."

Greaves' expression stayed polite, but the curiosity in his eyes lingered a moment too long.

"Well," Greaves said finally, stepping back toward the door. "If you do find something—anything—come to me first. I want to help you, Jack. You deserve answers."

Jack gave a short nod. He heard the words, but the tone? Still too smooth. Too careful. He stood in the doorway, watching as Greaves descended the steps and made his way down the quiet street, his figure melting into the night.

Something wasn't right. Jack closed the door—hard. He threw the deadbolt, then twisted the second lock for good measure. Without wasting another second, he crossed the room, then shut the secret compartment in the bookshelf.

He stood there for a moment, trying to calm the slow burn of suspicion gnawing at his gut. Why would the councilman care about a dead-end investigation? And the timing of it, the same night he had found the journal?

His fingers hovered over the desk drawer, but before he could open it—a second knock at the door rang out. Another visitor—so soon?

Grabbing his gun off of his desk, he crept to the door and pulled back the curtain just enough to see outside. A man stood there, tall and broad-shouldered, a dark coat hanging heavy against the wind. His face was lined and weathered by time.

Jack opened the door just a crack. "Who the hell are you?"

The man gave a faint smile that didn't reach his eyes. "Mr. Mason," he said, his voice carrying a thick Scottish lilt. "I'm here tae talk tae ye about yer wife. About Lily."

116

Jack's knuckles whitened around the grip of his gun. "You're my second uninvited guest tonight," he said sharply. "I don't know you. How do you know Lily? And who sent you?"

Mason's gaze flicked briefly to Jack's hand, taking in the gun without so much as a flinch. Instead, his expression softened with something that almost looked like understanding. "Aye, I ken that. But this isn't a doorstep conversation. I'm unarmed—and you, Jack, you've got the gun." Mason held up his hands slowly, fingers spread wide. "The advantage is yours."

After a moment, Jack motioned with his gun to come in, stepping back just enough to let Mason inside.

Mason gave a slight nod.

Jack led him down the hallway toward his small, cluttered office. Mason's gaze swept briefly across the desk—the scattered photos, the reports, the open coroner's notes—and the faintest sigh escaped his lips.

"Ye've been busy," Mason said quietly.

Jack ignored him and folded his arms, leaning back against the desk. "All right, start talking. Who are you really—and how do you know about Lily? About my family?"

Mason turned slowly, meeting Jack's guarded gaze. "I worked wi' Lily, though she likely never told ye about it."

"She didn't." said Jack. "And that's not much of an explanation."

Mr. Mason softened slightly. His voice dropped. "I know how it feels, Jack. Tae lose someone ye love . . . an' tae have no answers, nothin' that makes sense o' it. It eats at ye. Changes ye."

Jack folded his arms, leaning against the edge of the desk. "Don't act like you know what this feels like," he snapped. "I've been chasing ghosts for six months. Lily's dead and two of our agents are missing. The cops . . . and my colleagues say it's a dead end, but I know they're wrong. I just . . . I don't know what I'm missing . . . and now . . . you're here."

Jack's eyes locked onto Mason. "So tell me, if you know so much, what am I missing?"

Mr. Mason stepped closer to the desk, his gaze narrowing as he studied the photos. His expression darkened as he picked up one of the coroner's reports, scanning the printed words quickly.

Mason turned to Jack. "I'm no' here tae question yer grief, Jack, or tae make this more difficult. I'm here tae give ye answers." Mason reached for one of the crime scene photos—a shot of the gouges in the walls of Jack's home. He held it up, his voice lowering. "The kind ye won't find in police reports or forensics labs."

Jack frowned as he tried to read Mason's expression. "I'm listening."

Mason's eyes locked onto his. "First off, Jack, ye need tae understand somethin'—Councilman Greaves? That man is no friend tae ye."

Jack's stomach turned. "What are you talking about?"

Mason took a slow step closer to the desk. "Greaves is no' just a politician stickin' his nose where it doesn't belong. He's part of the reason Lily was taken from ye."

Jack's pulse kicked up. "Greaves showed up here not even an hour ago," Jack said, voice low and sharp. "Acting all sympathetic. Offering to help push the investigation forward. You telling me that was all an act?"

"Aye." Mason's face darkened. "Greaves works for someone else. Someone who's been pulling strings long before Lily died. Greaves didn't come here tae help ye—he came tae see what ye know. What ye might've found."

Jack's blood ran cold. His hand unconsciously drifted to the desk drawer where Lily's journal was hidden. "How do you know all this?"

"Because I've been watching him for years," Mason said. "Lily—though she likely never told ye—she knew what Greaves was mixed up in too. She spent years tryin' tae stay one step ahead of him . . . and his master."

Jack's throat tightened. "His master?"

Mason's voice dropped lower. "Azazel Blackthorn. Name mean anythin' tae ye?"

Jack shook his head. "Should it?"

Mason exhaled sharply. "Ye'll want tae remember it.

"Greaves, and a few others, are his eyes and ears in this town. It's no coincidence Greaves knocked on yer door." Mason paused, his brow creasing, ". . . He's lookin' for something. Something Lily had. A journal."

Jack froze. He fought to keep his expression neutral, but Mason's words hit too close.

"A journal?" Jack echoed, keeping his voice carefully flat.

Mason nodded. "Aye. It's more than just her thoughts, Jack. That journal holds names, maps, coordinates . . . secrets she never told even you. It has information Azazel wants. And if Greaves gets his hands on it, there won't be a safe place left for ye or yer daughters.

119

They won't stop until they have it—and they'll burn through anyone standing in the way."

Jack forced himself to keep his expression blank.

"If ye find it," Mason continued, "ye'll need to get it somewhere safe. Somewhere Greaves—and anyone workin' for him—can't get to it. Do ye have anyone ye trust for that kind o' thing?"

Jack let out a short, bitter laugh. "Trust? I'm not sure I even know what that word means anymore. Everyone's been closing doors in my face for months. If this thing's as dangerous as you say . . . maybe I don't have anyone."

Mason stepped closer. "That journal . . . It's a guide to who she was, who she was up against, and why she died. If ye want real answers, Jack—the kind ye cannae get from crime scene reports or coroner's notes—they're in that book. But I won't lie tae ye . . ." Mason's gaze was steady, almost mournful. "Some of what's in there will be hard tae take. It'll change how ye see her. How ye see everything."

Jack's throat tightened.

Mason gestured toward the desk, to the pile of dead-end files Jack had been chasing for months. "This investigation of yours—it's hit a wall, aye? That journal . . . it's the key tae breakin' through it. What's inside will take ye from a dead end to a new beginning."

Jack shrugged, keeping his tone casual. "Well, if I ever stumble across it, I'll figure that part out when I need to."

Mason gave a slight smile, seeing through the act but choosing not to push. "Fair enough," he said softly. "But when the time comes, Jack, ye'll want somewhere quiet—somewhere safe—to open it. Because once ye do . . . there's no going back.

". . . And when you do find it, Jack . . . you'll also need help decipherin' some of it. Lily's notes—some are written in ways only certain people would understand."

Jack's brow lifted. "And you just happen to be one of those people?"

Mason gave a small nod. "Aye."

Jack ran a hand over his face. It was too much, too fast—but every instinct he had told him Mr. Mason told the truth, or at least his version of it. And Jack had spent enough years reading people to know when someone was lying. Mason wasn't lying—but that didn't mean Jack trusted him. Not yet.

"I'll keep it in mind," Jack said flatly.

"Good." Mr. Mason took a step back toward the hallway. "But be careful, Jack. If they even suspect you've got it—or that you're close to findin' it—they won't hesitate. They'll come for ye. And they won't knock next time."

Jack's jaw tightened. "That supposed to scare me?"

Mason shook his head. "No. It's supposed ta keep ye alive."

There was a beat of silence between them. Jack exhaled slowly. "Well . . . thanks for the warning. But it's late—and I've had about enough surprises for one night."

Mason gave a slow nod, turning toward the door. "Aye." He reached the doorway, then paused, glancing back over his shoulder. "One more thing."

Jack raised an eyebrow. "What now?"

Mason reached into his coat pocket and held out a

small, ornate key. It was old, its handle adorned with a delicate engraving of intertwined leaves and vines. The faintest shimmer pulsed along its surface, almost like it was alive.

"If and when ye do find the journal," Mr. Mason said, "ye'll need this." He held it out.

Jack didn't move to take it right away. "Why would you give me this?"

Mason's smile was faint, tinged with something Jack couldn't place. "Because I knew Lily," Mr. Mason said. "And whether ye believe it or not, Jack—we're on the same side."

Jack took the key carefully, its warm metal buzzing faintly against his skin. He forced himself to stay neutral, nodding once. "Thanks."

"Aye," Mason said softly.

He turned and walked down the hallway to the door. He stepped out into the night, leaving Jack standing alone in the dimly lit office, the key warm in Jack's hand and his mind racing with more questions than answers.

CHAPTER 18

Sara's voice broke the silence first.

"So . . . what do we do?"

No one answered right away. The weight of Lucy's warning still hung in the air.

"Alert: Unauthorized tracking signal detected. Temporal signature identified. Source—Riftstone Beacon."

Eli's jaw was tight, his usual sharp wit replaced with cold focus.

Smith stood by the nearest window, arms folded, his eyes scanning the darkness outside like he expected shadows to come alive at any second.

Jo let out a sharp breath. "Okay. Wait. Back up. What exactly does that message mean?"

Mr. Mason leaned heavily on his staff, his face grim. "Voidwalkers."

Devin laughed slightly. "Seriously? What even is that? Sounds like something from a B-movie."

"No," Eli said quietly. "They're worse."

Stacy frowned, glancing toward Sara. "Okay . . . but *worse how?*"

Eli turned toward them—the humor drained from his face. "Voidwalkers are hunters. Azazel doesn't send them to negotiate. He sends them to drag you out of this world, piece by piece—body, mind, and soul."

Jo's face paled, "Okay . . . this has been real fun everyone, but we need to go . . . Now!! Come on, Sara!"

She grabbed Sara's wrist, already turning toward the door.

But Smith's voice cut through the tension. "That won't work."

Jo stopped, spinning toward him. "What do you mean, 'That won't work?'"

Smith didn't look at her—his gaze still locked on the darkened warehouse windows, his posture rigid. Waiting. Listening.

"I mean, they already know exactly where we are."

Jo's grip on Sara's arm tightened. Devin and Stacy both went still.

Sara swallowed hard. "So . . . running doesn't help?"

Smith shook his head. "They don't track movement. They track presence. As long as that Riftstone Beacon is feeding them our signal, it doesn't matter where we run."

Devin rubbed his forehead. "So you're saying we're just stuck here?"

"Not stuck," Smith corrected, finally turning to them. "We just need to break the signal—long enough to open a portal they can't trace."

Eli was already moving, his fingers flying over his keypad. "Lucy, we need a disruption now."

Lucy's holographic projection flickered to life above Eli's wrist. Her voice, cool and measured.

"Analyzing . . ." A pause. "The Riftstone Beacon is emitting a fixed-phase temporal signature. Likely routed through multiple relay points. Manual disruption would require at least six minutes."

Jo began to pace. "Okay, let me get this straight. We have to survive six minutes while soul-stealing monsters try to rip us apart? That's the plan?"

Mr. Mason exhaled sharply, gripping his staff. "Aye, lass. It is."

Sara shifted closer to Jo.

Devin huffed. "Six minutes? Yeah, okay, no big deal. Let me just check my watch and—"

Eli slammed his fist onto the workbench, making everyone jump.

"This isn't a joke." His voice was sharp, his usual sarcasm gone. "If Lucy doesn't jam that signal, we die here."

That shut Devin up.

Smith calmly raised his hand toward Eli. "Peace, Eli . . . This is all new to them."

Eli yanked open a metal crate, shoving it toward them. Inside, small glass spheres pulsed with golden light.

"Sunburst grenades," he said. "Light-based detonation, three-second blind effect on Voidwalkers. Aim for their face."

Stacy grabbed one first, rolling it over in her palm. "This . . . actually works on them?"

Eli nodded. "If it didn't, I wouldn't be handing them out."

Sara took one hesitantly, the faint warmth pulsing against her fingertips. Jo and Devin each grabbed one too.

Mr. Mason lifted his staff, testing the faintly glowing crystal at its top. A deep crack ran through the core—splintered from too much overuse, too little time to repair.

He muttered under his breath. "She won't hold up fer long, but she'll have tae do."

Smith, still near the window, pulled out a key hanging around his neck on a chain. "We hold them off just long enough for Lucy to jam the signal. After that, I'll open the portal."

Devin scoffed. "And what, we just jump through a random hole in space?"

Smith shot him a glare. "Better than getting dragged into one of theirs."

The lights flickered. Then died.

A deep, unnatural cold slithered into the room. The kind that curled in through the bones, rattled against the soul.

Sara felt her breath fog in front of her face.

Then came the sound—low, grinding, like wet bone scraping against stone.

From the farthest corner of the warehouse, a shape peeled itself out of the darkness.

Sara's pulse skyrocketed.

The first Voidwalker had arrived.

The being moved wrong. A silhouette stretching and shifting, edges dissolving like smoke. Its face—if it could be called that—was hollow, empty sockets staring through them. Its mouth opened, too wide, in a soundless scream.

Sara couldn't move.

Jo stumbled back into the crate. Devin went rigid, the blood draining from his face. Stacy gripped Devin's arm so tightly it hurt.

For the first time, they understood.

This wasn't a fight they could win.

The first Voidwalker lunged.

Smith shoved Eli forward. "MOVE!"

Everything happened at once.

The warehouse erupted into chaos—the Voidwalkers slipping through the walls, through the floor, their shifting forms half-solid, half-shadow. Their movements were jagged and flickering like a badly spliced film reel.

And then—the cold. A deep, soul-shaking chill that bit through skin, through muscle, through something deeper.

Jo was the first to snap out of it. She fumbled with the Sunburst Grenade in her palm, then threw it hard.

BOOM.

The grenade detonated in a flash of golden light, blasting outward like a miniature sun. The Voidwalker reeled back, its silhouette convulsing, body warping as if the light burned through its form.

For three seconds—it disappeared into the wall.

Smith slashed out with his blade, the blue light flickering erratically. His sword sliced through the mist of one Voidwalker. It screamed in pain, but the thing simply reformed a second later, whispering something in a language that made Sara's skin crawl.

Mr. Mason swung his staff in an arc of golden energy, knocking two Voidwalkers backward. But the crystal at the top cracked wider, pulsing dangerously.

He cursed, thinking, She won't hold up fer much longer.

BOOM. Eli's grenade lit up, forcing another Voidwalker to twist away.

Jo's hands shook as she yanked another grenade from her pocket.

Devin barely ducked in time as a Voidwalker whipped

its elongated fingers at him. He hit the ground hard, rolling to the side.

Stacy ran over to him and helped him up. "Come on!!—MOVE!"

The world blurred around Sara. She barely heard Jo screaming her name before she was shoved sideways—a Voidwalker had slipped between them, cutting her off from the others.

The thing moved toward her, arms stretching, mouth opening impossibly wide. A deep, unnatural pull reached out for her, like it tried to rip her soul straight from her skin.

Sara threw up her hands.

"NO!"

A burst of blinding blue light exploded from her palms, raw and unrefined.

The Voidwalker shrieked—its body catching fire where the blue light touched it.

It reeled back, sinking into the wall like a retreating nightmare.

Sara stumbled back, gasping. Her hands still glowed faintly.

Jo, Devin, and Stacy stared at her.

"What the hell was that?" Devin choked out.

Sara had no answer.

Then—Eli's comm crackled.

Lucy's voice cut through the chaos, cool and controlled.

"Signal disruption active. Estimated window—one minute, twelve seconds."

Eli's head snapped up. "Smith! We're good! They can't track us!"

A Voidwalker lunged toward Smith, its clawed hands stretching too far.

Smith turned, slashing out with his blade.

The sword's blue light flared, slicing through the creature's shifting form. The Voidwalker reeled back, hissing, its form unraveling—but not gone. It twisted, reforming along the wall, its empty sockets locking onto him once more.

No time.

Smith spun and ran toward the back wall, yanking the chain from around his neck.

He grabbed the iron key and jammed it into a nearly invisible slot in the concrete.

For a second—nothing.

Then—a deep, guttural grinding sound rumbled through the room.

The wall split apart, light bleeding through the cracks like something had torn through the fabric of reality. The air warped and twisted violently, the portal shuddering and unstable.

Smith didn't hesitate.

"TO THE PORTAL! NOW!"

Jo ran over and grabbed Sara's hand, yanking her forward.

Devin, Jo, Sara, and Stacy sprinted toward the portal. Eli and Mr. Mason followed behind them.

Stacy turned at the last second.

She struggled for a moment but grabbed her Sunburst Grenade and threw it directly at the closest Voidwalker.

BOOM.

The flash blinded the creatures for a split second—just enough time for the others to escape.

But Stacy slipped.

Her foot caught on the broken concrete. She tumbled hard, her breath punching from her lungs.

Devin turned.

"STACY!"

He began to run toward her—but Smith caught him.

"NO!" Smith's voice cracked.

Devin fought him, screaming her name.

Stacy looked up at them, dazed—just as a Voidwalker's claw speared through her chest.

For a moment—she smiled.

"Go," she whispered.

And then—the Voidwalker pulled her into the dark.

She was gone.

Devin screamed. Jo collapsed through the portal, sobbing.

Sara stood frozen at the portal entrance, tears streaming down her face.

Smith pulled her inside.

The last thing they saw before the portal closed was the Voidwalkers consuming the light where Stacy had been.

CHAPTER 19

Coach Conner leaned against the door frame of his office, his arms crossed as he stared out at the nearly empty practice field. A couple of the guys still lingered around, tossing a ball back and forth, but it was quiet—too quiet for his liking.

Devin Thompson hadn't shown up to practice for the third day in a row. For anyone else, it might have been concerning, but for Devin? It was downright shocking. The kid hadn't missed a practice since he was eight years old. Football had been his world for as long as Coach Conner could remember. Heck, he'd practically grown up on that field. They'd spent years together, with Coach Conner coaching him from peewee football all the way to high school and now college. Devin was a kid who lived and breathed the game.

Coach Conner sighed. This was a strange turn of events, one he couldn't quite make sense of. Something had changed in Devin, and it wasn't just him missing practice. There had been a shift lately, something deeper that Coach Conner couldn't put his finger on.

Coach Conner pushed himself off the door frame, making his way across the field to where Demetri was finishing up some throws with a couple of the other guys. As one of Devin's closest friends and his teammate, Demetri had to know something.

"Hey, Demetri," Coach called out, waving him over.

Demetri jogged up, holding the football loosely in one hand, his expression tense. "Yeah, Coach?"

Coach Conner folded his arms, studying the young man in front of him. "You heard from Devin? He's been missing for three days now."

Demetri shifted on his feet, avoiding Coach's gaze. "No, not since the weekend."

Coach frowned. "It's not like him. You've known him as long as I have. Kid's never missed a practice in his life. You've got any idea where he might be? His parents haven't heard from him either."

Demetri swallowed hard. He didn't want to lie, but what could he say? There was that weird incident in the park with those men in suits, but they had all agreed not to talk about it. Even Devin had said they should keep it quiet, like none of it had ever happened.

"Coach," Demetri began slowly, "I don't know exactly. Just . . . the last time we were hanging out, there was this . . . incident. We were at the park, playing a pick-up game, and some stuff went down. Devin's been weird ever since."

Coach's eyes narrowed. "What kind of stuff?"

Demetri shifted again, his grip tightening on the football.

"Look, Coach," Demetri said, lowering his voice. "It was weird. I don't even know how to explain it. There were these guys in suits, and they were surrounding this girl who was painting. Devin got involved, and . . . things got out of hand."

Coach raised an eyebrow, his concern deepening. "Did anyone get hurt?"

"No," Demetri said quickly. "At least not that I saw.

But it was intense. And after that, Devin's been . . . different. Like, really different."

"Why didn't you say something sooner?"

Demetri shrugged helplessly. "We all agreed not to talk about it. Devin didn't want anyone knowing. He said it was better to just pretend it didn't happen."

Coach Conner was silent for a moment, his mind racing. This didn't sound like anything typical—not for Devin, not for any of the kids he coached.

"You think he's okay?" Demetri asked. "Like, I don't know, Coach . . . What if this is serious?"

Coach sighed deeply, rubbing the back of his neck. "I'm not sure yet. Let me think on it a bit more. The last thing Devin needs is more pressure if this is something he can handle on his own. But three days with no contact . . . that's pushing it."

Demetri nodded.

Coach Conner clapped Demetri on the shoulder. "I'll do whatever I can to help him. But if he doesn't show up soon, we're going to have to take this to the next level. You let me know if you hear anything, all right?"

"Yeah, Coach. I will."

As Demetri jogged back to his friends, Coach Conner stood there for a moment, watching the field, lost in thought. He couldn't shake the feeling something much bigger was at play here—something that went beyond football, beyond anything he'd ever had to deal with.

He just hoped that when he found Devin, it wouldn't be too late.

Matt Halbridge let out a slow breath, drumming his fingers against the worn wooden table of Winker's Tavern. His wiry frame hunched slightly forward, restless energy evident in the way his fingers tapped an uneven rhythm. "So let me get this straight . . . You're saying there's more to this than just an old police file with an unsolved murder?" His dark hair, streaked with early gray, was swept back in that haphazard way of someone who spent more time chasing leads than grooming. He narrowed his sharp eyes at the woman across from him, skepticism laced in his tone. The smell of aged whiskey and fried food lingered in the air, mixing with the occasional burst of laughter from the bar.

Matt leaned forward, his voice lowering. "You know, I've been chasing this story for years—FBI agents disappearing, weird connections to Sweeney's case—always felt like something bigger was at play, but no one ever took it seriously." He studied the woman carefully. "And now, after all this time, *you* reach out to me. That tells me I wasn't just chasing ghosts. There's something real here, isn't there?"

Janice Fowler stirred her drink slowly, watching Matt with a patience that unnerved him. "I'm not saying anything yet," she responded, her voice calm but firm. The way she held herself—poised, deliberate—made it clear she was used to controlling the pace of a conversation. She was attractive in that understated way, her dark hair tucked neatly behind one ear, revealing striking green eyes holding more weight than her polished exterior let on. She sat with her back to the wall, positioned so she could see the entrance.

Janice continued. "But what I *am* suggesting is that

Jack Sweeney didn't just vanish because of his investigation into his wife's death. He was onto something bigger. Something he didn't fully comprehend at the time."

Matt raised an eyebrow, smirking. "Bigger than
uncovering why his wife was murdered? What, like aliens
or some secret government project?" He let out a short,
humorless chuckle. "Come on, Janice. I know you're into
some strange stuff, but this is—"

Janice cut him off, her voice dropping to a near
whisper. "Jack wasn't the only one looking into these
things. There's a reason I reached out to you specifically.
You've followed the patterns in this town for years—
disappearances, unexplained accidents, things that the
police can't—or won't—explain."

Something in her tone sent a shiver down Matt's
spine. The easy dismissal he had prepared suddenly
didn't feel right. He studied her more closely, watching the way she held herself. No fidgeting. No nervous
glances. Just quiet, unwavering certainty.

"Okay, I'll bite." He leaned forward, resting his
elbows on the table. "But what does this have to do with
that old FedEx package Sweeney sent out before he disappeared? No one's ever been able to track it down. Not
the Feds. Not even the conspiracy nuts online."

Janice arched an eyebrow, a smile tugging at the
corner of her lips. "Isn't that the pot calling the kettle
black?" she said dryly. "I mean, if you ask most people,
you're one of those conspiracy nuts, Matt."

Matt scoffed but couldn't hide the amused glint in
his eyes. "Yeah, well, I like to think I'm a *journalist* with
a healthy dose of suspicion."

Janice's fingers tapped lightly on the table, a subtle

tell beneath her otherwise composed demeanor. "That package," she said carefully, "ended up in my hands."

Matt blinked. "Wait—you *have* it? You've had it this whole time?"

She nodded slowly. "Jack sent it to me so what he had uncovered would not fall into the wrong hands. He knew I would understand what he found—or at least know where to start. But this isn't something I can just hand over, Matt. There are pieces of this story that most people couldn't handle. If I'm going to show you any of it, I need to know you're ready for the truth, no matter how . . . strange it might seem."

Matt let out a breath, rubbing his temples. He thought he'd seen it all in this town—corrupt officials, cover-ups, inexplicable crimes—but this felt different. He wasn't sure if Janice was leading him into another rabbit hole or onto something real. Either way, he *had* to know.

"So?" he said, choosing his words carefully. "What exactly was in the package? What did Jack find?"

Janice hesitated, her fingers lightly tapping the edge of the table. "It wasn't just evidence," she said at last, her voice deliberate. "There was a journal. Jack found it in his house hidden in a place Lily kept secret, even from him—it contains information that ties back to events that help explain her death." Janice paused, allowing the weight of her words to sink in. "This journal . . . it talks about things that defy logic. Places and people that shouldn't exist—but do."

Matt frowned. "Places? What, like secret government bases or something?"

Janice shook her head, her eyes darkening slightly.

"No. Not government. Not anything from . . . this world."

Silence settled between them. For the first time in a long time, Matt didn't have a snarky response. He *wanted* to laugh it off, to roll his eyes and call this another one of those wild theories he made a career out of exposing. But there was something in Janice's voice, in the way she held herself, that made him hesitate.

"And you've seen this journal?" he asked finally. "You've read it?"

"Yes . . . It reveals everything that helped Jack put all the pieces together. It was enough to know that it was putting him—and his daughters—in danger," Janice said. "There's a reason no one can find him. He was getting too close to something, and *they* wanted him out of the picture."

Matt's pulse quickened. "*They?*" he repeated. "Who's *they?*"

Janice paused, her green eyes narrowing. She measured him again, deciding how much to reveal.

"I'll tell you in time," she said finally. "But for now, just know that they're powerful. More powerful than you or I can imagine. And they're still watching."

A chill ran down Matt's spine. He stole a glance at the door, half-expecting to see a shadow lurking just beyond the frame. Paranoia was a reporter's worst enemy—but also his greatest asset.

He turned back to Janice. "All right," he said, voice steady. "I'm in. But you're gonna have to give me more than that if you want me to be able to write about this. If Sweeney was onto something bigger, something dangerous, I need proof."

Janice leaned back, the faintest hint of a knowing smile playing at the corners of her lips. Outside the booth, the quiet clinking of glasses and murmured conversations continued, the world going on as if nothing of consequence was happening. "You'll get proof, Matt," she said. "Soon enough."

CHAPTER 20

The cold hit first.

Not the unnatural, soul-draining chill of the Voidwalkers, but a raw, biting wind sweeping across them as they tumbled onto solid ground.

Jo landed hard on her knees, gasping. Her hands scraped against rough, dry earth. The scent of damp soil filled her nostrils as she shook uncontrollably, her breaths coming in ragged sobs.

Devin hit the ground rolling, barely catching himself on his hands. His body trembled from exhaustion, but his mind—his mind was still in the warehouse. Still with Stacy.

Sara stood frozen, staring at the empty space where the portal had been. Tears streamed down her face.

The light had vanished.

Stacy was gone.

The wind howled across the barren hills, kicking up loose dirt and swirling mist around them. The Shadowland Hills stretched out in all directions—vast, open, and eerily quiet.

Jo clutched her arms to her chest, shaking violently. Not from the cold, but from the crushing weight of what had just happened.

She choked out, "She—she was just—" Her voice broke, her eyes stinging with tears.

Devin wasn't listening. He was already pushing himself up, shoving past Smith, stumbling back toward where the portal had been.

"No," he rasped. His chest heaved. "No—open it back up. We have to go back! We can still—"

Smith grabbed his arm, stopping him.

Devin shoved him away. Hard.

Smith barely budged. "Dev—"

"DON'T TOUCH ME!" Devin's voice shook with rage. His eyes wild, desperate.

Sara flinched at the sound.

Devin turned to Eli. "You—You can track them, right? You can find them! Stacy's not—" His breath hitched. "She's not gone. We can still—"

Eli's face was stone.

"There's nothing left to track." His voice was quiet but final.

Devin's hands clenched into fists. His body tensed like he was going to hit something—someone.

But there was nothing to hit.

Sara couldn't move.

Her heartbeat pounded in her ears, drowning out everything else.

Her hands still tingled—a lingering warmth in her fingertips, faint traces of blue energy still flickering beneath her skin.

She flexed her fingers, but they felt foreign.

Like they didn't belong to her anymore.

Her throat felt tight.

This was her fault.

She had been the target. Azazel's creatures had come for her.

And now Stacy was dead.

Jo's breathing grew erratic. She pressed her hands to her face, squeezing her eyes shut.

"I—" she gasped. "I should have—I could've—"

Her whole body shook with sobs.

Mr. Mason stepped forward, his usual firm expression softening. He placed a steadying hand on her shoulder, but Jo jerked away from him.

"Don't—Don't touch me!"

She turned, stumbling back, arms wrapping tightly around herself, as if she was trying to hold in everything threatening to break.

"We left her."

The words barely escaped her lips.

Smith stood a few feet away from them all, silent. His gaze fixed on the spot where the portal had been.

He'd made the call.

He'd left her behind.

His grip on his blade tightened, knuckles turning white.

Stacy wasn't the first person he'd had to leave behind.

But that didn't make it any easier.

Finally, he spoke—his voice quiet but firm.

"We need to move."

Devin's head snapped toward him.

His expression twisted into pure fury.

"Move?" His voice cracked.

Smith met his eyes but said nothing.

That silence was the final straw.

Devin lunged at him.

"YOU LEFT HER!"

His fist connected with Smith's chest—once, twice. Again. Again.

Smith didn't fight back.

Devin kept hitting him.

"YOU LEFT HER! YOU LEFT HER!"

His punches grew weaker. Slower. Until, finally—his body gave out.

His hands gripped Smith's jacket, his forehead pressed against his chest.

And he sobbed.

Gut-wrenching, broken sobs.

Smith finally placed a hand on the back of Devin's head. Not to restrain.

Just to hold him together.

"I know, Devin." Smith's voice was raw. "I know."

The wind whistled through the hills, carrying silence with it.

After several minutes, Sara finally forced herself to speak.

"What . . . do we do now?"

Eli exhaled sharply, rubbing his face.

Mr. Mason's gaze turned to Smith.

Smith took a slow breath. "We head into the hills."

He glanced at the sky, the sun already sinking toward the jagged horizon. "We need to reach the cabin before nightfall."

His gaze swept over them—Jo still trembling, Devin hunched in silent grief, Sara staring at her hands, lost.

"We rest. We recover." He hesitated, his voice lower now. "Then we figure out our next move."

He turned away from the dying remnants of the portal, looking toward the distant hills.

". . . Before we lose anyone else."

The wind continued to howl across the barren hills, carrying the sting of dust and cold air as the group moved forward in silence.

No one spoke.

There was nothing left to say.

Smith led the way, his posture rigid but steady. His gaze stayed forward, locked on the rolling hills ahead, every step purposeful. His blade remained sheathed, but his hand hovered close—just in case.

Behind him, Mr. Mason walked with measured steps, his staff gripped tightly. The crystal at its top flickered weakly, cracks still glowing from the warehouse battle. He looked over the others with quiet concern, but even he knew this wasn't the time for words.

Jo walked beside Sara, her arms wrapped tightly around herself, her head down.

Sara noticed but said nothing.

Jo's usual sharp remarks, her frustration, her tough exterior—it was all gone.

They walked for nearly an hour before anyone spoke.

The hills stretched on in rolling waves of jagged rock and dry earth, the occasional twisted tree crooked against the darkening sky.

The sun dipped lower. Shadows stretched long and distorted.

Smith finally slowed his pace.

"We'll reach the cabin soon," he said, his voice calm but firm. "We rest there tonight. Get warm. Regroup."

He glanced back at the group, noting their exhaustion, the weight of grief pressing on them all.

"After that, we talk."

Devin let out a harsh laugh, but there was no humor in it.

"Talk?" His voice was raw. Hoarse. He shook his head. "What's there to talk about? That we failed? That she's—" His breath caught. "That she's gone?"

His voice cracked on the last word.

Sara flinched.

Jo rubbed her arms, looking like she wanted to say something. But she stayed silent.

Mr. Mason exhaled, his voice low and steady.

"Lad . . . I know ye're hurtin'." His accent was softer than usual. "We all are."

Devin looked away.

"She shouldn't have died," he muttered. "It should have been me."

Sara's breath caught.

Jo's head snapped up.

"Don't you say that."

Devin's expression twisted. "Why not? It's true. I was right there—" His voice broke. "I could've—should've—"

"You think Stacy would have wanted that?" Jo's voice was sharp but not unkind.

Devin looked away.

No one had an answer.

Because they all felt the same.

Smith watched them quietly.

He had seen grief like this before.

He knew there were no right words. Nothing would make this easier.

But he also knew one thing.

If they let it break them now, they'd never stand a chance against what came next.

144

He turned back toward the path.

"We keep moving."

The hills sloped downward, and suddenly, there it was.

A cabin, tucked into the hillside. Small, unassuming. The wood weathered from time, the stone chimney dark and cold. It looked like nothing more than an old shelter, forgotten by the world.

Jo frowned. "This is it?"

Smith said nothing. He stepped forward, pausing at the door.

A red door.

It was the only thing that stood out—vivid and rich in color, almost too new against the worn exterior.

Sara's eyes widened.

She had seen a door like this before. At Smith's townhouse and the warehouse.

Smith took a deep breath and reached into his coat, pulling out his ring of skeleton keys.

He ran his fingers over them, choosing one. A key with a carved leaf at its head.

With careful precision, he inserted it into the lock and turned gently to the left.

Click.

The door shuddered, the faintest ripple spreading outward from where the key had turned, like water disturbed by a single drop.

Smith exhaled and motioned with his hand for everyone to go inside.

No one hesitated.

Jo stepped inside first.

And froze.

Her eyes widened.

The inside of the cabin was not at all what she had expected.

The space was massive—impossibly so. The walls stretched high above them, with vaulted ceilings and large windows that looked out onto . . .

Something else.

Not the misty hills they had just walked through.

Instead, the view showed rolling forests, deep valleys stretching endlessly beneath a violet-tinged sky. It was too vivid, too surreal.

"This . . . This isn't possible," Jo muttered, turning back toward the red door they had just entered through. Her expression was tight, conflicted.

"How is this—"

She looked back at the room, her breath catching.

Devin barely looked up. He stood near the entrance, his arms folded tight, his grief too deep to care.

Eli exchanged a glance with Mr. Mason. A knowing look passed between them.

They had seen this before.

Sara, however, wasn't surprised.

She had seen this kind of magic before.

Smith's library. The impossible door to another world.

"It's . . . different inside," Sara murmured, her voice still shaky. "I've seen it before. In Smith's house."

Jo's brow furrowed. She turned toward Sara. "What do you mean? How is this all even possible? First the warehouse and now . . . this."

Smith stepped inside, closing the door behind them. He slid the key back into his coat and turned to face the group.

His expression was weary but resolute.

"It's a sanctuary."

Jo crossed her arms. "That doesn't explain anything."

"The outside world cannot touch you here," Smith continued. "Not while we're inside."

Jo shook her head. "That's what you told us about the warehouse!!" Her voice had an edge of frustration.

Smith didn't answer immediately.

Instead, he let the silence stretch.

Finally, he said, "Rest. Regroup. Then we'll talk."

Jo's lips pressed into a thin line, but she didn't argue.

Not yet.

They didn't eat.

No one spoke.

The only sound was the crackling fire, the occasional shift of wind outside.

Sara curled up against the wall, her fingers still glowing faintly blue as she clenched her hands into fists.

Devin sat near the door, his back against the wall, eyes vacant.

Jo rested her forehead against her knees.

Smith leaned against the table, eyes locked on the fire.

Mr. Mason let out a quiet sigh.

Tonight, there was nothing left to say.

The Voidwalkers knelt in a half-circle before their master, their shifting, tattered forms flickering against the dim glow of a mural that stretched across the chamber's wall. The painting was unfinished, but its twisting

shapes and writhing figure hinted at something monstrous yet to come.

Azazel stood before them, silent, watching.

"My Lord," one of the Voidwalkers rasped, its voice
a whisper of smoke and ruin. "We engaged them at
the warehouse. Smith's team resisted. They fought . . .
harder than expected."

Azazel's expression did not change, but a slow breath
left his lips, measured, calculating. "And the orb?"

The Voidwalker hesitated before bowing its head.
"We could not locate it. The vault was already gone. It
was not in the warehouse when we arrived."

The chamber seemed to darken at the weight of
Azazel's displeasure, the mural behind him deepening
in shade, the imposing figure in the picture shifting,
twisting as if feeding off his fury.

Another Voidwalker stirred, attempting to salvage
the moment. "We claimed the life of one of their own,"
it offered. "One of the women fell. The old one and the
artificer were also with Smith."

Azazel's fingers twitched, though whether in interest
or irritation was unclear. "The old one," he murmured,
his mind already cycling through the implications. "Mr.
Mason."

A slight tilt of his head. "The artificer. Whitaker?"

He considered them for a moment longer, then
exhaled, shaking his head. "You do not even know the
name of the one you took from them."

The Voidwalkers remained silent.

Azazel turned away, stepping toward the mural, his
gaze lost in its swirling, shifting shapes. "And their
weapons?"

One of the Voidwalkers shifted uneasily. "They fought with light, but the energy drained faster than in the past."

"Yes," he murmured. "Of course." said Azazel.

"They are weakening. Their connection to Valoria fades with every moment they remain here. Their exile has severed the tether they once held to their true . . ."

Then, one of the Voidwalkers interrupted. "But there was . . . something else. Another girl. She—she . . ."

Azazel turned sharply. "She what?"

The Voidwalker's form wavered. "She unleashed the blue light. Strong. Pure. It struck one of us directly . . . and it is no more."

His fingers curled into a fist. "Bring me Sykes."

Footsteps echoed through the chamber, measured and deliberate. Sykes entered, his presence one of quiet authority, a man who had long since abandoned the need for theatrics. His gaze swept the room, taking in the kneeling Voidwalkers, the dim, shifting light of the mural, and finally, Azazel himself.

Azazel did not waste time. "There was a death," he said, his voice as steady as iron. "That complicates things." His eyes burned into Sykes. "A cleanup is needed. No loose ends."

Sykes inclined his head. "Understood."

Azazel continued, his tone measured but firm, "The authorities in Muxley must not ask questions. You will ensure that." He stepped forward, shadows curling at his feet. "I want their grief turned against them. Let them be too burdened to see what is coming."

Sykes exhaled sharply. "That won't be a problem."

Azazel regarded him carefully. "See that it is done."

Sykes turned and left.

Azazel watched him go, then shifted his gaze back to the Voidwalkers. "The vault. It must be found."

The Voidwalkers bowed their heads in unison.

Azazel's gaze turned toward the unfinished mural, its shadows moving, ". . . And the girl."

CHAPTER 21

Matt Halbridge sat frozen, his mouth slightly open as he stared at Janice across the table. The dim lighting cast sharp shadows on his face, deepening the furrow in his brow. For a moment, he said nothing—his mind grappling with the weight of her words. His fingers curled around the edge of his notepad, knuckles whitening. The notes he had scribbled so meticulously just moments ago now felt useless.

"You can't be serious," he finally muttered, his voice hoarse, almost a whisper. "A portal? You're telling me that Jack was investigating people—or things—coming through some kind of . . . interdimensional doorway?" He shook his head sharply, like a man trying to wake from a dream. "This is—this is insane."

Janice didn't flinch. Her piercing green eyes held him steady, unwavering. Calm. It was the kind of calm that only came from someone who had already made peace with the impossible.

Silently, she slid a document across the table. The paper was old, its edges curled and yellowed with time. She tapped a single finger on it, her nails clicking lightly against the worn surface. "You wanted the truth, Matt. This is part of it."

His gaze flicked downward. He hesitated, then slowly reached for the paper, his fingers brushing against its brittle edge. The ink was faded, but the words stood out with eerie clarity.

Portal Confirmed. Entity Emergence. Incident Report #297.

A chill scraped down his spine. His throat tightened as he scanned the page, his mind scrambling for an explanation—any explanation—that made this *not* real.

"This . . ." His voice faltered. "This has to be some kind of hoax."

Janice exhaled through her nose, the sound more pity than frustration. "Jack thought the same thing—at first. Until the evidence kept piling up." Her voice lowered, carrying a weight he couldn't ignore. "Until they silenced him."

Matt swallowed hard. He leaned back, running a hand through his hair, searching for solid ground where there was none.

"If this is real . . . if things are coming through these portals . . . then why isn't this all over the news? Why hasn't anyone noticed?"

Janice's eyes flickered, almost imperceptibly. "Because it's being covered up." Her tone was even, but there was something underneath it—something colder.

Then she let out a breath, shaking her head. "Come on, Matt. *You're* the conspiracy guy. You of all people should know how this works." She leaned forward, fixing him with a look like a teacher watching a student struggle with something obvious. "You think the people in charge would *ever* let something like this go public? You've built half your career exposing the things they don't want people to see. But this?" She tapped the document on the table. "This is bigger. And it's controlled by people with more power than you can imagine."

He stiffened, the heat of embarrassment rising in

his chest. She wasn't wrong. He'd spent years piecing together cover-ups, hunting down corruption, revealing the cracks in the system. And now, when it landed right in front of him, he was the one second-guessing?

Janice studied his face, reading his hesitation. Then her voice dropped. "Jack was getting too close, and that's why he disappeared." She hesitated, then added, "It's why *they* took him."

Matt exhaled sharply, shaking his head. "All right . . . but if Jack gave you all the information he discovered, if you had everything you needed to blow this case wide open *years ago*—why the hell did you wait?" His voice edged with frustration. "Why *now*?"

Something in Janice's expression shifted. The hard-edged confidence softened, just slightly. The kind of shift that only came when something *personal* entered the equation.

"Because," she said, her voice quieter now, "Jack asked me to protect his children."

Matt stilled. He hadn't expected that.

Janice looked away for the first time, her fingers pressing lightly against the table as if steadying herself. "If I had exposed everything back then, it wouldn't have just been Jack who paid the price. They would have come for his daughters." She let out a slow breath. "And they would have never stopped."

Matt absorbed her words, the weight of them sinking in. His mind turned over the possibilities, the implications.

His voice was cautious when he finally spoke. "Were they . . . somehow involved in all this?"

Janice shook her head. "Not directly." A pause. "But

they're tied to it. More than they know." She met his gaze again, something unreadable in her eyes. "I'll show you more answers, Matt. But not here. I'll take you to where you can *see* for yourself."

Matt hesitated. He had gone deep into rabbit holes before, but this—this was different. He was on the verge of stepping into something that defied everything he knew about the world.

He exhaled through his nose. "I need something more. Some kind of proof before I just follow you down this insane road."

Janice studied him for a moment. Then, with a sigh, she reached into her coat pocket and pulled something out.

A key.

But not just any key.

It was intricate, its metallic surface marked with curling leaf symbols, patterns so fine they almost looked woven into the metal itself. A soft glow pulsed from its edges, faint yet undeniable, like embers breathing in the dark.

Matt's breath caught.

He had seen a lot of strange things in his career— government leaks, classified files, things hidden from the public—but this? This wasn't manmade.

He swallowed, unable to tear his eyes from it. "What . . . What is that?"

Janice tilted the key slightly, the glow catching in the low light. "Proof."

Matt licked his lips, the hesitation still there, but weaker now. "It looks . . ." He shook his head. "It looks *otherworldly*."

Janice gave a small, knowing smile. "Because it is."

Matt let out a slow breath. His fingers drummed against the table once before he leaned back. "Yeah . . ." He ran a hand down his face. "Okay . . . I'll go."

And then, before he could process what he had just agreed to—

His phone buzzed against the table, jolting them both.

Unknown Caller.

Matt blinked, tearing his focus away from the key, and glanced down at the screen. A spike of unease shot through him. He hesitated, then swiped to answer.

"Halbridge."

A rough voice crackled through the speaker, tense and breathless. "Matt, you're gonna wanna get down here. It's bad."

Matt's pulse kicked up a notch. "Who is this?"

"Detective Hayes," the voice replied. "We've got a situation on the south side of Muxley. A body. Young woman." He hesitated. "You're gonna want to see this. It's . . . strange."

Matt stiffened. He didn't like that pause. "What do you mean, strange?"

"I'll explain when you get here." Another pause, this one heavier. "And bring your new friend. You've got about twenty minutes before this place is swarming."

The line went dead.

Matt lowered the phone slowly, his gut twisting.

Janice, still focused on their conversation, studied his face. "Something wrong?"

"A body." His voice came out tighter than he intended. "South side of Muxley. Young woman. The detective said it was . . . strange."

She didn't react immediately. "Do you need to go?"

"Yes." He hesitated. "He said to bring you with me."

That made her pause. Then she slid the key back into her pocket and reached for her coat. "Then let's not waste time."

As they stepped out into the night air, Matt stole a glance at her. "You think this is connected?"

Janice didn't answer right away. But when she did, her voice was quiet. Steady.

"I don't believe in coincidences, Matt."

CHAPTER 22

The soft crackle of the fire and the faint scent of something warm and savory drifted through the air as Sara stirred beneath the thick blanket draped over her. The cabin was quiet.

For a moment, she didn't move.

The exhaustion from the night before still clung to her, heavy and lingering, but something about the morning air felt . . . different.

She sat up slowly, her blanket slipping from her shoulders. The others were still asleep, curled up on the couches, their breathing deep and slow.

Jo was tucked beneath a thick woven throw, arms still wrapped tightly around herself. Devin's face was turned away, his posture rigid even in sleep.

Sara's eyes drifted toward the center of the room.

Mr. Mason stood near the stone hearth, his back to her as he tended to a pan over the fire. The scent of freshly cooked eggs and something rich—maybe sausage—filled the air.

Across the room, Eli sat at the wooden table, his fingers moving rapidly over a sleek black keyboard.

His comm device was connected to a series of small monitors, and Sara could hear Lucy's soft, artificial voice murmuring in response to whatever he was doing.

She rubbed her eyes, pushing herself to her feet. The floor was cool beneath her toes as she padded toward the large window stretching across the far wall.

And then she saw him.

Sara pressed her palm lightly against the glass.

Outside, the morning light bathed the valley in gold and soft blues, the landscape stretching far beyond what should have been possible. The distant hills rolled into deep forests, the sky painted in soft violet hues.

And there, at the edge of a rocky outcrop, Smith knelt before something.

An altar.

She frowned, leaning closer, squinting through the glass.

The altar was made of dark stone, worn with time, its surface etched with what looked like symbols she didn't recognize. A soft mist curled around it.

Was he . . . praying?

She had never seen Smith like that before.

Then, something shifted.

A second figure.

Sara couldn't make out the features, but the figure stood tall and still, draped in flowing robes that rippled with the wind.

A woman?

She wasn't sure.

Smith looked up at her, speaking in low tones, his posture still kneeling, his head slightly bowed.

Sara squinted harder, trying to see who—or what—he talked to.

But the sunlight seemed to bend strangely around the figure, obscuring the details.

And then—just like that—the figure was gone.

Sara blinked.

Had she imagined it?

She turned away from the window, feeling a slight unease curling at the edges of her mind.

She found Mr. Mason still tending to breakfast, his movements slow and deliberate.

"Is Smith with someone else out there?" she asked quietly.

Mr. Mason didn't look up immediately.

Instead, he stirred the pan thoughtfully, the sound of sizzling filling the silence between them.

Finally, he exhaled, reaching for a plate.

"Might be."

He scooped the eggs onto the plate, turning slightly to glance at her.

"Or might be ye just caught a glimpse of someone who's only seen when they wish to be."

Sara frowned. "What does that mean?"

Mr. Mason simply smiled faintly, setting the plate aside.

"Means I wouldn't worry about it, lass."

That answer only made her more uneasy.

She glanced back toward the window—toward the altar, the empty space where the figure had stood.

The valley was quiet once more.

Smith was still outside, but she knew he'd be back soon. And when he was—she wanted answers.

She still wasn't sure if what she had seen was real or if her mind played tricks on her.

Before she could turn back from the window, the door creaked open.

The cold morning air rushed in as Smith stepped inside.

His expression was neutral, unreadable as he closed the door behind him and shook the lingering chill from his coat.

Sara parted her lips, ready to ask—

But before she could, Jo stirred from the couch.

A soft groan slipped from her lips as she blinked awake, rubbing her face with tired hands.

For a moment, she seemed disoriented, like she had forgotten where they were.

Then—it hit her.

Sara saw the moment yesterday's events crashed back into Jo's mind.

The way her shoulders tensed. The way her fingers curled against the blanket.

Jo swallowed hard before sitting up. She exhaled sharply, forcing herself forward, forcing herself to move.

"Food's ready," Mr. Mason said gently, his voice softer than usual. He handed Jo a plate.

Jo took it without speaking. She didn't look at anyone as she picked at the food.

Sara sat beside her, her own plate in hand, but neither of them truly tasted what they ate.

The sound of shifting blankets drew Sara's attention toward the couch near the door.

Devin sat up slowly.

He didn't look disoriented.

He didn't look tired.

He just looked . . . empty.

His movements were stiff, methodical, as if he were running on autopilot. His jaw was locked, his eyes dark and unfocused.

He glanced toward the plates of food.

But he didn't reach for one.

Instead, he lifted his gaze toward Smith.

"I don't want breakfast." His voice was hoarse,

cracked from disuse. He exhaled slowly, then said, "I want answers."

Jo froze mid-bite.

Sara set her plate down.

The tension in the room shifted.

Smith met Devin's gaze, studying him carefully before nodding once.

He pulled out a chair at the wooden table and sat down, resting his arms against the worn surface.

Eli closed his laptop and leaned back, arms crossed, waiting.

Mr. Mason didn't say anything, but he sat down beside Smith, his face solemn.

Jo slowly put her plate down.

For the first time since waking, she truly looked up.

Her voice trembled, the edge of desperation clear beneath her words. "What are we even involved in?" Her arms folded against her chest, her shoulders tense. "We've lost a friend . . . We deserve to know."

"I know this is hard. The loss of Stacy . . . tragic, but you've been caught up in this from the time you were infants."

Sara and Jo exchanged a wary glance, while Devin sat forward.

Smith's eyes landed on Jo first.

"You're your mother's daughter, Jo," he said, his voice quieter now. "More than you realize."

Jo scoffed, arms still tightly crossed over her chest. "Yeah, well, knowing her didn't exactly help me understand any of this."

Smith held her gaze.

"Your mother was what we called an Overseer in

Valoria. She was one of twelve who served King Thalion. But she wasn't just any Overseer. Lillianna was the Keeper of Gateways—the one who wove the connections between realms, ensuring Valoria's light could touch every world. She shaped portals, doorways of passage, and guarded the delicate balance between dimensions. But she was also a warrior, fierce and loyal, wielding Valorian weapons to defend the Crystal City when the need arose. And that power—that calling—didn't die with her."

Jo's fingers tightened against her arms. "But I don't feel anything," she muttered. "I don't have magic like Sara. I don't—"

"Not yet . . ." said Smith.

Devin let out a sharp breath.

"Okay, great," he said, his voice edged with frustration. "So Sara's got this fancy portal-making, realm-bridging, light-channeling magic passed down from her mom, and Jo's turning into some kind of Valorian weapon-slinger or whatever. But me? Why the hell am I here?"

Smith hesitated.

"Smith," Devin pressed, his voice low. "Tell me."

Smith met his gaze, and for the first time, Devin saw something behind those sharp blue eyes.

Pity.

Smith leaned forward, resting his elbows on the table. "Your family isn't from Earth, Devin."

The words hit like a hammer.

Devin stared at him, unblinking. "What?"

"You weren't just pulled into this by chance," Smith continued. "Your ancestors . . . your bloodline . . . comes from a realm that is . . . .unfortunately merely a shadow of what it was."

Devin's heart slammed against his ribs.

"You're lying," he said, his voice sharp.

Mr. Mason interjected, "Aye, there was once a realm called Draegora," he said, his voice low and steady. "A proud land, it was, known far and wide for its warriors. Its people—they were strong, resilient folk. We called them the Shadowforged."

"Shadowforged?" asked Devin, clearly confused.

"Aye," Mr. Mason continued. "They were Thalion's greatest defenders, they were. His finest warriors, no doubt. And at their head stood the fiercest, most loyal fighters of them all."

"Your ancestors, Devin," said Smith.

Devin felt like the room was closing in on him.

His blood pounded in his ears.

"No," he muttered. "No, that's not possible."

"You've felt it, didn't you. Back at the warehouse?" Eli asked, leaning forward now. His expression wasn't mocking or dismissive. It was knowing.

"The way you were drawn to the red orb. The way your hands itched every time you were near it. The way you felt like something inside you was . . . pulling you toward it."

Devin's stomach twisted.

They knew.

They knew about the pull. The strange compulsion he had felt when the red orb was on the table at the warehouse.

He swallowed hard.

"But if my ancestors were Thalion's warriors," he

forced out, "then why am I drawn to something that belongs to Azazel?"

The room was too quiet.

No one spoke at first.

Then, Smith exhaled slowly.

"Because the Shadowforged . . . became the Voidwalkers."

Devin felt like the floor had vanished beneath him.

His entire body went numb.

Jo's head snapped toward Smith, her expression one of complete shock.

Sara's breath hitched, and she covered her mouth.

"You're saying . . ." Devin's voice felt detached from his body. "My family—my ancestors—became Azazel's monsters? The ones that killed Stacy?"

Smith didn't look away.

"Yes."

Devin shoved back from the couch, the legs underneath scraping against the wooden floor. His breath came in ragged gasps, his chest tight.

Jo flinched at the sound.

Sara's fingers curled against her lap, her own grief still raw.

Devin pressed a hand to his forehead, his mind spinning.

"This—This is a joke, right?" He let out a hollow, bitter laugh. "Tell me this is just some sick joke, Smith."

Silence.

It wasn't a joke.

"I could have saved her." His voice was hoarse. "I should have saved her."

Jo stood up abruptly, her chair nearly tipping over. "Don't do this again, Devin."

His head snapped toward her.

"Don't what?" His voice was sharp, laced with anger and grief. "Don't blame myself? Don't— she died at the hand of my . . . people."

"It wasn't your fault." Jo's voice shook, but there was steel underneath it. "And if you say it was, then you're saying it was Stacy's fault too."

Devin froze.

Jo was stunned at the words that came out her mouth. Her hands trembled at her sides.

"She knew the risks. She chose to stay, to fight. And I hate it—I hate that she's gone—but . . ."

He shook his head. "That doesn't make it easier."

Jo's expression softened—just slightly.

"I know."

Sara finally spoke, her voice barely above a whisper.

"She wouldn't want us tearing each other apart over this."

Devin swallowed hard.

His arms fell limp at his sides.

The guilt was still there, curling deep in his chest, but the anger had nowhere to go.

He looked back at Smith, his voice rough.

"Fine," he muttered. "Tell me how it happened. How my ancestors turned into monsters."

"Aye," Mr. Mason said, his voice heavy. "Azazel needed an army. But he didnae want mercenaries or weak men who would break under fear. He wanted soldiers already trained for war. And the Shadowforged— your ancestors, Devin—were the strongest in all the realms."

Eli picked up where Mason left off. "But strength

wasn't enough. Azazel knew they would never serve him willingly." He tapped his fingers against the table. "So he used the red orbs. Corrupted magic. He bound the Shadowforged to his will—against their own."

Devin looked at Eli. "So what you're saying," he forced out, "is that my family wasn't just part of this fight. They were the ones who lost it."

Mr. Mason shook his head. "Nae, lad. They weren't just soldiers. They were prisoners. The first victims of Azazel's corruption."

Devin was silent.

His entire world had just fractured.

Smith watched him carefully.

"You asked how you fit into this, Devin," he said, voice measured. "This is how."

Devin scoffed softly, shaking his head. "I don't even know what I am anymore."

Smith, Mr. Mason, and Eli glanced at one another. Then Smith glanced at Devin. "Give it time, Devin."

Devin let out a slow, shaky exhale.

For the first time, he didn't know what to say.

Jo and Sara watched him carefully.

There was nothing more to be said for now. Sara looked Smith and in his eyes. She could see there was more to know. More to this story. But it would have to wait.

CHAPTER 23

The scene on the south side of Muxley was already roped off by the time Matt and Janice arrived. Yellow caution tape flapped in the light breeze, cordoning off the alleyway where a small group of officers milled about. The glow of red and blue police lights bathed the area in a surreal, almost eerie light. A few onlookers had gathered near the perimeter, whispering in hushed tones as they tried to catch a glimpse of the crime scene.

Matt flashed his press pass, and after a brief exchange with one of the officers, he and Janice were allowed past the initial barricade. As they stepped closer to the scene, Matt's gaze fell on the body lying beneath a thin white sheet, its edges smeared with streaks of red.

A knot formed in his stomach.

Janice's sharp eyes scanned the area, taking in every detail—the positioning of the body, the blood pattern, the tense expressions on the officers' faces. Something wasn't right here.

Detective Hayes spotted them and made his way over, his face set in a grim line. He was a grizzled man in his forties, with deep lines etched into his weathered face and a no-nonsense demeanor that immediately set the tone. "Halbridge," he greeted curtly, nodding to Janice as well. "Glad you could make it."

Matt kept his voice low. "What are we looking at, Hayes?"

Hayes' gaze darkened. "Young woman. Looks to

167

be in her early twenties. Cause of death isn't clear yet, but it's . . . strange. We've got blood here, a lot of it, but . . ." He trailed off, rubbing his temple. "There's no sign of trauma that could explain that kind of blood loss. No visible injuries. No gunshot wounds. It doesn't add up."

Janice's eyes flickered, her mind already racing. "Any witnesses?"

"None," Hayes replied. "But that's not the weird part." He glanced around, lowering his voice. "There's something off about the scene. It feels . . . staged. Almost too clean, you know? No personal effects, no sign of a struggle . . . and no ID."

Matt's frown deepened. "You're thinking someone moved her here? Set this up?"

"Maybe," Hayes said, his eyes hard. "Or someone's trying to make this look like something it's not."

Janice crouched down, her fingers carefully brushing over the ground near the body. "What is this?" Her eyes locked on the faint shimmering marks near the girl's hands—like a strange residue glowing faintly in the fading light.

Hayes shook his head. "No idea. We've never seen anything like it. Forensics will need to take a closer look, but whatever it is, it's not normal."

As Janice examined the scene, Matt's eyes scanned the crowd of onlookers behind the police tape. That's when he saw them—two familiar figures standing off to the side, faces pale and stricken with shock.

Coach Conner and Demetri.

Matt's pulse quickened as he recognized them. Demetri's hand was clutching the fence, his eyes wide as he stared at the covered body, and Coach Conner looked like he'd aged ten years in the span of a few minutes. They were clearly distraught.

Matt turned back to Janice, his voice tense. "Oh no, I think I know who this girl is."

CHAPTER 24

"THE LONG ROAD TO EARTH"
FLASHBACK OF HOW LILY GOT TO EARTH
AFTER AZAZEL'S REBELLION:

The dim glow of a single lantern illuminated the cramped stone chamber, its flickering light casting long, restless shadows along the walls. Smith paced in tight circles, his face taut with frustration, as Lily knelt by an open chest, carefully selecting items to bring with her. The faint scent of damp earth clung to the air, a stark reminder of the underground refuge they'd been forced to retreat to.

"You don't understand what you're risking, Lily," Smith said, his voice low but laced with urgency. His usual calm demeanor was frayed. "The Abyssal Key is not a relic—it's a weapon. It destroys indiscriminately. It consumes the one who wields it. You can't take it."

Lily didn't look up, her slender fingers brushing over the intricate carvings of the Abyssal Key before wrapping it in cloth and tucking it into the satchel at her side. "If I don't take it, and Azazel finds it, what then?" she countered, her tone steady but firm. "He'd use it to tear through whatever stands in his way, including you."

Smith stopped pacing, his sharp blue eyes narrowing. "If you take it and he finds you, he'll use you to get to it. Don't you see that? This isn't just about the artifact. It's about you, Lily. You're . . ." He paused. "You're too important."

Finally, Lily stood, her gaze meeting his. Her dark eyes, filled with both resolve and a hint of sorrow, softened as she studied the lines of worry etched into Smith's face. "I know what I'm risking," she said quietly. "But this is bigger than me. Bigger than both of us. If we don't take the risk, there won't be anything left worth protecting."

Smith's hands clenched at his sides. "And what about the journal? You're already taking the burden of hiding it. Isn't that enough?"

Lily's lips curved into a faint, bittersweet smile. "The journal is knowledge, Smith. The key is power. We can't let him have either."

The lantern flickered, the shadows on the walls dancing like restless spirits. Smith's shoulders sagged. "I hate this plan," he muttered. "I hate that you're putting yourself in harm's way again."

"Not just harm," Lily replied softly, pulling the strap of the satchel over her shoulder. "I'm putting myself in his path. If that's what it takes to protect the realms, so be it."

The sound of distant footsteps echoed faintly through the chamber, drawing their attention. Smith stiffened, his head snapping toward the narrow staircase leading out of the hideout. "They've found us," he said. His hand instinctively moved to the hilt of the dagger at his side.

Lily's expression didn't falter. Instead, she moved swiftly to the far wall, where a faint, nearly imperceptible outline of a mural could be seen. Her fingers brushed the wall's surface, and with a whisper of blue light, the mural began to come alive, its edges glowing as the portal within it awakened.

"We have to split up," she said.

"No," Smith shot back, his tone sharp with finality. "We're stronger together."

"We're also easier to find together," Lily countered, turning to face him. "You said it yourself—this isn't about just one of us. If one of us falls, the other has to keep going. That's the only way this works."

The footsteps grew louder, closer, accompanied by the faint clang of metal against stone. Smith's gaze flicked between Lily and the staircase. "Lily—"

"Go," she said firmly, her hand pressing against the mural as the light from the portal grew brighter. "Find the others. Regroup. If I can keep them off your trail— and off the child's—you'll have a chance to get back to Valoria . . . and free yourself."

Smith hesitated for a heartbeat, his hand twitching toward her shoulder before he let it fall. "Be well, Lily. And stay safe," he said softly, his voice steady but laced with unspoken concern. "We still have a fight ahead of us."

Lily's smile was faint but genuine. "Always," she said, her gaze lingering on him for a moment before she turned and stepped through the portal. The glow intensified, a cascade of blue light enveloping her figure before the mural sealed itself shut, leaving only the faintest trace of its former glow.

The sound of voices and clanging weapons broke through Smith's thoughts. He turned, his dagger drawn, as the first of Azazel's agents burst into the chamber.

"Come on, then," he muttered, his grip tightening on the hilt of his blade. "Let's see how far you get."

As he charged toward the intruders, the faint glow of the mural faded completely, leaving the chamber shrouded in shadow.

CHAPTER 25

After a long pause, Smith's eyes darkened with memory. He leaned forward, elbows on his knees, voice low. "There was a time before the war," he began, "when the realms existed in balance. Not perfect peace . . . but order. That balance was held by the Twelve Overseers."

Jo shifted, arms still crossed, but her brow furrowed. Devin leaned back, lips pressed tight, while Sara's gaze stayed locked on Smith, her hands curled in her lap.

"They weren't kings," Smith continued, glancing at each of them. "Not rulers. Guardians. Each chosen for something rare, something the realms needed. And they stood together under Thalion—the High King of Valoria, the beating heart of that balance."

Jo's voice cut in, quiet but firm. "Our mom . . . Lillianna. She was one of them?"

Smith gave a slow nod.

"Yes. She was the Keeper of Gateways, weaving the connections between worlds, making sure Valoria's light touched every realm—and guarding those paths from falling into the wrong hands."

Mr. Mason stepped closer, arms folded. "Each Overseer had their own burden, aye," he murmured. "Seraphis, the Keeper o' Secrets . . . Thariel, the Guardian o' the Blue Orbs . . . and Azazel—the Warbringer. Valoria's greatest general, he was. A fierce one . . . till he turned on us all."

Mason's eyes hardened.

Smith let the words settle, his gaze dropping for a beat before lifting again. "And above them, their king— Thalion. The heart that bound them together, the soul of Valoria itself."

Sara couldn't believe it.

Azazel had been an Overseer?

She glanced at Jo and Devin and could tell by their stunned silence that they had come to the same realization.

Smith continued.

"Azazel was not always the monster he is now," he admitted. "Once, he was Thalion's most trusted warrior. His closest friend."

"But war changes men."

Mr. Mason's face darkened. "When the first great war near shattered Valoria, Azazel lost faith in Thalion's vision. He believed the Overseers were too passive, aye— that they shouldnae just protect the realms, but rule 'em. Bend 'em to their will. Make 'em stronger . . . or so he thought."

Smith exhaled. "Azazel tried to convince the others that Thalion was weak. That the Overseers should take control. But he wasn't alone."

Eli leaned against the table, his voice calm but sharp. "Seraphis agreed with him."

Jo stiffened. "The Keeper of Secrets?"

Smith nodded. "Seraphis had spent centuries collecting knowledge—things no one else knew. He bought into what Azazel thought he saw— cracks forming in Thalion's rule. He believed that hidden knowledge should no longer be hidden, that they should use the forbidden magic locked away in Valoria's vaults."

"Aye, when Thalion wouldnae give his blessing to their plans," Mr. Mason said grimly, "Azazel and Seraphis made their choice. Turned their backs on us, they did."

"The first strike came swift," Eli said, voice low. "Azazel and Seraphis, working in secret, overpowered the Overseer tasked with guarding the blue orbs . . . Thariel. They nearly took all of them."

Smith looked down. His fingers tapped against the table, his eyes dark. "But they didn't just want to use the orbs as they were. They wanted to change them. Corrupt them, turning them into something unnatural. A perversion of their original power. The first red orbs."

Devin then sat up and asked, "So the Shadowforged? My Ancestors? That's when they were . . . corrupted?"

Smith's expression didn't change. "They were Valoria's warriors. Thalion's finest. But when Azazel turned, he took them with him."

"Not willingly," Mr. Mason clarified. "Azazel corrupted them, bent their minds, enslaved them with the red orbs."

Devin's stomach twisted violently.

Jo rubbed a hand over her face, her mind racing.

"So let me get this straight," she muttered. "The Twelve Overseers kept the balance. Azazel and Seraphis turned on them, twisted the blue orbs into the red orbs, used them to create the Voidwalkers, and dragged Devin's ancestors into this nightmare."

Smith nodded.

"And my mom . . . she was one of the few Overseers who stood against them."

"Yes," Smith said. "She and the others fought to stop them. And for a time, they succeeded."

Jo's arms tightened around herself.

"But not forever."

Smith didn't deny it.

Sara, looking up at Eli, Mr. Mason, and Smith, asked, "So how do you three fit into all of this?"

Smith glanced at his partners and was quiet for a moment. "Well . . ." he began.

But before he could answer, Eli's wrist communicator beeped softly.

The small screen lit up with a familiar alert: "Media Alert: Muxley Local News - Significant Developments."

Lucy's voice cut through the quiet.

"Eli. There's breaking news from Muxley. It's about Stacy Davis."

Eli's entire body tensed.

He exchanged a sharp look with Mr. Mason. The older man gave a slow, measured nod.

"Pull it up, Lucy," Eli muttered.

The holographic display flared to life, hovering just above Eli's wrist.

Everyone turned to face it.

The voice of a local news anchor came through the small speakers, tense with urgency.

"Breaking news today from Muxley, where police have discovered the body of a young woman identified as Stacy Davis. The discovery was made in the south side of town. Authorities are investigating the circumstances surrounding her death, but sources indicate there's no immediate cause of death evident at the scene . . ."

Sara inhaled sharply.

Devin's hands clenched against his knees.

The screen switched to a press conference.

A stern-faced man stood at a podium outside the Muxley Police Department.

Chief Scroggins.

His expression was tight, unreadable.

"We are treating this case as highly suspicious," Scroggins said. "Currently, we have no cause of death, but we're working with forensics to analyze all the evidence at the scene. We are asking anyone with information on the whereabouts of Devin Thompson, who we believe may have been one of the last people to see the victim alive, to come forward immediately."

The moment his name left the police chief's mouth, the air in the cabin shifted.

Devin froze.

His football team headshot flashed across the holographic display.

Sara's heart stopped.

Jo's slowly shook her head. "What?"

Devin stood so fast couch nearly toppled over.

The words came out in a whisper—

"They think I did this?"

The news report continued mercilessly.

"Devin Thompson is known locally for his successful football career, but speculation is growing about his involvement in the death of Stacy Davis. While authorities have not officially named him a suspect, Thompson has not been seen since her death was discovered, leading to increasing concern. If you have any information, contact the Muxley Police Department . . ."

Devin couldn't breathe.

His face—his name—plastered across the screen.

His life—shattered in real-time.

The newscast shifted to interviews with local residents. An older woman—one of his neighbors.

"He was such a good kid," she said, shaking her head. "I just can't believe he'd be involved in something like this . . . but . . . I guess we never really know anyone, do we?"

A second voice chimed in.

"I mean, you always hear about these kinds of things, right? Something bad happens, and then the boyfriend's the first suspect."

Devin's fingers dug into his palms so hard his nails nearly broke the skin.

Eli cut the feed.

The hologram flickered out, leaving only silence in its wake.

His face was unreadable, but his voice carried an unmistakable edge.

"This isn't speculation anymore. They're looking for you, Devin."

"I didn't do anything." Devin's voice shook. "How can they even think that? I wasn't even—how are they—"

He couldn't finish.

Jo stood up beside him, her face flushed with anger.

"This is insane!" she snapped. "They have no idea what's really going on. How could they? No one would ever believe the truth anyway."

Smith's face was dark, unreadable.

"They're looking for answers, Devin," he said quietly. "They don't know the truth. How could they?"

"So what, I'm supposed to hide while the whole world thinks I'm a murderer?"

"It's not forever," Smith assured him, stepping forward. "But right now, yes. We need to keep a low profile until we can clear this up."

He met Devin's burning gaze head-on.

"We have bigger problems than the media's false assumptions."

Devin knew Smith was right.

Mr. Mason stepped forward.

"Lad, ye need tae lay low for now," he said. "Let us work this out. We ken the truth, and ye've got nothin' tae prove by rushin' out there. Stay wi' us, and trust we'll set this right."

Devin glanced at Jo, at Sara, and finally back to Eli.

"I don't have much choice, do I?"

Smith's expression didn't change.

"No," he said gravely. "You don't."

The room fell into a heavy silence.

The weight of it settled over them like a storm waiting to break. And Devin Thompson was now the most wanted man in Muxley.

CHAPTER 26

The locker room buzzed with the usual after-practice chatter—guys snapping towels, joking around, the clatter of cleats hitting the floor. But beneath the surface, an uneasy tension gripped the space. The whispers had grown louder since the news broke about Stacy's death and Devin's sudden disappearance. And now, everyone talked, but not to each other.

Demetri sat on the bench, leaning forward, elbows on his knees, staring at his cleats. His mind wasn't on the practice they'd just finished. It hadn't been for days. He couldn't shake the gnawing thoughts—the memories of that strange day at the park, the suits, the girl painting, the men surrounding her. Something about it all had felt . . . wrong. And then Stacy . . . now Devin . . .

He looked up, eyes scanning the locker room, settling on a couple of the guys who had been there with him and Devin that day.

"Hey," Demetri called out, his voice quiet but urgent. The two players, Marcus and Tyler, glanced over at him, knowing exactly what he was about to ask.

"You ever think about what happened at the park?" Demetri continued, his brow furrowed in concern. "Like . . . do you think that has anything to do with . . . Stacy?"

Tyler shifted uncomfortably on the bench, rubbing the back of his neck. "Man, I dunno. We all agreed not to talk about it, remember? Devin said to just forget it."

Marcus shook his head, his voice low. "I haven't really thought about it, D. It was weird as hell, sure, but what're we supposed to say? I mean, those dudes were freaky, but none of us know what was really going on. We don't even know what they wanted with that girl."

Demetri gritted his teeth, his frustration bubbling up. "Exactly. We don't know. And now Stacy's dead, Devin's gone, and everyone's lookin' at him like he's guilty." He slammed a fist into his palm, the anger seeping into his voice. "Something's not right, man. We saw something that day. We saw how Devin acted. He's been different ever since. I just . . . I think there's a connection. There has to be."

Marcus looked over at Tyler, the two sharing an uneasy glance. "Maybe," Marcus muttered, clearly not wanting to dive into this conversation. "But none of us know for sure."

Demetri was about to say more when another voice cut through the locker room, loud and taunting. It was Jamal, a wide receiver who'd never particularly liked Devin.

"You ask me, it ain't that complicated," Jamal said with a smirk, his voice carrying over the usual locker room noise. "Devin's gone 'cause he knows he's guilty. Cops probably gonna find him holed up somewhere, runnin' scared. Just wait. That boy's gonna get what's comin' to him."

Demetri's entire body stiffened. His fists clenched so tight his knuckles turned white. He stood up, his heart pounding with fury. Jamal leaned against his locker, grinning like he'd just told the best joke in the world.

"What'd you say?" Demetri growled, taking a step toward him.

Jamal raised an eyebrow, looking unbothered. "You heard me. Devin's guilty. I don't care what y'all say. You think he just disappeared for no reason? That dude snapped, man. Probably couldn't handle her breakin' up with him or somethin'."

That did it.

Demetri lunged at Jamal, rage boiling over. "You shut your mouth!"

Before he could reach Jamal, Tyler and Marcus were on him, grabbing his arms and holding him back. "Whoa, whoa, chill, man!" Marcus shouted, struggling to keep Demetri from throwing a punch. "It's not worth it!"

Jamal just laughed, but there was a hint of nervousness in his eyes as Demetri fought to get free. "What, you mad 'cause you know I'm right? Devin ain't some hero, man. He's a killer. And y'all out here defendin' him like fools."

"Shut up, Jamal!" Tyler barked, his own patience wearing thin as he held Demetri back.

The locker room had gone dead silent, all eyes on the scene unfolding in the middle. Some of the guys looked uncomfortable, others clearly curious about what Demetri was going to do next. But before anything else could happen, a new voice cut through the tension.

"Enough!"

Everyone froze. Coach Conner stood at the door to the locker room, his presence demanding immediate attention. His arms were crossed, his face stern, but his eyes held a deeper disappointment. Slowly, he made his way toward the center of the room, his gaze moving between Demetri, still being held back, and Jamal, who had the sense to shut up now that Coach was there.

Coach Conner stopped in front of Demetri, his voice low and calm but firm. "I don't know what the hell's goin' on here, but this stops. Now." He turned to look at Jamal, his expression hardening. "And you," Coach pointed at him, "better keep your damn mouth shut about things you don't know. You don't know a thing about Devin, or what's goin' on. So quit spreadin' rumors."

Jamal opened his mouth to argue, but the look in Coach's eyes stopped him cold. He snapped his jaw shut, clearly irritated but smart enough not to push it.

Coach Conner's gaze shifted to Demetri, and he gave him a slight nod, signaling for Tyler and Marcus to let him go. They did, and Demetri took a deep breath, trying to calm himself down, though his fists remained clenched at his sides.

"Listen up," Coach Conner said, turning to address the entire room now. "I know tensions are high. I know y'all are wonderin' what's goin' on with Devin and this whole situation with Stacy. But right now, what we need is to focus on what we can control. The truth is gonna come out. Devin's one of us, and until we know different, we're standin' by him. You got me?"

The room was silent, the weight of Coach's words settling over everyone. No one dared argue with him— not even Jamal.

Coach's eyes swept the room, his voice softening just a little. "I know this is hard. Stacy was one of us too. But we gotta stick together. That's the only way we're gonna get through this."

Demetri nodded, his anger slowly ebbing away. But even as Coach's words calmed the room, the uncertainty lingered. Devin was still missing. And the longer he stayed gone, the more that doubt would grow—both inside the locker room and out.

CHAPTER 27

The ride to Janice's house was silent, the radio filling the space between them with grim details—the tragic death of Stacy Davis and a public plea for any information on the whereabouts of Devin Thompson. Combined with everything Janice had told him back at Winker's Tavern, it left Matt feeling overwhelmed, his mind spinning too fast to find words. He kept his eyes on the road, while Janice steered the car quietly beside him.

The car rumbled to a stop in the driveway, the low hum of the engine fading as she threw it into park.

For a moment, neither of them moved.

Then Janice turned in her seat, fixing Matt with a look that made it clear—*this was the moment.*

"You wanted answers," she said, her voice even but weighted. "Well, you're about to get 'em. But let me tell you something, Halbridge . . ." She rested an arm on the steering wheel, her fingers tapping against the leather. "What you are about to see . . . it's going to change things. Some of it's gonna be hard to take. Some of it's gonna make you wish you never asked in the first place."

Matt swallowed but didn't look away.

Janice's gaze sharpened. "So before we go in, I need you to swear to me—*what you learn tonight stays under your hat* until the time is right. No running off to publish some half-baked story, no trying to play hero. You wait.

You listen. And you *understand* what's at stake before you even think about what comes next."

Her tone wasn't a plea. It wasn't even a warning. It was a *command.*

Matt exhaled slowly, glancing toward the house. His instincts screamed at him to push back—*no one told him how to do his job.* But something about the way she said it, the gravity in her voice, made it clear.

Finally, he gave a small nod. "All right," he said. "You have my word."

Janice studied him for a beat longer, then nodded once and pushed open the door.

"Good," she murmured. "Then let's get to it."

The house itself was nothing remarkable—an unassuming single-story structure with weathered brick, tucked away in a quiet part of town. It was the last place Matt would have expected to hold *answers.*

Janice led him around the side of the house to the garage.

That's when he saw it.

A red door.

Matt halted mid-step. The hairs on the back of his neck prickled. Something about the color—deep, almost blood-like—sent an involuntary chill down his spine.

Janice didn't hesitate. She pulled out the ornate key she had shown him at Winker's Tavern. The same one with the intricate leaf symbols carved into its metal surface, the faint glow pulsing from its edges.

She fit it into the keyhole and turned.

A soft *click* echoed in the air, followed by a low, resonant *hum.*

Then the door opened.

Matt expected the dim, dusty interior of an old garage. What he got instead stole the breath from his lungs.

It was massive.

A vast, towering library stretched out before him, its walls lined with bookshelves climbing impossibly high. The scent of aged parchment, ink, and something faintly floral filled the air. An enormous wooden terrace extended outward, leading to an elegant round table overlooking a breathtaking view—a lush, thriving garden that shouldn't exist in a garage. Waterfalls cascaded down rocky cliffs, feeding into crystal-clear streams that wound through the greenery.

Matt took a step forward, his pulse hammering.

"This . . . This *isn't possible.*"

Janice closed the door behind them and locked it. "Possible or not, it's real."

Matt turned slowly, struggling to process the sheer *wrongness* of it all. The garage was maybe *twenty feet wide* from the outside. Inside? Janice led him across the upper terrace, past the overlook where the lush garden spread out below. Without a word, she guided him to the far right, toward a stone wall tucked beside the garden's edge.

She pressed her hand against a panel he hadn't noticed, and with a faint click, a hidden door swung open.

Wordlessly, she motioned him forward.

Matt followed her through the narrow passage into a second chamber, the air cooler, the stone walls rougher. That's when he saw it.

A mural.

It stretched across the entire surface, depicting something almost dreamlike—a swirling landscape, stars entwined in its painted sky, a bridge that led into a realm he couldn't quite place. The colors seemed to shift, subtly, like an optical illusion.

Janice lifted her hand. A vial sat on a small pedestal beside the mural. Inside it, a substance shimmered—a blue energy, softly pulsing like liquid light.

"Watch," she said.

She uncorked the vial and let a single drop spill onto the mural.

The paint reacted instantly. The colors pulsed. The stars in the sky shimmered and brightened. The bridge within the painting deepened, taking on a three-dimensional form.

The air in the room *shifted.*

Matt felt it. Like the subtle change in pressure before a storm.

The bridge in the mural . . . it wasn't just *paint* anymore. It looked real. Solid. A doorway.

Janice stepped back, letting the mural settle back into stillness. "It's a portal," she said quietly. "Now, you've seen it for yourself."

Matt couldn't speak. He swallowed hard, forcing himself to break his gaze away from the shifting, impossible image before him.

Then, finally, he found his voice.

"Where does it go?" he asked.

Janice glanced at him, then back at the mural. A knowing look crossed her face, like she had been waiting for that question.

"This particular mural takes you where you *need* to be," she said. "At the moment you need to be there."

Matt frowned. "So it changes?"

Janice nodded. "It's not just a picture—it's a door-way that responds to *purpose*. One day it could take you across a city. Another day, to a place no one's ever heard of. The image shifts, but the rule stays the same."

Matt stared at the mural again, feeling some-thing tighten in his chest. The idea that this *thing*—this painted bridge, this *living* artwork—could change depending on need rather than want made his head spin.

His mind turned over what she had just said, some-thing clicking into place.

He exhaled sharply. "Wait—" he turned to Janice, brow furrowed. "The mural at Walter's General Store. The one that's been all over the news . . . the one people said started *glowing* before things went sideways . . ." His voice trailed off, realization dawning on his face.

Janice's expression didn't change. She simply gave a small nod.

"Yes."

Matt's stomach dropped.

"That was a portal too?" His voice came out quieter than before.

"Yes," Janice confirmed.

Matt swallowed hard. He remembered the news stories—people claiming the mural *came to life*, the unexplained flashes of light. He had dismissed it as sensationalism, media hysteria.

"So . . . is this what Jack found?" He turned back to her, his voice steady but edged. "You said he was inves-tigating something dangerous. *This*—all of this—what did he actually uncover?"

Janice didn't answer right away. Instead, she gave a small, silent motion for him to follow, turning and leading the way out of the hidden chamber. Together, they stepped back through the narrow passage. Janice crossed the room, heading toward one of the massive bookshelves lining the walls.

She ran her fingers along the spines of the books— old tomes, leather-bound with gold lettering, some written in languages Matt didn't recognize.

Then she stopped.

From one of the higher shelves, she pulled out a weathered journal.

She turned back to him, holding it in both hands.

"This," she said, her voice quiet but firm. "This is where it all started."

Matt narrowed his eyes. "What is it?"

Janice's fingers brushed over the cover, tracing the name embossed on the worn leather surface.

Lilianna.

She held it out to him. "Everything Jack learned came from here."

Matt hesitated before taking it. The book was heavier than it looked, the leather cool beneath his fingertips. He flipped it open, scanning the first page. The handwriting was precise, elegant, but hurried, as if written by someone who had more thoughts than time to put them down.

The first few words stopped him cold.

"Murals are more than art. They are doors."

He lifted his gaze to Janice. "Murals like this . . . they're *all* portals?"

Janice nodded. "Not all of them are active. Some are hidden. Some lost. But the ones that *are* open? They connect places, worlds, people. Jack was only beginning to understand that when he—" She stopped herself. Exhaled. "When he was taken out."

She hesitated, then continued. "But the murals weren't the only thing he found."

Matt's brow furrowed. "What do you mean?"

"He discovered that there were . . . beings in Muxley. People—at least, they *looked* like people—who weren't from here. They came through the portals. Some hiding. Some scouting. And some . . . came here to do harm."

Matt felt a slow chill creep up his spine.

Janice met his gaze. "Jack found out that some of them weren't just passing through. They were *staying*. Covertly embedding themselves in places of power. He believed they were working toward something—slowly, carefully, planting themselves inside our institutions, waiting for the right moment to take control."

Matt let out a slow breath. "And you're saying Jack figured all of this out?"

Janice nodded. "Not all at once. It took him *years*— years to separate the truth from the paranoia, to gather enough evidence to believe it himself." She glanced down at the journal in her hands. "And that's when he uncovered the hardest truth of all."

Matt clenched his jaw. "Which was?"

Janice looked up. "Lily—his wife—was one of them."

He blinked. "Wait—*what?*"

Janice nodded. "She wasn't from here, Matt. She came through a portal. And she wasn't just hiding. She was *running*."

Matt's breath felt thin.

Janice pressed forward. "Lily was hiding from her

enemies. And in the end, they found her. They killed her."

A long silence stretched between them.

Matt looked down at the journal in her hands. "Jack never knew?"

"No," Janice said. "He didn't *know* the full truth until after she died. After he started digging."

Matt exhaled sharply. "Wow."

Janice's expression darkened. "Jack's last priority before he disappeared was protecting his daughters. Because they carry their mother's blood. Which means . . ."

Matt met her gaze.

"They're targets too," he finished.

Janice gave a slow nod.

For the first time in his life, Matt Halbridge felt like he was truly in over his head.

"There's something else you need to see," Janice said.

Matt followed her as she approached the smooth, polished pedestal. Resting at its center was a glowing orb pulsing softly, its silvery glow shifting as she placed her hand on it.

"This is the Seers Eye," she said. Images flickered to life inside.

A dimly lit apartment. A girl pacing. Another curled up on the couch, hugging her knees.

Matt frowned. "Who are they?"

Janice didn't look away. "The girls Jack left behind. I raised them after he died."

Matt's stomach tightened. This wasn't just some grand conspiracy. It had a *face*.

Then the image inside the Seer's Eye shifted.

A street. A young man running.

Sirens flared in the distance. Red and blue lights bounced off the buildings as police vehicles rounded the corner, cutting off his path. The boy skidded to a stop, his chest rising and falling in sharp, panicked breaths.

Matt tensed. "That's Devin Thompson. Looks like they caught him."

Janice's face darkened. "No." She exhaled slowly. "This isn't happening *right now.*"

Matt shot her a sharp look. "What do you mean?"

Janice hesitated, eyes narrowing as the image in the orb shifted again.

A warehouse. Dimly lit. Dust swirling in the beams of light cutting through the cracked windows. The same young man—*Devin*—stood at a round table. His hand reaching out toward something glowing in the middle of the table.

A red orb.

The pull was visible—his body leaned toward it, almost against his will, like the thing had a gravity all its own.

Janice blinked.

". . . Well, I'll be," she murmured under her breath.

Matt glanced at her. "What?"

She turned to him, clearing her throat.

Janice hesitated, then met his gaze. "This is showing us a *potential future.*"

Matt ran a hand down his face. "Great. So now you're telling me this thing predicts the future?"

Janice didn't flinch. "I'm telling you that this is telling us that if we don't step in, that's what *will* happen."

Her tone had shifted. "We need to protect him. And we need to get him *here*."

Matt stared at the shifting images in the Seer's Eye—Devin, the warehouse, the red orb.

He exhaled. "Okay. What can I do to help?"

CHAPTER 28

Her tone had a sharp edge to it. Blue. Annoyed.

head to get it inside.

Matt stared at the shifting breasts in the Sector

Ovi - Devin, the warehouse, the red orb.

He exhaled. *Okay. What can I do now?"

After the news report, the group sat in heavy silence for a while. But before long, Jo stood abruptly, unable to hold it in any longer. "What about our dad?"

Smith and Mr. Mason exchanged a glance.

"We've learned the truth about our mom," she continued. "But what about Dad? He . . . he had to have known something, right? Or was he part of this too?"

Sara looked up, the same question burning in her mind.

"Did Dad know about Mom's secret life? Did he know about Valoria, about all of this?"

Then—Smith leaned forward.

His elbows rested on his knees, his hands loosely clasped together. His expression was different now—not just burdened, but guarded.

"Your father . . . Jack Sweeney, wasn't an ordinary man."

Jo stared at Smith.

Sara gripped the edge of her chair.

"What does that mean?" Jo pressed. "Are you saying he was one of you? One of the Overseers?"

Smith shook his head.

"No. Jack was from Earth—just like you."

Sara's heartbeat quickened. "So . . . he knew about our mom?"

Mr. Mason took over.

"Jack didnae know who yer mother truly was until after she was gone, lass."

Smith confirmed. "Lilianna never told him the full truth. She wanted to leave that life behind—to protect all of you from it. And for a while, she succeeded."

Jo swallowed hard, her arms wrapping around herself.

"So when she died . . ."

Smith nodded. "That's when everything changed."

Mr. Mason's gaze darkened.

Yer father didn't accept what happened tae Lilianna. Not at face value. He knew somethin' was wrong. He dug deep—askin' questions, pushin' for answers. But everywhere he turned... he was met with resistance."

Sara's stomach twisted. "Who resisted him?"

"The very people who should've helped him," Smith answered grimly. "Law enforcement. Government officials. Old contacts. He thought they'd want to know the truth, but the more he searched, the more doors slammed in his face."

"For six months," Mr. Mason added, "he was fightin' against a wall. Nothin' made sense. He was chasin' ghosts."

Jo felt a lump in her throat.

"So what happened?"

Smith's expression softened- "Then I sent Mr. Mason to him."

Jo and Sara's eyes snapped to Mr. Mason.

"Wait," Jo said slowly. "You went to him?"

Mr. Mason nodded.

"What did you tell him?" asked Jo.

He exhaled slowly. "I gave him a key."

Jo and Sara exchanged a sharp glance.

"A key? To what?" Jo asked.

Mr. Mason's eyes met theirs. "To the very thing that would help yer father understand what had happened tae yer mother. He deserved tae know da truth."

He let the silence settle for a moment.

"Her journal."

"She had a journal?" asked Sara.

Smith nodded. "She documented everything. Not just her life on Earth, but her past—her mission, the things she couldn't tell anyone. The journal contains answers to the full restoration of Valoria and its people. She knew she was in danger, and she wrote it all down, knowing that one day, someone might need to read it."

Jo shook her head, her mind spinning.

"And you just . . . gave it to our dad?"

Mr. Mason's expression was grim. "Aye. But no' directly. I gave him the key. The journal was hidden— locked away, where only he could find it."

"Why did you wait so long to help him?" Jo asked.

Smith and Mr. Mason exchanged a heavy glance.

"As much as we wanted tae help him, lass," Mr. Mason said quietly, "we knew that if yer father learned the truth, it would put him in danger—and more than that, it could endanger you and Sara as well."

Smith nodded, his voice low. "We wrestled with it, Jo. But in the end . . . we decided to take the risk. To help relieve your father's burden, even knowing the cost."

Sara's heart pounded. "And did he find it? Did he read the journal?"

A shadow passed over Mr. Mason's face. "He did."

Jo's voice came out hoarse, shaking as the weight of the revelations crashed over her. "He didn't die in a car accident . . . did he?"

Smith's gaze was like steel. "No."

Jo's tears filled her eyes.

Sara's chest ached.

For a moment, no one moved.

Then, Jo abruptly pushed back her chair, the legs scraping sharply against the floor. Her hands shook. Tears burned in her eyes, but she refused to let them fall. Without a word, she turned and stormed toward the back door.

No one stopped her.

The door swung open, and she stepped out into the cool air, disappearing onto the back porch.

Sara instinctively moved to stand.

But before she could take a step, Smith's voice stopped her. "Let her go."

Sara turned, her eyes wide. "But—"

"Give her time," Smith said, his voice firm but not unkind.

"She needs a moment to feel this. To be angry. Let her have it."

Finally, she sank back into her chair, staring at the door Jo had just walked through. Tears began to fall.

Silence overtook the cabin once more.

CHAPTER 29

Jo sat in the creaking rocking chair on the wraparound porch, its rhythmic groan folding into the hush of the wind through the towering pines. The air carried the scent of damp earth and resin, crisp and biting against her skin. Beyond the porch, the landscape stretched endlessly—rolling forests and deep valleys, gilded in the fading light. A breathtaking view, but Jo barely saw it. Her eyes were fixed on nothing.

The weight of Smith's words pressed against her ribs. The truth had landed like a boulder.

Her father wasn't killed in a car accident. He had been murdered.

The thought sent a shudder through her, and suddenly, she was small again, standing in the doorway of his study, watching him sift through stacks of notes, his fingers trailing across the worn pages like they held all the answers in the world. He used to ruffle her hair without looking up, a quiet sign that he knew she was there. That she mattered. That he was always watching out for her. She could still hear his voice—low, steady.

"I'll figure this out, Jo. I promise."

But the storm had come anyway, ripping him away before she had the chance to understand what he fought for. Now all that remained were scattered memories and a raw, gaping wound where his presence used to be.

Jo wanted to feel something—anything—other than

this crushing helplessness. Doubt slithered through her mind. Smith. Mr. Mason. Their part in all of this loomed over her like faceless shadows. Had they really tried to help her father? Or had they been the reason he had a target on his back in the first place?

The thought churned her stomach, bitter and relentless.

A floorboard creaked.

Jo tensed, but she didn't turn right away. She had felt his presence before she heard him.

"Jo?" Smith's voice carried through the quiet. He stood at the edge of the porch, hands in his pockets, his silhouette shadowed against the twilight. The usual sharpness in his features had eased. "Mind if I join you?"

Jo dragged a hand across her face, wiping at the dampness she refused to acknowledge. She straightened, a steel edge sharpening her posture, as if sitting taller could force the emotions back where they belonged.

"Shouldn't you be inside, strategizing or something?" The bite in her words wasn't as sharp as she wanted it to be, but she didn't care.

Smith didn't flinch. "There's someone here who needs a hug from her sister."

Jo's turned.

Before she could process the words, the cabin door creaked open.

Sara.

She stepped out slowly, her face pale, eyes red-rimmed. She hesitated only for a moment before moving, closing the distance between them in a rush.

Jo barely had time to brace herself before Sara's arms

wrapped around her, holding on with a desperation that shattered what little resolve she had left.

Jo exhaled sharply, her chest tightening as she pulled Sara close, their bodies trembling against each other. Neither spoke. There were no words big enough for this—no words that could unravel the pain clawing at their insides.

And so they wept.

Sara buried her face against Jo's shoulder, gripping her like she was afraid to let go. Jo pressed her cheek to the top of Sara's head, rocking them slightly, the way their mother used to.

For the first time in what felt like forever, Jo allowed herself to break.

The wind hummed around them, weaving through the trees.

After what felt like an eternity, Jo loosened her grip just enough to look at Sara's tear-streaked face. She brushed a strand of hair from her sister's cheek, swallowing the lump in her throat.

"We're going to be okay," she whispered, not sure if she believed it but needing Sara to hear it anyway.

Sara sniffed, nodding as she wiped at her face.

Smith lowered himself into the rocking chair across from them, watching quietly, allowing them the space they needed.

Jo let out a breath she hadn't realized she'd been holding, her fingers tracing the worn cracks in the chair beneath her. She finally met Smith's gaze and was surprised to find understanding there, not pity.

She swallowed, her voice quieter than she intended. "I don't know what to believe anymore." Her fingers curled around the arms of her chair. "Everything you said in there . . . it changes everything. And now I don't know if I should trust you or blame you."

Smith nodded. "Yes, I know you're confused," he said, his voice calm but weighted. "I know why you left, Jo. And I'm sorry. You've heard a lot today—more than anyone should have to bear."

Jo swallowed hard. "It's not just today," she murmured. "It's everything. It's losing Mom and Dad. It's trying to be strong for Sara when I feel like I'm breaking apart inside."

The admission barely made it past her lips before her throat closed up again.

Smith didn't speak for a moment, then his gaze drifted past them, out toward the landscape. "That's why you need the Hallow," he said, nodding toward the endless green beyond the porch. "This place isn't just a safe haven. It's a place of healing, of renewal. The Healing Hallow has the power to help you face the grief that holds you down and come out the other side ready for what's ahead."

Jo turned, studying the view for the first time. It felt impossible—the rolling emerald hills, the golden light pooling in the valleys, the gentle whisper of the trees. The warmth of the breeze carried scents of pine and wildflowers, a stark contrast to the cold mist of the Shadowland they had walked through earlier.

"How is this possible?" Jo asked.

Smith reached into his coat and pulled out a ring of keys, the metal glinting as he turned them over in his palm.

"With these," he said simply, holding them out for Jo and Sara to see.

Jo frowned, leaning forward slightly as the keys caught the light. They weren't ordinary keys. Some looked ancient, their metal worn smooth, while others gleamed as if freshly forged. A few had intricate symbols etched into them, strange patterns curling along their edges.

Sara, still gripping Jo's sleeve, peered at them with wide eyes. "They look like the ones we use for your door at your house."

"Because they are," Smith replied. "Each one is unique, forged for a specific purpose. They don't open just any door—they each open the right door, to the right place."

Jo's brows furrowed. "So that red door we passed through . . . it wasn't just part of the cabin?"

Smith shook his head. "No. That door was an entrance to this realm. Without the key, you would just walk into a normal-looking cabin. With the key, it gives you access to this place. Just as the door here opened up the Healing Hallow, there are others scattered across Earth that open into different realms."

Jo exhaled, shaking her head slightly. "So you're saying these keys can open . . . other places? Other worlds?"

Smith's faint smile returned. "This place exists between realms, a sanctuary hidden from sight. The red door you passed through is one of many across the realms, each leading to a place of refuge or power."

Jo stared at the keys again, trying to wrap her mind around what he said. "And you just . . . know which key goes where?"

"I do," Smith said, slipping the ring of keys back into his coat.

Jo shook her head slightly. "This is all so weird."

She hesitated, her gaze drifting back to the golden light filtering through the trees. "It's not just weird—it's like I've been here before. I don't know how, but . . . it feels familiar. Like a place I should remember, even though I know I've never seen it."

Smith's expression turned serious again. "It's no coincidence that this place feels familiar. Places like this echo what is familiar to those who need them. It's a place for reflection, for finding strength in what was and what could be."

Jo's gaze flickered back to the golden-lit forest. There was something about it—something that both beckoned and unsettled her. The way the light pooled between the trees, the rhythmic sway of the branches, the whisper of the wind that barely stirred the porch but seemed alive within the woods.

Sara, still holding Jo's sleeve, asked, "Then . . . what are we supposed to do here?"

Smith heard her—but his eyes stayed fixed on Jo. His voice softened, directed at Jo. "Go," he urged quietly. "Let the Hallow do what it was meant to."

Jo's eyes shifted back toward the towering trees. A hush had settled over the forest—not silence, but something deeper. The rustling of leaves wasn't just wind; it was movement, deliberate and fluid, like a breath drawn through unseen lungs.

Then she heard it.

Not words. Not a voice. A feeling, like a distant memory stirring at the edges of her mind. It wasn't calling her. It was pulling. Like a tether deep inside her chest, gently tugging her forward.

As warmth brushed against her skin, an almost imperceptible shift occurred in the air, like someone reaching out—like fingertips grazing the edge of her thoughts.

A wave of something—grief, longing, recognition—rose so fast and fierce inside her that she swayed.

"*Jo?*" Sara's voice cut through the moment, grounding her.

Jo blinked hard, the world snapping back into focus. The forest was just a forest again. The wind, just wind. But the feeling remained.

"I can't." The words tumbled out before she could stop them. She rose from her chair abruptly, gripping the porch railing. "Sara . . . I need to check on Sara."

Sara frowned, tugging lightly on Jo's sleeve. "Jo, I'm right here."

Jo forced a smile, but it barely held. She took a step back. Then another. Away from the Hallow. Away from the unknown. As she turned toward the cabin, Smith's voice stopped her.

"Jo."

She hesitated.

When she looked back, Smith held something out to her. A key.

Not just any key. It was smaller than the ones she'd seen him use before, its metal cool and smooth —with patterns like winding roots, like flowing water.

"Take it."

Jo swallowed, glancing between him and the key. "What for?"

"Because you'll be back."

His voice wasn't forceful, not a command, just a quiet certainty.

Jo hesitated, then reached out, fingers brushing against the cool metal before curling around it. A strange sensation washed over her—like warmth seeping into her palm.

But she ignored it.

Without another word, she turned and walked back into the cabin, leaving the Hallow—and whatever it was trying to show her—behind.

CHAPTER 30

The warmth of the cabin did little to chase away the weight pressing on Jo's chest as she stepped back inside. Her limbs ached, not from any physical exertion but from the sheer exhaustion of holding herself together.

She barely made it a few steps before her knees felt weak. Without thinking, she sank into the nearest couch, the worn cushions swallowing her whole.

The weight of the past few hours pressed into her bones—the grief, the rage, the ache of Stacy's death, the unbearable revelation of their father's fate, the strange pull of the Healing Hallow, and the way she had felt something stir inside her there.

And Sara.

They had clung to each other, their grief shared, woven together like it had been since the day their mother died.

Jo closed her eyes for a brief moment, letting her head sink back against the couch. Just one breath. One moment to just—

The back door creaked open.

Her eyes fluttered open as Sara and Smith stepped inside, closing the door softly behind them.

For a brief moment, no one spoke.

Then, from down the hall in the cabin, a distant, muffled voice stirred through the room.

"Lad," Mason finally said, his voice steady, low. "You did nothing wrong."

Devin let out a sharp, humorless laugh. "Yeah? Well, tell that to the cops. Tell that to Greaves. Tell that to anyone who sees my face and thinks I'm some kind of murderer."

Smith exhaled through his nose, taking one look at Jo, slumped against the couch. His gaze glanced toward Devin's voice down the hall, who was heard pacing like a caged animal. Then to Sara, still standing near the door, watching it all unfold with quiet, weary eyes.

Smith made his decision in an instant.

"We need to rest," he said firmly, leaving no room for argument.

"We leave tomorrow. Get some sleep while you can."

Eli woke to the sharp chime of his communicator.

His eyes snapped open, heart hammering from the abrupt pull from sleep. The room was dark, save for the faint embers in the cabin's fireplace, casting long shadows across the walls.

For a brief moment, his mind was sluggish, still caught in the hazy edges of sleep, but then the chime came again—urgent, insistent.

Lucy.

Eli sat up, rubbing a hand over his face as he reached for the slim, silver device on the table beside him. With a flick of his thumb, the projection flickered to life, casting a faint blue glow across the room.

Lucy's voice came through immediately, clipped and urgent.

"Eli. Warehouse vault made visible."

The last remnants of sleep vanished from Eli's mind in an instant. His body tensed, his breath stilling.

"What?" he muttered, fingers already moving over the interface to pull up the data.

"The Riftstone beacon," Lucy continued. "Azazel's operative used beacon to trace the vault's exact coordinates. Transmission intercepted—Councilman Greaves is with them. Outer chamber breached. Red orb retrieved."

Eli sighed deeply, swinging his legs over the side of the cot. His boots hit the wooden floor with a dull thud as he scanned the readout in front of him.

The confirmation was there. The beacon's signal had flared across multiple channels before disappearing. The vault had been exposed, just long enough for Azazel's forces to take what they came for.

The red orb was in their hands.

Eli shut off the projection, his jaw tight as he pushed to his feet. There was only one thing to do now.

Wake Smith.

"What is it?" Smith asked. He didn't need warmth in his tone. The fact that Eli had woken him at all meant it was serious.

Mr. Mason followed, sitting up and throwing a cloak over his shoulders.

"The vault's been breached," Eli said finally, his voice low. "Greaves and Azazel's operatives used a Riftstone beacon. They've recovered the red orb."

Smith's breath left him in a quiet exhale, shoulders sagging.

"Then he can activate another mural," Mr. Mason muttered. "Bring through more of his twisted kin . . ."

Eli nodded. "That's why we need to respond in kind. We have to activate the mural Sara painted—at Walter's Market. Open the portal."

Smith didn't speak at first. His gaze dropped to the floorboards.

"She has Valorian energy in her now," Eli continued. "She painted that mural for a reason. And if we can find even one active blue orb—"

Smith turned, a look of something old, tired, and uncertain in his eyes.

"And what then?" he asked quietly. "Even with a blue orb in hand . . . do you expect Sara, Jo, and Devin to lead the charge into a war they barely understand?"

Eli frowned. "That's not what this is about."

Smith looked away. "They're just kids, Eli. That's a lot to ask of the young ones."

But Mason interjected, "Aye, but we've seen what they are . . ."

Eli interrupted, "Devin's connection to the red orb— don't pretend you didn't see it. That wasn't chance. That's Draegora in his blood, and it stirred for a reason. Sara's vision. The Mural. Jo's pull to the Hallow. This is no coincidence, Smith. This is the will of Thalion pushing back. We're not alone anymore."

Smith was still. His eyes dropped to the ring of keys at his side.

He clenched his fist and looked away.

"Even if that's true," he said after a long pause, "Even if we use one of our remaining blue orbs. You know that I . . . we . . . can't . . ." Smith couldn't finish.

Mr. Mason and Eli looked at each other slowly nodding.

After a moment Smith continued. "Azazel has the orb, and now that the beacon's been activated . . . it's only a matter of time before they track us here."

Eli exhaled. "Then we keep moving. But we move with purpose. With eyes open. And if there's even a chance the blue orbs might stir again, we have to try."

Smith said nothing for a breath, then gave a single, firm nod.

"Wake the others," he said, voice low. "We leave within the hour. If we're going to protect whatever hope we have left, we need to stay ahead of Azazel—and out of his shadow."

CHAPTER 31

The moon hung low, casting silver light over the clearing. Their breaths fogged in the cold night air, vanishing into the silence as they gathered just beyond the edge of the forest.

Sara stood near the edge of the group, arms wrapped tightly around herself, her hair tousled from sleep, cheeks flushed with the cold. She blinked slowly, still groggy, her body shivering in the crisp night air. Her hoodie did little to block the chill, and she rubbed her hands along her arms in a futile attempt to warm up.

Jo stood beside her, a few feet ahead. She flexed her fingers, the leather of her jacket creaking as she clenched and unclenched her fists.

Footsteps crunched softly over frostbitten ground.

Devin stepped up beside Sara, glancing at her with concern. Without a word, he reached out and gently rubbed her arms, trying to generate some warmth.

"You okay?" he asked quietly, his breath clouding between them.

Sara nodded faintly, teeth chattering just enough to betray her answer.

Devin gave a half-smile meant to be reassuring, then turned to Jo, as if silently asking if she needed the same.

But Jo met his gaze with a look that said all he needed to know. A firm, quiet 'I'm fine.'

He gave a subtle nod and turned to Smith, adjusting the strap of his bag across his shoulder.

"So where are we headed?" he asked. "And how do I keep a low profile so I don't get snatched up the second someone recognizes me in Muxley?"

Before Smith could answer, he stopped and put up his hand.

The night stretched around them, quiet . . . too quiet.

A whisper of wind.

A shudder through the trees.

Then—

The forest held its breath.

And he stepped through the darkness like he had been there all along.

Azazel Blackthorn.

His robes moved like liquid night, silent as the grave.

The air warped around him, thick with something unseen, something unnatural.

His eyes glowed a deep, malevolent red, burning like embers.

A slow, knowing smile curled his lips.

"So," he drawled, his voice smooth as polished glass, "this is what remains of Thalion's 'champions.' The last line of defense, clinging so desperately to a fractured cause."

"Hey, that's the guy from the . . . park," said Devin wishing he had kept his mouth shut.

Smith stood firm, his gaze fixed on Azazel.

Azazel's gaze drifted, slow and deliberate.

His eyes looked past Jo, lingered on Devin, then finally settled on Sara.

A dark gleam sparked in his gaze.

"Ah, the children of Lilianna . . . how poetic." He

tilted his head, mock pity threading his voice. "I almost feel sorry for you."

Sara swallowed hard, her pulse thundering against her ribs. Cold sweat gathered at the nape of her neck, but she forced herself to stand tall. She felt an unusual resolve in herself to not be afraid. She would not look away. Not from him.

As she looked down at her hands, she saw a faint blue glow emerging.

She looked up and Azazel had shifted his focus back to Smith.

"You, of all people, should know how this ends . . . Overseer," he spat, the title laced with venom.

A silence dropped like a stone between them.

Sara's mouth dropped open slightly. Overseer?

Her gaze snapped to Smith.

Devin stiffened, his expression twisting in confusion. "Wait . . . what did he just call you?"

Smith's jaw tightened, but he did not look away from Azazel.

Azazel chuckled. "Haven't you told them?" He stepped forward, the shadows slithering at his feet. "They deserve to know why you're here, stranded on this forsaken Earth, bound by ancient spells and reduced to hiding behind mortals."

"Smith . . . is it true?" Sara asked.

Smith finally nodded, slow, weighted. "Yes," he said, voice rough. "But that was a long time ago."

Azazel's grin cut through the cold.

"And now look at you," he murmured, mocking, gloating. "A ghost clinging to a past that can't be reclaimed."

215

His gaze turned back to Sara, his voice turning soft. "But the past isn't all that matters, is it?"

Smith's posture shifted, a storm rising behind his eyes.

"I may be bound," he said, his voice steely, "but I am far from powerless."

In one swift motion, he pulled a glowing amulet from beneath his coat—the blue light pulsing in his palm like a heartbeat. The air snapped with energy as he reared back and hurled it toward Azazel.

But—

The shadows moved faster.

Two figures emerged from the dark, black-cloaked operatives of Azazel, their forms unnaturally fluid. One of them lashed out with a whip of red energy, striking the amulet midair. It exploded in a burst of sapphire sparks, showering the clearing in brilliant fragments.

Before the light had even faded, Azazel lifted his hand.

The ring on his finger flared—deep crimson light coiling and pulsing with malevolence. With a flick of his wrist, a lance of red energy surged forward and slammed into Smith's chest, hurling him backward like a rag doll.

He hit the ground hard, skidding through leaves and dirt.

"SMITH!" Sara's scream tore through the clearing. Her voice cracked, raw with shock and fear.

Mr. Mason was already moving, diving toward his fallen comrade. "Smith—!"

Eli's hands were on his communicator in a flash. "Lucy—Lucy, we need help to get out of here, now!"

But Azazel's cold gaze flicked toward him.

With a casual wave of his free hand, a surge of red lightning arced through the air and struck Eli's earpiece with a pop of smoke and a burst of sparks. The device sizzled, then fell silent—dead.

Eli winced, swatting it from his ear. The metallic scent of burned circuits stung the air.

Jo stood frozen, heart jackhammering, her mind spiraling. This wasn't like the fight with the Voidwalkers—this was something else. Bigger. Worse. She looked at Sara, at Smith crumpled on the ground, at the red light still glowing in Azazel's hand. Panic twisted her chest so tight it hurt to breathe.

"No . . . no, no, no . . ." she whispered.

Devin didn't move.

He stood locked in place, just like he had in the park—the moment that dagger pressed to his throat, helplessness had rooted itself into his bones. Now it rose again, paralyzing.

He stared at Azazel, eyes wide, every instinct screaming to run, to fight—but his muscles wouldn't respond.

"You're all so predictable," said Azazel mockingly.

His gaze swept over them again, eyes gleaming with cruel amusement.

"Did you really think I wouldn't anticipate this?" He scoffed, tilting his head. "I knew the moment I reached the vault, it would bring you out of hiding."

He exhaled, mockingly shaking his head. "You play your roles so well. The rogue guardian. The lost heirs. But in the end, you're just pieces on a board."

Before anyone could react, shadows surged from the ground, coiling around Sara's arms and legs like living chains.

Sara screamed, struggling, panic flashing across her face.

"Sara!" Jo lunged, instinct taking over, but with a wave of Azazel's hand, an invisible force slammed into her, sending her sprawling.

Devin charged forward, but something unseen struck him like a hammer, knocking him onto his back.

"No!" Mr. Mason's voice cut through the night, raw with desperation.

Azazel turned back to Smith, his smile cold.

"If you want her back, you know what you must do," he said. "The journal . . . or her life."

Smith's body twitched, muscles tight with pain as he forced himself to move. He dragged in a breath and rolled onto his side, then pushed up onto one elbow, his coat torn and smoldering where Azazel's blast had struck him.

His hand pressed into the dirt, eyes blazing despite the pain.

"Let her go," he growled, his voice rough.

Azazel smirked, stepping back into the shadows, dragging Sara with him.

"Tick-tock," he whispered.

A wave of dark energy exploded outward, hitting like a storm

And then—

Silence.

Azazel was gone.

And so was Sara.

The emptiness that followed was suffocating.

Jo lay still, the cold seeping into her bones, her ears ringing.

Her sister. Gone.

She pushed herself up, her body shaking. She turned to Smith, who lay on the ground rigid, staring into the space where Azazel had vanished.

And then—without a word—she turned and ran.

"Jo!" Devin shouted.

"Let her go." Smith's voice was low.

Devin froze, staring at him. "But she—"

"She's following the path she needs to," Smith said as his eyes followed the path Jo had vanished into.

He blinked slowly, as if seeing beyond the present moment.

"Sometimes stepping away is the first step toward becoming who you're meant to be."

Mr. Mason turned, eyeing Smith curiously—but said nothing.

And for just a heartbeat, something flickered behind Smith's eyes. A spark.

With Mr. Mason's help, he stood up, straightened with effort, dust and ash clinging to his coat. He looked at Mr. Mason, Eli, and Devin.

"This battle is far from over," he said, louder now. Then Smith turned to Devin. "Young man . . . if we are going to have a shot at rescuing Sara and defeating Azazel . . . I'm going to need your help."

CHAPTER 32

Jo's feet pounded the earth. The moonlight slivered through the canopy in broken streams, painting the woods in silver streaks. The forest surged around her in a blur with leaves whipping past her face, branches clawing at her arms like desperate hands, but she didn't stop. Couldn't.

Somewhere behind her, Sara's scream still rang in her ears.

She didn't know how long she'd been running, only that she had to get back—to the place that had once whispered peace to her, even if just for a moment. The Healing Hallow.

Nestled deep in the Shadowlands, hidden behind a red door and a veil of strange energy. She had stood at its threshold with Smith and Sara, had felt its silent call, but she had turned away.

Now Sara was gone, torn from them by a monster who had already shattered their family once. And Jo couldn't let herself lose her sister too. Not after everything. Not after Mom. Not after Dad.

She pushed harder, faster, dodging gnarled roots reaching across the trail. Pain flared in her ribs with every breath, her lungs raw, but she didn't stop. A jagged branch slashed across her cheek, but she barely registered it.

The cabin had to be close.

She felt the weight of the skeleton key bouncing

lightly against her thigh with every stride, tucked safely in her jacket pocket.

"Because you'll be back," he'd said, calm and certain, like it wasn't a question. Like he *knew*.

At the time, she hadn't wanted to come back. And yet . . . here she was. Running through the dark, drawn by something she didn't fully understand.

How did he know? she thought.

The ache, then, in her chest wasn't just for Sara. It was older than that. Deeper.

She broke through a final thicket, out of breath.

There it was.

The cabin stood in silence, tucked between ancient pines. The red door shimmered faintly under the moonlight.

But then . . .

Voices.

She froze, her heart slamming against her ribs. Shapes moved around the cabin. Two men, shadows slipping between the trees. One of them stepped to the window, peering inside.

"Check the place," one said. "Make sure no one's hiding."

Jo ducked low, scrambling behind a nearby tree. Her breath came in sharp gasps, loud in the stillness.

The men's footsteps crunched through the underbrush, too close. Her eyes darted around until she spotted a rotted log nestled between roots just off the path. She dropped flat, belly to the dirt, and crawled into the hollowed space, the wood damp and foul against her skin.

She curled into the darkness, barely breathing.

A twig snapped. Boots paused.

"Did you hear that?"

The silence was so thick for a moment it rang in Jo's ears.

"I guess it's nothing. Let's report back."

The figures lingered a few moments longer before finally retreating, their footsteps fading into the forest. Jo didn't move. Not yet. Not until the last echo of danger was gone.

When she finally uncurled herself, every muscle protested. She emerged stiff and scratched, blinking at the cabin through strands of her own hair. Her body screamed to turn back—to find Smith, Devin, anyone. Warn them.

But something held her.

The pull.

It hadn't gone away. If anything, it had only grown stronger.

Her fingers found the key again. She pulled it from her pocket, tracing the intricate carvings with her finger.

She looked up. The door stood waiting.

She stepped forward, letting out a sigh. Her hands shook, but her eyes were set. "No," she whispered. Not this time. She wouldn't run.

She walked up to the door, slipped the key into the lock. A soft *click*. The red door opened without resistance.

And Jo, heart pounding, stepped through the door.

CHAPTER 33

The tension in Smith's townhome was a living thing. Rain battered the windows in hard sheets, the occasional rumble of thunder rattling the panes. The soft, mechanical murmur of Lucy's interface offered the only rhythm in the silence.

They hadn't risked opening the library.

The skeleton key remained untouched in Smith's coat pocket. They couldn't chance being detected again by the Riftstone Beacon. If Azazel's agents caught wind of where they were—it would all be over.

Devin sat hunched on the edge of a leather chair, his broad shoulders folded in. His eyes, locked onto the floor with the kind of intensity reserved for those trying to make the world stop spinning.

He hadn't said a word since they returned.

Eli's fingers paused mid-keystroke beside a flickering console. "Devin, we need to focus," he said quietly, not looking away from the screen. "Sitting here stewing won't bring the others back. We need a strategy."

Devin's head snapped up. "A strategy?" His voice cracked on the word. "Stacy's dead. Jo's gone. Sara's . . . we don't even know if she's still alive. And you want to talk strategy?" He surged to his feet, eyes blazing. "You all *dragged* us into this, and now everything's falling apart! Even if we wanted to help Sara—do we even *have* what Azazel wants? Do we even have this journal?"

A tense silence settled over the room for a beat.

Eli's voice was quiet but clear from the corner. "It's been missing for years," he said grimly. "We've been searching. But without it . . ."

Devin let out a sharp, bitter laugh. "Great. Just great."

"Devin," Mr. Mason said, stepping forward with a steady hand. "Ye've every right tae grieve, lad. But anger's a fire that cannae be fed—it'll consume ye."

"Don't," Devin spat, shaking him off. "Don't act like you get it. You're not the one they're hunting. You're not the one who lost—" His voice caught. He turned, dragging a hand over his face as if trying to erase what had just escaped.

Eli turned in his chair now. "None of us asked for this, but the threat is real—and so is your role in it."

"I didn't *ask* for a role!" Devin shouted. "I didn't sign up for this war or magic or demons. And now Stacy's gone because of it. Because of *you*." He jabbed a finger toward them.

Smith, until now silent in the corner, pushed off the wall and stepped into the light.

"Enough," he said.

The command in it sucked the heat out of the room. Devin's glare darted to him, but Smith didn't flinch.

"You're angry. You should be," Smith said, walking forward slowly. "You're carrying loss, fear, guilt—and you're right to feel all of it. But throwing blame like shrapnel won't heal you. And it won't bring Stacy back."

Devin barked a bitter laugh. "You've got all the right words, don't you? Calm and composed. Must be nice to feel nothing."

Smith's eyes narrowed, just slightly. "You think

I don't feel it? I brought you into this because I *do* feel it. Because I *see* what's coming. And because I believe you're the only one right now who can help stop it."

Devin's voice was a whisper now. "Help? Help with what, exactly? Another plan no one understands? Another mission no one survives?" He was now pacing like a caged animal. "My team . . . my friends back home . . . I haven't seen them in days. They think I'm some kind of fugitive. My coach probably thinks I snapped. The town might believe I killed Stacy." He swallowed hard. "And you want me to be *your* soldier?"

A long silence passed.

Smith took a step closer. "They might not know what's going on. But they remember who you are. The question is—*do you?*"

Devin turned away. His reflection glared back at him from the rain-streaked window.

"I don't know if I can do this," he said, his voice barely audible. "All of this . . . it feels like I'm drowning. Like the more I try to help, the more people I lose."

Smith didn't answer right away. Instead, he walked over to the mantle, retrieving something from beneath a stack of aged documents—something faintly glowing, veined with ancient markings.

He held it out, not revealing it fully, just enough for Devin to catch the shimmer of light across its surface.

"Draegora was a realm forged in the crucible of war. Honor and loyalty were their currency. You come from that bloodline, Devin—not just by name but by something deeper. Something rare."

Devin's eyes flickered toward the artifact, then away.

"You keep saying stuff like that, but you never explain what it means."

Smith paused for a moment, then spoke, "Just know this—there are things in this world that can only be found by a son of Draegora. And we're running out of time to find one."

Devin stared at him. "Why me?"

Smith didn't blink. "Because you're still standing. You're one of your kind that hasn't been made into a Voidwalker."

Devin turned away, his hands gripping the edge of the table. "I don't know . . ."

A long silence.

Then, without warning, Devin pushed away from the table and strode toward the door.

"Devin," Smith called after him. "You can't leave. It's not safe. If they find you—"

Devin turned. "I don't care."

Smith stepped forward. "You should. Because if you go running off half-cocked, you'll just be handing yourself over to them. Is that what you want?"

Devin hesitated, his hand on the doorknob. For a moment, the anger drained from his face, replaced by a flicker of fear and uncertainty. Without another word, he opened the door and stepped into the rain-soaked night.

Smith started to follow, but Mr. Mason placed a hand on his arm. "Let him go," he said quietly. "Like ye say sometimes, ye've got tae find yer own answers."

Smith stared after Devin for a long moment before nodding. "Let's hope he finds the right ones."

CHAPTER 34

The cell was cloaked in shadows, its damp chill seeping into Sara's skin and settling deep in her bones. Iron bars loomed in front of her like teeth, and beyond them, the faint flicker of torchlight from the corridor outside cast trembling shadows across the stone floor. High above her, a small, grated window let in the barest breath of night air—too narrow to escape through but wide enough to offer a sliver of moonlight from the world beyond.

She hugged her knees to her chest, the cold stone beneath her sending shivers up her spine. Her mind raced with fractured images of what had just transpired in the woods: the sudden rush of wind, Azazel's eyes gleaming with cruel satisfaction, the way Jo's voice had screamed her name as everything went dark.

A lump formed in her throat as she recalled the last fleeting glimpse of Jo.

Sara traced her fingers along the rough surface of the wall. The air reeked of damp stone and something metallic that made her stomach queasy.

A whisper stirred in the back of her mind: *You never should have been part of this story.*

The words hit her harder than she expected.

She thought of that afternoon in the Savor Street Market—how normal everything had seemed. Her biggest worry then had been finishing a drawing and spending time with Jo. Then she'd run into the mysterious man,

Smith—and felt that surge of blue energy rush through her.

She'd tried to ignore it. To explain it away.

But then the dreams began. The empty look on people's faces. And then . . . the mural. What was she supposed to make of that?

And Smith again. Taking her to his home—no, *his library*—in the middle of a tropical paradise. How that place even existed, she still couldn't explain.

And the park. Gosh, the park. The strange men. The way Devin and his friends had stepped in to protect her without hesitation.

Then the safe house. The warehouse. The vault. The red orb pulsing like a heartbeat in stone.

The Voidwalkers—silent, monstrous. The fight. The fear.

Stacy stepping between them and her . . .

And the last time Sara—or any of them—would ever hear her voice.

Then the Shadowlands. The truth. Finally learning what really happened to her parents. And then—just like that—back on the run.

And now she was here. Behind bars. Trapped. Alone. With no idea where she was, who might come next, or what Azazel truly wanted from her.

Her hands trembled as exhaustion crept over her like a slow-moving fog, unwelcome and relentless. She squeezed her eyes shut, trying to block out the echoes of everything she'd just relived.

Her eyelids fluttered. She pulled a threadbare blanket laying near her around her shoulders just as sleep took her, and the torchlight outside her cell flickered and fell away.

CHAPTER 35

13 YEARS AGO—LILY'S LAST STAND

The familiar warmth of Lily's home was shattered by the encroaching darkness seeping through every crevice, casting ominous shadows across the walls. The rooms she once knew as safe now felt like a prison. She could feel the cold dread pooling in her stomach, knowing he was close—Azazel, the man who had turned against everything he once stood for.

Cradling baby Sara against her chest, Lily's heart hammered as she made her way to the closet. She wrapped her daughter in blankets, tucking her into the corner, her wide eyes barely comprehending. "Shh, my little one," she whispered, brushing a tender kiss on Sara's forehead. "Stay hidden, stay quiet. I'll keep you safe. I promise." Her voice trembled on the last word, but she forced herself to remain steady. There was no room for fear now.

A creak echoed down the hallway, and her head snapped up. Shadows gathered at the doorway, growing darker and deeper until Azazel's silhouette filled the frame. His hollow, predatory eyes fixed on her, and a sinister smile curved his lips. Two of his trusted allies, Sykes and another enforcer with a jagged scar across his cheek, followed closely behind. Flanking them were several Voidwalkers, spectral figures cloaked in black armor, their weapons glinting ominously.

229

"Lily," Azazel's voice was smooth, mocking. "I hope you've had your fill of this charade. Did you truly believe you could hide from me forever?"

Lily's response was swift and silent. She extended her hand, and with a surge of raw energy, a sword materialized in her grasp, shimmering into existence as if called forth from the very air. Its blade glowed with a faint, ethereal light, and she raised it, unwavering, to meet Azazel's gaze.

Her grip tightened on the hilt of her sword, a fierce light sparking in her eyes. "My secrets weren't for the likes of you, Azazel," she replied, voice steady, defiant. "I won't let you desecrate what I've protected—not while I draw breath."

Azazel's hollow laughter echoed through the room, chilling her to the bone. "Oh, I think we'll change that soon enough." His eyes turned to her, gleaming with malice. "Hand over the journal, Lily, and maybe I'll be merciful."

She clenched her jaw, a fire of defiance blazing within. "Mercy isn't something you understand. You lost any claim to that word long ago."

Azazel's face twisted with anger. "Enough!" he barked, gesturing to his cohorts.

Sykes and the scarred enforcer lunged at her, flanking her from both sides. Lily's sword moved in a graceful arc, deflecting their attacks with a speed defying the laws of physics. She danced between them, her movements fluid yet deliberate.

As she turned, she nearly deflected a thrust from a Voidwalker's blade; a thrust aimed at her heart. She parried, ducking beneath another swing, her blade

230

finding its mark in the Voidwalker's side. But another was already upon her, striking with a force that nearly knocked her off balance.

Azazel watched from the doorway, his expression one of dark amusement. He leaned casually against the frame, as if savoring the spectacle of her struggle.

Lily summoned a protective barrier, a shimmering shield of energy pulsing around her, repelling the Voidwalker's next strike with a crackling burst of light.

But the magic was draining her—*fast*. Each pulse of the shield siphoned her strength like water from a cracked vase. Her breathing grew ragged, her grip tightening as her muscles screamed for rest.

Sykes moved in, blade flashing. She twisted to block, the barrier flickering at the edge of his strike. Another Voidwalker lunged—then another. Their blades hammered against the shield in quick succession, pounding like a war drum.

A high-pitched *crack* echoed through the room. The barrier faltered. A spider web of fractures rippled across the magical dome.

Lily's eyes widened. She pushed more energy into the shield—but it didn't hold.

With a shattering burst, the barrier collapsed in a rush of broken light, dissipating into the air like shattered glass caught in the wind.

A blade sliced across her arm. Another tore through her side. She cried out, stumbling back, blood spilling as she clutched her wound. Her sword wavered, but she didn't let it fall.

Gritting her teeth, she swung again in a wide arc,

forcing the Voidwalkers to retreat. Her body trembled, her vision blurred—but she stood . . . barely.

Azazel stepped forward, his smile widening as he saw her falter. He nodded to the Voidwalker closest to her, who seized her, twisting her arm behind her back and forcing her to her knees. Lily cried out in pain, her sword clattering to the floor.

Azazel loomed over her, his gaze cold and unfeeling. "Still so defiant," he murmured, almost admiringly. "Give me the journal, Lily. Spare yourself further suffering."

She glared up at him, defiance blazing in her eyes even as her strength waned. "You'll never have it," she spat, her voice hoarse but resolute.

The Voidwalker's hand moved to her shoulder, a dark energy radiating from his touch as he began to drain her life force. Pain seared through her body, weakening her further. She cried out in pain as she felt the vitality leeching from her. Her vision blurred.

With a trembling hand, she reached into her pocket, feigning surrender. "Fine . . . I'll give you what you want," she said, her voice a mere whisper, her gaze fixed on Azazel.

Azazel's eyes gleamed with triumph, and he leaned closer, his focus solely on her, expecting her to reveal the key to accessing the journal. But instead, she drew out an object, its surface gleaming darkly in the dim light—a small, intricate artifact pulsing faintly, an object Azazel recognized all too well.

"No . . ." he breathed, his face twisting in horror as he realized what she held. "You wouldn't dare!"

A fierce smile crossed Lily's face, a final act of defiance. "See ya!" she whispered, her voice resolute.

She summoned the last of her strength, pouring her will into the object. It responded instantly, flaring with an intense, pulsating, blue light. The air around her vibrated, a deep, resonant hum filling the room as the portal to an abyss began to form behind her.

The Voidwalkers recoiled, their spectral forms trembling as the portal's force grew. Sykes stumbled back, his face pale with terror as he felt the pull of the abyss. Azazel's calm shattered, his expression twisted with rage and desperation.

"No! Stop!" Azazel lunged forward, but the portal's pull was too strong. Tendrils of shadow wrapped around him, dragging him toward the abyss. His cohorts screamed, their forms dissolving into the dark energy, sucked into the void with no escape.

With a final, blinding pulse, the Abyssal Key closed. The room fell silent, the last traces of the vortex dissipating into thin air. Azazel, his cohorts, and the Voidwalkers were gone, trapped beyond the veil.

Lily collapsed to the floor, her body drained, the world fading around her. She lay motionless. "Sara . . ." she whispered. Lily began to crawl, inching her way to the closet where Sara lay, still wrapped in blankets, undisturbed by the chaos. Her fingers brushed the soft fabric as she whispered, "Be safe, my love . . . always . . ."

Her hand fell, her final breath escaping her lips as silence settled over the room once more, the only sound being the faint, gentle coos of her sleeping daughter.

CHAPTER 36

Sara stood barefoot on cracked earth. The sky above churned in deep reds and black, clouds swirling with a menacing life of their own. Ahead, a monolithic fortress rose, its twisted spires clawing at the heavens like skeletal fingers.

Then, a voice emerged from the shadows.

"What was sealed shall be set free . . . and from it, a new order shall rise."

From the swirling dark stepped a robed figure. His face was hidden. Shadows rippled across his form, cloaking him like living ink. He raised a hand, and a red orb bloomed above his palm—pulsing, flickering like a beating heart. The glow spilled over his features, catching on sharp angles, eyes that shimmered like burning coals.

Symbols spiraled in and out of view around him—glyphs Sara couldn't understand. The figure stood motionless, lips moving in silent incantation, eyes fixed on something unseen.

The ground trembled beneath her feet.

Behind him, wraithlike forms stirred wavering-like reflections in broken water. Voidwalkers.

Sara felt paralyzed.

And then she saw it.

A mural forming on the fortress wall, lines of paint stretching and twisting across the stone as if guided by an invisible hand. It showed a massive chain, splintered.

Each link curling like a serpent at the feet of the robed figure.

Sara took a shaky breath, her voice rising unbidden, quiet but laced with awe and fear: "Who is this . . . that I see?"

The robed figure's head snapped toward her, his eyes cutting through the distance.

And then he began to move. Each step was deliberate, slow. He was coming toward her.

Sara began to panic.

Just as his pace toward her began to accelerate, the sky above split.

A break in the swirling clouds. A glimmer of light.

A voice, familiar and warm, rang out: "Sara, don't tell them what you've seen!"

Her eyes widened.

A woman stood on the horizon, radiant. Her dark hair flowed and her eyes, those eyes, mirrored Sara's own.

"Mom . . . ?"

Sara reached out.

But the woman was already fading.

Sara jolted awake.

"Mom!" she gasped.

Sara sat up. Her heart pounded like a war drum in her ears.

The dim torchlight beyond the iron bars flickered, casting long shadows across the cell. Her chest rose and fell in rapid, shallow breaths. She clutched the thin blanket around her shoulders.

The woman's voice still rang in her ears, warm, urgent, real. But how could it be? Her mother was gone. Gone.

And yet . . . this was the second time now. The first dream had felt just as strange, just as impossible—until the pieces of it began showing up in the real world. The storm. The mural.

What if this was more than a dream too? But what had she seen? A prison? A prophecy? A warning?

She tightened the blanket around her, trying to shake the chill.

A soft rustle broke the silence.

Sara flinched and turned toward the sound.

Outside her cell, beyond the iron bars, a larger chamber stretched into shadow. And there—just at the edge of the torchlight—a boy sat curled in the corner of the room. His arms were loosely wrapped around his knees, his hands streaked with dried paint. Eyes wide. Watching her.

He didn't move. Just stared.

Slowly, cautiously, Sara rose from the cold floor and crossed the cell. Her fingers curled around the bars, the iron cold against her skin. She leaned forward, trying to get a better look.

"Hey," she whispered.

His eyes shifted, but he remained silent.

She swallowed, her throat dry. "Do you know where we are?"

No answer. His stare held.

Sara tightened her grip on the bars. Her eyes fixed on the boy.

"Why does he keep you here?"

Still nothing.

She searched his face, looking for anything. An expression. A look.

He blinked once.

Then, slowly, he rose.

His movements were smooth, eerie in their silence. Step by step, he crossed the small space beyond the bars, the echo of his bare feet ghosting against the stone. Sara watched as he approached a large tarp draped over the far wall. Dust and grime lined its edges. The boy reached for the tarp. Paused.

Then, without a word, he yanked it down.

The tarp fell with a heavy sigh, kicking up a cloud of dust—revealing what lay beneath.

Sara stood breathless.

A mural sprawled across the wall, a mass of jagged shapes painted in deep reds and inky blacks. But it wasn't still. The colors shifted—subtle, writhing, alive.

Her pulse quickened.

The storm. The sky. The fortress.

It was the dream.

Rolling darkness churned across the mural like a living sea, tendrils of shadow snaking through grotesque landscapes—cracked earth, twisted spires, and skies that looked ready to bleed.

Her gaze moved to the center.

There, in the midst of the chaos, stood a figure. Half-shrouded in shadow. One arm outstretched. A red orb hovered above his palm, pulsing faintly.

And near his feet, nearly lost in the chaos of lines and color, coiled a broken chain. Its links snapped and frayed. Curled like a serpent, waiting to strike.

Sara staggered back a step.

It wasn't just a dream. It was a reflection. A window.

No . . . a warning.

Her eyes turned back to the boy. He hadn't moved.

Sara's lips parted. A question formed on her tongue.

But the memory of the woman's voice struck again, clear and urgent.

"Don't tell them what you've seen."

She closed her mouth. Swallowed the words.

The boy stepped backward, retreating into the shadows without a sound.

And Sara stood alone, the mural before her whispering truths she couldn't speak—not yet.

CHAPTER 37

The Healing Hallow stretched before Jo, bathed in colors of gold and emerald.

The moment her boots touched the moss-laced earth, the air shifted. Time slowed. The world hushed. Towering oaks and pines stretched skyward, their ancient branches swaying in silent communion. Leaves rustled above her, whispering secrets and memories wrapped in the wind.

Jo walked forward, each step soft against the velvet moss. Wildflowers sprang up along the edges of the path, their petals pulsing through a dance of color. Blue to violet, violet to rose. A breeze brushed her cheek, and for a breathless second, she swore she heard laughter. Her father's deep chuckle. Sara's bright giggle.

The deeper she moved into the Hallow, the more she felt it; not just *her memories, but the Hallow's.* The land itself carried echoes: children splashing by a stream, lovers dancing under stars, mothers whispering lullabies into the dusk. Moments imprinted like scars in the soil, too soft to haunt, too sacred to forget.

Then, she reached a clearing.

The trees widened, giving way to an ancient circle of stone and silence. In its heart sat a pool, unnaturally still, its surface a perfect mirror of the shimmering sky above. Energy hummed in the air, subtle but undeniable. It crawled across her skin like the first drop of rain before a storm.

Jo took a cautious step forward.

Then, laughter.

Faint, carried on the wind. But not just any laughter.

Her father's.

Then Sara's.

She froze, whipping around. "Dad?"

Silence.

Then laughter again. Lighter now, distant but real. The sound was *coming from the water.*

Her feet moved before her mind could catch up, guiding her toward the edge. The surface shimmered, and within it, faint ripples of light began to swirl.

She knelt, heart pounding, as the laughter faded into a hush. Her reflection looked back at her —but not as it should have. The eyes staring up from the water seemed older, haunted. The edges of the pool began to ripple faster, forming rings of light pulsing outward. The colors shifted from silver to violet to black.

And then, without warning—the water reached up.

Jo gasped as her balance tipped forward. Her hands hit the surface, expecting resistance—but there was none.

She fell *through.*

The pool swallowed her whole, and the world turned to motion.

Jo tumbled, spun, weightless, through a vortex of color and memory. Voices echoed around her—some hers, some not. Images flickered past: her mother's smile, Sara's hand slipping from hers, her own face twisted in fury and fear. Light flashed.

Then stillness.

She landed softly—feet on cool, solid ground.

The air was hushed and thick with silver mist, the world around her silent. No Forest. No sky. Just an endless stretch of fog pulsing faintly with light. She stood—barely able to tell where the ground ended or the sky began.

And from that mist . . . two figures emerged.

Their hoods were drawn, their movements fluid. They stopped in front of her.

And then, with mirrored precision, they pulled back their hoods.

A look of shock appeared on Jo's face.

Both were her.

She took an instinctive step back, her eyes wide.

For a heartbeat, she couldn't breathe—couldn't comprehend what she saw. It wasn't just their faces. It was the *knowing* in their eyes.

Her lips parted in a whisper.

"What . . . ?"

One of the figures—bathed in quiet light, eyes full of warmth, sorrow, and something deeply knowing.

The other—sharper, colder. Her sneer twisted like a scar across her face. Her eyes burned like stormlight.

The dark figure stepped forward.

"Well," she said, "here we are."

Jo's stomach tightened.

The shadow raised a hand, pointing straight at her chest. "Failure."

The word hit Jo like a slap.

"You pretend to be strong," the dark figure went on, circling her. "But you're a scared little girl hiding behind sarcasm and silence. Always watching. Always judging. Always . . . alone." And you wonder why no one sees you."

Jo took a step back, chest heaving. "Stop!!"

The dark figure ignored Jo. "You're not strong, Jo. You're afraid. Of losing. Of being seen as WEAK!

Lightning cracked above them, and the silver mist darkened into storm clouds. Wind howled through the emptiness.

The shadow laughed but continued to press. "And you *never* ask for help. Oh no," said the figure sarcastically. "You *endure. How valiant.*"

The storm surged. The dark figure lunged, slamming Jo to the ground atop jagged rock. The air ripped with cold.

Jo gasped, pain blooming in her shoulder.

"Cry out," the shadow taunted, holding Jo down. "Let's see who comes to your rescue."

"*I HATE YOU!!*" screamed Jo. A sob tore from Jo's throat.

The dark figure only leaned in closer . . . "And then you blame the world when it doesn't come running." The words of the dark figure pierced Jo's heart.

Jo sobbed hard now, her strength failing.

"Why?" Jo whispered. "Why am I always the one left holding everything?"

The storm surged darker, wind roaring, the ground beneath her trembling as if Jo's despair reshaped the space itself. Through the mist, cracks spread, jagged edges splitting beneath their feet—a cliff's edge forming where none had been before.

The shadow's grin widened. "You're breaking, Jo. Just like you always feared."

Jo's fingers curled into fists against the rock. Her body shook—not just from pain but from something rising inside her.

And then, through the storm, the other figure stepped forward. The one bathed in light. She didn't speak. She didn't fight. She simply reached out her hand.

Jo stared. And in that moment, she *understood.*

This wasn't just about pain.

It was about choice.

Jo's voice trembled as she turned back to the shadow. "You're right. I am scared. I shut people out. I don't trust anyone—because I don't even trust *myself.* But I'm still here."

The shadow tilted its head, eyes narrowing.

Jo pushed up on shaking legs. "Still standing. Still fighting."

The dark figure blinked, faltering for the first time.

With a grimace, Jo stepped forward, ignoring the pain as she grabbed the shadow's throat. ". . . And YOU don't get to define me anymore."

She drove the figure back, step by step, toward the waiting cliff—the dreamscape shifting with her will. The wind screamed, the edge crumbling underfoot.

With a final push, she drove the dark figure back. The wind screamed as the shadow stumbled toward the edge—and fell.

Silence.

The storm broke apart, leaving stillness in its wake.

Jo collapsed to her knees , gasping for breath.

The silver mist returned, gentle and cool.

The light-cloaked version of herself stepped beside her.

Jo looked up.

And this time, reached for her hand.

CHAPTER 38

Farley's barn loomed in the distance, its wooden frame weathered and brittle in the silvery light of the moon. The fields around it were slick from the earlier rain. Devin's breath clouded in the cold night air.

He crept through the tall grass, walked up to the barn, and opened the old wooden door. He slipped inside, boots crunching softly over the straw-strewn floor. Inside, shadows hung thick, stretched long across rusted tools and broken bales. He wasn't sure if Demetri would actually show.

Then, footsteps.

"Devin?" came a voice, just above a whisper.

Devin turned toward it, relief crashing through him like a wave as Demetri stepped into a slant of moonlight filtering through the barn wall.

Without hesitation, Demetri strode forward and pulled Devin into a tight embrace, slapping a hand against his back.

"Man, where the hell have you been?" Demetri said. He pulled back, gripping Devin's shoulders as he scanned his face. "Do you even know what's happening out there? The whole town's losing it. People think you—" He hesitated, shaking his head. "People think you killed Stacy."

Devin swallowed hard. "I know what they think," he said. "But I didn't do it, Demetri. I swear."

Demetri's brow furrowed as he studied Devin. "So

what happened, man? Talk to me. You vanished, Stacy's dead, and now everyone's saying you just snapped."

Devin turned away, dragging a hand down his face. "Do you remember that day in the park? When we saw those guys surrounding that girl?"

Demetri's eyes narrowed, his expression turning serious. "Yeah . . . the creepy ones in black? What about them?"

Devin gave a slow nod. "That's where it started," Devin said. "They weren't just random guys. They were after that girl . . . And that was only part of it."

He shifted, gaze falling to the hay-covered floor. "I was trying to explain it to Stacy—what we saw—just talking it through one day at the college library. That's when this girl overheard us. Turns out she was the little girl's older sister."

Demetri blinked. "That's random . . ."

"But it felt . . . like it wasn't random. Like we were supposed to meet her. She asked us for help—to find her sister— make sure she was okay. And I figured . . . after what we saw at the park, maybe we should."

"So you just went with her?"

Devin nodded slowly. "We tried to help her find her sister. And that's where everything just . . . spiraled."

"What do you mean 'spiraled?'" asked Demetri.

"We met some people. Serious people. Like, not just 'concerned citizens.' They knew who those men in the park were. They knew things—*explained* things. Said the girl was being hunted."

Devin's voice lowered. "They weren't just guessing, Demetri. They showed us things. Stuff I still can't fully wrap my head around."

His eyes lifted, catching the moonlight. "Things you wouldn't believe. I didn't either. Not until I saw them for myself."

Demetri blinked, unsure if he was hearing right. "Wait—? Like . . . this is who you've been with this whole time?"

Devin nodded. "But it all went sideways. Fast." His voice cracked. "I didn't kill her, Demetri. But I was there. I saw what happened, and I couldn't stop it."

Demetri's eyes narrowed as he processed Devin's words. "Then who did it? Who killed her?"

Devin's eyes welled with tears, and he shook his head, unable to answer. "It's not that simple," he said. "It happened so fast. And it wasn't just some person, Demetri. It was something else. Something dark."

A beat passed.

Then Demetri stepped forward again, placing a hand on Devin's shoulder, his voice softer than it had been all night. "Look . . . I don't know what's going on. But I believe you. I've known you since we were six, man. I *know* you didn't do this." His grip tightened slightly. "But you can't keep running. You need to tell someone the truth."

"I don't even know what the truth *is* anymore," Devin whispered. "Sara's missing. Jo disappeared. Smith thinks I'm supposed to help him with something . . . something big."

Demetri tilted his head. "Who's Jo, Sara, and Smith?"

Devin sighed. "Long story."

Demetri opened his mouth to ask more, but the crunch of gravel outside the barn cut through the quiet.

"What's that?" Demetri whispered, his voice low and tense.

Devin crept to a narrow gap in the wall and peered out. Headlights swam across the open lot like searchlights. A police cruiser pulled up and rolled to a stop just outside the barn. Two officers stepped out, flashlights slicing through the darkness.

"They're here," Devin hissed, backing away from the wall. His pulse thundered. His body locked between flight and freeze.

Demetri looked toward the back of the barn, eyes wide. "How the hell did they find you?"

"I don't know. Doesn't matter," Devin said. "We have to go. Now."

CHAPTER 39

Sara watched, her gaze shifting between the boy's mechanical strokes and the living shadow on the wall.

Gathering her courage, she whispered through the bars, "How did you get here? Did he bring you?"

The boy didn't answer. His brush moved with precise, practiced strokes—each one careful.

Sara swallowed hard. "When did you start painting the murals? Have you ever . . . seen what's behind them?"

The boy paused and turned toward Sara.

Just for a breath.

His hand trembled.

Sara noticed. "You have . . ." For the first time since waking, something real passed between them. A crack in his stillness.

But then—he returned to the mural. His shoulders dropped, and he kept painting. A single tear slid down his cheek, catching the torchlight like a falling star. Sara's fingers tightened around the bars. She wanted to speak, to offer something—anything—but the words stayed lodged in her throat.

Then came the sound of boots. Echoing down the corridor.

Sara stiffened, every muscle tensing as Azazel stepped into view. He didn't enter—he *arrived*, like a storm crossing a horizon. His presence filled the room before he said a word.

The boy didn't flinch—but his brush moved faster.

Azazel's gaze swept across the mural with a look hovering between awe and possession. "Magnificent," he murmured, his voice low and smooth, like oil over glass.

Sara met his gaze with fire. "Why him?" she demanded, her voice shaking but clear. "Why do you need a child to do this for you?"

Azazel smiled.

He turned toward the mural. "The boy was just a wanderer. A child playing in fields he didn't understand. He stumbled across an old object—something long buried, long forgotten. In touching it, he opened a door . . . a portal . . . and in doing so, he touched me."

Sara's eyes narrowed. She recalled the article Jo read to her at breakfast the other day about the missing boy.

He's the one, she realized.

Azazel continued, his voice growing quiet, almost coaxing.

"And the red energy welcomed him. Not because he was worthy. Not because he was chosen. But because he was *there*. Right place. Right time. That's all fate really is. Coincidence dressed in robes."

He turned to her, eyes catching the torchlight in cold glints.

"You want it to mean something, don't you? That moment in the market with Smith. The mural. The blue light. You were told it wasn't random. That you were . . . *meant* for something."

His eyes shifted back to Sara. "Am I right?"

He stepped closer, voice tightening.

"But what if it *was* random? What if Smith just happened to be there that day? What if you were just another curious girl with a brush in her hand? No prophecy. No calling. Just timing."

Sara's breath caught. She hadn't expected him to speak of *that*. Not in that way. But he had seen it. All of it.

Azazel's icy words wormed under her skin.

"Your mother believed in Thalion's myths. So does Smith. But belief doesn't make something true. You think there's a grand design? A higher will at work?"

He leaned in, voice dropping like a stone.

"There is no design. Only chance. And those with the strength to bend it to their will."

Sara stared at him, a storm rising behind her eyes. But inside . . . she felt something shift. Because when he said it like that . . . Her meeting with Smith *did* look like chance.

It hadn't felt holy or orchestrated. It had felt strange. Sudden. *Random.*

Just like the boy.

She gripped the bars tighter.

Azazel studied her for a moment longer, then said with a thin smile, "That's the truth no one dares to say aloud. There is no fate. No balance. Just power—earned or taken. And you . . . you've already taken your first step. You just haven't admitted it yet."

Sara said nothing.

Azazel's words lingered like smoke in her lungs.

What if he's right?

What if there was no higher plan? No destiny? Just her—caught up in something ancient and brutal because she happened to be standing in the wrong place at the wrong time?

She gripped the bars tighter, her knuckles pale against the cold iron.

The silence stretched.

But then . . . something stirred within her.

A *memory.*

The dream. The fortress. The storm. The figure with the red orb—and then the break in the clouds. The voice. Her voice.

"Sara, don't tell them what you've seen."

And that woman—*her*—standing in the light like a beacon in the darkness. Her mother.

Not just a dream. Not a fantasy spun from grief.

It had *felt* real. More real than Azazel's presence in this room.

Her heart thudded.

If all of this was chance—if there was no design—then why had she seen what she saw? Why had her mother come to her, again and again, through dreams that felt more like messages than nightmares?

Sara lifted her eyes.

The boy had stopped painting.

He hadn't moved. But now—he looked at her.

Really looked.

His gaze locked with hers. Quiet. Watching.

And in his eyes, she saw more than fear. She saw recognition. Like he was asking the same question she was:

Could all of this really be random?

Azazel's voice pulled her back.

"Your mother believed in Thalion's lies too," he said, more quietly now. "She thought she could outwit fate. She thought sealing me away would stop what was already in motion."

Sara looked at him sharply. "You knew her?"

He didn't deny it.

Something shifted in his eyes—not triumph. Not cruelty. Something older. Deeper.

For a heartbeat, the room changed.

Azazel's gaze drifted to the mural, but he wasn't looking at it. Not really. He was *remembering*.

And then—like a gate slamming shut—his jaw tightened, and the softness vanished behind a wall of pride.

"She was strong," he admitted, almost reluctantly. "Stronger than most."

He turned his head, as if the words cost him something. "But strength without vision is wasted."

Sara stepped closer to the bars.

"She had vision," she said quietly. "She saw through you. She gave her life to stop you."

Azazel's lip curled—not in anger but in disdain. "She . . . delayed me. That's all. And now she's gone."

A quiet fire emerged from behind Sara's eyes. "You really believe that, don't you?" she said softly. "That it's all random. All chance. That power is the only thing that matters."

Azazel tilted his head slightly, watching her.

She pressed on, voice steady but rising. "But at the end of the day . . . it wasn't random. Not then. Not now. Because Thalion's power—"

Azazel's face twisted in an instant, his voice cracking like a whip. "Never speak of Thalion's power in my presence!!!"

Sara flinched slightly but stood her ground, heart pounding. And then, a small, knowing smile touched the corner of her mouth.

"That's it, isn't it?" she whispered. "That's what you can't stand. That after all your power, all your schemes . . . the King's will *still* endured. His light couldn't be snuffed out."

Something dark flashed across Azazel's eyes.

Sara leaned in. "You're the one who's been deceived, not me. You *think* you're bending fate to your will—but you're already tangled in the one thread you'll never break. And that's what's setting you up for your biggest fall."

Azazel was silent.

Sara felt her breath catch in her throat. *Where had those words come from?* For a moment, her own heart pounded with confusion. She was just a girl—thirteen, scared, standing in a prison cell facing down a monster centuries older than her. And yet . . . those words had come so easily.

A shiver passed through her. Azazel's words echoed in her mind: *"And now she's gone."*

But no. No, she thought, gripping the bars tighter. Her mother's voice in her dreams. The blue energy that had lit her hands. They weren't accidents. They weren't hallucinations. Sara lifted her head, her voice trembling but clear.

"She's not gone," she said. "Not really. I've seen her. Felt her. She's still guiding me. You saw it too, didn't you?"

Azazel's gaze sharpened.

But he said nothing. He turned and left the room.

The boy's eyes hadn't left hers. He was still watching. Still listening.

And somewhere inside Sara, something settled.

Not certainty. But a *choice.*

She didn't have to believe Azazel.

Because even if she didn't understand the dreams . . . or the blue energy . . . or the mural that had come to life beneath her brush . . . Even if the story of Valoria still felt too big, too impossible . . .

She *had lived* it.

She had *felt* it move through her. Seen the way light bent toward her hand. Heard her mother's voice—*not in memory*, but in warning. Watched shadows crawl from paintings, and creatures pulled from nightmare tear through the veil of reality.

These weren't just feelings. They weren't metaphors or symbols or lucky guesses.

They *happened.*

And if something was happening beyond reason, beyond chance— Then maybe her mother was right. Maybe Smith was right.

And maybe she wasn't here by accident. Maybe she was here because she was part of something bigger than what Azazel could see.

Something not random.

Something *real.*

"Police!" a voice boomed outside the barn. "We know you're in there, Devin Thompson! Come out with your hands up!"

Devin's mind raced, calculating his options. He glanced at Demetri.

"They've got you," Demetri whispered, his voice tight with fear.

"No, they don't," Devin whispered back. "But you need to stay here. Don't get involved. This isn't your fight."

"Devin—"

"Trust me, D." Devin gripped his friend's shoulder. "I'll figure this out. Just . . . don't let them catch you with me."

Before Demetri could argue, Devin ducked low, moving quickly between the hay bales. Voices and footsteps thudded outside—boots on gravel, flashlights cutting through the barn slats like searchlights.

"There's no way out of this!" one officer called. "Come out peacefully, and no one has to get hurt!"

Devin ignored the voice. His eyes scanned the dark interior. There—a narrow window high on the back wall, half-obscured by a rusted plow. It wasn't much, but it was something.

He dragged over a wooden crate and scrambled onto it, his fingers cold and slick with sweat as he shoved the warped window open. The old wood groaned. Somewhere outside, a flashlight beam swept past. He hesitated for half a heartbeat—

Then vaulted through.

As soon as his feet hit the ground outside, he bolted, not daring to look back. The tall cornfields of Farley's pasture loomed ahead, their stalks swaying gently in the night breeze. Devin plunged into the field, the corn engulfing him like a protective cocoon. The muffled shouts of the officers faded behind him, but he knew they weren't far.

His boots hit wet earth and he landed hard, pain jolting up his legs. He didn't stop. He ran.

255

Behind him, shouts erupted. A flashlight caught the edge of his movement. A voice yelled—he didn't hear what. He was already gone, swallowed by the towering cornfield at the edge of Farley's pasture.

The stalks closed in around him, tall and whispering with the breeze. He plunged deeper, the slap of wet leaves on his face and the thud of his footsteps on the uneven muddy ground. His breath came fast and ragged. The corn swallowed sound, but he knew they were following. Somewhere.

He zigzagged, doubling back, weaving between rows. No pattern. No trail. Just movement.

Then—ahead, he saw the faint glow of lights cutting through the darkness. He slowed, chest heaving. Panic set in—had they circled around? Were they waiting for him on the other side?

As he came to the end of the rows of the cornfield, he realized the lights belonged to a single car idling on the shoulder of a quiet highway. The driver's window rolled down slowly. A man leaned out, one hand on the steering wheel. "You got guts, kid," he said. "Now get in."

Devin's chest heaved as he stared at the man. It took him a moment to recognize the face—Matt Halbridge, the local reporter in Muxley.

"You've got to be kidding me," said Devin. "How did you even—?" Devin started backing up a step.

Halbridge lifted a palm. "Been watching Farley's since I heard whispers the cops were headed this way. Figured if they knew, you'd probably know they knew. Figured you'd run."

Devin's brow furrowed. "You *staked out the barn?*"

"I staked out the road behind it," Halbridge corrected. "Not the kind of place you leave on foot unless you want to get caught. There's only one way out unless you're planning on digging a tunnel. So I waited."

He reached over and pushed open the passenger door. "Now's your chance to keep running. Or your chance to start figuring out what the hell is really going on."

Devin hesitated, glancing back toward the cornfield. Faint shouts. Flashlights. Maybe dogs.

He looked back at Halbridge. "Why you? Why are you here?"

"You want answers? To what happened to Stacy?" Halbridge's eyes found his in the dark. "You'll find the truth, Devin. But you won't like all of it. Now get in."

Devin hesitated. Then he glanced back at the cornfield, hearing faint shouts growing louder, closer. Devin stepped toward the car door and climbed in, slamming the door behind him.

The car lurched forward, tires spitting gravel, and they roared onto the dark highway.

Inside the car, silence held for several minutes, broken only by the engine's low hum and Devin's breathing slowing.

Halbridge broke the silence first. "You're in deeper than you realize, kid. But stick with me, and I'll show you what you're up against."

Devin glanced at the reporter. "Where are we going?"

Halbridge gave a faint, humorless smile, his eyes fixed on the road. "You'll see soon enough."

CHAPTER 40

THIRTEEN YEARS AGO, RIGHT AFTER LILY SWEENEY'S DEATH

The sleek, unmarked FBI sedan sped along the dark road, its headlights piercing through the quiet night. Inside, two agents sat in silence, each lost in thought as the vehicle cut through the deserted landscape. The day had been a long one, filled with paperwork and unsettling details from the crime scene where they had recovered Lily Sweeney's body.

Agent Collins gripped the steering wheel, his gaze occasionally darting to the evidence bag resting on the seat beside him. A strange, intricate object lay within.

Beside him, Agent Reynolds shifted, glancing at the bag with narrowed eyes. "This case just gets weirder and weirder," he muttered.

Reynolds shivered, a grimace tightening his face. "Hard to believe that something like this happened to him. Lily's death . . . it doesn't feel right, you know? Feels . . . wrong."

Collins didn't reply, his gaze returning to the evidence bag. He tried to brush off the unease gnawing at him, but the strange artifact seemed to pulse with a quiet, ominous energy.

Silence settled in the car, broken only by the low hum of the engine and the rhythmic sweep of the wipers cutting through the night drizzle.

Then the air shifted.

Collins felt his chest tighten, a bead of sweat trickling down his brow despite the chill in the car. "What . . . What is happening?" His voice was barely a croak, fear clawing its way up his throat.

Before either of them could react, the key began to pulse—a sinister, blood-red glow seeping through the fabric of the bag, painting the car's interior in shades of crimson. Shadows stretched and twisted, moving with a life of their own, curling around the men like dark tendrils.

Reynolds' eyes widened, his breath hitching as he reached out instinctively. "Collins, get rid of it!"

But it was too late. The glow intensified, the red deepening, becoming a churning vortex of light and shadow that filled the car, swallowing the men's screams as they were pulled into the darkness.

The sedan swerved, lurching as it lost control. Tires screeched against the pavement, and then the car veered off the road, tumbling down the embankment. Metal groaned and glass shattered as it rolled, finally coming to a stop in a field, upside down, with its headlights casting a feeble glow over the tall grass.

In the stillness that followed, only the whisper of wind disturbed the night.

Among the debris, a small, twisted object lay half-buried in the grass—its glow now extinguished, as though nothing had happened.

HOURS LATER: The scene was a chaos of flashing lights and hushed voices. FBI agents and local law enforcement cordoned off the wreckage, the twisted metal of the sedan gleaming under the harsh beams of floodlights. Officers and paramedics moved around the site, the tension in the air palpable. There was no sign of the two agents who had been driving the car—only scattered files, crumpled papers, and personal items strewn across the field.

Matt Halbridge stood at the edge of the perimeter, notebook in hand, his sharp gaze fixed on the scene. A seasoned investigative journalist, he'd arrived on the scene within hours, tipped off by a source who knew he thrived on the unexplained and the sinister.

He approached an FBI official, a man in his late forties with a rigid stance and a no-nonsense expression, whose name tag read "Sanders." Halbridge noted the man's steely gaze and decided to tread carefully.

"Agent Sanders, any news on the condition of the agents involved in the crash?" Halbridge asked, his voice polite but edged with curiosity.

Sanders hesitated, his mouth a hard line. "I'm afraid that's classified information, Mr. Halbridge. We're handling it internally."

Halbridge arched an eyebrow, unfazed by the brush-off. "Classified? All right, then. But could you at least tell me if they're alive?"

Sanders' eyes flickered, just for a moment, but it was enough for Halbridge to pick up on the uncertainty lurking beneath his official veneer. "We're still assessing the situation," Sanders replied tersely, his words deliberate, evasive.

Halbridge pressed on, undeterred. "Assessing the situation? With all due respect, Agent Sanders, this is a rural road, not a high-security facility. Two of your men vanish without a trace in a simple car accident, and you're telling me there's nothing to report? No sign of them at all?"

A muscle in Sanders' jaw twitched, but his expression remained stoic. "That's correct. As I said, this is an internal matter."

Halbridge scribbled in his notebook, jotting down the agent's words, his mind already racing with theories. He shifted his approach, turning to a young police officer nearby who appeared more rattled by the scene.

"Excuse me," Halbridge began, lowering his voice to a more conversational tone. "You were one of the first responders, right? What can you tell me? Did you see anything . . . unusual?"

The officer hesitated, glancing nervously at Sanders before nodding slightly. "We got here pretty fast after the call came in," he murmured, barely loud enough for Halbridge to hear. "But when we searched the car, there was . . . nothing. No bodies, no blood, no sign of them at all. It was like they'd just . . . vanished."

"Vanished?" Halbridge's pen hovered over his notebook, his pulse quickening at the hint of something inexplicable. "So where do you think they could have gone? Were there any footprints or trails?"

The officer shook his head, his brow furrowing. "That's just it. The ground around the car was undisturbed. It doesn't make sense."

Before Halbridge could probe further, Sanders stepped between them, his tone clipped and final. "That's enough. I suggest you keep your speculations to yourself, Officer. And Mr. Halbridge, if you continue to interfere, I'll have you removed from the scene."

Halbridge smiled thinly, holding up his hands in mock surrender. "Of course, Agent Sanders. Just doing my job."

As Sanders and the officer moved away, Halbridge took one last look at the wreckage. His instincts screamed there was more to this than a simple car accident, something dark and unexplainable lurking just beneath the surface.

CHAPTER 41

The car slowed as Halbridge turned down a narrow dirt road, the headlights cutting through the thick canopy of trees. Devin sat rigid in the passenger seat.

"Where are we going?" he demanded.

Halbridge kept his eyes on the road. "Somewhere safe. There's someone you need to meet."

"That's not an answer," Devin shot back. "How do I know I can trust you?"

Halbridge let out a dry laugh. "You don't. But if you want answers, you'll want to meet her."

Devin glared out the window, watching the dense forest blur past. As they emerged into a clearing, a modest house stood at the center, its weathered exterior blending into the shadows of the trees. But it wasn't the house that caught Devin's attention—it was the large garage beside it, with a bright red door that seemed to glow faintly in the moonlight.

Halbridge parked the car and turned off the engine. "Come on. She's waiting."

Reluctantly, Devin followed Halbridge to the red door. Halbridge pulled out a small skeleton key. Its metallic glint in the moonlight caught Devin's eye.

"Where did you get that key?" Devin asked

Halbridge looked at Devin but didn't answer. Without a word, Halbridge unlocked the door and pushed it open, motioning with his arm for Devin to enter.

The moment Devin stepped inside, the air changed.

The scent of pine and parchment wrapped around him. The room beyond was vast—impossibly vast. Towering shelves reached into shadows above. Strange artifacts, glowing crystals, and books too large for any normal shelf surrounded him.

"Of course," Devin muttered under his breath. "Another place that's bigger on the inside. Why am I not surprised?"

Halbridge smirked but said nothing. He motioned for Devin to follow. As they walked deeper into the space, Devin caught flashes of his memories—Smith's library, the Healing Hallow, the vault, the orbs. All pieces of a puzzle he still could not explain.

They passed through a hallway and stepped out onto a broad wooden terrace. The space opened wide, over-looking a lush moonlit garden that defied logic. A soft waterfall trickled nearby. At a large circular table sat a woman with sharp, intelligent eyes and a commanding presence. A leather-bound journal rested beneath her fingertips.

Her eyes lifted to Devin as he approached.

"So you're the quarterback everyone's looking for," she said.

Devin hesitated. "Who are you?"

Janice gestured to the chair across from her. "I'm Janice. I worked closely with Jack Sweeney."

Devin tensed. "Jack Sweeney? . . . Jo and Sara's dad?"

Janice nodded. "He was a good man, one who sac-rificed everything to protect his family. To protect all of us, really."

Devin stared at the book on the table, the leather cover worn and weathered from years of use.

Halbridge leaned against the wall, his arms crossed. "Jack Sweeney wasn't just an FBI agent, kid. He was a good one. One of the best. And that's, unfortunately, what led to his demise."

Devin glanced up. "That's what I was told as well, but funny nobody mentioned you two in the discussion."

Halbridge shrugged, his expression unreadable. "It looks like that was by design."

Janice glanced at Devin, her fingers brushing the cover of the journal. "The reason you didn't hear about me is because Jack entrusted me with this journal. He trusted me with it so it wouldn't fall into the wrong hands."

She tapped the leather-bound book lightly. "This journal—it isn't just notes and stories. It's a blueprint. A record of everything Lily knew about Azazel, the realms, the orbs . . . and how to stop him."

Devin's eyes widened, his thoughts racing. "So that's why Azazel wanted it," he muttered under his breath, the pieces clicking together. "When he took Sara . . . he told Smith he'd trade her for the journal."

Janice's head snapped up. "He what?"

Her grip on the journal tightened, her face paling slightly. "Sara was taken?" she repeated, the words sharp with worry. For a moment, her eyes turned toward the garden below, as if calculating distances, dangers. "That means . . . he's closer than I thought."

She pulled in a breath, grounding herself, then leaned forward, her voice sharpening. "What else did Azazel say? Did Smith tell you what Azazel is after? What he's trying to do with the red orbs?"

Devin hesitated, then exhaled sharply. "Smith isn't

exactly a straight shooter with info. But he mentioned something . . . about a realm called Draegora."

Janice blinked, her focus narrowing like a lens. "He told you about Draegora?"

"Yeah," Devin said. "He said it was where the red energy comes from. That people from there were . . . protectors or something . . ." Devin's voice trailed off. ". . . and that my ancestors are from there . . . I don't know what to think. I'm not saying I believe it. I'm just saying . . . it's what he told me."

Janice studied him for a moment, then nodded slowly. "I understand why you'd doubt it. Anyone would." Janice slowly rose from her chair. "There's something you should see."

She stepped to the side of the large circular table, where a tall, ornate pedestal stood. Atop it sat a smooth sphere-like object suspended within a brass framework etched with ancient runes. The sphere shimmered faintly.

Janice gestured toward it. "This is the Seer's Eye. It reveals moments—threads of events that ripple through the realms when something . . . or someone . . . is about to change something."

Devin stood slowly, staring at the sphere.

Janice continued. "A few days ago, after Azazel's forces stirred in Muxley, the Eye began to glow and reveal multiple events. A few hours ago in one of the scenes . . . I saw *you*."

Devin turned sharply to her, eyes narrowing. "You knew it was me?"

"We did," Janice said, motioning toward Halbridge. "You were in a warehouse, the red orb glowing like it had a heartbeat. And the orb—it was calling to you. *Reaching* for you."

Devin's eyes got wide. "You saw that?"

Janice nodded. "That's when I knew . . . you were the one Lily wrote about. The one tied to Draegora. The one who could find the sacred text and free the guardian."

Devin was speechless. He didn't know how to respond.

He shook his head, as if trying to clear the fog. "Free the guardian? . . . What guardian?"

Janice's expression grew solemn as she closed the journal gently, her fingers still resting on the cover. "His name is Thariel."

She met Devin's eyes. "Lily wrote that he was once a protector of the realms—one of the Twelve Overseers. He stood between worlds, ensuring balance between light and shadow. Protecting the blue orb energy.

"But Azazel and another overseer named Seraphis feared him. He stood opposed to them and their plans to overthrow King Thalion. Together, they used ancient magic to bind him—stripping him of his power and exiling him from Valoria, hidden in a shell of his former self."

Devin stared at her, trying to process what she said. Then, slowly, his eyes narrowed as a memory stirred.

"The woods," he said quietly. "When Azazel showed up . . . he looked right at Smith and said something— mocked him. Said he was *bound*."

Janice nodded, already seeing where Devin was going.

"At the time, I didn't get it," Devin continued. "But

now . . ." He looked back at her. "Smith. You think *he's* this Thariel."

"I do," Janice said. "And if that's true, then Azazel taunting him like that wasn't just cruelty—it was fear. Because if Thariel is ever unbound, Azazel loses the one advantage he's clung to all this time."

Devin let out a sigh, his voice growing low. "So that's what Smith was trying to tell me. What he needed my help to do . . ."

Halbridge let out a low whistle, his arms crossed as he leaned against the wall. "A guardian bound by ancient magic," he said, shaking his head. "And here I thought uncovering corruption in city politics was heavy."

Janice offered a faint smile, but her eyes stayed fixed on Devin.

She opened the journal again, carefully turning to a marked page, the edges worn from revisiting. "Lily believed Thariel's binding could only be undone by retrieving a sacred text hidden in a place called the Library of Althea. Not just any library—it's a living place, woven into the realms themselves." Janice slid her index finger down the page. "She called it a 'sanctuary to the humble . . . but a maze to the proud.'"

Devin swallowed, listening intently now.

"She wrote that the key to entering the heart of the library—and retrieving the text that holds the words of unbinding—wasn't power. It was identity. Only one born of Draegora, uncorrupted, could retrieve it."

Devin shook his head, the enormity pressing in. "But Smith—he knew all this? If he's Thariel, then why didn't he just find another Draegorian warrior to do this?"

Janice hesitated. "Because he thought it was hopeless to find such a person."

Devin looked up sharply.

"After the fall of Draegora," she continued, "Smith believed all of the Shadowforged—the ancient protectors of his realm—had been corrupted by Azazel. That there were none left untainted. That the bloodline was gone . . ."

Janice closed the journal, her hands resting gently on the cover.

"Little did Smith know that Lily, after she came to Earth, had smuggled one child out of Draegora before it was sealed. A baby." Janice paused before continuing. "She hid him . . . in Muxley, placing him with a family she trusted."

Devin's mind froze for half a heartbeat before everything began racing at once.

Janice looked at him. "She saved *you*, Devin."

The words hit like a thunderclap.

"She believed, if you survived, you would one day be the one to free Thariel. Her closest companion . . . one of the Twelve. And in doing so, you wouldn't just restore him and give Valoria a chance at rising once again—you'd restore the legacy of Draegora. A legacy Azazel tried to erase."

Devin stood completely still. "No," he whispered. "That's not—my parents . . . they adopted me, yeah, but . . . I'm just a regular kid from . . ."

Janice stepped closer, her voice gentle but unwavering. "You're more than that. You've always felt it—haven't you? That sense that you didn't quite fit. That pull you felt in the warehouse? That wasn't coincidence. That was your blood calling back to its origin."

Devin's voice cracked. "Why didn't Smith tell me this before the warehouse? Why didn't he come to me sooner? "

"Because he didn't *know*," Janice replied. "Not until recently. Not until he saw how the orb reacted to you. And even then . . . I am sure a part of him still doubted. He still feared hope was too dangerous a thing to hold."

Devin shook his head. ". . . I don't even know if I could do this," he admitted. "I don't know if I have it in me."

Janice smiled as she leaned back slightly. "Well, lucky for you, your first mission is just going to a library," she quipped lightly, her tone shifting to something almost casual. "Pretty sure that's the least intimidating start to a heroic journey anyone's ever had. No dragons. No armies. Just a dusty old book."

Devin blinked, caught off guard by the sudden change in tone. For a moment, he just stared at her—and then, despite himself, his lips twitched into a small grin. A quiet chuckle escaped him, low and unsteady, but real. It was the first time in what felt like forever that he remembered the sensation of smiling . . . even for a fleeting second.

"Great," he said, shaking his head with a soft laugh. "So I'm saving the world with ancient literature? That's great."

Janice's smile lingered a moment longer, then faded as she straightened and walked to a tall, arched doorway at the far side of the chamber. "Come with me," she said, her tone shifting back to purpose. "There's something you need to see."

Devin followed with Halbridge following behind him.

270

They stepped through the doorway; the space opened into a stone-walled chamber. The air was cooler. Devin stopped in his tracks.

Against the far wall, the mural waited.

Swirling colors filled the painted sky—stars twisted into spirals, streaks of deep violet and cobalt threading through endless space. A bridge of stone and light stretched over what looked like a bottomless abyss, fading into a distant shimmer. Trees unlike anything from Earth bordered the edges, their bark glowing faintly, their leaves like shards of crystal.

Janice stepped beside him. "This is your way in."

Devin's voice was hushed. "This is the Library of Althea?"

"It's a threshold," Janice replied. "The mural will carry you close, but the library's heart is hidden. The journal doesn't map it clearly. Lily only ever saw pieces. It could take a few days to find what you need once you're on the other side."

Devin blinked, glancing at her sideways. "Wait— other *side*? You mean I'm actually going *into* that painting?"

Janice gave a small nod, her expression calm. "Yes. It's a portal. One of the few left that still responds to the blue orb energy from Valoria. It was painted by Lily herself—activated years ago, and kept hidden ever since."

Devin took a small step back, eyeing the mural with a renewed mix of awe and suspicion. "Okay, that's . . . insane. I mean, I've seen weird things lately— Voidwalkers, orbs, shadow realms—but walking into art? That's next-level strange."

Janice smiled faintly. "You're not wrong. But this

isn't just art. It's living magic—crafted by one of the last painters linked to the Overseers. This portal doesn't just respond to need; it responds to *purpose*. And now in this moment, it shifts and opens according to the path tied to the one who carries Draegora's spark."

Devin rubbed the back of his neck. "Right. That's me, apparently."

Janice moved to a nearby stone table and began assembling supplies—methodical, calm, like she'd prepared for this moment a hundred times in her head.

"You'll need food. Water. The journal isn't clear how far the library's edge is from where you'll arrive, so prepare for several days of travel."

She handed him a satchel, heavier than it looked. "There's enough here to last. Just pace yourself."

Devin took the pack slowly, his eyes still flicking back to the swirling mural.

Janice glanced at him. "Good luck."

CHAPTER 42

Jo stood in the quiet aftermath, the storm gone, the darkness retreating behind her like a fading nightmare.

The gentler figure—the version of herself bathed in quiet light—remained.

She held out a hand.

Jo hesitated . . . then took it.

They walked side by side into a part of the Hallow that hadn't existed a moment before. The mists parted to reveal a narrow path carved through amber woods, the trees ancient. The air shimmered, golden and hushed, and the ground beneath their feet was soft with moss.

Leaves drifted down from the trees like glowing embers, each one catching the light before landing gently in their path.

And then Jo saw it.

Each falling leaf held *movement*—not just color, not just shimmer, but *memory*.

A scene unfurled within the first as it passed by: a woman with long, dark hair stood on a battlefield, blades of light clashing against red lightning. Jo knew instantly it was her mother.

Another leaf floated past, spinning slowly, revealing a city of crystal towers under siege, surrounded by flying beasts and warriors cloaked in silver flame.

She reached out as a leaf passed close to her face. Inside it, a younger version of Smith stood beside Eli, both wielding ancient weapons, defending a gate glowing with murals etched in living fire.

"What is this?" Jo whispered, awestruck.

The light-being finally spoke. "The memory of Valoria. A history held in the breath of the Hallow. These leaves are echoes of what came before . . . of what is waiting to return."

Jo's heart pounded as more leaves fell, faster now— one showing her mother raising a blue orb high as a tide of darkness crashed against a golden shield; another revealing five robed women linking hands around a glowing mural, protecting it with song and light.

And then—in a falling leaf—she saw *herself* . . . or someone who looked like her. She was standing at the edge of a cliff, the wind in her hair, holding a bow carved from crystal and light.

"She looks like—"

"She is you," the guide said softly. "Not from the past. But from the truth you've not yet accepted."

Jo stopped walking.

"No," she said, shaking her head. "I'm not that. I'm not part of this. I wasn't raised in that world. I didn't grow up with swords and orbs and war councils.

"My mom never said a word—" Jo paused.

"How could she?" said the light being. "You were too young to understand. But now that you're older, you have been brought here to understand and to choose! Because the choice must be yours."

Ahead, the path opened to a glowing circle of stone.

And in its center pulsed a blue orb, resting atop a pedestal of polished silver.

Jo stared at the blue orb as she approached.

Around it stood five figures in flowing robes—each figure radiating a different aura. They watched her with quiet expectation.

Their presence felt . . . ancient.

"These are the Wardens of the Hallow," her guide said softly. "Guardians of the memory and the thread of Valoria."

Jo took a shaky step forward. "Why am I here?"

The Warden of Truth stepped forward. His face was lined with time, and Jo found it hard to keep looking into his eyes. "Because you are part of what was and what is still to come. The blood of Lilianna runs through you—not only through your sister. Your mother left you a legacy not of power . . . but of *choice*."

Jo's heart pounded. "I'm not a chosen one," she said quietly. "I'm not even sure I believe this is real."

The Warden of Compassion approached now. Her smile was gentle. "To believe in what you were born from does not mean you must stop grieving who you were. The protector, the sister, the girl who never had answers—that girl is not being left behind. She is being healed."

Jo's gaze turned back to the blue orb.

It pulsed.

"Touch it," said the Warden of Courage. "But only if you are ready to remember—to become who you truly are."

The soft hum of the mural faded as the last glow vanished into silence. Devin was gone.

Janice exhaled slowly, her shoulders sagging just

slightly. For a moment, she and Halbridge stood there in the quiet chamber.

Without a word, Janice turned and led the way back through the narrow passage, exiting the hidden room. Halbridge followed, casting one last glance at the now-still mural before stepping out behind her.

They reentered the main room, where the circular table sat waiting in the center. Janice moved toward it, sinking slowly into a chair as her eyes drifted toward the still-sealed journal resting there.

Halbridge remained standing for a long moment, his gaze lingering on the door they had just left before he finally spoke.

"You really think he's ready?" he asked.

Janice didn't look at him. "Courage always comes before confidence. That's how the process works."

Halbridge pulled out a chair and dropped into it with a groan, rubbing his temple. "I gotta say . . . if you'd told me even a month ago I'd be helping smuggle a kid through a wall-sized painting to go find a magic book, I'd've called for an ambulance."

Janice offered a tired smile. "And now?"

He met her eyes. "Now I'm scared."

Halbridge looked down at his hands. "It's not just what we've seen, Janice. It's what we *haven't* said. Azazel. These orbs. The corruption spreading through Muxley. I always suspected something was wrong, but this?" He tapped the table. "This is war. And we're not soldiers."

Before Janice could respond, the room dimmed slightly—and the Seer's Eye flared to life on its pedestal.

Both of them turned.

The surface of the orb shimmered, the darkness within parting to reveal a room—dimly lit, formal. Wood paneling. Suits. Familiar faces.

Janice leaned in. "City Council . . ."

Halbridge sat up straighter. "That's the Muxley Chamber."

They watched as more figures appeared around a long table. Most were city officials, but one—leaning in, whispering something that made the others nod—was unfamiliar. His posture stiff, face gaunt, but something about him radiated influence.

"I've never seen him before," Halbridge muttered. "But the others—they're listening to him. He's leading that room."

Janice's expression hardened. "The Eye doesn't show random events. If it's showing us *this*, there's a reason."

Halbridge leaned in, eyes narrowing. "Where is this happening?"

Janice didn't answer right away. Instead, she tilted her head, studying the image more closely. "The better question," she said slowly, "might be *when*."

Halbridge looked at her, confused.

"The Seer's Eye doesn't always show the present," she explained. "Sometimes it reveals what's coming— events not yet set in motion but inevitable unless something shifts the course."

Halbridge turned back to the vision, watching the gathered council members. "So this might not have happened yet?"

Janice nodded. "Possibly. If that's the Muxley Civic Center—"

Halbridge pointed suddenly. "Wait—zoom in on

that." He gestured toward the far wall in the vision, where a banner hung partially in view. "That's the Muxley Civic Center. I've reported from that room. It's the closed-session chamber, behind the main auditorium."

Janice's jaw tightened slightly, thinking fast. "Then maybe . . . maybe it hasn't happened yet. But if the Seer's Eye is showing it to us now, it's a warning. And it means we still have a chance to get there first."

Halbridge stepped back, absorbing the implications. "Then we'd better move. We might still have time."

Then Halbridge turned to her. "This could be it, Janice. Proof. Real evidence. Not hearsay. Not rumors. I've spent years trying to blow the lid off Muxley's power structure, and I've had nothing but theories and secondhand reports. If I can document this—names, agendas, alignment with Azazel's plans—"

"You'd have something real," Janice said quietly. "The kind of truth people can't ignore."

He hesitated, the fire in his eyes dimming with fear. "And it could get us both killed."

Janice didn't argue. "Yes. It could."

Halbridge leaned back, torn. "You know, part of me . . . yeah, part of me wants to finally prove I wasn't just a crackpot shouting into the void. That everything I've written—every warning, every accusation—they'll finally see it was true. But the other part?"

He looked back at the Eye. The unfamiliar figure on the screen was smiling now.

"The other part knows we're not dealing with just dirty politicians anymore."

Janice nodded slowly, her voice softer. "But the Eye

showed *us*. Not someone else. Maybe it's warning. But either way . . . it's calling us to act."

Halbridge looked at her, then back at the eye.

"Well," he said, standing. "Looks like we're not done chasing ghosts after all."

CHAPTER 43

Devin adjusted the straps of his satchel, the weight of his dwindling supplies pressing on his mind as heavily as his doubts. He unfolded the crumpled piece of parchment in his hand, his eyes scanning the faded ink in the dim light filtering through the dense canopy of trees.

> *"Find the gate where the serpent rests,*
> *Beneath the ivy's tangled crest.*
> *A door unseen by arrogant eyes,*
> *Revealed when the humble recognize."*

He read it again, muttering under his breath. "Gate, serpent, ivy . . . What does that even mean?" His voice echoed faintly in the oppressive stillness of the forest he was in.

It had been three days since he'd set out, following Lily's journal and the map Janice had marked with shaky confidence. The forest was unforgiving—twisted trees with bark like knotted hands reached out to him, and the air seemed heavier with each passing hour. His water skin was nearly empty, and his last bit of dried meat had been gone since the previous night.

Devin swiped the back of his hand across his brow, his steps faltering as hunger gnawed at his stomach. He pushed forward, his eyes scanning for any sign of the old stone farmhouse Lily's journal described. "Just a little further," he told himself, though the resolve in his voice was thin.

The journal had been frustratingly vague, only mentioning that the farmhouse would be hidden by nature, its walls nearly indistinguishable from the overgrown terrain. But the riddle implied there was more to finding the entrance than simply spotting the structure.

His boot caught on a root, and he stumbled forward, catching himself against the rough bark of a nearby tree. "What am I doing here?" he asked himself, straightening and brushing dirt from his palms. The parchment fluttered in his hand, and his gaze returned to the line about the serpent. *A door unseen by arrogant eyes . . .*

Devin exhaled, a slow, frustrated breath. "Well, I'm not exactly feeling arrogant right now."

He crested a small rise and froze. There, partially obscured by brambles and thick ivy, stood what looked like the remains of a stone wall. Time had worn the structure, its stones weathered and cracked, but it matched the description from Lily's journal. Heart quickening, Devin moved closer, his fingers brushing aside the ivy to reveal a faint, almost ghostly drawing etched into the stone.

An arched doorway.

His eyes traveled upward, following the curve of the arch until they landed on the faint outline of a serpent carved into the keystone at the top. Its body was coiled, its head resting as though it watched over the invisible door.

Devin swallowed hard. "This has to be it," he said. He reached out, running his fingers over the cool surface of the stone. The carving felt ancient, its details smoothed by centuries of weathering. But there was no obvious handle, no keyhole, nothing to indicate how to open the door.

He stepped back, scanning the wall for clues. The riddle from the paper echoed in his mind. *A door unseen by arrogant eyes, revealed when the humble recognize.*

"Recognize what?" he muttered, his frustration growing. "The door's right here. I see it." He let out a sharp breath and dropped to his knees, his fingers brushing the ground. "Humble. Humble . . ."

Devin paused, lowering his gaze. He shifted, bowing his head slightly, and let his hand rest lightly against the base of the archway. A faint vibration coursed through his fingertips, subtle but unmistakable. The air seemed to grow warmer, and a soft, golden light began to spread along the outline of the arch.

He froze, watching as the glow brightened, illuminating the serpent at the top of the doorway. Its coiled body seemed to move, unwinding itself as though waking from a long slumber. The glow intensified until the carved serpent blinked, its eyes glinting with life before the light faded, leaving the stone wall unchanged.

The faint sound of grinding stone broke the silence, and the ivy began to pull away from the wall, revealing the entrance—a weathered door of dark wood, its surface engraved with runes Devin couldn't decipher.

He sat back on his heels, his heart pounding. "Well, well," he whispered.

Slowly, he stood, brushing dirt from his hands as he stared at the door. His fingers trembled as he reached for the handle.

The door creaked open, and Devin stepped inside, leaving the forest behind.

Janice and Halbridge crouched in the shadow of the old archive alcove, tucked behind a row of long-forgotten city documents and a defunct speaker system mounted high on the wall. From their vantage point, they had a clear—if angled—view of the council chamber through the slats of a ventilation grate.

People were just beginning to gather.

Council members filed into the room in subdued clusters, their expressions unusually serious. As they took their seats around the long mahogany table, murmured greetings passed between them. Despite the soft voices, there was a current of anticipation in the air.

Janice nudged Halbridge and pressed record on the small, enchanted lens embedded in the brooch she wore at her collar.

Councilman Haldine sat, slowly tapping a brass gavel against the table once. The room fell silent.

"Thank you, all," he said. "Before we begin, I must remind you—this meeting is sealed. No disclosures. No leaks. Anyone found violating this sacred trust will be dealt with . . . swiftly."

There were murmurs of agreement, nods from the gathered officials. Janice and Halbridge exchanged a glance—so far, exactly as the Seer's Eye had shown.

Haldine smiled faintly. "It's time. The pieces have aligned. Lord Azazel's vision—what we've worked toward for decades—is about to be realized."

A low murmur swept through the room, followed by

283

scattered applause. The moment Haldine uttered *Azazel's* name, an electric thrill passed through the council. Some clapped softly. A few smiled with thin, gleaming satisfaction.

Halbridge and Janice exchanged a tense look.

Another council member, a woman with dark-rimmed glasses and a violet pin on her lapel, spoke up. "The east corridor has been cleared. All digital records erased. No trace of our prior meetings remain with our foreign contacts."

A man in a charcoal suit added, "The press has been fed the approved narrative. We've staged the economic diversion as planned—no one is watching us."

Another councilwoman leaned forward. "Security around the perimeter has doubled. Our contact in the local precinct says the department's fully aligned with our timeline."

Haldine gave a curt nod, then turned to a different official near the end of the table. "And what of the reports regarding the Riftstone Beacon? Was it not triggered near the old tree line?"

The man adjusted his collar. "Yes, Councilman. We detected a brief pulse—an anomaly tied to one of the ancient path markers near the Valwyn Grove. But the data was . . . inconclusive. The forest was marked long ago as a defunct channel—no active gateways have been recorded there in years."

Janice froze. She turned her head slightly toward Halbridge and whispered, "Devin."

Halbridge gave a single nod.

Haldine's expression darkened. "Inconclusive is unacceptable. Dispatch operatives to investigate immediately. I want eyes on that forest. If anyone has breached the threshold, I want them found and eliminated. There can be no mistakes—*no possibility* of any resistance rising against our agenda. Lord Azazel made CLEAR that doorway must not be accessed by our enemies."

The man nodded as the tension in the room deepened.

Haldine nodded approvingly. "Good. Very good. Our task was never simple—but loyalty has brought us here."

He stood, both hands resting on the table.

"And now," he said slowly, "our master approaches the final stage. Soon, he will bring the last piece to the table—the vessel that will unlock the flow of unlimited red energy. With it, we will create enough portals to stretch across this world's power centers undetected. Silent dominance. Complete assimilation."

The room broke into restrained, reverent applause—no cheers, but wide smiles and eyes glittering with ambition.

Janice closed her eyes, bile rising in her throat. Halbridge's hands shook, but the lens continued to record.

"Let us ready ourselves," Haldine intoned. "Our time is here. No more shadows. No more whispers. We become *the hand that guides the world*."

Haldine raised his arms.

The others stood.

One by one, they began to chant—low at first, then building in rhythm and intensity.

Cast off the shackles of Thalion's Throne
Let red fire rise and flesh be stone
Through painted doors and hidden light

We claim the day, we kill the night
The veil is torn, the watch is blind
Our master calls—his will, our mind
One world, one path, one silent reign
The blood of stars shall break the chain

As the last syllable faded, the room fell into a reverent hush.

Behind the grated alcove, Janice's breath came shallow. Her face turned white as she turned toward Halbridge.

"We have to move," she whispered. "Now."

Halbridge nodded, his eyes still fixed on the council. "We just watched them pledge allegiance to a being who wants to hollow out this world from the inside."

"And we recorded every word," Janice said, pressing a finger to the brooch still pulsing faintly with enchanted light. "This is the first real proof the world will *have*—if we can get out of here alive."

Halbridge peeked through the slats one more time as the council began to disperse, their expressions solemn and self-satisfied. Already, a few were checking devices or murmuring orders into comms.

Then a sound—metal boots against tile, moving toward the hall.

"They're sending operatives to Valwyn," Janice whispered, barely containing the panic in her voice. "They're going after him."

"Devin," Halbridge said through clenched teeth. "How do we warn him?"

Janice grabbed his arm, shaking her head. "We can't. He's beyond our reach now—between realms. No message would get to him in time."

Halbridge's expression tightened. "So we're just going to do *nothing* while they send killers after him?"

"No," Janice said firmly. "We shift the end of the path."

Halbridge blinked. "What does that even mean?"

She took a breath. "When Devin emerges from the library, there's still a window of influence—about where he appears. By default, he'd return to the last point of entry: Valwyn Grove. But I can anchor a new exit point using an old Overseer tether I've stored. A kind of . . . redirect beacon."

Halbridge narrowed his eyes. "Where?"

"My house," Janice said. "In the garage. Behind the red door. I've never used it, but Lily's journal gives instructions. She must have foreseen this possibility— and with the right sequence, I can calibrate it to pull Devin to another location instead."

Halbridge exhaled. "So we can't stop the Council's hit squad—but we can make sure they miss the target entirely."

"Exactly," Janice said, already moving toward the stairwell. "But we'll need to move fast. If they get to Valwyn before I shift the beacon's position, they'll be waiting for him."

"Then let's not waste another second," Halbridge whispered, following her into the dark.

They slipped from the alcove in silence, hugging the shadows along the edge of the stone walls. One council-man passed within a dozen feet, head down, muttering into a secure earpiece. Neither Janice nor Halbridge dared to breathe.

A narrow door loomed ahead, half-hidden behind a

broken display case. Janice reached for it, fingers trembling, and opened it, just wide enough to slip through. Halbridge followed close behind.

The stairwell was dark, tight, and cold. Their footsteps echoed faintly as they descended.

When they reached the tunnels, Halbridge finally spoke. "You realize if we publish this—if we actually release what we just recorded—we'll have targets on our backs."

Janice nodded. "We already do. At least now we'll give them a reason."

A sharp voice echoed from the far end of the tunnel. "Hey! You there—stop!"

Halbridge whipped around. Two figures in black uniforms emerged from the shadows, weapons drawn.

"Go!" Janice hissed, already turning.

They bolted down the side corridor, the lights above them flickering wildly as boots pounded the floor behind them. Shouts echoed through the narrow passage, but Janice and Halbridge didn't look back.

CHAPTER 44

Devin stepped through the doorway.

The air was cooler here, carrying the faint, earthy scent of old paper and moss. His boots clicked softly against a floor of smooth stone, worn by centuries of footsteps long gone. He froze in place, his eyes widening as he took in the vast expanse before him.

It wasn't just a library—it was a cathedral of knowledge. Towering bookshelves stretched upward toward an arched, glass ceiling partially obscured by creeping ivy and overgrown foliage. Sunlight filtered through the glass in soft, golden beams, illuminating floating motes of dust and the vibrant greens of the vines clinging to the walls. The effect was both serene and haunting, as though the library had been abandoned by its caretakers yet refused to be forgotten.

Stone staircases curved along the walls, their steps partially covered in moss and scattered leaves, leading to balconies lined with even more shelves. Some sections of the library appeared intact and pristine, while others seemed on the verge of collapse, as though time couldn't quite decide whether to preserve or destroy this place.

Devin's gaze lingered on the far corners of the room, where shadows pooled like living things, shifting and dancing just beyond the light's reach. The entire space felt alive—watchful, almost sentient. He couldn't shake the sense that the library studied him as much as he studied it.

He stepped forward cautiously, his fingers brushing

the spines of books on a nearby shelf. Many were covered in dust, their titles written in languages he couldn't recognize. One caught his eye—a leather-bound volume with an intricate golden emblem on its spine. He reached for it, but the book wouldn't budge, as though it were rooted in place. Frowning, he pulled again, harder this time, but it remained immovable.

"Figures," he muttered, letting his hand fall to his side. "Nothing in these places ever works the way you think it will."

Devin turned slowly, taking in the sheer scale of the library once more. The light streaming through the glass ceiling seemed to shift as he moved, following him like a curious companion. He exhaled deeply, the sound echoing faintly in the cavernous space.

"Hello?" he called out, his voice hesitant but clear. The word bounced off the walls, echoing back to him in distorted fragments—Hello . . . hello . . . hello . . .

He stood still, listening as the echoes faded into silence. For a moment, the library seemed to hold its breath. Devin shook his head. "Yeah, because that's not creepy at all," he muttered.

But as he turned to explore further, a faint sound caught his attention—a whisper, so soft it was almost imperceptible. It wasn't an echo; it came from deeper within the library, somewhere beyond the rows of towering shelves.

Devin froze, his hand instinctively tightening around the strap of his backpack. "Great," he said, his voice low. "Not alone after all."

Jo's breath shook. "If I do this . . . will everything change?"

"No," said the Warden of Justice. "Everything will finally *align*."

She looked at her guide—the version of herself bathed in light. The one who had walked beside her since the storm.

The guide stepped forward now, eyes full of compassion.

"You've always known this truth," she said. "Deep down, you've known that I existed. You just didn't believe you were *worthy* of it."

Jo's eyes filled with tears.

She stepped to the orb.

Her fingers hovered above its glowing surface. She turned to the light being beside her one last time.

And the light being—nodded.

Then she stepped toward Jo.

Jo touched the orb.

Their forms met—and in a soft surge of radiant light, they merged.

Jo gasped.

The moment the two became one, the orb flared. Her body arched as warmth spread through her core. A cascade of visions flashed behind her eyes—images of her mother and of Sara—but then she saw flashing images of *herself*.

She saw herself drawing the crystal bow, unleashing an arrow of pure light across a battlefield. She saw herself standing before a gathered crowd, her voice rising in defiance. She saw herself kneeling at Sara's side, and finally standing face to face with Azazel, unflinching.

Jo collapsed to her knees, hands pressed to the earth, tears pouring down her face —but not from pain.

From *release*. For the first time, the weight she had carried for so long . . . was gone.

She wasn't just Sara's older sister.

She wasn't just a girl who held it all together when everything fell apart.

She was now Jolene, daughter of Lilianna—Heir to the line of Overseers, called and claimed by Valoria itself.

A soul born of two worlds. A soul reborn.

The orb dimmed slowly, now quiet and calm. Jo, from her knees, reached out, this time not hesitating to hold it.

It settled into her palm with surprising ease.

The Wardens bowed their heads. One by one, they stepped back into the light, fading into the folds of the Hallow.

Jo rose.

The moss beneath her feet shimmered. Jo looked around and realized she was now back at the clearing by the pool.

But something had changed.

Everything around her—the trees, the air, the light—looked different now. Sharper. Deeper. The leaves glowed with a radiant intensity she hadn't noticed before, hues of gold and jade laced with threads of living energy. The stones beneath her feet pulsed with a soft luminescence, as if welcoming her. Even the breeze carried more than just movement—it carried *meaning.*

It had all been there before. But now, the veil was gone.

She hadn't realized how much she'd been seeing

everything through fear—through doubt. But now . . .
she saw the Hallow not as something strange or mystical
but as something that had always been . . . *home.*

Somewhere in the far distance, the sound of wind
through leaves called to her. The cabin and the red door
would soon be in view.

It was time.

But she turned once more to the pool behind her.

Her reflection stared back.

She was whole.

CHAPTER 45

The tires screamed as Halbridge took the corner hard, gravel spitting beneath them. The city lights blurred into streaks of red and gold behind the windshield.

"They're still on us," Janice said, twisting in her seat to glance behind them. Headlights swerved into view—two black SUVs gaining ground.

"I noticed," Halbridge gritted, slamming the gas. "Maybe next time we sneak out of a cult meeting, we take the *quiet* route."

"They're not going to stop," Janice warned. "If they catch us, that recording never sees the light of day—and Devin loses his shot. How are you going to outrun them??"

Halbridge gripped the wheel tighter, eyes locked on the road. "I'm going to drive really fast!"

Janice shot him a look.

"What?" he added. "You asked."

The road out of Muxley wound sharply into the woods as they neared the edge of town. Trees blurred past them like shadows with limbs. Halbridge swerved through the switchbacks, the engine growling in protest.

A bend.

A side road.

He killed the headlights and veered down the hidden turnoff.

The black SUVs sped past the fork, tires screeching.

Silence.

Janice and Halbridge sat still, barely breathing.

Then Halbridge exhaled. "Think we lost them."

"Not for long," Janice said. "Let's go."

They tore through the final stretch of wooded road. Janice's home came into view—quiet, dark, nestled behind its weathered fence.

They jumped out before the engine fully stopped, racing to the side of the house. The garage loomed ahead. At its center: the red door.

Janice reached into her coat, pulling free the worn silver key.

Halbridge turned at the sound of distant footsteps.

Shadows were moving down the street. Fast.

"They found us," he muttered.

Janice shoved the key into the lock. A subtle *click* echoed. The door shimmered, a pulse of light rippling across its surface.

"Inside. Now."

They stepped through the red door—and vanished.

The door clicked shut behind them, the magic sealing it once more.

Seconds later, the black-clad operatives stormed into the garage.

Guns raised. Eyes scanning.

Nothing.

Just an old, dusty garage with cobwebs, rusted tools, and a red door that no longer glowed.

CHAPTER 46

Devin narrowed his eyes toward the sound, the silence that followed pressing in around him. "Who's there?" he called out, his voice echoing faintly through the shelves.

No answer. Just the distant creak of wood and the soft rustle of unseen pages. He stood still for a moment longer, waiting—listening. Nothing.

Devin turned in a slow circle, his eyes scanning the towering shelves and winding staircases. He rubbed the back of his neck, muttering to himself, "Right. Just find the one ancient text in a place bigger than a stadium. No problem."

He sighed and slumped against a nearby table, setting his backpack down with a dull thud. His hand drifted to his pocket, fishing out the crumpled piece of paper that had helped him find the door outside. The edges were worn from his constant handling over the past few days, the ink smudged.

"Maybe you've got more to say," he murmured, unfolding it carefully. As he flattened the paper on the table, his brow furrowed. The riddle about the door was still there, but now the back of the paper caught his attention. Words had appeared that hadn't been there before.

He turned it over fully, holding it closer to the light streaming through the glass ceiling. The writing was faint, as though it had been burned into the parchment rather than written. He read aloud:

"To find the truth, face what you've hidden,
In mirrored halls where lies are chidden.
Where whispers test what your heart conceals,
And bridges ask what your soul reveals."

"What the hell does that mean?" He scanned the library, half-expecting the answer to jump out at him. Of course, nothing did.

He folded the paper and slid it back into his pocket. "All right," he muttered, his voice echoing faintly. "Mirrored halls, whispers, and bridges. Great. That clears it right up."

He picked up his satchel and took a step forward, his boots scuffing softly against the stone floor. The sound of his movement echoed faintly, but then . . . there it was again. The whisper.

It was so soft it could almost be mistaken for the rustling of leaves, but there was no wind here. Devin froze, straining to listen. The whisper seemed to come from everywhere and nowhere at once, just on the edge of hearing. Words brushed against his mind like a feather as though the library itself urged him onward. Devin turned his head, his gaze drawn to a faint glimmer of light flickering in the distance. It wasn't bright—just enough to catch his eye, like a star barely visible in the night sky. Without fully understanding why, he took a step toward it.

As he walked, the glimmer grew stronger, resolving into a staircase spiraling upward. The stone steps were worn and uneven, their edges softened by the passage of countless footsteps. Vines clung to the walls, their leaves a vibrant green despite the absence of sunlight.

Devin hesitated at the base of the staircase, his fingers brushing lightly against the cool stone railing. The whisper returned, softer now. It wasn't a sound so much as a feeling, a gentle nudge at the edge of his awareness, urging him to climb.

"All right," he muttered under his breath, gripping the railing. "Here we go."

The climb was steep, each step seeming to carry him higher than the last, as though the staircase defied the laws of distance and gravity. The light above grew brighter as he ascended, casting long shadows on the walls. His breath came in steady rhythms, but his mind raced, replaying the words from the riddle Lily's journal had pointed to: *Face what you've hidden.*

When he reached the top, the staircase ended abruptly in front of a tall archway. Its surface was intricately carved, depicting twisting vines framing a pair of mirrored panels on either side. Devin stepped closer, the faint glow from the arch highlighting the silver runes etched along its edges. The archway loomed ahead, dark and silent beyond its frame. Whatever lay beyond, it waited for him. He took a deep breath and stepped through.

Devin moved deeper into the labyrinth. In this hall, all of the walls were covered with mirrors that seemed to stretch endlessly in every direction, creating a maze of reflections that shifted as he walked. He couldn't tell if he was going forward, backward, or in circles.

He stopped and turned, hoping to see the faint light of the doorway he'd entered through, but there was only glass—his reflection staring back at him, fractured and multiplied.

"All right," he muttered. "Think. How do I get out of this?"

The mirrors rippled, and a scene began to take shape. He froze as he saw himself in the woods, standing helplessly as Azazel grabbed Sara. The memory unfolded in stark detail—Sara's screams, the cold, calculating expression on Azazel's face, and the way Devin's feet had felt rooted to the ground.

A sharp ache twisted in his chest, catching him off guard. The image didn't just *remind* him—it *reopened* something. Emotions he hadn't realized he buried began to rise—and grief that hadn't had space to speak.

The mirror then shifted, showing Smith stepping forward to pull Sara back just as the Voidwalkers descended. Devin saw the look on Smith's face—calm and composed. In Devin's mind he seemed almost indifferent. At the time, it had infuriated him. Before Devin could think, out came, "He knew more than he let on," Devin muttered. "If he'd just told us everything—if he hadn't kept all those secrets—we could've been ready. We could've stopped this."

As the memory faded, another mirror lit up. It showed the warehouse. Stacy's last moments. Devin saw himself again, yelling after her as she ran toward the Voidwalkers . . . to protect Sara. He remembered the desperate anger, the way he'd fought against Smith's grip, screaming that he could save her.

Smith's face appeared in the reflection. Devin saw himself struggling against him, shouting, "Let me go!" He remembered the bitterness that had surged through him when Smith had held him back.

"If he hadn't stopped me, I could've saved her,"

Devin said through gritted teeth. "I would've saved her."

The mirrors shimmered, as if responding to his thoughts.

If he'd just trusted me. I could have saved them. I . . . I would HAVE DONE what needed to BE DONE. I COULD HAVE SAVED THEM!

Devin's face was flush.

The corridor began to twist around him, the mirrors warping into jagged edges. Devin stumbled forward, the ground beneath him tilting. He didn't know where he was anymore.

The images in the mirrors blurred, fragments of these memories swirling together into a chaotic storm.

"You think you're better than him, don't you?" a voice whispered from the depths of his mind. It wasn't the warm presence he'd felt before—it was cold and relentless. "You think you'd have led them better. Saved them all."

"THAT'S RIGHT!" Devin shouted.

The corridor tilted again, and suddenly he stood on the edge of a vast drop. The mirrors framed the chasm like a twisted picture frame, their surfaces reflecting the same scene over and over: him, falling, reaching, grasping.

His foot slipped.

Devin gasped as the ground disappeared beneath him. He tumbled over the edge, his body weightless in the rush of wind and gravity. His hands flailed instinctively, and just as the momentum threatened to carry him into the void, his fingers caught the ledge.

The impact jolted through his arms, and he cried

out. His muscles straining as he clung to the stone. His legs dangled uselessly, the empty chasm yawning beneath him.

"Help!" The word tore from his throat before he could stop it. He gritted his teeth, shame rising like bile. He could feel the sweat on his palms, his grip on the edge slipping. "No," he muttered. "I can do this. I don't need—"

His fingers slipped further, his strength fading. "I—" His voice cracked. "I can't . . . I can't do this."

The whisper returned, gentle and steady, like a warm breeze brushing past his face. It wasn't audible, but he felt it all the same.

Devin closed his eyes. For the first time in what felt like forever, he let go of the fight inside him. "I need help," he whispered, his voice breaking. "Please."

The silence that followed was deafening. Then, just as his grip faltered completely, a hand shot out from above, clasping his wrist with unyielding strength. Devin's eyes snapped open, and he looked up to see a figure silhouetted against the faint light.

"I've got you," the figure said, their voice calm and resolute. It wasn't anyone Devin recognized—but the presence felt familiar.

Devin's muscles burned as the figure pulled him up, inch by agonizing inch, until he finally collapsed onto the ledge, his chest heaving. He rolled onto his back, staring up at the ceiling far above. The figure knelt beside him, their face obscured by the light.

"Even the strongest need help sometimes," said the figure.

The words hit Devin hard. Devin closed his eyes, the

weight of his bitterness finally giving way to something else. When he opened his eyes, the figure was gone. So were the mirrors.

Devin rose slowly, his legs trembling as he steadied himself. The ledge beneath his feet felt solid again. He looked around him. The mirrors were gone, their fractured reflections replaced by a clear, straight path ahead.

For a moment, he just stood there, letting the silence settle over him. His chest felt lighter somehow, as though the weight he'd been carrying had loosened its grip. But the quiet didn't last.

A faint sound reached his ears—a soft, rhythmic murmur that grew clearer as he focused on it. . . running water. Devin squinted into the distance. The path stretched forward, narrowing slightly. He adjusted his backpack and began to head toward the sound.

The hallway felt endless, its walls smooth and unmarked.

"Even the strongest need help sometimes," he whispered. He didn't know who—or what—had pulled him back up from the ledge, but something about the experience had shifted something deep inside him.

The sound of water grew louder, pulling Devin from his thoughts. The hallway widened abruptly, opening into a cavernous room. "Whoa," said Devin. His eyes widened.

The space was immense, its vaulted ceiling held aloft by towering stone pillars carved with intricate designs. The pillars stretched upward into gracefully arched beams, their surfaces etched with swirling patterns that seemed to shift subtly as the light played across them. The walls between the pillars were lined with massive, ornate frames, each one holding a portrait or painting. The frames were dark cherry wood, their polished surfaces gleaming faintly in the soft light that seemed to emanate from the images themselves.

The portraits were more vibrant than anything Devin had ever seen. Some depicted ordinary people—an old woman with kind eyes, a boy clutching a book, a merchant surrounded by wares. Others were grand and majestic, showing warriors clad in shining armor, queens draped in golden robes, and scholars holding scrolls that seemed to shimmer with light. Each figure seemed frozen in time, their expressions so vivid that Devin half-expected them to step out of their frames.

In the center of the room ran a shallow stream, its clear water flowing gently over smooth stones. The stream's surface reflected the portraits, turning the entire room into a kaleidoscope of color and light. The sound of the water was soothing.

As he moved deeper into the room, he approached the nearest painting—a young woman tending a garden—then a whisper.

"She gave her life to nourish the land," the voice said softly. "Her work fed generations."

Devin blinked, startled. He glanced around the room, but there was no one there. The voice seemed to come from the painting itself.

He turned to another painting, this one of a man in golden armor standing atop a hill, his sword raised high. The voice that followed was deeper, richer, but tinged with arrogance. "He ruled through strength, feared by all. His name will never be forgotten."

Devin took a step back, his eyes darting between the

portraits. More voices joined the first two, soft at first, then louder, until the room was filled with a symphony of whispers. Some were kind and encouraging, recounting tales of sacrifice, love, and perseverance. Others were sharp and cutting, boasting of power and dominance, or lamenting opportunities lost to pride and greed.

"You could be more," one voice murmured, smooth and low. "They'd all remember your name. Admire you. Need you. All you have to do . . . is keep chasing what you already are."

"Who do you think you are?" another voice hissed, cruel and mocking. "Who are you without their cheers? Without the spotlight? You're hollow. A shadow playing at purpose."

"You've already come so far," said a gentler voice, filled with warmth. "Finish the new path you've started."

Devin sighed. The stream rippled at Devin's feet. He glanced down, startled to see his own reflection among them. His face was fractured, each fragment showing a different version of himself—some strong, some defeated, some filled with anger, others with determination.

He thought, again, of the hall of mirrored reflections—the bitterness he'd carried, the fall that had nearly ended him, the hand that had saved him. And now, the voices in the gallery—some speaking of light and selflessness, others laced with vanity, ambition, and the fear of being forgotten.

"Who . . . are you?" a voice asked softly.

"I don't know," Devin whispered, his gaze fixed on the stream at his feet. "I don't know who I'm supposed to be."

He saw himself again, the quarterback under the stadium lights, the crowd roaring his name. He'd been everyone's golden boy—the leader, the star. He thought of Stacy by his side, her bright smile masking the pressures they'd both carried.

"But that isn't me," Devin murmured, his voice trembling. "Not anymore . . . It's what they wanted. What they needed me to be." Tears began to fall down Devin's face.

Some of his tears fell into the stream. The fractured image rippled, shifting into something new. He saw himself as the protector in the park, standing between Sara and Azazel. He saw Stacy, her determination as fierce as her love, charging forward to protect Sara. He saw Smith, his stoic resolve hiding a burden far greater than Devin had realized.

The whispers returned, but now they were different. "Who do *you* want to be?" one asked softly.

"Do you crave power?" another voice asked, low and seductive. "To rule? To be feared?"

"Do you want to serve others?" a gentler voice asked. "To give, even when it costs you?"

"Do you seek love?" whispered another. "Acceptance? Or just peace?"

He drew in a breath. "I don't want to live for someone else's dream," he said, his voice steady. "I've spent so much time trying to prove I was strong enough . . . that I was the best. Like if I could just be *great* at something, I'd finally matter."

He paused, voice softer now. "But that wasn't me. Not really."

The whispers quieted. One remained, soft and steady,

brushing past him like a breeze: *"And in what spirit will you live out that truth?"*

Devin swallowed hard, his throat tight. He thought of the reflections, of Stacy's sacrifice, of Smith's quiet strength, of the countless people who had come before him—their legacies etched in the portraits lining the gallery.

"Humbly, I guess" he said at last, the word small but resolute. "I want to be humble. A protector of those I'm responsible for—not for power or recognition but because it's the right thing to do."

The reflection of himself in the stream shifted slightly, and suddenly he thought of Smith. The man who had frustrated him endlessly with his stoic demeanor, his secrets, and his unwillingness to let Devin charge headlong into battles he couldn't win.

". . . Like Smith does," Devin murmured. His throat tightened as he spoke the words, the truth of them settling over him. "I was so wrong about him."

Devin's voice wavered as he let himself feel it—the bitterness he'd clung to, the blame he'd placed on Smith for Stacy's death, for Sara's kidnapping, for everything he thought he could've done better. But now, the pieces began to fit together. Smith had held him back not out of doubt or control but out of a protective instinct so much deeper than Devin had been willing to see.

Smith had been a protector all along. Not for glory. Not for power.

The words settled in the air like a quiet proclamation. Devin looked up, and for the first time, the gallery seemed to brighten. A soft glow appeared on a small table near the edge of the room. He walked toward it until he saw what lay there—a glass pitcher, its surface catching the light like liquid crystal. Beside it was a simple wooden cup.

In the corner of his eye, movement drew his attention. He turned to see a new painting on the wall—a group of people kneeling by a stream, their hands cupped as they drank. Their faces were serene, their postures unguarded.

He reached for the pitcher. Slowly, he poured some of the water into the cup and raised it to his lips. The water was crisp and cool, the taste clean and refreshing. As it slid down his throat, he felt a strange warmth spread through his chest, light but steady, like a flame that wouldn't burn out.

The gallery shifted around him. The portraits dimmed, their whispers fading into silence. Devin's gaze followed the stream as it snaked through the room. At the far end a large archway was now visible and a deep rumble could be heard. Devin stepped closer, his boots splashing lightly in the shallow water. He stepped through the archway and saw a narrow bridge suspended over a rushing waterfall.

The sound of rushing water hit him first, a low, thunderous roar. The room was vast, its ceiling rising high above in an open expanse. The small stream he'd followed fed into this massive waterfall that spanned the far wall. The waterfall flowed away from him, its sheer force drawing his eyes to the many sources feeding into it. Streams flowed from crevices in the stone walls, rivulets poured from above. Together, they converged into the roaring falls as it plummeted into the void.

Devin stopped at the threshold, blinking at the sight

before him. He let out a dry laugh. "This has got to be the strangest library I've ever been to," he muttered, shaking his head.

The roar of the waterfall drowned out the sound of his voice, but the humor lingered. He took a step forward onto the bridge, his boots skimming the mist-slicked stone. The edges were uneven.

The falls seemed alive, their thunderous roar drowning out everything else. He squinted, trying to see through the mist and spray. On the far side of the chasm, the bridge ended abruptly at a ledge just before the falls. Beyond that, there was nothing—no visible doorway, no steps, no path. Only the relentless cascade of water.

This is it, he thought. *The path ends here.*

As he reached the center of the bridge, the mist thickened, clinging to his skin like a second layer. The roar of the falls seemed to grow louder, echoing in his ears until it felt as though the sound was coming from within him. He stopped, his hand gripping the rough edge of the railing.

The whisper returned. "Surrender."

Devin stiffened. The word wasn't a command; it was an invitation. A choice. He glanced back at the path he'd taken—the gallery, the portraits, the stream that had guided him here. Every step had led to this moment.

He turned back to the falls, his gaze fixed on the rushing torrent. His heart pounded as understanding dawned. The only way forward was not across the bridge, but through the falls. To go over. To let go.

"You've got to be . . ." Devin exhaled. His instincts screamed against it. Don't. You'll drown. You'll die.

But beneath the fear was something else: a quiet certainty that this was the test. Did he believe this would lead to the book Smith needed? Or was all this for nothing?

Devin exhaled slowly, his grip on the railing loosening. "All right," he shouted, his voice barely audible over the roar. "Let's do this." He stepped forward, his boots slipping slightly on the slick surface of the bridge. As he reached the end, he paused, staring into the cascade of water.

He closed his eyes. "I surrender," he whispered.

And then he stepped off the edge.

CHAPTER 47

Janice leaned against the old wooden table in the protected garage, breathing heavily. Halbridge paced in tight circles nearby, his face tense as he ran fingers through his hair.

"So," he finally said, breaking the silence. "We've got the evidence, the Council exposed—but we're trapped. If we walk out that door, Azazel's goons are waiting. How exactly do we get this recording out?"

Janice shook her head slowly. "I don't know yet. But even if we did, that's not all we have to worry about.

Halbridge stopped pacing, exhaling sharply. "And Devin. You think he made it out of the library? I mean . . . is he even okay?"

Janice's face tightened, urgency flashing in her eyes. "I hope so—but like I said, the Council knows Devin breached the old pathway in Valwyn Grove. They've dispatched operatives there already. If Devin returns there, they'll capture him—and the book won't reach Smith."

Halbridge's shoulders stiffened. "Earlier you said you could redirect him. Can you still do it?"

Janice moved swiftly, reaching to one of the bookshelves and lifting out a small chest. Opening it carefully, she removed a small bag and a slender crystal.

"The journal said this crystal can anchor a new endpoint for someone returning from another realm—in this case, Devin. If I set this correctly, it should guide him away from Valwyn, to someplace safer. Someplace hidden."

Halbridge's brow furrowed. "Where exactly?"

"I'm not completely sure. I've never used it before," Janice admitted. She moved to the pedestal holding the Seer's Eye, opened the bag, and pulled out a small bundle of runic tokens, fingers trembling slightly as she sorted through them. "These need to align with the crystal's tether—otherwise the Eye won't stabilize the endpoint."

Halbridge watched as Janice carefully placed the tokens into shallow grooves on the pedestal, their carved surfaces beginning to glow faintly. She adjusted their positions with slow precision. Once the tokens were set, Janice took the crystal and slid it gently into a slot on the side of the Seer's Eye. She closed her eyes briefly.

The crystal flared brilliantly, the Seer's Eye spinning faster, pulsing waves of blue light outward across the room in expanding rings. A high-pitched sound filled the air as the tokens flared, matching the crystal's glow.

Janice leaned forward, adjusting one token just as it flickered irregularly—her fingers steady.

Finally, the glow softened, the crystal settling into a soft, steady rhythm.

Janice exhaled slowly, shoulders sagging with relief.

"It's done. Devin should come out somewhere safer now. The Council won't find him—not immediately, at least."

Halbridge exhaled in relief. "Good. Let's just hope wherever he lands—"

Before he could finish, the Seer's Eye flared brightly,

casting strange shadows across the walls, causing Janice to retreat from the pedestal.

Halbridge turned sharply. "What now?"

Together, they approached the Eye. The orb revealed a grim scene outside—Azazel's operatives moving swiftly, pouring fuel along the walls of the house and garage. One flicked a lighter.

"They're going to burn it down," Halbridge murmured, dread in his voice.

Janice went pale. "They know they can't enter, so they'll trap us. Eliminate our only exit."

CHAPTER 48

The fall was immediate and all-consuming. The water engulfed Devin, cold and unrelenting, pulling him into its depths. For a moment, he was weightless, suspended in the current. The roar of the falls filled his ears. He was utterly powerless, carried by the torrent.

And then, just as suddenly, the water released him. Devin broke through the surface with a gasp, the air rushing into his lungs. He floated for a moment, the cool water lapping at his skin as he caught his breath. His heart thundered in his chest. He swam toward the edge of the pool. The roar of the falls faded behind him as he climbed onto the stone ledge, water streaming from his clothes. He stood there, his chest rising and falling as he took in his surroundings.

The room was circular, its walls lined with towering shelves brimming with books and scrolls. Devin stood in the midst of it, water dripping from his clothes and pooling at his feet. The journey had left him soaked, exhausted, and raw.

At the center of the room stood a pedestal bathed in warm light. Atop it lay a single book, its cover embossed with intricate designs.

Devin took a cautious step toward the pedestal, his eyes drawn to the book resting on top of it. The golden light surrounding it seemed to intensify as he approached, illuminating the intricate patterns on its cover. He stopped a few feet away.

His gaze lingered on the shifting designs etched into the leather. At first, they were chaotic, moving like ripples in water. But as Devin stared, the patterns began to align, forming symbols and letters that slowly resolved into a single word: *Thariel*.

"Thariel . . ." Devin whispered. He remembered Janice's voice, calm but insistent as she'd spoken of the guardian stripped of his power.

"This is it," Devin said aloud. "This is the book."

He stepped forward, his hands trembling as he reached for the pedestal. The leather was warm beneath his fingertips. Slowly, reverently, Devin lifted the book. It was lighter than he'd expected, almost unnaturally so.

He let out a shaky breath, glancing at the cover again. Curiosity tugged at him, and he hesitated for only a moment before gripping the edge of the cover.

As he began to open it, a sudden gust of wind erupted from nowhere, swirling around him with a force that nearly knocked him off his feet. Devin staggered, clutching the book tightly. The pages fluttered but remained sealed.

"Whoa!" Devin exclaimed, taking a step back. The wind died down as suddenly as it had come. He stared at the book in his hands. "All right . . . guess that's a no." He shook his head, his voice edged with nervous humor. "What, is your name on the book, Devin? No? Just checking." Devin let out a soft chuckle, shaking his head.

He glanced down at his soaked clothes, water still dripping from his sleeves and boots. The book in his hands felt almost too precious to carry so casually, but he knew he couldn't hold onto it forever. Shifting his grip, he slipped his wet backpack from his shoulders, the straps heavy with dampness. He unzipped the main compartment carefully, making space between the few supplies he had left.

Devin zipped the pack shut, shouldered it again, and stood there for a moment, looking back at the pedestal. The golden light surrounding the room began to dim, soft and gradual, like the final notes of a song. Devin looked, his eyes adjusting as the towering shelves and their endless scrolls seemed to dissolve into shadows. The circular walls faded next, the intricate carvings and stone disappearing into nothingness.

The air around him shifted, cool and sharp. The earthy aroma of damp soil and moss replaced the faint scent of aged parchment. Devin turned in place, disoriented, as the last traces of the library melted away. He found himself standing on uneven ground of the Shadowlands stretching around him. "How did I get here?" Devin murmured. "Weird."

Devin adjusted the weight of the pack on his back, glancing over his shoulder at the spot where the library had been. There was nothing there now—just an expanse of dark woods, silent and still.

Devin glanced at the path ahead, the faint outline of a trail winding through the Shadowlands. He let out a breath, squared his shoulders, and started walking.

CHAPTER 49

The Shadowlands were quiet. Only the faint rustle of leaves and the occasional distant bird call broke the silence. Devin kept his steps light, his boots crunching softly on the uneven ground.

He adjusted the straps on his satchel, scanning the twisted trees around him. The cold mountain wind cut through his damp clothes like knives. Every inch of him ached—his muscles stiff from exhaustion, his stomach hollow with hunger. He had no idea how long he had been walking. Hours? A day? The last thing he ate had been before the Library of Althea, before he had taken the book.

The adrenaline that had pushed him through was finally burning out.

Then—a sound.

Footsteps.

Devin stopped.

The soft snap of twigs. The subtle shift of underbrush. Someone followed him.

Azazel's men? His pulse pounded in his ears. If they were tracking him, if they knew what he carried . . .

He needed to lose them. Quickly.

Devin ducked behind a large cluster of boulders, pressing his back against the cold stone. His breath came shallow, his fingers hovering near the small blade at his belt.

If it's one of Azazel's, I'll have to take them down first.

The footsteps grew louder. Closer.

Devin gripped the hilt of his knife, every muscle in his body coiled as he prepared to strike.

The figure emerged from the brush.

Devin lunged.

"Whoa—WHAT THE . . . ?!"

The figure stumbled back, arms flying up in surprise.

Devin barely stopped himself in time, his blade hovering midair, heart hammering.

"Jo? What are you doing here?"

Jo straightened, brushing her hands down her clothes with a scowl. "What am *I* doing here? What are *you* doing, jumping out like a maniac?"

Devin let out a shaky laugh, tucking the blade back into its sheath. "Yeah, that's kind of the point. I thought you were one of Azazel's goons."

Jo rolled her eyes but took a step closer, her expression shifting from irritation to something more thoughtful. She studied him, really looked at him—his damp clothes, the exhaustion in his face. ". . . Where have you been?" she asked quietly.

He hesitated, glancing down at his pack. "I could ask you the same thing. Where've you been?"

Jo's expression shifted. "At the cabin . . . the one we were all at recently with Smith and the others."

Devin frowned slightly. "You stayed there alone?"

Jo exhaled through her nose. "Not exactly. There is a place there . . ." She hesitated before she continued. " It's . . . called . . . The Healing Hallows. I . . . had some things to figure out."

Devin nodded slowly, recognizing the weight in her tone. He thought about the Hall of Reflections, the

Whispering Gallery, and the bridge. He didn't need to pry.

Jo's eyes narrowed slightly as she studied him. "Looks like you've been through something too."

Devin huffed a laugh, adjusting the damp straps of his pack. "Yeah, well. Waterfalls. Cursed books. You know, errands for Smith."

"What kind of errands?" asked Jo.

Devin hesitated. "The kind that *really* shouldn't fall into the wrong hands."

Her eyes glanced at the pack on his back, and she tilted her head. "You've got something important, don't you?"

"Yeah," Devin admitted. "But I think we both do, in our own way."

Jo nodded slowly.

For a moment, they just stood there, the tension between them easing into something warmer. Devin's stomach growled loudly.

"Been a while since you ate, huh?" she asked, her tone teasing.

"You could say that," Devin muttered, his cheeks reddening slightly. "Not sure a granola bar would've made it through that waterfall."

Jo blinked. "Waterfall? What waterfall?"

Devin hesitated, scratching the back of his neck. "Uh, yeah . . . it was in this . . . library."

Jo's expression grew even more incredulous. "Library? What kind of library has a waterfall?"

Devin chuckled dryly. "The kind that also has a Hall of Mirrors and . . . tests your soul every step of the way."

Jo stared at him for a moment, then shook her head

with a small laugh. "Okay, you officially win the weird-est story of the day."

"Look," Devin said. "I don't think we're making it back to Muxley tonight. I'm soaked, I'm starving, and if I don't eat soon, you might have to drag my body the rest of the way." He tilted his head. "That cabin still standing?"

Jo glanced down the path. "Not too far."

Devin nodded. "Good. Let's head there, and I'll fill you in on everything. I promise—waterfalls, libraries, and all."

Jo smiled. "All right, deal. But you better not leave out a single detail."

CHAPTER 50

Jo leaned back in the creaky wooden chair, eyes locked on Devin like she was still wrapping her head around what he'd just said. "So . . . riddles, traps, a waterfall that nearly killed you, and the book only responds to someone from Draegora?"

Devin sat by the fire, steam rising from the bowl of soup he cradled. He tore a piece of bread in half and gave a faint, tired grin. "Basically, yeah."

Jo didn't laugh—but her lips curled in something between awe and disbelief. "And you made it out alive."

"Barely." He took a sip from the bowl, letting the warmth settle into his bones. "But the book's here. That part matters."

"You think it'll really help Smith?"

Devin nodded, slower now. "Yeah. I think it's part of getting him back to full strength. And we're gonna need him at full strength."

Jo didn't argue. Her fingers tapped against the armrest, gaze drifting to Devin's pack.

"You've changed," she said finally, voice soft.

Devin glanced up. "You too."

Jo gave a small shrug. "The Healing Hallows . . . It showed me things. Not visions or magic tricks. More like . . . truth. About myself. About Mom."

Devin set his bowl down, listening.

"I always thought I had to be her. Be strong for Sara. Hold everything together." She looked at the fire.

320

"But I forgot how kind she was. Not just strong—gentle. Steady. I think I lost that part in trying to carry everything alone."

Devin nodded slowly. "Funny. I thought I had life all figured out. Ball, future, what mattered. But that library . . . it pulled something out of me I didn't know was there."

Jo studied him, surprised by the honesty.

"When I was near that red orb," Devin added after a pause, "something in me stirred. Not in a creepy way. More like . . . recognition. Like a part of me that was asleep started waking up."

Jo tilted her head. "And now?"

He met her eyes. "Now, I'm sure I'm not who I was a few days ago anymore. I know I don't want that life anymore.

Jo let a breath go, shoulders easing. "That's more than I could've said a few days ago."

Devin smiled faintly. "Guess nearly dying and finding out you might be from another realm'll do that to a guy."

"Yeah," Jo said, matching his smile. "Guess it will."

The fire crackled between them, casting soft orange light across the cabin walls. Outside, the faint glow of the Healing Hallows shimmered through the trees.

"I don't think we're meant to go back to who we were before," Jo murmured. "I think this world—Valoria, Draegora, all of it—it's calling us forward."

Devin leaned back, eyes closing for a beat. "Yeah. And this time, I'm not running from it."

Jo nodded, watching him with something like admiration.

"You really think we can stop Azazel?" she asked.

Devin's brow furrowed. "I think we have to try. And I think . . . we're not alone."

Jo was about to respond when she noticed Devin's head start to dip slightly. His breathing slowed.

"You know," she said gently, "I was thinking—"

A soft snore answered her.

Jo blinked, then laughed under her breath. "Figures."

She rose, grabbing a blanket and gently laying it over him.

Sitting back down by the fire, she stared at Devin and then into the flames of the fire.

For the first time in a long while, the weight she carried didn't feel like hers alone.

The sound of scraping metal echoed through the chamber.

Sara jolted upright, heart hammering.

Her cell door creaked open, the iron hinges groaning waking her from sleep.

Two of Azazel's guards stepped inside—black-robed, faceless. They moved like smoke pulled by unseen wind, feet barely brushing the ground. Effortless. Inhuman.

Sara pressed herself against the far wall, bracing.

They said nothing.

One stepped forward, pulling a delicate silver chain from beneath his cloak. It shimmered faintly in the flickering torchlight.

He reached for her.

Sara recoiled. "Don't touch me."

They didn't respond.

The second guard produced a small black vial and twisted the top off with long, pale fingers. A sharp scent filled the air.

"What is that?" Sara asked, voice cracking with unease.

No answer.

The first guard grabbed her wrist, fast. A quick prick of pain—just a drop of blood. The second guard tipped the vial and poured its contents onto her skin. The liquid hissed where it touched her. Not enough to injure—but enough to test.

Sara jerked her arm back, eyes burning. "Why are you doing this? What do you want from me?"

Still, nothing.

They turned. Silent. Slipping back through the cell door like shadows.

The door clanged shut behind them.

Sara staggered slightly, cradling her wrist. The faint sting of the prick pulsed under her skin, the strange scent of the liquid still sharp in the air. Her breath came fast, mind racing. *What was that?* She pressed her back harder against the wall, trying to steady herself.

But then—movement caught her eye.

Through the narrow bars, she watched them glide down the corridor — smooth, weightless. No footsteps. No sound. The air itself seemed to bend around them, carrying them forward.

I've seen this before.

The memory rushed in—*the park.* Azazel's men moving through the air like it obeyed them. No footsteps. No effort.

And then... a whisper in her mind.

Try.

It wasn't her own voice.

She flinched and shook her head. "I'm stuck in this cell..."

But then—she noticed it.

The door to her cell.

It wasn't fully closed.

CHAPTER 51

Jo and Devin stood before the familiar red door, the crisp morning air still carrying the chill of the night before. The city of Muxley was just beginning to stir, but here, in the quiet street lined with townhouses, the world felt strangely still.

Jo exhaled, shifting her weight. "So this is our plan? Just waltz in and hope they're here?"

Devin gave a half-shrug. "Worked out great last time."

Jo shot him a look, but he wasn't wrong.

She remembered the last time they were here—following Smith and Sara, desperate for answers. They'd stepped into what looked like an empty, lifeless house. Nothing but dust and shadows. And yet . . . moments later, Smith and Sara had appeared, seemingly out of nowhere, descending a spiral staircase that hadn't even been there before.

Jo bit her lip, glancing at the door. "For all we know," she murmured, "the others are elsewhere and Sara's . . . . still with Azazel."

Devin said nothing, just exhaled through his nose.

Jo shook her head quickly, as if pushing the thought aside.

"We don't have the key," she murmured.

Devin frowned. "Yeah, so?"

Jo turned to him, thinking aloud. "That's how it works. Every time we've been somewhere Smith brought us—something changed when he used his key." She began counting on her fingers. "At the warehouse, the key didn't just unlock a door—it led us into a whole operations center. Holographic maps. Ancient artifacts. An armory. A hidden vault."

Devin nodded.

Jo continued. "And the cabin? That wasn't just some rundown place in the hills. It became the Healing Hallows when the key was used."

She gestured to the door. "So this townhouse works the same way. The last time we were here, we saw an empty house because we didn't have the key."

Devin nodded slowly. "But Smith and Sara still showed up."

Jo's brows knitted together. "Exactly. We didn't see the **real** place—but it was still here. It was just hidden from our eyes."

Devin let out a breath. "Great. But are you saying the place the key shows is real and what we saw wasn't . . . .real?" Devin exhaled . . . "Don't answer that . . . ."

He rubbed his hands over his face. "So we show up without the magic key, and we're just standing in a boring townhouse. Meanwhile, Sara . . ." His voice trailed off.

Jo nodded. "Unless they're already inside. Maybe they will hear us."

Devin knocked. Three solid raps.

Silence.

They exchanged a glance.

"Only one way to find out," Jo muttered, turning the doorknob. It twisted easily, the door swinging open without resistance.

It was just like last time.

No furniture. No warmth. No sign that anyone lived here at all.

Devin let the door close behind them. He cupped his hands around his mouth and called out. "Smith? Eli? Mr. Mason?"

There was a long silence.

Jo sighed, rubbing her temples. "Maybe they really aren't—"

A shift.

The air rippled, almost imperceptibly, like the shimmer of heat off pavement. A low hum vibrated through the room, and then—

The ceiling shimmered.

A soft grinding sound filled the space as a spiral staircase unfurled from above, descending slowly as if it had always been there, waiting.

Devin took an unconscious step back, watching as the staircase came to a stop. "Okay. That's still so weird."

At the top of the staircase, standing in the dim glow of the hidden library, was Smith.

Arms crossed, expression unreadable, he looked down at them. "Took you long enough."

Jo and Devin turned toward the sound. Smith's sharp gaze studied them closely. Behind him, the dim glow of towering bookshelves and maps pinned to stone pillars flickered like lantern light.

Jo squared her shoulders. "Well, we had a long walk."

Devin adjusted the strap of his pack, stepping forward. "And we've got a lot to talk about."

Smith gave a small nod, his gaze steady. "Yeah. And not much time to do it."

CHAPTER 52

Jo and Devin settled into their seats at the large wooded table. Smith, Eli, and Mr. Mason sat opposite them, quiet and watchful.

Smith broke the silence. "Tell us what happened."

Jo took a slow breath, beating Devin to the draw.

"I'll go first," she said . Devin leaned back, nodding for her to take the lead.

"After I ran, I went back to the cabin and used the key Smith gave me. I went back into the Healing Hallows," Jo began, her fingers laced together in her lap. "And at first, it just felt like a dream. But the longer I stayed, the more I realized it wasn't a place to rest. It was a place to see."

She looked at Smith, then Mr. Mason. "To see myself."

Her voice wavered slightly, but she pushed forward. "I've spent most of my life trying to be a wall. For Sara. For everyone. I thought strength meant shutting everything else out. But in the Hallows, I saw Mom—not just the way I remembered her, but the truth of her. Not just fierce . . . but kind. Warm. Gentle."

Jo's eyes grew glassy, but she didn't look away.

"I saw the version of myself I was afraid to be. And I chose to step into it."

She paused—then a soft glow began to pulse around her. Blue, like the glow that once surrounded Sara. It spread gently across her skin like moonlight, and from

328

her chest, a shimmer of light extended outward—until in her hands, slowly, a radiant bow of crystal-blue light took form.

"I saw this in the Hallows," she said quietly. "It was waiting for me."

Devin eyes got wide. "Whoa . . . .you don't see that every day."

The bow flickered once, then dissolved into particles of light. The glow around her dimmed—but something of it remained in her eyes.

The room was still. Smith's gaze was not unreadable now. "You are your mother's daughter," he said. "She would be proud."

Jo nodded. "Thank you."

Jo turned to Devin, smiled gently, and nodded at him.

Devin exhaled, glancing at Jo before standing up to share. "I . . . owe you an apology, Smith."

Smith's eyes narrowed slightly, but he said nothing.

Devin leaned forward, setting his pack on the table between them. "Before I left . . . when you asked me for help, I wasn't ready. I didn't trust you. I didn't trust any of this." His voice caught for a moment. "But something changed. I guess it starts with me running for my life."

He hesitated for a moment, then continued. "After I ran from you guys, I met up with my friend Demetri at Farley's Barn and tried to tell him what was going on. Everyone's concerned because I've been missing. Anyway, the police showed up, and I had to run. That's when I ran into a guy named Halbridge—he's a reporter—found me. Said he'd been looking into all the

strange things happening and wanted to take me somewhere that could help."

Eli exchanged a glance with Smith but said nothing.

Devin continued, his voice growing more certain.
"Halbridge took me to this house—outside of Muxley,
down this narrow dirt road in the middle of nowhere.
Big lot, set back in a clearing. And it had a . . . a garage
with a bright-red door."

Jo, who had been idly tracing patterns on the table
with her fingers, suddenly stilled. Her head snapped up,
her eyes sharp. "Wait—what?"

Devin frowned. "Yeah, the garage side door was
red. And Halbridge had this key—looked just like yours,
Smith. He used it to open the door, and when I stepped
inside, it wasn't just a garage anymore. It was . . . different. Bigger. Like this place." He gestured vaguely at
the library around them. "A space that doesn't belong
in this world."

Jo's leaned forward. "That house . . ." she murmured. "That sounds like—" She stopped herself, swallowing hard.

Smith leaned forward slightly. "And inside? What
did you find?"

Devin hesitated, his gaze flicking toward Jo before
answering. "Janice Fowler."

Jo's eyes widened. "Janice?", a mixture of disbelief
and shock. "As in . . . Aunt Janice?"

Devin blinked. "Aunt—wait, you know her?"

Jo's expression darkened, emotions flickering across
her face. "Yes . . . She raised me and Sara after our dad
was killed. But Sara and I moved out a couple years ago,
and we haven't . . . seen her since . . . had a falling

out . . . long story. I had no idea she knew anything about any of this."

Devin nodded, a realization clicking into place. "That explains it," he murmured. "When I first met her . . . when I told her Sara had been taken, she reacted fast. Like she already had skin in the game. But she never said she raised you—just that she knew your dad."

Mr. Mason's voice was low but clear. "She did know about all of this. But she wasn't allowed to say so."

Jo's eyes turned toward him.

"It was yer father," Mason continued, his voice low. "Jack gave her strict orders before he died. If anythin' were tae happen tae him, Janice was tae protect you and Sara—but never involve ye, not till the time was right."

He drew in a slow breath.

"She was told not tae force the path, Jo. Not tae interfere—not even wi' good intentions. Jack knew what Lily had been part of. He kent what was comin'. And he asked Janice tae do the hardest thing of all—wait. Wait, and let the will o' Thalion guide the timin' . . . not her own."

Jo's mouth parted slightly as it all settled in. No anger came this time—only a quiet, dawning understanding.

"She was trying to honor him," Jo said, almost to herself. "Even when it meant staying silent."

Mr. Mason nodded. "Aye. It was nae easy for her, lass."

Jo exhaled slowly, sitting back. "Then I guess I was wrong about her too."

A beat of silence passed.

Devin continued, reaching for his pack, his fingers tightening around the strap. "She showed me something while I was there. A journal. It had a name written across the front—Lilianna."

The room went still.

Mr. Mason stiffened, his hand clenching into a fist against the table. Then, in a hushed, almost reverent whisper, he muttered, "By Thalion's beard . . . it has been found."

Eli leaned forward. "So Janice has had Lily's journal this whole time? Kind of a brilliant move by Jack. Keeping it from anyone who had a direct connection to Lily. That means—"

Smith held up his hand, and he and Eli exchanged sharp glances.

Devin continued. "Janice confirmed everything you told us, Smith. That you were one of the Overseers of Valoria. That Azazel and someone named Seraphis cast a binding spell on you and stripped you of everything." He paused. "But the journal . . . it had your name in it, Smith. And not just your name—your true name."

Eli and Mr. Mason looked at each other and smiled.

Devin glanced down, then back at Smith. "And then she told me something else."

Jo leaned forward slightly.

"She told me I wasn't from here," Devin said. "That my bloodline traces back to Draegora. To the Shadowforged, just like you said. She also told me that Lily smuggled me out of Draegora when I was a baby, brought me here to Earth. She hoped that I would grow up, learn the truth, and be the one to help you, Smith. To reclaim your place in Valoria."

Silence settled over the room. Then Devin continued.

"That's how I got to the Library of Althea. She

said only someone with Draegoran blood could retrieve what was needed. And that if I made it out . . ." Devin unzipped his bag and pulled out the book, ". . . to bring this book to you."

Devin set it in the center of the table.

He looked at Smith, and for the first time since they met, his voice carried no trace of sarcasm. Only humility.

"I was wrong. About everything. About you. And I'm sorry."

Smith stared at him for a long moment before finally nodding. "You came back. That's what matters."

Smith's features softened.

Smith reached out and laid his hand on the book but didn't open it.

Jo leaned forward. "Now that we have what we need—what's next?"

Smith looked up, the firelight reflecting in his eyes. "We find Sara."

Devin nodded. "Whatever comes next—we're in. Both of us."

Jo met his eyes and gave a small smile. "All in."

Smith finally looked at each of them. "Then let's begin."

CHAPTER 53

A FEW WEEKS AGO: THE BOY AND THE ABYSSAL KEY

Seasons had come and gone, and the field where the FBI vehicle had crashed lay quiet. Tall grass swayed in the breeze, wildflowers bloomed in patches, and the remnants of the wreck—any remnants that mattered—had long been cleared away. Only whispers lingered, the tale of two vanished agents woven into local legends.

On one summer evening, beneath the glow of a setting sun, a young boy wandered into the field, his steps light but purposeful. The "haunted car wreck," as kids called it, had always piqued his curiosity. With a flashlight in hand, he combed through the tall grass, his fingers brushing the earth, seeking any relic or token from the past.

He crouched down, the last rays of sunlight catching on something buried beneath a thin layer of soil among the tall grass. He began to dig with his hand while holding his flashlight in the other. The flashlight's beam traced over a small, intricate object, half-hidden among the blades of grass. He brushed it off with his hand, the cool metal rough against his fingers. It was beautiful, strange—a small artifact covered in swirling, delicate carvings seeming to shimmer under his touch. He held it up to the flashlight.

For a long moment, he simply stared, entranced by

the way the carvings seemed to twist and shift, drawing his gaze deeper, as though they were alive. He turned it over in his palm, feeling an odd warmth seep into his skin.

Minutes slipped by, turning into hours. He wandered the field, toying with his newfound treasure. He traced its lines over and over, letting his mind drift, imagining tales of heroes and villains, of lost treasures and hidden powers. The night deepened, stars pricking the sky, and still he held the artifact, his fingers absently running over its surface.

Then, without warning, a sharp jolt shot through his hand—a sudden spark, like static, snapping him from his trance. He yelped, the artifact tumbling from his grasp into the grass. His heart raced, the shock lingering in his palm, tingling with an energy he couldn't name.

He took a step back, staring at the object as if it had turned into a live creature. The calm curiosity from before had twisted into something darker. But he couldn't leave it. He reached down, hesitating, fingers trembling as they hovered above the metal. Then, with a shaky breath, he picked it up again.

The moment his fingers closed around it, a faint red glow pulsed from its center. His pulse hammered as the light intensified, casting eerie shadows across the field and painting his skin in shades of crimson. It grew brighter, hotter and all he could see was the light, filling his mind, his whole being with a fierce, otherworldly warmth.

Then, from the shadows, a figure took shape.

A towering form loomed before him, the dark silhouette sharpening into cruel edges and hollow eyes, staring down at him with a look that pierced through to his soul. Azazel, released from the prison of the Abyss, now stood in the world of the living. Two other figures also emerged with him.

The boy's mouth went dry, words failing him as he looked up, paralyzed with fear and awe. Azazel's gaze swept over him, a slow, calculating look.

"Ah . . . what do we have here?" Azazel's voice was smooth, dripping with dangerous curiosity as he took in the sight of the boy. Azazel's gaze shifted to the object in the boy's hand, his eyes narrowing in recognition. He extended a slender, pale hand, motioning for the boy to release it. The boy's fingers hesitated but obeyed, the artifact slipping from his grasp into Azazel's waiting palm.

Azazel turned the key over, studying it with a dark gleam in his eyes. "So . . . Lily's final attempt," he murmured, "failed . . ."

He lifted his gaze, a flicker of triumph crossing his face as he observed the boy. The red glow now seemed to throb faintly within the boy himself.

Azazel's expression shifted, a spark of intrigue mingling with his cold satisfaction.

"Interesting," he muttered, glancing back at the key, then at the boy. "It seems the orb has chosen to leave its mark." He tilted his head, a glimmer of something close to admiration in his gaze. "You have been . . . altered, haven't you, child?"

The boy didn't respond, his wide eyes locked on Azazel, now glowing with a faint red hue that mirrored the energy pulsing within him.

As Azazel turned back toward the darkness, two

figures emerged from the shadows behind him. Sykes, his loyal operative, appeared first. Behind him stood a burly man with a scar slashing across his cheek, his eyes narrowing as he regarded the boy with suspicion.

"Sykes," he called, his voice a commanding whisper cutting through the night. "Take the boy with us. An unexpected boon."

Sykes stepped forward, his hand hovering near the boy's shoulder but hesitant, almost uncertain. He shot a quick glance at Azazel, silently asking for confirmation.

Azazel's gaze was fixed on the boy, a dark glint in his eye. "He carries the power of the orb within him," he murmured, half to himself. "A tether to what lies beyond, a conduit." He turned his cold smile toward Sykes. "He'll be . . . useful to our cause."

Sykes nodded, understanding flickering in his eyes as he reached out to guide the boy. The boy followed without resistance, his gaze still unfocused, his body stiff yet compliant.

The scarred man cast a wary glance at Azazel. "Are you certain about this, sir? Bringing a . . . vessel like him with us?"

Azazel's smile grew colder, a hint of satisfaction in his gaze as he looked at the boy. "He has been chosen by the power itself. He is bound to it now, just as it is bound to him."

Azazel turned, gesturing for Sykes and the scarred man to follow. Together, they melted into the shadows, the boy trailing after them.

As they disappeared into the night, the field fell silent once more.

CHAPTER 54

Sara blinked.

The guards hadn't locked it.

Slowly, cautiously, she stepped forward. Pressed her palm to the iron. It creaked open—just slightly—with a tired groan.

She peered into the hallway. Empty. Quiet.

Her pulse raced as she slipped through the opening, her bare feet silent on the cold stone. She glanced left, then right.

No one.

Still—the voice . . .

Try.

Sara froze. "What are you?" she whispered.

But she received no answer.

She turned back, intending to run—*get out while she could*—but then her gaze landed on the mural chamber.

And the boy.

Still painting.

Still trapped.

Her legs moved before her fear could stop them.

He didn't notice her at first.

His brush moved with slow, agonizing strokes—each one as if pulled from him by force. The mural was near completion. The central figure stood tall and cloaked, the red orb above his palm glowing faintly. The broken chain below now glimmered like molten iron.

Sara crossed the room, each step deliberate.

She knelt beside him.

"Hey," she whispered.

No response.

She reached out. Her fingers brushed his shoulder.

He flinched—then stilled.

Sara's hand glowed softly. A pulse of warmth moved from her palm into his skin. The blue light traced up her arm, dancing along faint veins of energy beneath her skin.

The boy's hand paused mid-stroke.

He blinked.

And for the first time, he spoke.

His voice was soft. Raw. "It's almost finished . . ."

Sara leaned in, heart pounding. "What is?"

He swallowed. "The mural. It's a door. A prison seal. When the last mark is drawn . . . he says the gate will open."

Sara's blood ran cold.

Her dream. The fortress. The broken chain. The robed figure with the orb.

This was it.

She stared into the boy's face—his eyes clearer now, the red shimmer fading just enough to see *him* underneath. The fear. The weariness. The *understanding*.

"Why are you doing this?" she asked, voice cracking.

"I don't want to," he whispered. "But when the power takes over . . . I can't stop."

And then—

Footsteps.

Fast. Sharp. Too close.

The boy's head twitched. Panic flickered across his face.

"You have to go," he said. "Before it takes me again."

Sara shook her head, hand still on his shoulder. "I'm not leaving you here."

His voice trembled. "Please. I can feel it coming back."

"I'll come back," she whispered.

The boy closed his eyes.

Sara's hand slipped away.

The red shimmer returned.

And the boy lowered his head, falling silent once more as the brush resumed its slow, haunting path to complete its mission.

Sara backed away from the mural chamber.

The boy had gone silent again, his eyes glazed with red. The shimmer of blue still tingled faintly in her fingertips, but the warmth was quickly replaced by dread.

Footsteps echoed down the hallway. Shouts followed—garbled, harsh.

They knew.

They're coming.

Sara turned and ran—then stopped as she heard the voice again.

Don't run. Try.

She pressed her back against the wall, heart hammering. Closed her eyes.

Let go.

She focused—not on the ground beneath her, but the *space* around her. The memory of how the guards moved. How they had floated in the cell.

She bent her knees. Pushed. Nothing.

Then, suddenly, blue energy flared at her feet—and she lifted.

No hesitation this time. Her body moved *with* the air, not against it.

She launched forward, awkwardly trying to steady herself. "Whoa, Whoa, this is weird . . ." Sara flailed in midair. After a moment, she steadied herself, stopped midair, and closed her eyes. Then she slowly leaned forward.

A blur of torchlight began to streak past as she slowly began to glide through the winding halls—smooth, fast, *silent*. Her feet off the ground.

Faster.

Faster.

A shout rang out behind her.

"They've seen me," she whispered.

She turned sharply down a corridor, sparks of blue scattering behind her like comet tails.

The voices grew louder. Closer.

Sara's gasped as she rounded another corner—

Another wall.

A dead end.

"No!"

She turned. The corridor behind her glowed with moving torchlight—guards closing in.

Then—

Paint the door.

The voice again.

Calm. Still.

She was trapped.

Her breathing grew rapid, panic settling in. But then the voice spoke again—

"Paint the door."

"What?" she whispered.

The voice was patient. "Paint the door."

Her fingers trembled. "I—I don't have paint."

But even as she said it . . .

A memory.

Her mural. At Walter's General Store.

How the colors had flowed from her hands.

Slowly, she lifted her fingers to the wall.

And something glowed at her fingertips.

Not paint.

Light.

It dripped like liquid gold as she dragged her fingers across the surface. A shape began to form. A frame. Then a handle. Then . . . a door.

It wasn't perfect—but it was there.

The guards' shouts rang out behind her.

Sara didn't think.

She grabbed the handle—and pulled.

To Sara's amazement, the door swung open.

And she stepped through.

The library was tense with conversation. Devin, Jo, Smith, Eli, and Mr. Mason sat around the large wooden table, maps and documents spread before them.

Jo leaned forward, her brow furrowed. "We need a way in that doesn't end with us all dead."

Devin exhaled sharply, rubbing his temples. "Easier said than done. Azazel isn't just gonna hand her over."

Eli, arms crossed, nodded. "We don't even know where she's being held. Could be his fortress. Could be a moving stronghold."

Mr. Mason sighed. "Aye, an' let's nae forget—Azazel wants the journal in exchange. He'll be expectin' Smith tae make the trade."

Smith, standing at the head of the table, tapped his fingers against the wood. "We're not making that trade." His tone was firm.

Jo exhaled. "Then how do we get her back?"

Devin, glancing at the old book in the center of the table. "We have this," he said quietly. "We didn't go through all that to drag it back here just to stare at it. This book—it's supposed to restore you, right? Restore you to your rightful name."

Smith's jaw tightened, his fingers pausing mid-tap.

"If you're stronger—if you're whole—maybe you can stand against Azazel. Maybe *that's* our edge."

For the first time, Smith's steady mask slipped just slightly. "It's . . . not that simple," he said softly. His eyes flicked to the book, and something unreadable crossed his face—a mix of longing, doubt, and quiet restraint. "There's a cost. And we're not using it—not yet."

Devin let out a frustrated breath. "Then what? We sit here and wait?"

Jo threw up her hands. "Okay, well, we don't even have the journal. Maybe we give Azazel a fake—stall for time."

Mr. Mason shook his head. "Azazel's nae a fool. He'd ken the difference."

Devin rolled his eyes. "No. I've got it. We bait him."

Smith arched a brow. "With what?"

Devin hesitated before answering. "Me."

The room went still.

Jo blinked. "Excuse me? You?"

Devin nodded. "Think about it. The red orb? My connection to it? Azazel already has his eyes on me. If I make enough noise, he'll come looking."

Eli frowned, opening his mouth to reply, but before he could—

Lucy's voice chimed in from Eli's laptop, which had been left open nearby.

"That idea has an 87.3 percent chance of failure."

The room paused.

Devin blinked. "Excuse me?"

Lucy continued. "Calculated based on previous encounters, estimated enemy response time, and the average survival rate of humans engaging in reckless heroism. Would you like me to round up?"

Devin exhaled sharply, rubbing his temples. "Great. Even the AI thinks I'm an idiot."

Jo snorted, trying and failing to hide her amusement.

Mr. Mason coughed into his fist, his shoulders shaking slightly.

Smith, ignoring the laughter, folded his arms. "That's a risk I'm not willing to take."

The conversation grew heated, voices layering over each other as they argued the best way to get to Sara. Devin pushed for a risky approach, Jo was skeptical, and Smith remained stone-faced, refusing to sacrifice anyone.

None of them noticed the painted door appear.

At the far end of the library, just near the towering bookshelves, a faint glow flickered—a door, brushed into existence by streaks of golden light, materialized against the stone wall.

Then—

Sara stumbled through.

She barely had time to process where she was before her knees buckled, and she caught herself against the nearest bookcase. Her heart still hammered in her chest.

Her wide eyes darted around the massive library, the sprawling bookshelves, the massive ocean view behind the glass doors. She quickly recognized it was Smith's library. How was she here?

Sara turned, her hands still covered in faint, shimmering colors. The door she had created had already begun to fade, the last traces of its magic evaporating into the air.

For a long second, she just stood there, her mind trying to catch up.

She was so overwhelmed by what had just happened that she barely registered the very loud discussion happening at the table in front of her.

"—we'll need a diversion," Devin was saying.

"We dinnae have time for games!" Mr. Mason countered.

Sara cleared her throat.

No reaction.

She tried again. "Uh . . . guys?"

Jo turned her head—and froze.

She stared at Sara, eyes wide, mouth slightly open.

Sara stared back.

For a moment, neither of them moved.

Then Jo shot to her feet so fast her chair scraped across the floor. "SARA?!"

Sara barely had time to brace herself before Jo

345

launched across the room and wrapped her in a crushing hug.

Devin, still mid-argument, blinked at Jo's sudden outburst. "What are you—?"

He turned. His jaw dropped.

Smith slowly straightened from where he had leaned on the table.

Eli's chair clattered as he stood.

Mr. Mason let out a soft breath, shaking his head. "By the stars . . ."

Sara—overwhelmed, confused, and still a little winded from her escape—was suddenly wrapped in Jo's arms, held so tightly she could barely breathe.

Sara let out a half-laugh, half-gasp. "O—Okay—breathing—still a thing—"

"You're—You're here?!" Jo's voice cracked with relief, disbelief, and every bottled-up emotion she hadn't allowed herself to feel. "How—?!"

Sara blinked, still dazed. "I—I don't know. I just—" She swallowed, her voice unsteady. "I just walked through."

Devin, still frozen, ran both hands down his face. "You just—walked through?!"

Sara nodded slowly.

Smith, arms still folded, exhaled deeply, his gaze sharp and unreadable. But his voice, when he finally spoke, was gentle. "Welcome back."

The room fell into stunned silence.

Then Jo pulled back, hands gripping Sara's arms. "Are you okay? Did he hurt you? How did you get away? What happened?!"

Sara looked at their stunned, disbelieving faces.

Then, for the first time since she had been taken, she felt something strong inside her.

Something whole.

She straightened her shoulders, her voice steadying.

"I think . . . I just found out what I can do."

CHAPTER 55

The scent of roasted vegetables and simmering broth filled the air as the group gathered around Smith's long wooden table. The crackling fire in the hearth cast a warm glow over the ancient bookshelves, making the vast library feel almost cozy.

Sara sat between Jo and Devin, a steaming bowl in front of her, but she barely touched it. The events of the past day still weighed heavy and tangled in her mind.

She glanced toward the massive door-wall of glass, where the ocean stretched endlessly beyond the library's walls. The sky, once a brilliant shade of gold, had deepened into burnished orange and violet shades, the sun sinking slowly beyond the horizon. Even here, where the air smelled of salt and warmth, where the breeze whispered through the palm trees, the temperature shifted with the setting sun.

Sara pulled her sleeves down over her hands, suppressing a small shiver as the library's interior, seemingly untouched by the tropical air outside, cooled along with the fading light. The fire in the hearth crackled, its flickering glow casting long shadows against the towering bookshelves.

She exhaled, glancing at Jo and Devin before murmuring, "It's strange, you know? The sun still sets here."

Jo looked up from her bowl. "What do you mean?"

Sara's gaze drifted back to the glass. "The ocean.

The cliffs. It's like we're in some endless summer, but even here . . . the day ends. It gets colder at night. It feels real, but also like it shouldn't be."

Smith, seated across from them, rested his hands against the wooden table. "Because it is real," he said simply.

Jo leaned in, her arm brushing Sara's. "I'll fill you in," she murmured softly. "A lot happened while you were gone."

She told Sara about the Healing Hallows: how she'd walked through a forest bathed in silver mist, where the leaves shimmered like mirrors and showed her memories. She spoke about touching the blue orb, feeling its energy surge through her fingers, how its blue light pulsed with a warmth that felt familiar.

Jo's voice softened as she described the crystal bow—how it had appeared after she faced herself and laid down her old defenses.

Sara softened, placing a hand on her sister's arm.

Devin cleared his throat. "And me? Well, turns out I was chosen for a light jog through hell—otherwise known as the Library of Althea."

Jo rolled her eyes teasingly. "Oh, here we go."

Devin grinned before continuing. "Imagine a massive library filled with books that try to kill you. I had to pass all these ridiculous tests, dodge an actual death waterfall, and, oh yeah—turns out, I got the book we needed?"

Sara stared at him, "Book?"

"Yeah, and I'm the only one who could get it," Devin added.

Jo shook her head. "And he's so much more humble," she said sarcastically.

"What book?" asked Sara.

Devin turned to Smith, who had been silent, listening. "Tell her, Smith."

The room got quite. Smith sat with his hands clasped together, staring at the table as if gathering words from the wood grain.

He inhaled deeply. "There was a time when I was not Smith." His voice was quiet but steady. "A time when I walked among the Twelve as Thariel, Overseer of the blue orbs. and Guardian of Thalion's Council."

Jo, Devin, and Sara exchanged glances.

Smith continued, "But power is a dangerous thing. Even for those who believe themselves above corruption."

He lifted his gaze, but it wasn't to the others in the room—it was to the portrait of the young girl above the fireplace.

"I was loyal to Thalion. I swore my life to him, as did the others in the Council. And Azazel . . ." Smith sighed. "He was one of us, once. Respected, even admired. Until the whispers started. Until Seraphis partnered with him and believed they could offer something greater. 'Why serve,' they asked, 'when we could rule?'"

Smith let out a slow breath, his eyes dark with memory. "I dismissed it at first. We all did. Thalion was our king—his wisdom was beyond us. His vision stretched farther than ours could ever see. But Seraphis . . . he had a gift. He could twist truth so finely that, if you weren't careful, you'd mistake it for wisdom."

Sara swallowed hard. "What did he do to you?"

Smith's lips pressed together.

"Seraphis wove a spell, subtle but insidious. It clung to my thoughts, twisted my perceptions. Every word

Thalion spoke, every order he gave . . . it began to feel wrong. Corrupt. As though I had been blind and Seraphis had shown me the truth."

His fingers tightened. "I nearly believed it. I stood at the edge of betrayal, teetering on the precipice, not realizing how close I was to falling."

Jo's expression darkened. "But you didn't betray Thalion."

Smith shook his head. "No. But by the time I saw through the deception, it was already too late."

The fire crackled louder, sending embers swirling into the air.

"Seraphis and Azazel stripped me of my name that day."

Devin sat forward. "How?"

Smith exhaled. "The Council of Thalion each bore a Seal of Authority. It resided in us—not just as a symbol but as a force that bound us to the kingdom and to each other. It was our right, our burden, and our power."

His eyes darkened. "But when I stood against Seraphis and Azazel who had already turned . . . Serephis had already reached over to me and took My Ring. My Seal. My authority. My name."

A long pause.

"The moment it was gone, I could feel it. I became . . . lesser. Powerless. The weight of my voice, my command—it meant nothing . . . and I started to believe . . . I was nothing. I had been Thariel, but then, I began to believe I was no one."

Sara's throat tightened. "That's when you took the name of Smith."

Smith nodded. "When they also took my ring—the

351

last remnant of my authority—they cast it into a realm I could never access. One that my keys could never unlock."

Devin's brows furrowed. "And that's where the book comes in? The one I retrieved?"

Smith continued, "That book holds the key to opening the portal to the realm where my Ring is being kept under a watchful eye." Smith looked at Devin. "Seraphis hid the book away in the Library of Althea. He made certain only a Draegoran warrior could retrieve it, knowing that if the Shadowforged were truly lost, then no one ever would."

Silence thickened the air.

Then, Sara spoke, her voice hesitant. "But . . . that would make Devin . . ."

All eyes turned to her, but it was Mr. Mason who answered, "Aye . . ."

"Lily, your mother, knew what Azazel an' Seraphis were doin' tae the Shadowforged. She knew the bloodline was bein' twisted—turned into his army. But she also knew what the Draegoran warriors once were, before Azazel's corruption."

His weathered hands rested against the table, his knuckles white. "So she saved one."

The firelight flickered against Smith's face, casting deep shadows across his sharp features.

"He smuggled a child out. Kept 'im hidden on Earth. Knew that one day, he'd be the only one who could retrieve the book that holds the key to restoring Thariel's Seal."

Sara's gaze slowly slid to Devin.

Devin exhaled, offering a small, wry smile. "Yeah. Me."

Smith's eyes softened. "Because of your mother, Sara—because she believed when I no longer could—Devin was able to help me reclaim a chance I thought I'd lost forever."

A long silence stretched across the table.

Finally, Smith straightened, resting his hands firmly on the book before him. "I have to go into the realm."

Jo's head snapped up. "We'll go with you!"

Smith looked at Jo and smiled softly. "Thank you, Jo, but this task is for me alone."

He reached forward, placing a hand on the ancient book Devin had retrieved.

"My ring—my Seal of Authority—is locked away in another realm. If I'm going to fight Azazel, if I'm going to protect you all . . . I need everything back . . ."

Sara set her spoon down.

"There's something else you need to know," she began, her voice quiet but firm.

The room stilled. Smith, Eli, and Mr. Mason exchanged looks, sensing the shift in tone.

Sara took a deep breath. "There was a boy."

Eli straightened immediately. "A boy?"

Sara nodded. "He was trapped in Azazel's lair with me. But . . . he wasn't like me. He was . . . different. At first, he seemed afraid, but it was like he was under a spell. And it had everything to do with the red orb. Azazel was using it on him. Not just to control him but to change him. And now, he's painting . . . murals like me."

Jo frowned. "Painting?"

Sara nodded.

A sharp breath from Eli made Sara look up. Eli nodded slowly, glancing at Smith before turning back to Sara. "We've seen him before as well. In a video a few days back and again at the warehouse in Brakenridge Hollow."

Sara's stomach lurched. "What?"

Smith exhaled, rubbing a hand over his chin. "Lucy pulled a satellite feed from a field outside Muxley days ago. We saw him. A boy, standing alone. The energy readings from that night—they were off the charts."

Jo sat up straighter. "Yeah, Sara and I read about that online a few days ago! A boy went missing out past Mulligan Road. So that's why he disappeared? Azazel took him?"

Smith nodded. "The boy found an object in that field—an object that had been missing for years. A magical device called the Abyssal Key. Your mother, Lily, used it to trap Azazel in a place we call The Abyss."

Jo's hand reached for Sara's as tears formed in both of their eyes.

Smith continued. "It was during that event that your mother used it with her dying breath . . ." Smith paused as a tear rolled down his cheek, ". . . to imprison Azazel and protect you, Sara . . . .and really . . . .everyone . . . .until recently, when the boy found it. He accidentally activated it, opening the portal and freeing Azazel. The power of Azazel's Ring must have touched the boy when he was released. Azazel then took him into his service."

Jo wiped her yes. "That's where those two FBI agents disappeared years ago too, isn't it?"

A deep sigh came from Mr. Mason.

"Aye, lass." He folded his hands together, his brow furrowed. "When those agents collected the evidence from your mum's crime scene . . ." He hesitated, his voice dipping lower. "One of the objects they found was the Abyssal Key."

Jo nodded.

"They had no idea what it was," Mr. Mason continued. "They put it in their car along with the rest of the evidence and set off tae deliver it back to their facility for secure holdin'—but . . ." he exhaled through his nose, "somewhere along the way, the key activated."

The weight of his words settled like lead in the room.

"The portal opened, lass," Mr. Mason said gently. "An' it swallowed them whole. Just . . . gone."

Sara shuddered, imagining it.

"And the car?" Jo asked. "That's all they found, right?"

"Found abandoned in the very field where the boy disappeared," Smith confirmed. "The evidence that had been inside . . . scattered everywhere."

Eli ran a hand over his face. "And the Abyssal Key was lost until the boy stumbled upon it."

A thick silence filled the space.

Finally, Sara spoke. "Now, he's being used to bring Azazel's army into this world . . . and his final piece is almost here."

Smith met her gaze. "What?"

Sara's fingers clenched. "One night, while being held captive, I had a dream. Or . . . at least, I think it was a dream. I saw the boy painting. But then, in the mural—something moved. A figure. It wasn't just part of the painting. It was alive."

Jo stiffened.

Sara's breath came faster. "And then . . . this figure . . . he lifted his hand . . . and the red orbs just . . . appeared . . . as if he created them out of nothing."

Eli cursed under his breath.

"And when I woke up, the figure I saw in my dream?" Sara hesitated. "It was taking shape on the wall the boy was painting."

Smith whispered the name like a curse. "Seraphis."

Mr. Mason pushed back from the table, pacing. "Aye . . . by Thalion's name—Azazel's found the realm he was imprisoned in."

Sara's voice trembled. "What does that mean?"

Mr. Mason turned back to her, his expression grim. "It means Seraphis is nae hidden from Azazel anymore. Somehow, he's found him—and the lad's been used to paint the doorway to the cell we once sealed him in."

He paused, looking down like he was piecing together a puzzle. "With you dreamin' about it, lass, it seems Seraphis is already whisperin' through the cracks between realms. But soon enough . . . ."

He exhaled slow, heavy.

"Soon enough, he'll be takin' form in our world. And if Azazel succeeds in fully summonin' him . . . ."

Smith's voice cut through, sharp as steel. "Then he'll have an unlimited supply of red orbs."

Jo's stomach churned. "And with those . . . ."

Eli finished her sentence. "There will be no limit to the number of portals Azazel can activate. Azazel won't just have a link through all the realms—he'll rule them."

The finality of his words sank into the air, cold and unshakable.

Smith stood, his gaze locked onto the book resting on the table. "Then we don't have much time."

CHAPTER 56

Devin ran his fingers over the book's worn leather cover. Symbols shimmered faintly beneath his touch. He drew his hand back slightly.

"Yeah . . . not opening that again," he muttered, remembering all too well the surge of wind and power it had stirred back in the Library of Althea.

Eli moved quickly.

With a calm but deliberate motion, he took the book from Devin's hands. "We need Lucy to scan this first."

Devin raised an eyebrow. "It's a book. Since when does your AI need to scan *books*?"

Eli's expression was unreadable. "It's a book that led you through an ancient labyrinth filled with trials designed for warriors of a forgotten bloodline. A book that was hidden away so no one could access it. It's not just a book, Devin."

Devin shrugged. "Fair point."

Eli placed the book on a scanning platform. The sleek silver device hummed softly. A few beeps later, Lucy's voice crackled to life from the speakers.

"Analyzing . . . processing . . . The structure of this book is not merely textual. It contains a dimensional tether. The enchantments suggest it is bound to a spatial vault."

Jo's brow furrowed. "A vault?"

Smith leaned forward, hands laced together. "Not just a vault. A prison. A place beyond time and space where lost things—stolen things—are kept."

Mr. Mason nodded gravely. "Aye. It's called The Meridian."

Jo's gaze turned to Smith. "And what Azazel and Seraphis took from you is there?"

Smith exhaled slowly. "Yes."

Sara hesitated. "When will you be back?"

Smith hesitated just long enough for Jo and Devin to notice.

Then Smith responded, "Not long." His expression softened, just for a moment. "At least . . . that's the plan."

Eli stepped forward, sliding a small device onto the table. "Lucy will monitor energy fluctuations while you're inside. If something feels off, we'll pull you back."

Smith placed his hand on Eli's shoulder and gave him a look. "That won't work there. You know this."

Eli frowned as mist filled his eyes. "Just be careful, friend. The Meridian is a closed realm, Smith. If you don't retrieve the ring . . ." His voice dropped. "There's no coming back."

Sara's eyes widened. "Wait—what?" she blurted, sitting forward. "What do you mean, there's no coming back?!"

Eli turned to her, his voice low and careful. "The book takes him *in*, but only the ring can bring him back out."

Sara's heart thudded painfully in her chest. "So . . . if you fail . . ."

Smith offered her a faint, reassuring smile. "Then I suppose I'd better succeed."

Jo and Devin looked at each other. Then Devin reached out his hand to Smith, "Good luck."

Smith shook his hand and then gave each a small, steady nod—quiet, resolute, as though memorizing their faces.

Then he exhaled, walked over, and took the book off of the scanner. He laid it on the table and placed both hands on the book. Smith opened his mouth and spoke a phrase in a tongue that Jo, Sara, and Devin did not recognize.

A low hum resonated from the book, growing in intensity.

The pages turned on their own, flipping rapidly until they stopped at the center, where an inscription in glowing blue letters pulsed with life.

And then—

A vortex tore open, swallowing Smith whole.

The air in the chamber crackled, heavy with the stench of smoldering iron and ancient rot. A pulsing crimson orb sat cupped in Azazel's palm, casting eerie shadows across the mural. The painting twisted, shifted—alive.

Azazel's ringed fingers flexed, pressing the orb forward. "Come forth," he growled softly, voice thick with anticipation.

The chamber shook, tremors rippling through ancient stone. Veins of fiery red fractured the mural. A low, resonant whisper drifted outward, seeping like mist through the cracks.

"At last . . ."

A gauntleted hand, pulsing with dark energy, breached the painted veil. The wall shattered outward, shards clattering like crystalline bones. Seraphis stepped forward—towering, majestic, sinister. Black and crimson robes flowed like spilled blood. Silver eyes gleamed cold beneath his hood; upon his brow rested an intricate crown of interlocking metal.

Azazel smirked, a flash of triumph in his eyes. "Seraphis."

The towering figure inclined his head slightly, voice gravelly, carrying a deceptive humility. "Lord Azazel . . . By your will, I return."

Azazel strode forward, confidence radiating with every step. "Not a moment too soon. We have unfinished work, you and I."

Seraphis made no immediate reply, instead scanning the chamber slowly, as if cataloging every detail— the Voidwalkers lining the walls, and finally, the small empty cell.

Azazel's smile faltered slightly as Seraphis lingered there.

"The girl?" Seraphis asked quietly, voice unsettlingly calm.

Azazel's looked down. "Escaped. The daughter of Lilianna wields the blue orb's power. She doesn't fully understand it yet—but she grows stronger by the moment. A complication, but temporary."

Seraphis considered this silently, his expression unreadable beneath the shadowed hood. Then, softly, he pressed, ". . . And the journal?"

Azazel's eyes darkened further. "Still hidden. But we are close—I can sense it. An opportunity will present itself soon enough.

Seraphis retorted, " Without that journal, our ultimate goal remains . . ."

Azazel cut him off, "I am perfectly aware of what that journal means."

Seraphis considered that silently, his expression unreadable beneath the shadowed hood.

The uncomfortable silence broke as one of Azazel's operatives hurried forward, bowing quickly. "Lord Azazel, we received a report from the tunnels beneath Muxley's council hall—two intruders overheard the meeting. We pursued them back to a farmhouse. They fled into a protected realm."

Azazel's gaze sharpened. "A farmhouse? Who were these intruders—Smith's people?"

The operative hesitated, exchanging anxious glances with his companions. "My lord . . . we do not believe so. They weren't recognized as part of Smith's known associates. A man and a woman—the woman, none of us had seen before. The man, perhaps a local reporter."

Azazel's eyes narrowed dangerously. "Yet, they had access to a protected realm?"

Seraphis interjected quietly, tone carefully measured. "It would seem Smith's circle is larger than we believed. A most unfortunate revelation."

Azazel inhaled slowly, suppressing a wave of irritation. He fixed a piercing gaze on the operative. "And how, exactly, did you handle this?"

The operative swallowed hard, then quickly answered, "We burned it down, my lord. Trapped them inside—surely they're good as dead."

Azazel lifted a hand sharply, cutting off the man's eager reassurance. He hesitated, instinct gnawing at him, an unease he couldn't fully articulate. Finally, he forced himself to speak:

"Good," he said, though the word felt brittle, false on his tongue. ". . . Yet keep watch on the site."

The operative bowed hastily, retreating gratefully to the shadows.

Azazel exhaled, turning again toward Seraphis. The Voidwalkers surrounding them stirred restlessly. Azazel's eyes narrowed dangerously. "Smith, the girl, and their allies—they remain a thorn. Locate them, destroy them, and FIND Lily's journal."

Seraphis inclined his head again, his voice deep, reverberating with hidden meaning. "As you command."

Azazel turned abruptly, anger seething beneath the surface. His eyes settled on the boy, who stood nearby, pale-faced and shaking slightly. "Boy—come here."

The boy stepped forward hesitantly. Azazel gripped his chin roughly, forcing eye contact. The boy winced but didn't avert his gaze completely.

"You spoke to her, didn't you? The girl?" Azazel's voice dripped venom.

The boy trembled but didn't speak. His silence was defiant, quietly courageous.

Azazel shoved him away sharply. "Keep an eye on him," he growled to a Voidwalker nearby. "The girl's influence weakens my hold. We still have need of him."

Seraphis's silver eyes narrowed subtly beneath his hood. His gaze followed the boy curiously.

Azazel turned back to the operatives who'd failed in holding Sara. "Step forward."

They froze, sensing doom.

Slowly, trembling, they obeyed.

Azazel gave Seraphis a cold glance. A silent command. Seraphis raised his hand, conjuring effortlessly a swirling red orb, its glow illuminating the chamber with sinister light. The operatives collapsed, pleading, begging for mercy even as their forms unraveled, souls drawn agonizingly into the red sphere.

Their distorted, tortured faces flickered briefly upon the orb's surface, frozen in eternal horror.

Seraphis calmly tossed the orb back into the mural. The painted wall devoured it greedily, echoes of their screams rippling into silence.

Azazel nodded approvingly. "Impressive."

Seraphis turned slowly. "Failure demands consequence."

Azazel chuckled, cold amusement returning. "Indeed. Remember that—all of you. Now go. Find the journal. Find the girl. Find Smith and bring him to me crawling."

As the operatives scattered, Seraphis approached Azazel, voice lowered. "Do you believe these intruders at the town hall meeting pose a threat?"

Azazel scowled deeply. "No, but something feels off. Lily's bloodline has always been resourceful." He paused. "The fact that they had a protected realm reveals one that we missed. Somehow it was kept veiled to us. Whoever they are, they have a role in this somehow—but the fire ensures they can't leave easily. Still . . ."

Seraphis nodded slowly, thoughtfully. "You sense there is more?"

Azazel's lips twisted bitterly. "Instinct. Vigilance has kept me alive thus far."

Seraphis' silver eyes gleamed faintly in the dim torchlight. "Then trust that instinct, Lord Azazel. Trust it completely."

Azazel straightened, shoulders tense, nodding curtly. "Yes. Come. We must accelerate our plans."

He swept from the chamber, cloak billowing dramatically.

Behind him, unseen, Seraphis allowed himself the faintest hint of a cold, knowing smile. He glanced back once, his gaze resting thoughtfully on the boy, who stood pale and shaken.

And quietly, so only he could hear, Seraphis murmured, "Yes. We must."

CHAPTER 57

Smith landed with a jolt, his boots scraping against a worn stone floor.

Before him stretched the twilight expanse of The Meridian—a marketplace built from the ruins of a thousand forgotten places floating between the stars. Massive stone arches, crumbling but impossibly suspended, framed a city of shifting pathways, spiraling towers, and drifting platforms.

It was a trading post between worlds, where time had no master and lost things had a price.

And it was crawling with Voidwalkers.

Smith kept his hood low, moving swiftly through the throng of travelers, thieves, and smugglers who milled about.

The stall was exactly as Smith remembered—a chaotic clutter of stolen artifacts, enchanted weapons, and relics pilfered from fallen civilizations.

And behind it, perched like a vulture, was a man that Smith hadn't seen in centuries—and yet, hadn't forgotten. Finklestover Warren.

A spindly creature draped in layers of mismatched finery, the trader had a sharp nose that hooked downward, his skin pale with a faint gray tint. At least half a dozen rings adorned his bony fingers, each glinting with a different type of magic. But it was his eyes that were most unsettling—small, darting, and sharp with the kind of cunning that came only from years of outwitting desperate buyers and deceiving dangerous men.

He never chose a side.

He never owed loyalty.

That's why he was still alive.

Smith didn't speak his name. To do so would risk recognition, and right now, he needed to be just another trader looking for wares.

The short, wiry man grinned the moment he saw Smith. "A new customer, I presume?"

Smith kept his voice casual. "I deal in relics. I hear you're the best trader here."

Finklestover chuckled, rubbing his hands together. "Oh, flattery will get you everywhere, my friend. Now, what is it you seek? Artifacts? Ancient knowledge? Perhaps something a bit more . . . volatile?"

Smith allowed his gaze to drift over the artifacts, pretending to search.

A sealed glass case containing an obsidian dagger—its hilt wrapped in what looked like sinew and etched with runes he recognized.

He nodded toward it. "What's the price on that?"

Finklestover's grin widened. "Ah, a fine piece. But something tells me . . . you're looking for something far more valuable."

Smith tilted his head. "Am I?"

Finklestover leaned forward, eyes glinting. "Oh, indeed. Because no one comes to me without seeking the impossible."

He turned, moving to a small iron chest at the back of the stall.

Smith's heart steadied. This was it.

Finklestover unlocked the chest with a whispered incantation, and the air thrummed with unseen power. The lid creaked open, revealing—

Not the ring.

But a different artifact.

A golden amulet, shaped like an eye, with an emerald gemstone pulsing at its center.

Smith hid his disappointment instantly.

He forced himself to smile, crossing his arms. "Not bad."

Finklestover's smirk mirrored his own. "Not bad? This is a relic from the lost empire of Vaelthorne. A single drop of its magic can rewrite fate itself. And yet, I sense . . . it's not what you're after."

Smith feigned hesitation. "I deal in power. This looks useful . . . but I'm interested in something a bit more . . . personal."

Finklestover's grin faltered for a second. Just a second.

And Smith saw it.

Does he know what I want? But he's hiding it?

Smith took a slow step forward, lowering his voice. "You're a man of business, Warren. I'm here to make a deal."

Finklestover studied him carefully. "And what, exactly, do you offer in return?"

Smith glanced toward the Voidwalkers at the edge of the market.

They were waiting.

Watching.

If they saw Finklestover handing over the ring, the deal would be over before it began.

CHAPTER 58

The waves outside whispered, crashing against the shore beyond the glass. Inside, the glow of a low fire flickered across bookshelves and worn stone walls.

Eli sat hunched in a leather chair, poring over blueprints of something ancient. Jo stood by the window, arms folded, her gaze pinned to the horizon where the sun melted into the sea.

Mr. Mason moved quietly in the corner, his hands steady as he brewed tea.

Sara lay curled on the couch, a knit blanket draped over her like a second skin. The flames cast dancing shadows across her cheeks. Devin sat nearby, elbows resting on his knees, his eyes lingering on the blue orb tucked into an alcove next to the fireplace. It pulsed softly.

"He'll find it," Devin murmured to no one in particular.

"Aye," Mr. Mason replied. "He must."

After a while, one by one, the group turned in for the night. Sara's breathing slowed and the fire dimmed as she drifted off to sleep.

Sara found herself standing in a field of silver grass beneath a violet sky. The wind didn't move her hair—it passed through her like she was both there and not.

Then—just ahead—a familiar brick wall appeared out of nothing. It was Walter's Market. Or at least, a dream version of it. The structure floated without foundation, its red bricks worn and cracked. And there, painted across its surface, was the mural.

She recognized it instantly.

The woman in flowing robes, standing beneath an ancient, gnarled tree. Two towering figures loomed faintly behind her, their faces always hidden. In this dream, however, the paint on the mural began to move—swirling gently as if stirred by wind or breath.

Sara stepped closer.

The woman's eyes—blinked.

Then, slowly, she stepped out of the mural, the paint dripping from her robes like dew sliding off silk. She landed softly on grass, her presence rippling through the dream like a pebble dropped in water.

Her face, once obscured by shadow, was now half-lit and luminous. Her beauty was arresting, her eyes like constellations. At her waist, an emerald jewel glowed—pulsing faintly in rhythm with Sara's own breath.

No words were spoken aloud, but Sara heard her all the same.

"Begin."

The mural behind her faded. The sky turned a deeper violet.

The world shifted.

Sara now stood on the broad wooden terrace over-looking the moonlit garden. A waterfall trickled some-where nearby.

To her left, she saw Aunt Janice and a man seated at a wooden table. Their mouths moved, though no words reached her ears.

Ahead, among the flowerbeds, stood three blank walls, positioned apart.

The woman from the mural now stood at her side.
She raised her hand—not to speak but to direct.
"Paint."

Sara's feet carried her forward without command.
Her arms began to glow. Wisps of blue energy swirled
around her wrists, trailing down to her fingertips like
ink suspended in water.

She lifted hands.

As she reached toward the first wall, her hand moved
without thinking. The image unfolded like memory:

Devin, clothed in royal garb, stood before a city of
white towers, gleaming under a golden sun. Hills rolled
around it, and flags of cobalt and gold snapped in the
wind. He looked older. Weathered. Proud.

Behind him glowed an ancient seal. Sara knew that
it was the seal of Draegora.

Then—from a deep place inside Sara, emerged words
that she could not stop from coming out. She shouted
the words, "A crown unclaimed shall rise again, but first
must fall the shadowed men."

Sara's dream surged forward into a storm of visions.
Fire. Screams. Blades clashing. An army stood before her.
Sara gasped as she saw armored warriors—once noble—
standing shoulder to shoulder.

The Shadowforged.

Then—corruption. One by one, the red glow
consumed them. Their armor warped. Their eyes
dulled. They twisted into Voidwalkers, monstrous and
hollow.

A single child dropped a sword glowing faintly blue.
It hit the ground and vanished into ash.

Sara stumbled back, turning toward the second wall.

From the corner of her vision, she saw Aunt Janice, panic in her eyes, clutching a leather-bound journal.

"Help! We're trapped!" she cried. She painted quickly—desperately—a narrow hallway, dim and claustrophobic, ending in a flickering sign: "MOTEL HAVEN."

Janice reached toward her as the mural came to life. But then—faded.

A soft voice drew her attention.

A young girl, maybe eight, barefoot and wide-eyed, stood in a pool of moonlight, holding a book too big for her hands.

She closed it gently and looked at Sara. She walked toward the last wall.

As she stepped forward, she aged—each step accelerating her into young adulthood. She stopped beside the blank mural, turning back with familiar eyes.

"Daughter of Lilianna," she said, "I must ride."

Sara's arm moved before her thoughts could catch up.

She painted a horse—tall, noble, cloaked in starlight. Its mane flickered like fire. The final stroke shimmered—and the horse stepped forward, alive.

The girl mounted swiftly.

Sara reached out. "Wait! Who are you—?"

The girl smiled, her face achingly familiar. Then she galloped through the mural and vanished.

Before Sara could react, the world turned white. The sky cracked open.

From a cloud of mist and light, a presence descended—not quite human, not quite spirit. The being radiated kindness and terrible power. Its voice, a tapestry of many:

"What you have seen here—
What was,
What is,
And what is to come."

"When the ring returns,
And the name is restored,
It will be the sign:
Your life is about to change.
Do not be afraid."

When the presence finished speaking to Sara, rushing water roared behind her.

Sara jolted awake and sat upright, her chest rising sharply with every breath.

The fire beside her had dimmed to embers.

Then she heard a soft clink.

Mr. Mason stood beside the fire, pouring hot water into a teacup, steam curling upward.

He glanced over his shoulder with a warm smile. "Good mornin', lass," he said gently. "Sleep well?"

Sara blinked, still half in the dream. Her hands shimmered faintly—blue light fading with each heartbeat.

"I dreamed," she whispered. "And I think . . . we need to prepare."

CHAPTER 59

Back inside the hidden realm inside the garage, Janice and Halbridge waited in tense silence. Hours had passed since the blaze above had collapsed the building, sealing them inside this protected space.

Halbridge paced near the far bookshelf, running a hand through his hair. He turned sharply toward Janice. "How *are* we supposed to get out?"

Even if we survive down here, we've got the video—the proof from the council meeting—but it does us no good here."

His gaze turned toward the far chamber, where the mural Devin had passed was. "Could we use that? Could we go through it the same way Devin did?"

"No," she said quickly, shaking her head. "That mural is keyed to Devin right now. We have no idea where we would end up. If we tried to use it, we'd—"

Before she could finish, a sudden, fierce wind tore through the room. Papers flew off shelves, books toppled. The walls and floor seemed to shift, twisting slightly. The air filled with a sweet fragrance.

Then, as suddenly as it began, it ceased.

Halbridge spun around, bewildered. "What . . . What just happened?"

Janice stood perfectly still. "Something shifted. The room isn't the same."

Before Halbridge could question further, a faint, steady glow flickered from the garden below the terrace.

Janice stepped closer, staring in disbelief. "The garden," she whispered. "Something's happening down there."

Without hesitation, Janice moved toward the staircase leading down into the garden, Halbridge close behind. They emerged beneath the pale moonlight, its glow competing with a brighter, ethereal illumination from behind the flowerbeds. Three large murals now adorned the old stone walls, glowing with the unmistakable pulse of portal magic.

Janice stepped slowly forward.

The first mural showed a young man standing tall and strong, eyes focused ahead, red energy faintly visible in his outstretched hand. Devin. Older, stronger. Resolute.

"He made it," Janice said softly, her voice trembling with relief.

Halbridge glanced at the mural, confused. "How do you know?"

"Because this isn't just art—it's prophecy. Devin's destiny is unfolding. This proves he made it through the Library and onto the next stage. Lily was right about him."

She moved to the next mural: a girl on horseback, riding fiercely, wind whipping through her hair. Janice gave the scene a knowing nod, eyes thoughtful. "It looks as if my part in this story is almost complete."

Halbridge raised an eyebrow. "What does that mean?"

She smiled faintly. "It means this story is shifting beyond us now. The younger generation—Sara, Devin, Jo—they're stepping forward. Our role is becoming clear. We must ensure the truth reaches those who can act."

Finally, they came to the last mural. It depicted a long hallway, warmly lit, ending in a doorway beneath a familiar flickering neon motel sign.

Halbridge's eyes widened in recognition. "Wait—isn't that the old motel up in the northern part of Muxley? That's across town."

Janice's expression filled with quiet triumph. "Sara painted this. She came through for us. She's given us a way out."

Halbridge blinked, disbelief mingling with cautious hope. "A way out?"

Janice stepped toward the mural, lightly touching its painted surface, feeling its soft pulse of magic. "Yes. We obviously can't leave the way we came. But this mural—is a portal. A hidden path."

Halbridge stepped closer, looking skeptical. "We're seriously going to walk through a wall?"

Janice glanced back at him, eyes twinkling faintly despite the stakes. "Yes. We are. Like Devin . . . remember?"

Halbridge shook his head, disbelief melting into reluctant awe. "Yeah . . . Wow. This is really how we're getting out, huh?"

Janice nodded firmly. "It's not just a way out. It's a path forward. We take the evidence from the town hall meeting and Lily's journal. We get to safety, and we get this truth out to the public."

He exhaled sharply. "All right, then. Let's go walk through a painting."

Janice hurried back up the stairs, grabbed the journal and the recording, then returned without a word.

She and Halbridge stepped together toward the

mural, its glow intensifying as they approached, enveloping them in a soft, comforting brilliance.

As they crossed through, the image rippled—like the surface of water stirred by a breeze—before settling, returning to stillness behind them.

CHAPTER 60

The moment Finklestover Warren leaned forward, Smith knew he was being sized up. The trader was a master of reading intentions, a man who had survived centuries not by power but by cunning. He was sniffing out desperation.

Which meant Smith needed to play the part of a man with too many options and not enough time.

Smith exhaled sharply, rolling his shoulders as if he were bored. His eyes drifted over the assortment of trinkets, enchanted weapons, and volatile magical contraband littering the stall. Not too fast. Not too slow. Keep him guessing.

Finally, he nodded toward an iron chest, its lid partially open, revealing an array of relics inside. Some were useless. Some were priceless. And nestled among them— just barely visible beneath the clutter—was his ring.

The deep sapphire blue stone, infused with the essence of Valoria, flickered in the dim glow of the Meridian's eerie twilight.

But Smith didn't react.

He barely looked at it.

Instead, he pointed to something else entirely.

A set of bone dice, etched with ancient runes.

Finklestover's sharp eyes narrowed ever so slightly, but his grin remained intact. "An interesting choice."

Smith smirked. "Luck's been bad lately. Thought I'd change that."

Finklestover tilted his head, weighing the response. Then, with a slow, almost lazy movement, he picked up the dice, letting them tumble over his fingers like an old habit.

"This set's been through many hands," he murmured. "Some left rich, some left cursed. The question is—what will you leave with?"

Finklestover's grin didn't waver, but Smith saw the gears turning. The trader was always hungry for the bigger deal. He wasn't interested in selling a set of dice if he thought he could sell something more valuable.

Which meant Smith needed to let him make that decision himself.

The trader sighed dramatically, setting the dice down. "Perhaps I misjudged you. A mere gambler, not a man of fine tastes."

Smith feigned mild amusement. "Oh, I've got fine tastes."

Finklestover tapped a bony finger against his chin, then casually nudged the iron chest forward. The motion was almost too subtle—but Smith knew what it meant.

Finklestover wanted to see what Smith's eyes lingered on.

Testing him.

Smith let his gaze pass over the chest without stopping—as if nothing inside was truly of interest to him. Then, he gave a half-smirk. "Got anything in there worth a man's time?"

Finklestover clicked his tongue, shaking his head as if in mild disappointment. "A pity. I had thought you were a man who understood history."

Then, with an air of almost exaggerated reluctance,

he reached into the chest and pulled something free—a golden amulet, crusted with age but radiating power.

Smith's expression didn't change, but inwardly, he felt his pulse quicken.

Finklestover had reached into the chest, but not deep enough to disturb the ring.

That meant it was still there.

Smith leaned back, tilting his head. "That's old Valorian."

Finklestover's eyes widened, pleased Smith recognized quality. "Indeed. Pre-fall craftsmanship. Rare."

Smith kept his tone skeptical. "Rare, sure. But useful?"

Finklestover tut-tutted, waving a finger. "Everything has its use, my friend."

Smith stroked his chin, pretending to consider. Now came the gamble.

"You have something better," he said, his tone dropping just enough to sound like a man who knew more than he let on.

Finklestover arched a brow. "Do I?"

Smith gestured vaguely at the chest, making sure not to glance directly at the ring. "Something older. Something tied to power."

Finklestover hesitated for a fraction of a second—and that's when Smith knew he had him.

The trader's fingers drummed against the amulet, debating, calculating.

Then, with painful reluctance, Finklestover reached back into another chest, sifting through the different pieces.

This was the moment.

As the trader's hand sorted through the relics, Smith moved.

In a fluid motion, his fingers slipped inside his coat, brushing against the thin sliver of enchanted metal hidden in his sleeve—a sleight-of-hand tool crafted long ago for thieves and deceivers.

Smith flicked his wrist.

A pulse of energy rippled outward, shifting the contents of the iron chest ever so slightly.

Not much. Just enough.

Just enough for the ring to tumble free from its resting place and slide closer to Smith's side of the table.

Finklestover, oblivious, pulled out an object—a jeweled Valorian brooch—turning it over in his fingers with a smug grin.

Smith, meanwhile, let his hand casually drift toward the table's edge, where the ring now rested just within reach.

Finklestover saw nothing.

Smith snatched the ring in a swift, practiced motion, tucking it into his palm just as he reached for his belt pouch—a perfect misdirection.

Smith nodded at the brooch. "Impressive piece."

The trader was getting annoyed. "Of course it is."

Smith knew he needed to stay calm. "How much?"

"500 Valorian." Finklestover's tone was short. "Take it or leave it."

Smith dropped a few Valorian coins onto the table.

Finklestover barely looked at them. He handed the brooch to Smith, convinced he had just outmaneuvered another desperate buyer.

Smith rose to his feet, tucking his purchase away. "A pleasure."

Finklestover inclined his head, already focused on something else. "Come again . . . if you can afford to."

Smith didn't look back.

He had what he came for.

Smith moved quickly, slipping through the dimly lit corridors of the Meridian.

But he wasn't safe yet.

The Meridian was a place of shifting loyalties and hidden eyes. If Finklestover realized what had just happened—

Smith quickened his pace.

Behind him, the distant clink of trinkets and gold being shifted rang out, followed by a low, puzzled murmur.

Then—

A sharp intake of breath.

A chair scraped against the floor, toppling over.

"No . . . No, no, no." Finklestover's voice trembled.

Smith didn't stop, but he could picture it perfectly. Finklestover rifling through the iron chest, hands digging frantically through its contents.

Then the moment of terrible realization.

"The ring," the trader breathed in horror. "Where is it?"

Smith reached a narrow corridor leading to a dead-end wall.

Behind him, Finklestover shouted, knocking over more crates. "Guards! Seal the Meridian! No one leaves!"

Smith's pulse thundered. He was out of time.

But he had what he needed.

The ring.

And with it—the key to opening a portal home.

Smith placed the ring on his finger and lifted his hand. The blue stone in the ring flickered to life, its glow intensifying like a star reigniting.

He clenched his fist, and the air around him shuddered.

A tremor ran through the walls of the Meridian as the fabric of reality strained against the ring's command. Then—

A deep-blue rift split open before him, swirling like a storm caught in time.

Finklestover's voice cut through the air, desperate, furious. "No! STOP HIM!"

Smith didn't hesitate.

He stepped forward—

And the moment his foot crossed the threshold, the Meridian disappeared.

CHAPTER 61

Sara stood beside the hearth, her tea cooling in her hands, explaining her dream to the team.

"I saw her again," she said softly. "The woman from the mural at Walter's Market. She stepped out of it. She showed me things . . . places, people."

Devin rubbed the back of his neck. "The city you painted," he said slowly, "with the towers . . . that was Draegora?"

Sara nodded.

Devin looked down, eyes tracing the floorboards. "The journal and The Library of Althea showed me things . . . fragments—about my connection to Draegora, but this—" He paused. "A king?"

Eli's voice was low. "Not just a king. A restorer of the kingdom."

Devin shook his head, overwhelmed. "I don't know if I'm ready for any of that."

Sara stepped forward and continued. ". . . And I saw Aunt Janice. She was clutching a journal—Mom's, I think . . . She was with a man . . . trapped . . . scared. There was a hallway and a sign that said 'Motel Haven.' I painted it as a way out." She looked to Jo. "I think . . . it worked. The mural was their escape. From what I don't know."

Jo's eyes widened. "Aunt Janice . . ." Her voice cracked. "I left her on such bad terms. I thought she was just keeping us trapped when we were younger. I didn't understand."

"You do now," Mr. Mason said quietly. "She was protectin' you both, even if it meant bein' misunderstood."

Sara nodded. "She knew what was coming."

Mr. Mason tilted his head, a proud softness in his eyes. "You're your mother's daughter, right enough."

Eli offered a rare smile. "Lilianna would be proud . . . of both of you."

The room was quiet for a moment. Sara's eyes moved to the painting above the mantel—the girl in it now unmistakable. "And her. That's her. The girl with the book. She said she had to ride."

Eli and Mr. Mason exchanged a glance, unspoken meaning passing between them.

Jo moved closer, her brow furrowed. "You're sure it was the same girl?"

"In my dream—I painted a mural of the horse she would ride. She aged right in front of me," Sara replied. "By the time she spoke, she was . . . older. Familiar. She got on it and rode."

"Who was she?" Jo asked.

Just then, Lucy's voice cut through the conversation.

"Alert. Smoke detected. Coordinates: Just outside Muxley. Structure matches residence formerly occupied by . . . Janice Fowler. Visual feed available."

A window panel on the wall shimmered to life.

The house was in ruins, flames still smoldering against the gray morning sky.

Jo's hand flew to her mouth. "No . . ."

Sara's knuckles turned white around her mug.

Devin stepped forward, placing a hand gently on Sara's shoulder. "Maybe she made it to the garage. The hidden room. Let's not give up hope yet."

"What hidden room . . . ?" Jo asked confused . . .

Sara looked up, blue light dancing faintly beneath her skin. "I painted the hallway because the Lady from my first Mural knew the fire was coming. It wasn't random—it was protection. They're alive. They have to be."

Eli nodded gravely. "But if she has the journal . . . she's in more danger than ever. If she takes your escape route, it forces the journal out into the open."

Sara's jaw tightened. "Azazel wants it. Badly. But why? What's in it that's so important to him?"

"Aye, Lass," Mr. Mason began . . .

Devin interrupted . . . "But even if we wanted to protect Janice and the journal, Smith isn't back yet. We don't know if he can even get back . . . .and we need him if there's any hope—"

A pulse of blue light erupted near the entryway—gentle at first, then swelling like a tide. The temperature in the room lifted. Books fluttered open. The orb in the alcove hummed with power.

And then—he stepped through.

Smith—no, Thariel—returned.

But he was not the man who left. He stood taller, his presence heavier with authority and light. A sapphire-blue ring pulsed on his hand, glowing in harmony with the orb.

"Before we do anything," Thariel said, his voice clear and calm as if he had been listening the whole time, "a moment of alignment is required."

The room erupted with voices.

"You made it!"

"By Thalion's beard, I knew ye'd come back!" Mr. Mason boomed, half-laughing, half-tearing up.

Thariel smiled faintly. "We can celebrate once our work is finished. For now, we must prepare."

He stepped forward, raising the ringed hand. The orb in the alcove floated into the air, drawn to him.

"Blue orb. Ring. Lineage." He turned toward Jo. "The bow."

Jo stepped back instinctively—then gasped as the space around her chest began to glow. From light, the crystal bow formed in her hands, humming with energy.

Thariel turned to Sara.

Blue light surged around her—but this time, it was more than blue. Radiant hues—violet, green, gold, red—flowed over her skin. A spectrum, like sunlight split by crystal.

The three of them—Thariel, Jo, and Sara—stood together.

A circle of light bloomed beneath their feet.

Thariel's voice rang like a bell.

"The bond of Valoria is restored.
The daughters of Lilianna stand ready.
The heir of Draegora has returned.
And the hour of reckoning begins!"

The circle of light dimmed slightly, but the aura of power remained.

Thariel lowered his hand, his voice softening—not losing its strength, but drawing closer.

He turned first to Jo, her hands still trembling slightly around the crystal bow.

"Jolene Sweeney," he said, "you carry more than your mother's name—you carry her spirit. The fire in you once burned with bitterness, but now it burns with purpose. You are her shield. Her strength. And you have become your own." He reached out and lightly touched the bow. "This weapon answers to your will because it was forged by your courage."

Jo swallowed hard but stood taller.

Then Thariel turned to Devin.

"Devin Thompson," he said, his tone deepening with solemn weight. "You were born with a fractured legacy—but you are not bound by it. You were chosen not because of your blood but because of your heart. Draegora will rise again only if its heir refuses the pride that once doomed it." He locked eyes with him. "You are not just a product of the past. You are the one meant to redeem it."

Devin took a breath, shoulders squaring. A quiet resolve filled his chest.

Then Thariel stepped toward Sara.

The room seemed to shift.

"Sara Sweeney. The hope of Valoria does not rest on your shoulders—it rests on Thalion, the true Light. But His power flows through you, because you have chosen trust over fear."

The orb above them pulsed gently, echoing the truth in his words.

"The blue orbs were not meant to glorify those who carry them," he continued. "They are vessels of Thalion's presence. And you, Sara, have become the first in a long time to bear it . . . not with pride but with surrender."

He stepped closer, the warmth of his presence wrapping her like a memory she hadn't known she'd lost.

"You are not just an artist. You are a mirror. A window. A path."

He smiled gently.

"You do not need to become Lilianna. You only need to become fully yourself. That will be enough."

Tears welled in Sara's eyes, but she didn't look away. The rainbow glow on her skin flared briefly, as if in quiet agreement.

Thariel then turned his attention to Mr. Mason and Eli.

He clasped Mason's shoulder firmly. "Your wisdom has steadied us more times than I can count. You speak little, but every word plants roots. Your loyalty has been the spine of this mission."

Mr. Mason gave a small nod, his throat tight. "Aye, and I'll see it through to the end."

Thariel faced Eli and extended his hand.

"Eli Whitaker. Without your mind and your heart, none of this could have begun. You built the bridges— across dimensions, across doubts. You've never stopped fighting for what might still be."

Eli smiled faintly, a rare humility in his eyes.

"And we're not done," Thariel said. "Azazel wants Lily's journal which is now in the open. They want it so they can find the secret it holds."

"Which is?" asked Devin.

"The location to Thalion's Vault. It contains the most sacred things of Valoria. We can't let that happen."

There was silence in the room for a few moments.

"All of you," he said. "You are no longer simply survivors. You are no longer just defenders. You are keepers of the flame of Valoria. And with the light restored . . . we move forward. Together."

The orb pulsed once, in perfect harmony with the ring, the bow, and the glow on Sara's skin.

Beyond the windows, the ocean stirred. The tide was shifting.

And somewhere, the enemy felt it.

CHAPTER 62

Janice and Halbridge step through the mural, emerging in a dimly lit hallway with worn carpet and the faint buzz of an old neon sign outside. The air was stale, carrying the distant hum of traffic. They exchanged silent glances before quickly securing a room at the front desk.

They arrived at their room, the door clicked shut behind them, sealing away the outside world. Halbridge moved swiftly, checking windows and drawing the curtains tightly.

Janice placed the small recorder carefully on the table, exhaling deeply. "Okay. We're safe—for now."

Halbridge flicked on the television, adjusting the volume to a low murmur. He turned back toward Janice, arms crossed, face grim.

"You realize this won't be easy," he said quietly. "They'll have spun their story already. Who's even going to believe us?"

Janice shook her head, frustration building. "We'll have to find someone. There's got to be at least one news outlet still not under their thumb—"

Suddenly, Halbridge's attention snapped to the television. His expression darkened as images flashed across the screen:

"Breaking News: Outrage Grows in Muxley. Citizens Demand Justice for Stacy Davis."

Footage showed angry crowds outside the Muxley

Police Station. Signs waved, bearing slogans like "Justice for Stacy" and "Devin Must Pay!"

Halbridge shook his head. "It's already started. They've framed Devin perfectly. They're controlling the narrative."

Janice studied the screen, her voice steady but tense. "It's not just about framing Devin—it's about distraction. Remember what Haldine said in the meeting? They mentioned 'economic diversions.' This chaos is probably part of their strategy to keep everyone focused elsewhere while they finalize Azazel's move."

Halbridge sank into a chair, eyes locked on the recorder. "We have the proof that they're working with Azazel, but if we just post this online or try a small publication, it'll be dismissed as conspiracy theory."

Janice leaned forward thoughtfully. "Not if we don't present it alone. If we tie this directly to something undeniable—something tangible and immediate—we might get attention."

Halbridge frowned. "Tangible how?"

Janice's eyes brightened, determination dawning. "The economic diversion—something big enough to prove the Council knew ahead of time. Think. If they planned an economic event, it had to be something significant, right? Some policy change, a project, or maybe a business collapsing suddenly—something publicly noticeable."

Halbridge snapped his fingers. "The industrial plant outside of town—Weyland Industries. They employ hundreds in Muxley. There've been rumors for weeks that the Council's been quietly negotiating with foreign investors—not to grow jobs but to take over the company, dismantle it, eliminate the competition, and pocket the profits. If the deal goes through, hundreds of people here will lose their livelihoods overnight."

Janice nodded sharply. "Exactly. And if we can prove they're not just allowing it but actively *helping* it happen—sabotaging their own town's economy in exchange for kickbacks, all while collaborating with Azazel? People will have no choice but to listen."

Halbridge nodded slowly, excitement mixed with anxiety. "But how do we get that proof fast enough?"

Janice tapped the recorder. "We have their meeting recorded. If we carefully comb through this audio, there must be references to that economic disruption—at least indirectly. That, combined with the direct mentions of Azazel, could be enough."

Halbridge exhaled slowly. "And we have to release it strategically. It can't come from just you and me—we're too easily discredited alone. We need credible allies."

Janice considered this carefully. "What about outside journalists—someone from a major outlet outside Muxley? You must have contacts. Someone who's trusted, credible, and can't easily be bought or threatened."

Halbridge's gaze sharpened, realization dawning. "There is someone. Caitlyn Monroe. She's an investigative journalist with a national reputation. She and I started in journalism together before I came here. She's been digging into corporate and political corruption for years. They can't touch her easily."

Janice smiled faintly. "Then that's our play. We get this recording to her. But we need to move quickly—they're already winning public opinion."

Halbridge stood abruptly, pacing again, energy

renewed. "I'll contact her securely tonight. We have to lay low until we can set this up. Once she gets this, it'll be national news."

Janice nodded slowly. "Maybe. But one thing at a time. Let's handle the evidence first. Caitlyn Monroe is the key."

Halbridge nodded firmly, already pulling out a burner phone from his bag. "Let's do this. No more lies, no more cover-ups. Time to fight fire with fire."

Janice's voice dropped. "If this doesn't get out—if they catch us first—then all of this dies with us."

Halbridge gave a dry chuckle, locking eyes with her. "Then we'd better not get caught."

The crowd outside the Muxley Police Department surged and swelled like a tide of restless anger. Signs bobbed in the air—*Justice for Stacy! Bring Him In! No More Lies!*—each word sharp, each chant louder than the last.

Janice pulled her hoodie lower over her head. "We need to stay sharp. One wrong glance, and someone recognizes you from your columns."

Halbridge kept his head down, weaving them through a knot of shouting teens. "I've pissed off most of this town already. No one would be surprised to see me caught in the middle of a riot."

They reached a quieter side street where the roar of the protest dimmed behind rusted fire escapes and chipped brick. A man leaned casually against the side of a pawn shop, a thin cigarette dangling from his lips. He wore a denim jacket too clean for the neighborhood and eyes too alert for a lazy smoker.

"Applegate," Halbridge said under his breath.

The man smirked and pushed off the wall. "Still paranoid, Halbridge. Good to see it hasn't dulled."

His gaze turned to Janice. "Friend of yours?"

"Old friend," Halbridge replied. "One I trust more than most."

Applegate gave a short nod. "Come on. You've got ten minutes."

Inside the pawn shop, past dusty glass cases and shelves of outdated electronics, Applegate led them through a cramped hallway. At the far end stood a steel door with keypad access. He tapped out a quick code, and it clicked open.

The room beyond was dim but alive with cold light— eight monitors, humming routers, cables wound like ivy across concrete walls. It felt like stepping into a bunker built for digital warfare.

"Secure line," Applegate said, pulling a chair away from the desk. "No one taps it but me. You've got band-width and a little time."

Janice sat first. Halbridge moved quickly, plugging a small black drive into the central terminal. The monitors flickered, blue bars crawling across the screens as the files began transferring.

"This better work," Janice said, eyes on the progress bar.

"It will," Halbridge replied, his voice low. "Caitlyn Monroe's been waiting for years to blow something wide open. This is it."

91% . . . 93% . . .

Janice leaned forward, as if she could will the files faster. Halbridge stepped back, stretching his neck and cracking his knuckles. He turned to Applegate.

"I might need one more favor."

Applegate sighed through his nose. "Favor?"

Behind him, the steel door creaked open.

Three men entered—black coats, no insignia, boots too quiet for their size.

Applegate stepped aside without flinching.

"Sorry, Halbridge," he said, voice flat. "My loyalties . . . aren't what they used to be."

Halbridge's eyes darted to the screen. 97%.

"You son of a—"

The blow came fast—a dull, sickening crack against the side of his skull. Halbridge dropped like a sack of bricks.

Janice stood, shouting his name—but another figure moved behind her, swift and silent.

For Halbridge, the room spun. Darkness fell.

CHAPTER 63

The ancient stone beneath Muxley's city hall groaned as heavy doors creaked open, revealing a vast underground chamber—part war room, part temple, part throne hall. Torchlight danced across blackened steel, red banners, and broken crests from forgotten realms.

Voidwalkers lined the perimeter, dozens more than had ever been seen together before—each armored in the jagged relic gear recovered from Draegora. Their eyeless helmets glowed faintly with red streaks. Along the elevated platform stood the shadowy members of the Muxley City Council, with Haldine standing in front of them relishing this moment.

Sykes stood to the right of the dais, flanked by several senior agents—hooded, armed, loyal. Seraphis stood just behind Azazel, silent, regal, unreadable. The ring on Azazel's hand pulsed gently, in time with the dark orb hovering near his throne.

Azazel stepped forward to the edge of the dais, arms wide.

"Brothers. Sisters. Shadows of the New Order . . ."

A wave of silence swept over the room. Every entity present turned to him.

"The hour has come," Azazel declared, his voice deep and commanding. "Every maneuver, every preparation, every sacrifice—it has all led to this." His voice boomed, echoing through the stone. "And now, *we* are the fire on the horizon."

He began to pace, every step echoing with force.

"The final remnant of Valoria still clings to false hope. The daughters of Lilianna rise as if destiny is on their side."

He raised his hand—the orb flared red.

"We have opened the portals. Our warriors—the Voidwalkers—have crossed through. And now? They are legion." He gestured toward the walls where the armored figures stood still as statues. *"Armed with the strength of Draegora. Ready to crush Thalion's light forever."*

Azazel's tone darkened.

"Let them tremble. Let Smith weep in the ashes of his failures. For today, we strike the final blow." He turned, eyes gleaming. "We will sever Valoria from the realms, and then . . ." he lowered his voice to a rasp, "we will move through city by city, neighborhood by neighborhood, until this world bends at last."

The chamber erupted in cold, thunderous applause— Voidwalkers pounding fists against armor, agents nodding with savage pride, council members applauding with glee.

But then—a commotion at the far end.

Two guards shoved open the main entry door.

Between them stumbled Halbridge, blood trickling down his temple, a massive goose egg rising above his eye. Janice followed, her clothes torn, face bruised, but eyes burning with defiance.

Behind them, one of the guards held out a small collection of items: a flash drive, a compact recorder, two cracked phones . . . and a thick leather-bound journal.

The air shifted.

Azazel descended the steps, every movement slow and deliberate.

His eyes landed on the journal. His lips turned into a serpent's grin.

He plucked it from the guard's hands and opened it briefly, scanning a few pages. His hand trembled, but not from weakness—from elation.

"At last," he whispered. "Lilianna's journal."

He turned toward the room, holding it aloft.

"The final piece!! The words of the traitor herself. The secrets that have eluded us—now, in my hand."

He turned to Seraphis, voice swelling with pride.

"Smith has failed. His beloved counsel is scattered. His secrets exposed. His strength, broken." He looked to the council. "Now let us go and destroy the final portal to Valoria. Let us burn the gateway. Let us erase Thalion's reach from every realm, forever!"

The room erupted into a deafening roar.

But somewhere beneath the noise, just for a breath— Seraphis did not cheer.

He watched Azazel from behind, silver eyes glowing faintly, the corners of his mouth twitching into the ghost of a smile. One hand slowly touched the ornate ring on his finger.

Suddenly, one of Sykes' lieutenants approached, weaving through the crowd. He leaned in and whispered something into Sykes' ear.

Sykes straightened, his expression tightening. He stepped forward and turned to Azazel, raising his voice just enough to be heard over the fading cheers.

"My lord—word just came in from Brakenridge Hollow. Smith and his team . . . they've appeared at the mural in town. With a blue orb."

The chamber went still.

Azazel scoffed, waving the comment off at first. "So? He cannot activate the portal without his—"

His voice stopped.

He blinked.

Then, slowly, his expression changed—confusion hardening into realization.

". . . Seal."

The word hung in the air like smoke.

"No . . . Impossible."

His eyes darted, wild with calculation. "He couldn't have . . . he doesn't have the—" A flicker of dread passed through his gaze.

Then, fury surged forward to cover the fear.

"Get out there. Now!" he roared, voice cracking like thunder.

He turned to Sykes, pointing toward the upper chambers. "Send every available squad. No one waits. If Smith has regained his seal . . . he can open the portal."

The Voidwalkers hissed in unison, armor groaning as they began to move. Operatives barked orders. The ground itself seemed to tremble under the rush of boots and blades.

Azazel's face twisted into a mask of rage.

"Crush them before it opens. Burn the mural if you have to." He stepped down the dais. "If that portal connects . . . Valoria will answer. And we will lose everything."

Behind him, Seraphis did not move. He merely watched.

And ever so faintly . . . he smiled again.

CHAPTER 64

The wind stirred softly down the street, carrying the scent of rain and distant smoke. The air had a strange weight to it, as if the town itself knew something was coming.

Sara stood beside the outside wall of Walter's Store, where her mural stretched wide across the brick—a painting that had once just been a girl's dream made real. But now, it was something more. Every stroke shimmered faintly, the colors breathing in and out, almost as if the mural was waking up.

Thariel stood beside her, no longer hiding within Smith's familiar frame. His presence seemed larger. In his hand, he held the blue orb. It pulsed faintly like a living heart.

Sara looked at the orb. "Are you sure this will work?"

Thariel's gaze rested on the mural. "This orb was entrusted for this very purpose. Now, Valoria will answer."

He pressed the blue orb against the mural.

The mural reacted instantly. Blue light seeped into every crack and brushstroke, veins of energy spreading outward until the whole wall radiated with its light. The whole wall began to pulse, the light spilling out into the street like liquid dawn.

The portal was opening.

Through it, shapes began to form—glimpses of Valoria breaking through the veil. Fields of gold. Spires of crystal. And standing at the threshold, warriors clad in silver and azure, their weapons pulsing with the same blue energy that now linked Sara to this ancient place.

Mr. Mason stood just behind Thariel. Eli stood beside him, hands in his pockets, his eyes misty.

"We thought this day would never come," Eli whispered.

"Aye," Mr. Mason said softly. "We thought we broke it forever."

The two men stood there in silence, witnesses to the mending of something that had been broken. And yet, here it was—open again—not because of the Overseers, but because of a young girl who had the courage to believe.

As the glow from the mural spilled across the street, it began flickering against windows and drawing eyes from every direction. Neighbors wandered out of their homes, squinting at the brilliant blue light. Cars slowed. Shop doors creaked open.

Word spread fast.

"What is this? Some kind of stunt?"

But others stared in silent wonder—faces lined with fear and awe.

Back at the store, Thariel turned away from the mural, facing the group. "Valoria's warriors will hold the line on their side . . . for now," Thariel said. "But this battle is ours. The story will be written here."

Jo stood nearby, her arms crossed tightly over her chest, though her foot tapped restlessly. "What if we need them?"

"They will come," Thariel said simply. "Valoria does not abandon those who carry her light."

Devin stood further back from the others, just out-side the reach of the mural's glow. His hands were stuffed deep into his jacket pockets, shoulders hunched from the weight of too many eyes, too many whispers.

But this time, the whispers weren't just in his head.

"Hey! There he is!"

A voice cut through the murmuring crowd, sharp and accusing. Heads snapped in Devin's direction.

"Call the police!" someone shouted.

"Grab him before he runs!" yelled another.

The first few people surged forward, but they never reached him.

Because at that precise moment, the sky tore open.

The air split with a shriek, like metal being ripped in half, and a jagged seam appeared directly above the mural. Red light poured through the crack. The earth trembled beneath their feet, knocking several people off balance as frost curled along the edges of windows and pavement.

And out of that scar in the sky, Azazel strode for-ward like a conquering general, coat flaring behind him. When he landed, the cane in his hand tapped rhythmi-cally against the pavement. His smile stretched wide.

Azazel spread his arms wide, relishing the spotlight. "You want justice? I'll give you justice. You want to know who's responsible for your misery—who brought death to your doorstep? There he stands!"

He swung his cane like an accusing finger, pointing it straight at Devin.

Gasps rippled through the crowd. Some people lurched forward again, emboldened by Azazel's words, while others hesitated, their fear of Azazel himself tem-pering their anger.

Devin tensed, fingers curling near the Shadowblade Eli had given him at his hip, but Mr. Mason's hand found his shoulder, the old Keeper's grip gentle but firm. "Easy, lad," Mr. Mason said softly. "They dinnae ken what they're doin'. Fear's a sharp knife—it cuts at anythin' close enough."

But Azazel wasn't done.

"And there!" Azazel's cane swung again, this time pointing to the mural itself. "That cursed doorway! The girl's paintings—the Sweeney witchcraft—all of it! It's all connected! The death, the disappearances, the monsters—they brought it here! And tonight . . ." His grin sharpened. "We end it."

The people wavered, caught between their simmering rage at Devin and the sheer unnatural force of the scene unfolding before them. And then—the sky ripped open further.

Through the widening tear, Seraphis descended.

He drifted down slowly, his feet never touching the earth, his cloak trailing behind him like a bleeding wound in the air. The crimson ring on Azazel's hand pulsed, and the very ground beneath their feet shuddered, like the earth itself wanted to back away.

Azazel stepped aside, his arm sweeping toward Seraphis in mock invitation, pretending this was all part of his grand plan. "Behold the true force of justice. The reckoning you've been waiting for."

But even as he spoke, the Voidwalkers spilled out behind Seraphis. They flowed toward the mural like ink running downhill, drawn to the portal Sara had painted.

At the sight of the Voidwalkers, the crowd erupted into chaos—screams, scrambling feet, parents grabbing children and dragging them away. Whatever anger they'd carried toward Devin was instantly replaced by primal terror at the things now pouring into their streets.

Sara stood frozen. She'd seen Seraphis before—but never like this. Out in the open, in her town, with no veil between her nightmare and reality.

This wasn't just a battle anymore.

This was a reckoning for everyone.

Janice and Halbridge stumbled through the storm drain exit behind the council hall—wet, limping, but alive.

They had escaped only minutes earlier. Janice had spotted the old maintenance grate in the floor of the lower chamber, half-buried beneath storage crates and rusted chains. Likely forgotten by the men who dragged them in.

She had pried it open while Halbridge distracted the guards.

Now, they ran.

Halbridge's temple still throbbed, a dull pounding from where one of Azazel's men had cracked him with the butt of a rifle before their capture.

Janice kept moving, one arm wrapped around Halbridge's waist.

"Come on, kid," she muttered through gritted teeth. "You're not bleeding bad enough to stop now."

"Not bleeding bad enough?" Halbridge groaned. "You've got a gift for comfort."

She offered the ghost of a smile. "You're lucky I didn't leave you back there."

As they emerged into the alley near the square, they froze.

The mural across from Walter's General Store was glowing—and something was happening in the square.

Janice looked up, scanning rooftops and storefronts. "We're not too late. Let's go."

CHAPTER 65

Azazel and Thariel stood at the heart of the battlefield, the mural at their backs, the fate of realms before them.

The Voidwalkers, once men, swept through the streets like a storm of living shadows. Their armor—reclaimed from Draegora—gave them shape, but their faces were gone, erased by death and magic.

The citizens of Muxley, who had only minutes before gathered in protest, now screamed and scattered in panic. Shouts turned to cries as darkness poured from alleyways and rooftops.

Through it all, Jo and Devin moved like twin flames—cutting through the chaos, shielding civilians, drawing the attention of the creatures away from the vulnerable.

Devin slammed into a Voidwalker with a pipe torn from a scaffold, knocking it back. Jo, her crystal bow shimmering with light, launched a radiant arrow that exploded into blinding mist, allowing a small group of civilians to escape.

"Go!" she shouted. "Back to the square!"

They were outmatched, but they held the line.

Meanwhile, at the mural, the real storm brewed.

Azazel conjured a jagged crimson blade, shaped from raw hatred and red orb energy. Thariel answered, raising a glowing spear of sapphire light, born of restored authority.

Their weapons clashed with a sound like shattering bells.

Azazel sneered, pressing forward. "You never saw the truth, Thariel. You clung to your order. To Thalion's *pathetic* vision for the realms."

Thariel parried, grounding himself. "That vision held the realms together. It gave the strong purpose and the weak protection."

Azazel snarled, his voice rising. "No. I brought *clarity*! I gave the weak purpose! The people didn't need a protector—they needed a *ruler*." He swung wildly, red sparks trailing behind each blow.

Thariel caught one of the strikes and locked weapons, staring directly into Azazel's eyes.

"At what cost?" he said coldly. "You hollowed out an entire race. The Shadowforged were Draegora's honor. Now they're your foot soldiers. Wraiths. Dead as dead can be."

Azazel's eye twitched, rage sparking behind his smirk.

Thariel pushed off, his voice resolute.

"You didn't elevate them. You *consumed* them."

Azazel's eyes blazed. "You think Valoria will save you? That they still believe in you? You were cast out. Stripped of your name."

"And yet," Thariel lifted his hand, blue light dancing between his fingers, "here I stand."

Azazel faltered—only for a heartbeat. And in that heartbeat, Seraphis stepped forward.

His voice was calm, colder than frost. "Enough."

Azazel turned, catching his breath. "Together?"

Seraphis gave a slight nod. "For now."

They attacked as one.

Azazel's crimson blade clashed with Thariel's spear. Seraphis summoned chains of dark flame that shot from his fingers, wrapping around Thariel's limbs. Thariel grunted, forced to one knee.

They overwhelmed him.

Memories of the last time—when his seal was stripped, when his name was silenced—flashed across his mind.

Thariel's knees scraped against the ground as Seraphis's burning chains coiled tighter around his limbs, pinning him in place.

Azazel hovered over him. "You always thought faith could sustain you. But look around—this world doesn't believe anymore."

Thariel spat blood and raised his chin. He grunted as the chains binding his arms and legs flared again. Azazel's crimson blade hovered inches from his throat, vibrating with power. And above him, Seraphis stood still, coiled like a serpent watching its prey.

Azazel turned slowly, withdrawing something from the folds of his cloak.

Lilianna's journal.

Thariel's heart dropped. "No."

He strained against the bindings, his seal glowing. "You can't—Azazel, you don't know what you're unleashing."

Azazel's smirk grew wider.

"On the contrary. Lily always hid her secrets in riddles. But I knew her mind better than anyone—once."

He opened the journal with reverence, flipping through pages marred with cryptic marks and diagrams. Then, with careful precision, he began folding some the pages—one corner here, a crease there—creating a layered, angular shape like an origami key.

Thariel's struggle intensified. "Stop! That vault is not for you. You forfeited its trust the moment you betrayed your calling!"

Azazel didn't even look up. "And yet . . ." he whispered, tracing the final fold into place. "Only an Overseer once entrusted with it can open it."

He turned the journal toward the mural—and uttered the ancient words.

The language was older than language itself.

The street rumbled.

The sky split.

The ground behind them shuddered. A rift split open—and out of it manifested a massive structure of light and stone: Thalion's Vault.

It stood like a cathedral fallen from the heavens, sealed by symbols.

Azazel stepped forward, shaking with anticipation. "At last . . ."

He stepped toward the vault, lips parted, arm extended.

But the closer he drew, the more resistance he met.

His hand stopped short—*as if a wall of unseen force stood between him and the gate.*

Azazel grunted, forcing forward. Nothing.

His arm trembled. No matter how hard he strained, his hand would not cross the invisible threshold.

"What?" he breathed. He tried again, growling this time. Then struck at it with his ring's energy. The force rebounded, knocking him off balance.

"What is this?! I opened it!" he roared.

From behind him, Seraphis began to float forward slowly.

"Indeed, you did," he said softly.

Azazel froze. "What?"

"You brought us to the door," he said softly.

He moved past Azazel and floated to the threshold of the vault.

And then, with no resistance at all, Seraphis passed through.

Azazel staggered backward, his chest heaving. "How . . . ?"

Seraphis turned, holding out his hand toward Azazel, who instinctively clutched his chest.

"You fulfilled your purpose."

Azazel turned slowly. "What . . . do you mean 'fulfilled?'"

Seraphis smiled—a cruel, elegant thing. "You were always a means to an end, Azazel. Led like a beast on a leash."

Suddenly memories poured into Azazel's mind.

Him finding the first red orb, thinking it fate.

The whispering that led him to Seraphis' mural.

The ring placed on his finger, its glow matching the whispers.

The dreams that weren't dreams, but commands.

The ring . . . was never his.

Azazel staggered. "You . . . you deceived me."

Seraphis raised his hand.

The ring on Azazel's finger began to glow, then burn. Azazel screamed as it seared his flesh—and with a subtle flick of Seraphis's fingers, the ring slipped off, flying into Seraphis's palm.

Azazel collapsed as the light left him. His robes lost their luster. His skin turned ashen. His frame shrank. His voice, once commanding, barely a rasp.

"You used me . . ."

Seraphis smiled, closing his hand around the ring. "Thank you for your service."

Azazel said nothing more.

CHAPTER 66

Jo stood with her back to Devin, crystal bow drawn tight, her breath shallow but focused. Her arrows weren't made of wood; they were formed from light, shimmering and radiant.

Around them, Voidwalkers slipped through shadows, wraiths in armor, striking without mercy. People fled in every direction. Screams rang from storefronts. Explosions echoed across the town square.

Jo turned and fired—an arrow of pure energy cutting through the dark, striking a Voidwalker mid-lunge. It howled, then disintegrated in a cascade of red dust.

Devin glanced back. "Nice shot."

Jo didn't reply. Her eyes were wide—not with fear but with something else. *Focus. Intensity.*

She'd felt it just before the Voidwalker struck—*a flicker*, like time skipping half a beat. She'd seen the attack a moment before it happened.

Another scream. Jo turned.

A Voidwalker raised its blade over a young man crawling beneath a broken bench. Jo didn't think—she just *knew*.

She fired again.

The arrow struck just as the creature brought its weapon down. The man looked up, blinking in disbelief, untouched.

Jo exhaled sharply. What . . . was that?

A second later, another flicker. This time—a fire escape above her, cracking loose.

"Devin—move!"

She tackled him just as the metal staircase crashed behind them.

Devin rolled to his feet. "How did you—?"

"I don't know!" Jo snapped, not angry—just over-loaded. She clutched the bow tighter. "I just . . . saw it. Before it happened."

Before Devin could respond, the air behind Jo shifted.

A Voidwalker appeared from the smoke. Fast. Close.

Jo spun—but not fast enough.

The blade slashed across her shoulder, sending pain down her spine. She gasped, stumbling.

The Voidwalker loomed over her, blade drawn back again.

And then—it spoke.

"This is how your mother Lily felt . . . when she screamed."

The words coiled around Jo's spine like ice.

The world tilted.

In that instant, a flash overtook her mind

She wasn't in the street anymore.

She saw it.

Her small house she grew up in. Lily—her mother— standing at the center of the room, her body glowing with blue energy. Facing a group of tall, dark, shifting beings—a figure cloaked in red shadows.

A blade of red energy.

Her mother's scream.

Then blackness.

Jo gasped—eyes wide as the memory slammed back into the present.

She staggered, the pain in her shoulder now distant beneath a rising storm inside her.

"You . . ." she breathed, her voice shaking, ". . . don't get to say her name."

Her grip tightened on the bow.

The crystal pulsed.

Light shot up her arms, her chest, her jawline.

Her bow lit up—not just with blue light but white fire. She drew the string, and the arrow formed.

The Voidwalker laughed.

And Jo released.

The arrow tore through its chest—not piercing, but unraveling. The creature screamed, its body disintegrating into burning threads, vanishing in the wind.

Jo fell to one knee, breath ragged. Her hands shook.

Devin rushed to her side. "Jo! Are you—?"

"I'm fine," she lied, holding her shoulder. "Just . . . tired."

But as she looked down at the bow in her hand—still pulsing faintly—she knew something had changed.

Sara sprinted across the rubble-strewn intersection, blue light trailing from her hands. Every time she lifted her palm, a burst of orb-light shot outward, knocking back the Voidwalkers surging toward her.

Her breathing was steady. Her focus razor-sharp.

She had never felt more awake.

Then—

A crashing sound. Shouts.

She turned and saw them.

Jo and Devin, emerging from the smoke.

Jo held her bow tight, limping slightly but alive—eyes burning.

"Sara!" Jo shouted, already moving toward her.

Relief washed over Sara as she saw them.

They met near a collapsed awning.

"Are you okay?" Sara asked.

Jo smiled faintly. "Took a hit. Gave one back." Jo winced, gripping her shoulder where the Voidwalker's blade had slashed through moments before.

"Let me see it," said Sara.

Jo hesitated. "I'm fine."

Sara stepped closer, raising a glowing hand. "You're not. But you will be."

Jo put her hand up. "I'm fine!

"Stop being so stubborn," scolded Sara.

She placed her palm gently over Jo's shoulder. The blue orb-light flowed from her hand like liquid fire.

Jo gasped—not in pain, not exactly. It was something deeper. *The wound lit up from within,* threads of glowing light weaving into her skin, sealing what had been torn.

Jo's knees buckled.

"Hurts," she whispered, eyes watering. "But it hurts . . . good."

"It's healing," Sara said softly.

Jo grabbed Devin's arm to steady herself. Devin caught her easily, arm firm around her waist.

But as Jo leaned into him, still wrapped in Sara's healing light, something shifted.

The blue energy arced—flowing into Devin.

His eyes went wide.

He was thrown back as if struck by lightning, crashing into a crate across the way.

"Devin!" Jo shouted.

He groaned, sitting up. "I'm okay . . . I think."

He looked at Sara, dazed. "What was that?"

Before anyone could answer, a new Voidwalker emerged from the smoke—eyes burning, blade raised.

Devin was trapped. No weapon. No armor.

The blade swung hard—*straight for his chest.*

Jo and Sara screamed.

And the blade—shattered.

The Voidwalker recoiled, as if struck by something invisible. Its hand trembled. It looked confused. Then afraid.

Devin stood, untouched.

He stared at the creature. Then down at himself. Then back at it.

Before anything else was said, Jo lifted her bow and shot a blazing arrow, taking out the Voidwalker.

Jo and Sara ran over to Devin, who stood there dazed. "Dev, are you okay?" Jo asked, grabbing his arm. "Are you hurt?"

Devin turned to them, breathless, shaking his head. "I'm . . . I'm fine. I think—" He paused, frowning. "It's like the blade couldn't touch me . . ."

A flicker of realization crossed his face. "Maybe . . . maybe because I'm from the same lineage. Maybe they *can't* touch me."

"Wow," said Sara.

"That would be nice," said Jo, rubbing her shoulder that now felt much better. "Maybe next time you

417

can stand in front of me when one of those . . . things attacks."

Devin smiled, then looked up. He then looked back at them both, then nodded toward the mural in the distance, still glowing. "Smith . . . eh . . . Thariel's still fighting. We need to get to him."

Sara's face shifted.

"Then let's go. Together."

CHAPTER 67

The static cleared, and the glow of a dozen screens flickered in the back of a storage unit deep beneath an abandoned newspaper building.

Eli Whitaker sat hunched over a patched-together control rig, his sleeves rolled up, sweat beading on his brow. His fingers flew across the keyboard like a composer.

Above him, a voice—calm, precise—spoke from a portable speaker.

Lucy.

"Main uplink is stable. Auxiliary drone relays are online. Tracking blue signal . . . confirmed. Sara, Jo, and Devin are fifteen meters east of the mural site."

Eli exhaled. "Keep feeding me their locations. If they get pinned, I'll reroute guidance."

He tapped a few keys, switching feeds. One screen showed a drone's-eye view of the town square. Another tracked the energy signatures of the Voidwalkers, pulsing red dots moving like hungry blood cells.

Then, a chime.

"Eli," Lucy said, her voice shifting. "There's a high-priority signal incoming. National broadcast frequency."

Eli froze.

"Patch it through."

The center screen blinked—then cleared.

Caitlyn Monroe appeared. Calm. Composed. Radiating conviction.

"This is Caitlyn Monroe reporting with breaking news from Muxley, where the town council has been implicated in an underground operation tied to illegal experimentation, a cover-up of supernatural activity, and the death of at least one local teenager, Stacy Davis . . ."

Eli sat forward.

". . . Leaked footage and internal documents provided by investigative sources—some of whom risked their lives to make this public—paint a picture of corruption that reaches into every part of this town's leadership . . ."

"Lucy—can you override the local broadcast system?"

"Already bypassing encryption."

"Patch it to the plaza. Feed it to every screen, every speaker still intact."

Lucy replied, "Broadcasting now."

As they approached the plaza's edge, Janice stopped in her tracks.

Halbridge followed her gaze.

Across every storefront screen, every static-ridden speaker, Caitlyn Monroe's face appeared. "This is Caitlyn Monroe reporting with breaking news from Muxley . . ."

Halbridge dropped to a crouch, eyes wide. "No way. No way it got out."

Janice stood. "It got through . . ."

They stood frozen, listening to the broadcast unfold. The people of Muxley were beginning to gather, some turning toward the screens in silence. Others murmuring. Whispering. *Wondering.*

Janice's eyes burned. Then she straightened.
"This is the moment."

Sara, Jo, and Devin moved together, cutting through pockets of Voidwalkers, clearing space for people to flee toward the safer blocks.

The plaza trembled with the aftermath of battle—shattered glass, rising smoke, and civilians frozen between fear and fury.

Caitlyn's voice poured into the plaza like sunlight after a storm. Then, the broadcast ended.

The final words of Caitlyn Monroe's exposé still echoed in the minds of the crowd:

". . . Muxley's leadership has been compromised. The corruption is deeper than we feared—and the danger is real."

Then a voice could be heard above the clamor. Aunt Janice stood atop an overturned transport cart, dust and blood on her clothes.

"You heard the truth!" she cried, voice shaking with strength. "You saw it with your own eyes—this council has *betrayed* us!"

Jo, Sara, and Devin paused near a fallen wall, hearing the voice they all knew too well.

"Is that—?" Sara whispered.

Jo surged forward, eyes wide. "Aunt Janice."

They reached the edge of the plaza just as Janice turned in a slow circle, speaking not just to the people—but to their hearts.

"Look around you . . . This is what their leadership brought to our doorstep! This is the cost of silence!" "

She gestured to the chaos—the Voidwalkers prowling the streets, the buildings cracked and scorched.

"This . . . is what they brought into our world."

Her voice grew tighter, grief behind the fire.

"They didn't just allow evil to enter—they *invited* it. They made deals with it."

The crowd stood silent. Listening.

"And because of that—because of *them*—Stacy Davis is gone."

A ripple passed through the crowd. Her name meant something. She was one of them.

Janice's voice broke—but only for a moment.

"This is hard to believe, I know. It sounds like madness. But truth often does—until it's too late."

As Eli watched all of this unfold from his monitor. He saw a woman standing on an overturned cart

He tapped Lucy's console. "Give me an audio boost on her location—center feed."

"Done."

He leaned closer, listening as Janice's voice carried through the plaza.

"Look around you—this is what their leadership brought to our doorstep! This is the cost of silence!"

Then—

A new energy reading.

Eli turned pale as the screen turned red.

"No. No—Lucy, don't tell me—"

CHAPTER 68

"But it's not too late. We can still fight back. Stand up. Take our town—*our lives*—back!" Janice shouted.

Some began to step forward.

Nods. Shouts of agreement.

Then—

The sky cracked.

A rush of wind pushed inward, swirling dust and debris.

Seraphis descended—his dark robe drifting like smoke, his face unreadable beneath that ancient crown.

"Enough."

The word alone silenced the crowd.

From the ledge, Jo's breath caught in her throat. "No. No—Janice, *move!*"

Sara grabbed her hand, already knowing.

Seraphis raised his hand with barely a flick of effort.

A blast of crimson energy surged forward.

It struck Janice in the chest, lifting her off her feet and hurling her like a rag doll into the stone wall behind her.

The impact shook the square.

She fell—still, silent.

Halbridge rushed to her side, crying out, but the sound was drowned beneath the thunder in Jo's chest.

"Aunt Janice!"

She bolted forward, but Sara caught her by the arm.

"Jo—stop!"

"We'll get to her a different way so we are not seen." Sara's voice trembled, but held.

Down below, the crowd wavered—panic and fury rising at once.

And above it all, Seraphis hovered, watching with cold detachment.

Jo turned back toward him, tears burning.

Halbridge dropped to Janice's side, cradling her broken form, yelling for help that wasn't coming fast enough.

"Janice! Janice!"

Her breathing was shallow. Her eyes fluttered. Blood trickled from the corner of her mouth.

Halbridge choked. "You're okay. I've got you. Just stay with me."

He looked up. People were still watching.

Some of the people scattered—some screamed, others froze, caught between terror and disbelief.

A shadow emerged from the smoke.

A man. Calm. Weathered. Walking slowly with purpose.

Halbridge spun, eyes wild. He grabbed a rusted pipe from the debris and pointed it with trembling hands.

"Stay back!"

The figure stopped a few paces away, raising his hands in peace.

"Easy now, lad," the man said gently, voice laced with a soft Scottish lilt. "I've no quarrel with ye."

Halbridge's grip tightened. "Who are you?"

The man took one more careful step forward.

"Name's Mason," he said. "I was a friend to her—" he nodded toward Janice, "—and to the ones she's been protectin'. I reckon I'm here to help."

Halbridge's breath caught. The fight in him wavered.

Mr. Mason lowered to one knee beside Janice, eyes full of quiet grief and strength. He reached out with two fingers and gently checked her pulse, closing his eyes for a breath.

"She's still with us. Barely . . . but aye, there's still breath."

Halbridge's arms tightened around her, his voice cracking. "She stood up for all of us. And he—he just—"

Mr. Mason looked him in the eye, firm but kind.

"Aye. And she's not the first to pay dearly for standin' in the light. But she's not gone yet, lad. And she's nae alone."

He glanced back toward the mural and the battle still raging near it.

Mr. Mason gave Halbridge's shoulder a steady squeeze. "Stay with her. I'll send word to a friend of mine. He's nearby. We'll try to get help."

Halbridge's eyes glistened as he held Janice closer. "Can we save her?" he whispered.

Mason rose slowly, his face lined with quiet resolve. "We have tae try, lad."

CHAPTER 69

Jo's heart pounded. She kept glancing toward the plaza, where she'd last seen Seraphis standing over Aunt Janice's fallen body.

"Sara," she breathed. "We have to get to her."

"I know," Sara replied, not stopping. "But not through the open square. If Seraphis sees us—"

"Then how do we get there?" Devin asked, staying close behind.

Sara slowed in front of a wall—half-collapsed, scorched black—but still intact. Her hand rose.

"This'll do."

The glow in her arms brightened, threads of blue light weaving from her fingertips like ink in water. She drew quick, precise strokes across the wall.

"It looks like a door . . ." said Devin confused.

Jo blinked. "What are you doing?"

Sara nodded. "This is how I escaped from Azazel and ended up back with you guys."

The final line connected, and a glowing archway appeared, filled with swirling light.

"This will take us straight to her," Sara said softly. "Unseen."

Jo and Devin exchanged a look—then followed her in.

They emerged not onto a battlefield—but into a shadowed alley near the plaza.

And there, just ahead—a man knelt on the stone, cradling a broken form in his arms.

Aunt Janice.

Halbridge startled at their sudden appearance, his grip tightening on Janice. But then he looked closer. Recognition flickered in his eyes.

"Devin? . . . And you . . . you're Jo and Sara."

Jo didn't respond—she was already moving.

"Aunt Janice!"

She dropped to her knees, hands trembling as she reached for her. Sara was beside her in a blink.

"No, no, no—please be okay . . ."

Jo placed a hand gently against Janice's neck.

A pulse. Faint.

Tears spilled freely now. "I'm sorry," Jo choked. "I'm so sorry—for how I left. I wasn't kind. I didn't understand, and you didn't deserve that. You were trying to help us, and I—"

Janice stirred.

Her eyelids fluttered open, just barely. Her face was pale, lips cracked—but she managed to lift a shaking hand to Jo's cheek.

"Don't waste a moment . . . in regret," she whispered. "All is forgiven."

Jo wept, pressing her forehead gently against her aunt's hand.

Sara knelt quietly beside them, her breath shallow, tears flowing down her cheeks. She just reached out and took Janice's other hand, holding it in both of hers.

Janice's voice cracked. "You have no idea how proud I am . . . of you both."

Sara's lips trembled. She closed her eyes.

Janice turned her head—just slightly—and her fading gaze landed on Devin.

She motioned weakly. "Come here . . ."

Devin stepped forward, hesitant, his usual strength faltering under the weight of the moment.

Janice's hand found his. Her grip was frail—but warm.

"You made it," she breathed. ". . . The Library . . . accepted the truth of who you are."

He nodded, blinking quickly. "I still don't know if I'm ready to carry it."

Her eyes softened.

"No king ever is . . ."

She squeezed his hand one last time. "Stand strong, Devin. Draegora . . . will need you."

The breath left her slowly.

Her eyes drifted shut.

And in the plaza, beneath the cracked sky of Muxley, Janice Fowler— keeper of Jack and Lily Sweeney's legacy—was gone.

CHAPTER 70

The light from Thalion's vault pulsed with a low, ancient rhythm, casting shadows across the ground.

Thariel knelt near the entrance, still bound in thick red chains pulsing with Seraphis' dark magic. His shoulders heaved, his breath shallow. Blood traced the corner of his mouth, and his spear—dimmed and flickering—lay just out of reach.

Azazel crouched nearby, collapsed against a large stone. His ringless hand trembled, pale and exposed, as though haunted by the absence of power he once held, his eyes glassy, unfocused.

Thariel forced himself upright against the chains, his voice hoarse but steady. "Azazel . . . look at me."

Azazel didn't move.

"Look at me, old friend."

Slowly, Azazel turned his head, his eyes dull with disillusionment.

"You still have a choice," Thariel rasped. "Seraphis played you. He played all of us. Help me stop him before it's too late."

Azazel let out a ragged breath. "There's no stopping him now." His gaze drifted past Thariel to the looming vault doors. "I gave him everything. And in the end, I was just a pawn. Same as you."

Thariel's jaw clenched, the blue glow under his skin flickering faintly. "We are not the same."

But before another word could pass between them—

The air shifted.

A ripple of dark power surged through the plaza, and Seraphis materialized near the vault, his cloak billowing behind him, his face lit with cold triumph.

His gaze swept over the scene—Azazel crumpled, Thariel chained, the vault still sealed—and a sharp smile came across his face. "Ah," Seraphis murmured. "Still right where I left you."

He lifted a hand, preparing to deliver the final blow—

And that's when Thariel moved.

A sudden, blinding surge of blue light burst from his chest, crackling up the chains, racing along their length like fire down a fuse. The chains shuddered—once, twice—before shattering in an explosion of shards and energy.

Thariel caught his breath, rising slowly to his feet. His hand stretched toward his fallen spear —and it flew to him, snapping into his grip, reignited with brilliant blue fire.

Seraphis's smile faded, replaced by a sneer. "So . . . you still have fight left."

Thariel leveled his spear, his voice a low growl. "I have more than that."

They moved at once.

As they faced off, Azazel—pale and panicked—began crawling backward, dragging himself away from the confrontation. His body shook as he turned and tried to scramble toward the shadows. Whatever remained of his pride was gone; only the desperate urge to survive remained.

Thariel lunged, driving his spear forward with a

blinding arc of light. Seraphis countered, his arm sweeping up—black energy flared, clashing against the blue, shaking the ground beneath them.

Blow for blow. Light against shadow. Old power against ancient treachery.

Seraphis snarled, twisting, slamming Thariel back with a burst of raw force. Thariel rolled, landed hard, pushed up again—blood in his mouth

He launched forward, spear thrusting for Seraphis's chest—but Seraphis vanished, reappearing behind him, claws slashing across Thariel's back.

Thariel staggered, gasping—then spun, catching Seraphis across the jaw with the haft of his spear.

Seraphis stumbled, lips curling into a twisted smile. "You're slowing, old friend."

Seraphis raised both hands. Dark sigils flared along his arms as he muttered a forbidden incantation. Shadows bled from the ground, twisting into jagged tendrils that lashed toward Thariel's chest.

Thariel's eyes snapped wide, his hand slamming against the spear's shaft. Blue light erupted outward in a shockwave, dissolving the shadow tendrils midair.

He surged forward, driving the spear's tip straight through the dark magic, grazing Seraphis' side—the first clean hit.

Seraphis snarled, twisting with a backhand crackling with red lightning. Thariel ducked, the energy slicing past his head, searing the stone wall behind him.

Grimacing, Thariel raised his palm, summoning blue orb glyphs that pulsed and spun—a shield wall of light. He slammed the shield forward, battering Seraphis back a full step, drawing a surprised grunt.

They crashed together again—Seraphis driving a spear of shadow toward Thariel's heart, Thariel parrying with the shaft of his glowing spear, twisting, driving an elbow into Seraphis's ribs, knocking the breath from his chest.

The ground beneath them shuddered, cracks racing outward from the vault doors.

Thariel gritted his teeth, twisting his spear free and slamming the butt of it into Seraphis's knee—a brief stumble, a rare opening. He drew back for another strike, but Seraphis roared, shoving him back with a burst of red energy, sending Thariel skidding across the ground.

Breathless, Thariel braced himself, blue sparks flickering around his form. He forced himself to his feet, legs shaking. His chest burned. His vision blurred at the edges.

Seraphis straightened slowly, rolling his neck, dark power coiling thickly around him. His gaze was sharp, cruel—and unshaken.

And then—

A new energy surged across the plaza.

From the far end, two figures appeared—one rising into the air, surrounded by a halo of blue light, the other steady on the ground, a crystal bow crackling in her hands.

Sara. Jo.

Thariel's heart twisted in his chest. "No . . ." he rasped, panic knotting in his throat. "Stay back . . . stay back, you're not ready . . ."

But they kept coming.

Jo's voice sliced across the open space, sharp and sure. "We're not running."

Sara floated higher, her eyes glowing, her hands burning with the light of creation.

Seraphis turned slowly, his grin widening as he took in the sight of them. "Ah . . . the daughters of Lilianna." His voice curled with venom. "I've been waiting for you."

Without hesitation, Jo loosed three arrows in rapid succession—they streaked through the air, striking Seraphis's shoulder, his ribs, his arm, each one flaring with white-blue light.

Seraphis staggered back.

Sara rose even higher, spinning midair, painting a glowing glyph—a massive hammer of crystal and light. With a fierce cry, she hurled it down, striking Seraphis's back with a thunderous crack.

Seraphis dropped to one knee, a growl rumbling from his throat—not in pain but in rage.

Sara formed another glyph, this time a spiked chain of blue energy, whipping it toward him and wrapping it tight around his torso.

Jo knelt, breath steady, and fired one more arrow, piercing the center of his chest. It stuck, hissing and sizzling.

For a moment, the plaza fell still.

It looked—just for a breath—like they had him.

Seraphis's head lifted slowly, eyes burning with dark fury. "Enough."

In a blur, he snapped the chain, tore the arrow from his chest, and lunged toward Thariel.

He slammed into him, lifting Thariel off the ground and driving him brutally into the stone. A crack echoed, sharp and violent.

Thariel cried out, his spear skidding from his grasp.

Sara screamed. "No!"

She shot forward, desperate, glyphs flaring in her hands.

Jo fired—but Seraphis turned, backhanding her across the plaza like swatting a spark. She crashed into a stone pillar with a sickening thud, dropping motionless to the ground.

"Jo!" Sara's cry split the air, her focus splintering with panic.

Seraphis turned on her, hatred blazing in his eyes. A blast of red energy tore from his hand.

Sara braced midair, forming a glowing shield—but the force shattered it, blasting her across the plaza, straight into . . . the mural. The moment she hit it, the blue light flared —and she vanished.

"SARA!" Thariel roared, lifting his head with the last of his strength. "No!"

Silence fell.

CHAPTER 71

Sara stirred.

Her body felt weightless, yet whole—rested in a way she had never known. Her eyes opened slowly, blinking against a soft light that had no source and no shadow. She had no sense of how long she had been asleep—only that it had been long, and deep, and necessary.

She sat up, her breath steady, her heart calm.

She stood, and her bare feet touched down on something impossibly smooth and warm —as though she walked on the surface of sunlight itself. The air shimmered with a gentle glow, pulsing in time with her heartbeat. The weight of a past she barely remembered was gone, replaced by silence so perfect it felt alive.

She looked around slowly, blinking again. There was no pain. No fear. Only light.

A soft whisper escaped her lips.

"Where . . . am I?"

The words felt unfamiliar on her tongue. A language she had once spoken but nearly forgotten.

In its place stretched a meadow of luminous grass, each blade glowing with a faint bluish-green light that shifted when she breathed. She knelt, running her fingers over the grass, and felt it respond, like it knew her touch. Coolness, warmth, life . . . and something deeper—a connection, ancient and unbroken.

Far ahead, the horizon curved upward into something wondrous: a city bathed in light, its spires and

domes gleaming like pearls in a sky painted with laven-
der, crimson, and gold. The entire city seemed to hum—
not with sound but with presence, like a living heartbeat
woven into its stones.

Sara's steps carried her forward as if guided. But in
her mind something troubled her.

She slowed.

There was something else ... wasn't there?

She pressed a hand to her chest

A battlefield.

A cry.

A name?

What was the name?

She closed her eyes. The light swirled around her.
She could see faces—but they blurred like watercolors
bleeding together.

One came into focus—then another.

Jo . . . Devin . . . Mr. . . . Mason . . . Thariel!! . . .

Her breath caught.

"Thariel warned me . . ." she whispered. "He said if
I crossed through, I might not be able to go back."

The words came like a thread yanked loose from a
tapestry, unraveling pieces of memory with it.

A sudden beam of radiant light descended from the
sky, pooling into a column of swirling energy. From
within it, a figure emerged—wrapped in brilliance so
intense that its form constantly shifted, as though made
of liquid sunlight. A veil of mist swirled gently around
its face, obscuring its features.

Sara should have felt fear.

Instead, warmth bloomed in her chest—a comfort
deeper than words, a recognition that had no name.

The figure extended a hand.

Sara stepped forward. "Am I . . . dead?"

The figure did not speak aloud. Instead the air itself seemed to reply—a warmth that wrapped around her, like a voice she once knew in childhood and had long since forgotten.

Then the voice came, within and around her:

"No, child. You are alive—more fully than you've ever been. But time here does not flow as it does in the world you left."

Sara's brow furrowed. "Then how long . . . have I been here?"

The being did not answer immediately. Instead, it raised a hand and swept the air beside them.

The figure gestured, and a mirror shimmered into being beside them—tall, glowing, its frame carved from living wood threaded with silver light.

"Look," the voice instructed.

Sara stepped closer and gasped. It was her—but older. Wiser. Her eyes gleamed with clarity. Her posture radiated quiet confidence. Her hair bore subtle streaks of silver, not from age, but from being in the presence of pure light.

"How long have I been here?" Sara asked again.

The figure gave no answer.

Instead, memories began to surface and manifest in the mirror.

She saw herself training alongside radiant beings, sparring with light-forged weapons, walking the halls of the gleaming city, speaking the language of stars, meditating beneath crystal arches. She stood before a mountaintop throne, crowned in radiance, her voice shaping things as she spoke them. She lived years of discipline, insight, heartbreak, and healing—and it had all become part of her.

"I've been here for years . . ." whispered Sara.

"I . . . I love it here," she confessed, tears filling her eyes. "It feels like home."

The figure's light dimmed faintly, like a sigh of affection.

"But why can't I remember my world? Why was I forgetting Jo? Devin?"

The being's tone softened.

"This is what Thariel feared. Not that you would be trapped here—but that you would be *untethered*. Time here is not linear, not anchored. Its glory is so full, it can cause even the deepest memories from your world to fade . . . if you let them."

Sara's eyes filled with more tears. "But I *don't* want to forget. Jo is back there. Devin. Thariel . . . there was a battle . . . They need me."

The figure nodded once, slowly.

"That is why you must choose. Not by force. Not by prophecy, but because of what is in your heart to do," the voice said gently.

Sara turned back to the mirror.

Behind her reflection, the mural connecting her to Earth shimmered—not just as a portal but now as a painting of her life. Scenes of her past, her fears, her love, her sacrifices—woven together. And yet the final strokes remained unwritten.

"Who are you?" she asked, facing the figure again.

The mist thickened briefly.

And in that moment—just for an instant—she saw it:

A crown of woven light resting on the figure's brow.
She gasped softly, but the image faded.
The light surged—
And the entire world collapsed into a single point.

Sara's eyes flew open.
She lay against the same shattered wall from before.
She stood slowly.
Her posture was different. Her features refined.
Footsteps echoed nearby—then Devin appeared, rounding the corner with blood on his forehead and urgency in his eyes.
He froze the instant he saw her.
"Sara . . . ?"
He stared, wide-eyed, taking her in.
"We saw you go through the Mural. Are you okay?" Devin paused as he looked at Sara. Her features clearly different than he remembered. "You . . . look older."
Sara glanced down at her hands—blue energy gently flowing across her skin like threads of living color.
"It's a long story," she said softly, a faint smile crossing her lips.
She stepped forward, eyes lifting toward the battle-field in the distance.
"But we've got a battle to win first."
The light along her arms flared brighter than ever.
And this time—it was hers to command.

CHAPTER 72

Thariel was slumped to one knee, blood running down his brow, his breathing slow but steadying. The pain was sharp, but his body—infused with the authority of the ring—was already beginning to mend.

He lifted his gaze.

Seraphis stood at the entrance to Thalion's Vault, bathed in its otherworldly light. His silhouette cast a long shadow across the plaza.

"You're actually going to take it," Thariel said, his voice ragged. "The Crownshard."

Seraphis paused, not turning yet.

"So it still sings *your* name, does it?" he said softly. "Even in your defeat."

"It doesn't sing," Thariel murmured. "It warns. You know what that shard holds—Thalion's authority, yes, but also his judgment. It was never meant to be *wielded*—only borne by one who walks in harmony with his purpose."

Seraphis turned, his expression cold and burning.

"I *was* his purpose!!" His voice echoed like a fault line splitting. "He chose me. You forget that."

"He chose you once," Thariel replied. "Before your hunger poisoned everything you touched. That shard is a remnant of a throne—not a weapon. Try to wield it, and it will consume you in return."

Seraphis stepped into the vault, undeterred.

"All your reverence. All your caution. It's why the

440

realms rot beneath you. You still kneel while the world burns. Me? I will burn it clean."

He raised his hand—and summoned it. The Crownshard. Jagged and brilliant, it pulsed with fractured threads of gold, white, and violet. Symbols swirled across its surface, not etched but alive.

"You think it will make you more," Thariel said. "But it will only reveal what you truly are."

"Then let it show the world," Seraphis snarled.

He pressed the shard to his chest.

The light screamed.

It didn't explode—it *sank*—melting into his body like fire into steel.

Seraphis convulsed.

Then rose.

Changed.

His robes blackened. His limbs elongated and cracked. Horns of jagged crystal curved from his brow. His voice no longer echoed—it *shook*. Wings of burning shadow fanned out from behind him.

"Now," he growled, "let the last of Thalion's faithful stand against me."

Thariel inhaled slowly.

The ring on his finger glowed.

His spear reformed in a flash of searing blue.

And he rose.

"Then come," Thariel said, "and let's see whose throne you think you're claiming."

CHAPTER 73

Jo stirred.

Lying among broken stone and scattered glass, her body ached, her breath shallow—but her heartbeat remained steady. Alive.

Her eyes fluttered open.

Through blurry vision, she saw a shape wreathed in blue light—hovering.

"Sara . . . ?" Jo coughed, slowly pushing herself upright.

Sara turned, still midair, her eyes glowing like sapphires lit from within.

"You're awake." She dropped to the ground beside Jo, kneeling. "Easy. Are you hurt?"

A second figure knelt beside them—Devin. His clothes were torn, blood on his temple, but his eyes were alert. He gave Jo a quick nod, relief washing through his features.

Jo smiled faintly at him, then turned to Sara. Her voice was ragged, disbelieving.

"Sara, you look . . . like you walked out of a tanning salon."

Sara cracked a smile. "I know."

Jo blinked hard, trying to sit up. "How . . . ?"

Sara took her hand. "We'll talk soon. But first—let's get you up. Then . . . we end this."

She rose, extending a hand—pulling Jo to her feet. As she did, a pulse of blue light flowed from Sara's hand

442

into Jo's frame—mending bruises, strengthening limbs, restoring what had been broken.

"Wow," Jo breathed. "What's gotten into you?"

"Later," Sara said, focused.

Jo tilted her head. "You're starting to sound like Smith . . . er, Thariel."

Sara smiled but said nothing.

Jo drew her bow—its crystal thread already humming with fresh energy.

Devin stepped forward beside them, scanning the chaos. His eyes locked on Seraphis.

"My God," he murmured. "Look at him." His voice tightened. "How are we going to stop that?"

Together, they turned toward the clash at the center of the square, where Seraphis roared, wings spread wide, locked in a fury of blade and flame against Thariel.

Jo looked to Sara. "What do we do?"

Sara's gaze burned with clarity.

"I've got an idea."

She turned.

"Devin . . . I need you to do something . . ."

CHAPTER 74

Sara's eyes never left Devin.

"There's someone else we need."

He turned to her. "The boy?"

She nodded. "Azazel's painter. He's still out there—somewhere near the council hall. But he's behind the Voidwalkers."

Jo glanced toward the east side of the square. "It's a wall of them. No one's getting through that."

Sara looked at Devin, her voice calm but charged with something new—authority.

"You will."

Devin blinked. "What?"

She stepped toward him, eyes glowing.

"You already felt it. When that Voidwalker tried to strike you and the blade broke?"

He nodded slowly. "Yeah. It was like . . . it couldn't touch me."

Sara's expression softened, but her voice grew stronger.

"Because you're Draegoran. The Voidwalkers were forged from your bloodline, but still bound to it. To *you.* They can't harm what they're tied to."

Devin glanced toward the blockade in the distance.

"So I can walk through?"

"You've already done more than that," Sara said. "But now you run—because this time, it matters."

Jo raised a brow. "You sound like an old general. Whats gotten into you?"

444

Sara almost smiled, her gaze locked onto Devin.

Devin let out a breath. "All right. I'll get him."

Sara laid a hand on his shoulder—a spark of blue light pulsing between them.

"Find him. Bring him here. Then I will tell you what's next."

Devin nodded and took off—racing into the heart of what should have been death . . .

The ground cracked beneath Devin's boots as he sprinted past the edge of the square.

Smoke coiled through the lower quarter of Muxley. The buildings were scorched, twisted, and caved in where Voidwalkers had passed. But they were thinning. The battle had drawn them toward the center, toward Thariel, Jo, and Sara.

Which gave Devin the window he needed.

He ducked through the broken frame of a side alley, muscles burning, lungs sharp with heat. A Voidwalker turned to intercept—its face a cracked mask of red-glowing hatred—but it froze the moment it sensed him.

Its blade half-raised . . . then slowly lowered.

Devin didn't flinch.

He moved past the creature, heart pounding, eyes forward.

Then he saw him.

The boy sat alone, hunched beside the blackened steps of the old records building—knees to his chest, arms wrapped tight. His eyes still glowed faintly red.

Devin slowed, chest rising and falling with effort.

"Hey," he said gently.

445

The boy didn't look up.

Devin stepped closer. "I'm not here to hurt you. Sara—she sent me. She needs you."

That caught the boy's attention.

He lifted his head slightly, eyes uncertain. "She . . . touched me once."

Devin nodded. "And it changed something, didn't it?"

The boy hesitated. "I still feel it. But everything else . . . it's loud in here." He pressed his fingers to his temples. "Azazel's voice, the red orb's pull. Like echoes that won't stop."

Devin crouched in front of him.

"Sara believes in you. She sent me to tell you she needs your help."

The boy's lower lip trembled. His hands glowing with a red glow.

"I'm scared," he whispered.

"Yeah," Devin said. "Me too." He reached out a hand.

The boy stared at it for a long second . . . then slowly reached out and took it.

CHAPTER 75

Steel clashed. Arrows flew. Shadows screamed.

Jo fired an arrow into the chest of a Voidwalker leaping from a crumbling rooftop, the impact throwing it backward into a shattered window.

Sara sent a burst of radiant energy through a group of Azazel's remaining cohorts, the wave of light peeling them away from the edge of the square like ash on the wind.

"We should be fighting with Thariel!" Jo shouted, knocking another arrow, her braid snapping behind her like a banner.

"When the time is right," Sara called back, her voice calm, eyes scanning the eastern perimeter.

"Time is sort of *bleeding out on the pavement*, Sara!"

"We're clearing a path," said Sara.

Jo loosed another arrow. "A path for *what*, exactly?"

Sara smiled faintly, never taking her eyes off the buildings beyond the square.

"You'll see."

Jo groaned. "You're literally *impossible* now."

Before Sara could answer, movement drew her attention—Devin, emerging from the smoke with someone beside him.

The boy.

He looked smaller than she remembered, fragile in the shadow of everything that was breaking around them.

447

Sara stepped forward to meet them.

Devin gave a curt nod. "They didn't lay a finger on me."

"I told you they couldn't," Sara said, touching his shoulder briefly before kneeling in front of the boy.

He looked at her with a kind of reverence.

"You came back for me," he said softly.

He blinked rapidly, trying not to cry.

Sara gently took his hands in hers.

"You know how to paint what needs to be seen," she said. "And that's what I need from you. Just once more."

The boy nodded slowly.

"What do I paint?"

Sara leaned in close.

Her lips brushed his ear.

She whispered.

He nodded again quickly, more certain now.

Sara smiled and rested a hand on his chest.

"You were never just a pawn."

Then she turned to Jo and Devin.

"Keep him safe. He's about to change everything."

Far from the center of the chaos, Eli sat hunched over a bank of glowing screens, his fingers flying across a broken keyboard patched with wires and tape. Lucy's voice chimed softly in his earpiece.

"Pulse readings in the plaza are fluctuating again— blue light signatures increasing near the mural and inner square. One new source . . . . strong."

Eli's eyes narrowed as data scrolled across his monitor.

"That's not just a spike. That's a *return* signal."

A pause.

"Lucille . . . is that . . . Sara?"

Lucy's responded. "It's her . . . but not as she was. Something's changed. Her energy's refracting through multiple planes. She's—Eli, she's *not tethered to Earth's time signature anymore.*"

Eli leaned back slightly, stunned. "Hmm? That could change things going forward."

Away from Eli near the town Square on Muxley, Mr. Mason stood still, arms crossed, staring at a live feed from one of Eli's aerial drones hovering above the battlefield.

He watched as Sara knelt by the boy.

He watched as Jo stood protectively beside her, and Devin lingered nearby.

He watched the boy's hands begin to move—paint blooming on the wall.

Mr. Mason's expression shifted. A spark igniting behind them.

"Aye," he whispered. "I see what she's doin', the clever lass."

Eli answered in the earpiece. "What is it?"

Mr. Mason stepped forward.

"She's not just fightin'. She's *weavin' somethin' bigger*. And by the looks of it, it's nearin' its final stroke."

Lucy's voice came back through the feed. "Routing Thariel now. Message relayed."

Then—

Mr. Mason touched his earpiece and muttered:

"Y'know, Lucy . . . ye're soundin' more like a person every day . . . an' less like a machine. I dinna know if I should be impressed or deeply disturbed."

449

Lucy's tone perked. "It's okay, Mr. Mason. I'm still programmed to like you."

He snorted. "Well, that makes one of ye."

Eli laughed under his breath as he patched the signal to Thariel's ring.

"Let's hope she's right. Because if Sara's plan works, this battle's about to shift in a very big way."

CHAPTER 76

The clash between Seraphis and Thariel shook the square.

Sara stood at the edge, blue energy rising like a storm around her. Her hands glowed. Her eyes tracked every movement of the battlefield, but she didn't move. Not yet.

"Sara!" Jo shouted over the noise, loosing another arrow. "We've got the boy. We need to go help Thariel, now!"

Sara didn't turn.

Her gaze sharpened.

"Not yet . . ."said Sara softly.

Sara looked at the boy in the distance. His brush moved with strange precision—each stroke glowing faintly, forming a new mural along the far wall of Old Parson House—a former chapel long boarded up.

Before Jo could press further, Sara stepped forward—into the middle of the plaza, where the wind seemed to bow away from her. The sounds of battle quieted as the very air waited.

Then Sara spoke.

Not in English.

Not in any human tongue.

But in something older—a command wrapped in melody and power.

The words rippled out, foreign to Jo and Devin, unintelligible . . .

Across the way, Mr. Mason froze.

His eyes widened.

"Did she just . . . ?"

Eli looked up from the monitors. "What did she say?"

Lucy's voice was low. "Translation not available. Words match harmonic patterns from the Overseers' archives."

Mr. Mason's voice dropped to a whisper.

"She invoked the Rite of Return."

Seraphis faltered mid-swing, eyes narrowing.

His body tensed. His wings stopped beating.

And then he saw her.

His eyes locked on Sara—standing radiant, fearless, hovering midair, her eyes locked on to his.

His face contorted in disbelief.

"Impossible . . ." he breathed.

He took a step forward, not in anger—but in pure astonishment.

"You . . . crossed through." His voice was low, sharp. "You were *untethered*. That realm rewrites what you were. *No one* comes back from that."

Sara said nothing.

Her gaze didn't waver.

Seraphis tilted his head slowly, searching her expression for weakness, for fracture. He found only light.

His awe turned cold.

"But no matter," he snarled, straightening. "You think you can invoke that? *You* think you bear the right to call such power?"

452

He pointed toward the horizon.

"Only those who carry Thalion's authority can give such a command."

He moved to strike her—

But Sara was already gone.

In the blink of an eye, she swept her hand in a broad arc—blue energy flowing like a ribbon through the air. A glowing doorway spun into existence, pulsing with light and painted swirls. She stepped backward through it just as Seraphis's blade of shadow came crashing down.

It passed through empty air, splintering the stone beneath in a violent burst of red energy.

Seraphis snarled, twisting, searching—

Another door burst open behind him.

Sara stepped through, calm, focused.

Her boots touched down lightly on a raised platform overlooking the square. She didn't say a word—just stared him down.

Seraphis whirled around. He moved to strike again, but a loud noise came from the direction of Walter's General Store.

The mural at Walter's General Store ignited with blinding blue and gold. Light poured from its seams.

Burning. And then it opened.

"No!", shouted Seraphis

Figures emerged.

Warriors—clad in silver and deep blue, bearing the emblems of all the realms.

Archers. Spear-bearers. Riders of light.

The regiments of Valoria, long hidden, long silent.

Mr. Mason, watching from afar, stepped back in awe. His voice cracked as he spoke.

"Valoria... answers."

Eli's mouth dropped open. "Are those...?"

Lucy interrupted, "Confirmed. Reinforcements arriving."

Thariel, in the square, staggered back and dropped to one knee—not in defeat, but in *reverence*.

He recognized the banner. The crest. The faces.

Sara stood tall, her voice like thunder wrapped in light. She looked straight at Seraphis.

"You were wrong, Seraphis."

"I *am* a daughter of Valoria."

CHAPTER 77

Seraphis let out a roar that cracked windows across the square. Sara's trick had worked—but it had also enraged him.

He launched into the air, wings of black flame spreading wide. His body twisted, blades forming in both hands as he dove for her.

Sara spun, conjuring a shield of blue light just in time. It absorbed the first blow—but she staggered from the force.

Thariel was already moving, vaulting up the stairs of the old Bastion Hall, his spear flaring with white-blue fire.

"I'll flank him!" Jo shouted, drawing her bow and sprinting toward the far wall, loosing arrow after arrow toward Seraphis as he twisted in midair.

The battle erupted again.

Steel met fury. Light clashed with darkness.

All around them, Valoria's soldiers surged into the square—formations moving with precision and discipline, shields rising, swords cutting through Voidwalkers like light through smoke. Seraphis's remaining cohorts scrambled, outnumbered and unprepared for the counterassault.

And in the chaos, the boy kept painting.

Brush strokes danced across the stone wall of Old Parson's House—a glowing archway now taking shape.

The battle raged behind him, but Devin stepped away, drawn by something else—a whisper at the edge of the square.

Across the plaza, past the wreckage of a shattered fountain and the rising flames of a broken cart, he saw it: A fallen statue, once noble, now half-sunk into rubble. Its face was cracked, its hand outstretched toward nothing.

And leaning against it . . . was Azazel.

The former lord of shadow sat hunched, shoulders slumped forward, eyes hollow.

He was talking to himself.

Muttering in a low, guttural voice—half riddles, half regret.

"They took it . . . no, I gave it. Thalion's flame . . . always out of reach. She painted the door. I never understood the door . . ."

Devin stepped closer, cautiously.

He remembered the night in the warehouse. The Voidwalkers. Stacy's scream.

He remembered Azazel had ordered their deaths— *cold and sure.*

And yet . . .

Standing here now, watching this broken husk of a man claw at his own thoughts like shadows, Devin didn't feel rage.

He felt . . . *pity.*

Azazel wasn't a threat anymore.

Devin looked back toward the battle. Toward Sara.

He looked down and saw a small piece of mirror glass on the ground. He picked it up and angled it toward the square, and caught the flare of sunlight through the smoke.

A flash of blue caught Sara's eye.

From across the battlefield, she turned—met his gaze.

He pointed. Once.

To the statue.

To Azazel.

Sara nodded.

And with a single swirl of her hand, a blue portal bloomed around her.

She stepped through and disappeared.

The blue portal shimmered behind her as Sara stepped onto the crumbled stone, just beneath the shadow of the fallen statue.

She approached slowly.

Azazel didn't look up.

He was still muttering, hands trembling at his sides.

Sara stopped a few feet away, watching him carefully.

His once-regal form now slumped like loose fabric over broken bones.

He noticed her at last.

His eyes—no longer glowing—searched hers with confusion.

"You . . ." he whispered.

Sara nodded. She saw what looked like shame flicker in his eyes.

"You are your mother's child," he said. "Too much light . . . even when the war broke her."

Sara knelt slowly, never taking her gaze off him.

"Azazel . . . I'm not here to punish you."

He blinked.

"No?"

"You've done enough damage. But this moment . . . it's not about you anymore," said Sara.

He let out a rattling breath. "Then why come?"

Sara's voice softened. "Because you still have something we need."

"What makes you think . . ." Azazel paused, looking at the ground.

Sara tilted her head.

"I know you kept one. You always planned for a backup . . . in case the others failed you."

His jaw clenched, but he didn't move.

Sara leaned closer, voice gentle but unyielding.

"Do something right, Azazel. Just once more. You knew my mother. You saw her fight for something better. You walked away from that—but you don't have to stay away."

A long silence followed.

Then, slowly, Azazel reached beneath his tattered cloak.

His hand emerged, trembling.

In his palm sat a single red orb, faintly pulsing with the last vestiges of power—dormant, like a spark in waiting.

He held it out to her.

"Don't waste it," he rasped. "You've got one chance."

Sara took out a cloth and wrapped the orb in it.

Azazel's voice dropped, almost reverent.

"You really are her daughter . . ."

Sara stood, orb in hand, and nodded.

And with a sweep of blue light, she vanished through another portal.

Azazel was again alone at the broken statue. He leaned his head against the stone and began to weep.

CHAPTER 78

Seraphis stood tall, his form towering now—twisted by the Crownshard, wings of shadow crackling, body plated in blackened armor that shimmered with infernal veins of red light.

"You think this is over?" he roared, his voice booming across the plaza.

He raised both hands and conjured an obsidian axe, its double-bladed head laced with veins of molten gold. The weapon thudded into his grasp.

Thariel moved in first.

He spun his spear and struck—the impact blinding—but Seraphis caught the blow midair with the flat of the axe and drove Thariel backward with a single crushing swing.

"You've already lost," Thariel growled. "Valoria is here. You're standing on borrowed ground."

Seraphis laughed.

"Let them come. Let them watch as I burn the heart from their children."

With a roar, he slammed the axe down—the ground cracked open, a shockwave blasting outward like a cannon.

Valorian troops were flung from their posts—one regiment hurled into the steps of the Bastion Hall, another scattered near the burning remnants of Walter's Store. Shields shattered. Weapons clattered from stunned hands.

Thariel moved to intercept again, his spear a radiant

blur. He struck fast—precision over brute force—but Seraphis blocked and twisted, countering with terrifying ease.

Their weapons collided, and for a moment it looked like Thariel had the upper hand.

Until Seraphis stepped inside the arc of the spear and dragged his axe across Thariel's side, slicing deep into his ribs.

"THARIEL!" Jo's voice cracked across the square as he stumbled back.

She tried to reach him—but Seraphis wasn't done.

With a roar, the dark god spun and brought the full weight of his axe down across Thariel's chest, the impact booming like a drum of war.

Thariel was launched clear across the plaza, his body crashing into the base of the Bastion Hall with a sickening crunch. Dust exploded around him.

He didn't rise.

Jo froze.

Seraphis turned toward her.

"You're next."

He raised the axe again.

Jo reached for another arrow, but her hands trembled. She stepped back—tripped over shattered stone.

Then—from above—a figure descended in a slow arc of blue fire.

Sara.

Her voice rang out like a bell forged from storm: "Enough."

She unleashed a bolt of radiant power—blue and white, threaded with light—and it struck Seraphis square in the chest.

The shockwave blasted outward.

Seraphis hit the ground with a thunderous thud, skidding across the cracked stone.

Jo scrambled to her feet and ducked behind a column, catching her breath.

Sara floated down slowly, boots touching ground.

Seraphis groaned as he stood, smoke curling off his shoulders. He glared at her.

"You . . ." he growled.

Sara stood tall, eyes glowing, arms relaxed but ready. "Me."

Seraphis rose from the crater Sara had struck him into, his cloak tattered, flames dancing along his pauldrons.

"You think you're something new? You're a shadow of your mother. A spark flickering in the dying breath of Valoria. You speak their words. You carry their hope. But you're too late. The Crownshard burns in *me* now."

He slammed the butt of his axe into the stone—cracks split outward.

"Thariel has fallen. Your allies scatter. Your portal is open—but it leads to nowhere. And soon, neither will you."

Sara tilted her head slightly, voice soft.

"You talk like someone who's already lost."

Seraphis sneered. "I hold the power of Thalion in my chest!"

"No," Sara said, her voice steady but low. "You hold its *echo*. You forced it into a vessel that was never meant to carry it."

Seraphis roared and lunged toward Sara.

Sara's hands lifted—not to attack but to resist.

A wall of blue light erupted between them, curved like a great shield summoned from the soul of Valoria itself. Seraphis slammed into it with the full weight of the Crownshard's fury.

The ground beneath them cracked, splintering outward in jagged veins.

Sara gritted her teeth, every muscle in her body bracing as Seraphis pressed forward, step by brutal step.

"You cannot hold me back forever!" he snarled, pushing harder, his gauntlets sparking as they pressed into the barrier.

Her arms trembled. The shield flickered but held.

"I crossed through what you feared," she said, breath shallow. "I spent years in the light of the one you betrayed."

The blue light around her flared—ribbons of it spiraling up her arms, into her hair, her eyes glowing brighter than ever.

"And what did it teach you?" Seraphis hissed, digging in harder. "How to delay the inevitable? How to polish your mother's broken crown?"

"No."

The light surged.

"I learned that power isn't in possession . . ."

Sara staggered forward a step, forcing him back.

"It's in *purpose*."

The barrier pulsed. Seraphis reeled, stunned for the first time not by strength, but by certainty.

He screamed in frustration, the ground burning beneath his boots, cracks glowing red.

"And what purpose do you think you serve, little flame?"

Sara, still straining, managed to lift her eyes—beyond him.

To the boy.

To Jo, crouched behind broken stone.

To Thariel, bloodied but watching, waiting.

Then she looked back, her voice quiet . . . and absolute.

"Restoration."

"Restoration."

Her voice echoed through the plaza like the toll of a final bell.

For a moment, Seraphis stared at her, eyes wide—not in awe, but in dawning understanding.

Then—he saw it. The boy off in the distance. The mural was complete.

Seraphis's eyes widened.

"No—"

He twisted away from Sara and surged toward the boy.

That was his mistake.

Sara's power dropped from defense to offense in a single, fluid motion. She gathered her energy and released it in a searing arc—and drove *him back.*

The blast hit Seraphis in the side, knocking him into a broken column. His axe skid across the stone.

Sara landed, breathing hard.

And in one smooth motion—from beneath her cloak—she drew the red orb.

She didn't show it off.

She didn't say a word.

She palmed it quietly . . . and turned.

Devin saw it.

He was already watching.

He gave her the nod.

Sara's eyes narrowed.

She spun, shifted her weight—

And faked the throw toward the mural.

Seraphis, seeing the motion, screamed, "No!" He lunged again. One gauntlet outstretched—but not for the orb. For *her*.

Before Sara could adjust her stance, he unleashed a savage arc of red energy, jagged and screaming like a whip of molten glass.

It struck her square in the chest.

She was lifted off her feet and hurled backward, crashing into the ground with a cry. Dust exploded around her.

Jo gasped. Thariel stirred. Mr. Mason swore under his breath.

Sara hit the stone hard and slumped—still.

Seraphis advanced.

"I've got it now." His voice dripped with triumph, twisted with hunger. "The painter's breath, the orb of judgment—it ends in my hand!"

He reached toward where the red orb had rolled—

But then—

Sara moved.

Slowly. Weakly.

But with purpose.

She looked up—blood at the corner of her mouth, dust in her hair—and saw Devin.

Their eyes met.

Devin's hands were already raised—ready.

Sara exhaled . . . and summoned every last shred of strength.

Her fingers curled.

Blue energy surged through her palm like a river.

With a flick of light, the orb lifted, shot across the air—

And landed cleanly in Devin's grasp.

Seraphis's head whipped around.

He pivoted, ready to chase—

But Sara was faster.

With her final reserve, she slammed her hand to the earth, and a burst of blue vines of energy shot from her body—wrapping around Seraphis' limbs, his torso, his throat.

He strained, roared, fought—

But he was bound, long enough for one last throw.

Devin caught it clean—no hesitation.

And in the instant his hands wrapped around the orb—a vision flashed through him.

Him on a throne. A city behind him.

He almost lost himself in it.

"Devin!" Jo's voice broke through the fog.

Sara too, "Now!"

He blinked. Refocused.

Stepped back.

Set his feet.

Like every throw he'd ever made . . . only this one would change the world.

He cocked his arm.

Focused on the mural and threw.

The orb sailed like a comet.

A perfect spiral.

It struck the center of the painting and exploded in light.

The wall shivered and cracked open—not like a painting, but like reality itself had been peeled back.

And from it came wind—not natural wind but pull.

A vortex.

The Voidwalkers shrieked as they were lifted off the ground, drawn screaming into the portal. Their armor crumpled, their forms warping.

Seraphis turned.

He planted his feet, snarling as wind and energy clawed at his form.

"No! I AM THE BEARER! THE CROWN IS MINE—"

But something shifted.

The Crownshard in his chest began to glow—then tremble—then burn.

Seraphis clawed at it, but it was too late.

With a sound like splitting crystal, the shard erupted from his chest—ripped away by the portal's rejection. Everything tied to red energy began to unravel.

It tumbled to the ground, glowing dimly, untouched by the pull.

Seraphis's body shrank—folding inward, his armor shattering, his form twisting down to what he was before power ruined him.

"This isn't over!" he screamed, his voice wild with hatred. "Do you hear me, daughter of Lilianna? *This isn't over!*"

And then—he was gone.

Swallowed into the portal with the last of his broken army.

As the wind roared louder, the boy stumbled.

The mural's glow illuminated his eyes—and for a second, the faint red still pulsed in him lit like a beacon.

He gasped as his feet lifted off the ground. The boy grabbed hold of lamppost nearby.

"Sara!" Devin shouted.

Sara turned, eyes wide.

"Devin—*help him!*"

Devin sprinted as fast as he could across broken stone, dodging a fallen banner, and lunged just as the boy was nearly airborne.

He grabbed the boy's wrist with both hands.

"Hold on!"

The vortex tugged hard—so hard Devin's heels lifted. His muscles screamed.

But he didn't let go.

"You're not going with them," Devin said through clenched teeth.

The boy's body trembled. His fingers dug into Devin's arm. "I can feel it; it's still in me!"

Devin looked into the boy's eyes. Something began to shift.

A glow—subtle at first—began to rise from the boy's chest. Red tendrils of light coiled up through his skin like smoke escaping a burning house.

The portal pulsed in response.

The red light lifted—drawn upward and outward—

The boy screamed, not in pain, but in release.

And Devin held tighter.

The tendrils detached, trailing from the boy's hands, his temples, his heart—and were sucked into the swirling portal, vanishing like ash in a cyclone.

The red was gone.

The boy collapsed into Devin's arms—exhausted but free.

The portal shimmered one last time—then blinked out of existence.

A soft wind passed through the square.

And then there was silence.

CHAPTER 79

The portal collapsed with a final shudder, leaving only silence in its wake.

Smoke drifted lazily over the cracked stone of the plaza. Shattered pillars and toppled banners framed the battleground, but the air was still—almost reverent, as if the world itself were pausing to exhale.

The boy stood quietly near the mural, his small shoulders trembling. His hands twitched, as though testing the absence of the red glow that had long clung to his skin.

Sara approached softly.

She knelt before him, meeting his wide, uncertain eyes.

"You were never meant to carry that burden," she murmured, placing a glowing hand on his forehead.

The light shimmered—not to bind but to release.

The boy let out a shaky breath, eyes welling up, before throwing his arms around Sara in a fierce, grateful hug.

She pressed a steady hand to his back, eyes briefly closing in quiet peace.

When they parted, the boy offered her a trembling smile, wiped his face on his sleeve, and turned. He walked slowly across the plaza—toward the edge of the square.

He never looked back.

Near the far side of the square, Azazel was slumped, surrounded by a ring of Valorian soldiers.

Thariel approached slowly, limping, hand pressed against his ribs where Seraphis's axe had struck.

Azazel lifted his eyes, dark and hollow.

"So you've come to gloat."

Thariel gave a faint, pained smile.

"No. I've come to watch you stand trial for the lives you shattered."

Azazel huffed a bitter breath.

As the soldiers moved in, Thariel placed a hand briefly on Azazel's shoulder—not in forgiveness but in finality.

"Your reign is over, old friend."

Azazel was led away.

At the center of the plaza, the Crownshard lay on the ground, pulsing faintly. No longer claimed by Seraphis, no longer connected to the dark pull of the portal, it sat like a discarded relic—silent and unyielding.

Thariel approached, reverently lifting the shard with both hands.

As he turned, a glow filled the square.

The light brightened—pure, radiant, woven through the very fabric of the air.

And from the mural, Thalion emerged.

Tall, robed in shimmering white and gold, his presence filled the space with the hush of majesty. The Valorian army straightened, heads bowed in reverence.

Thalion moved first to Thariel.

"My loyal one," he murmured, resting a hand on the wounded man's shoulder. "You stood when others fell. Be restored."

Light flowed through Thariel, mending bone, sealing wounds, returning strength to his battered frame.

Thalion turned next to Mr. Mason and Eli, who stood together near the outer edge, awe clear on their faces.

"Faithful builders, quiet stewards . . . well done."

Eli blinked hard, barely holding back emotion.

Mr. Mason gave a modest nod. "Aye."

Thalion's gaze fell on Devin.

The young man instinctively straightened, his chest tight, heart pounding as the ancient eyes settled on him.

"Son of Draegora," Thalion said softly. "Courage is not the absence of fear. It is standing anyway."

Devin swallowed hard.

Thalion stepped just a little closer.

"The time of your people's restoration draws near."

Devin's eyes widened.

"There is much to rebuild . . . much to reclaim. The enemy has been set aside for now—but not forever."

Thalion offered the faintest of smiles, as if letting the words settle directly into Devin's heart.

"Your path lies yet ahead, Devin of Draegora."

At last, Thalion turned to Sara and Jo.

He looked at them as if seeing their mother's face reflected in two living mirrors.

"The grace, the fire, the beauty of Lilianna . . . endures in you both."

Jo's eyes shimmered with unshed tears.

Thalion's voice softened, his words trailing just enough mystery to stir the heart.

"Jolene . . . you will be the voice here. A keeper of memory, a light among your people. And Valoria . . . may yet call on you."

Jo blinked, startled.

Sara tilted her head, sensing something deeper in his gaze.

Thalion stepped closer.

"And you, daughter of the light . . . your heart has already chosen. Your path waits beyond."

Sara's chest tightened—but she did not look away.

As Thalion lifted his staff, the Valorian troops assembled.

Azazel, bound and escorted, was led to the mural's threshold.

With one last brilliant flare, the Valorian army stepped back through the portal, carrying their prisoner and the Crownshard with them.

The mural shimmered once more.

And when the light dimmed . . . the devastation of the battle was gone.

The square was whole.

Trees rustled gently. Birds sang.

Jo stood beside Sara, staring in quiet awe.

"Amazing . . ." Jo whispered.

Sara smiled faintly and nodded. "It is amazing."

As the last rays of Valorian light faded from the square and the mural sealed shut, a strange hush settled over Muxley.

And then—the sound of tires on gravel.

Black SUVs rolled up the road to the plaza, brakes hissing softly as federal agents stepped out, black windbreakers flashing gold FBI lettering under the lamplight.

One agent paused, looking around.

"I thought they said this place looked like a war zone?"

His partner frowned, glancing at the neatly swept stones, the unbroken windows, the rustling green trees overhead.

They shrugged.

"Guess they exaggerated."

Without further hesitation, the agents moved in, fanning out toward City Hall.

Jo and Sara stood quietly at the edge of the square, watching as Greaves, Haldine, Sykes, and several others were led away in handcuffs.

The councilmen protested—voices sharp, sputtering—but the agents were firm, reading them their rights, stacking boxes of seized documents into waiting vans.

Jo exhaled, a shaky laugh bubbling up.

"Poetic, isn't it?" she murmured.

Sara gave a faint, bittersweet smile. "Feels right. Dad spent his whole career with the FBI. It's almost like he's finally finishing what he started."

Jo's eyes shimmered softly. "Almost feels like he's still here."

Sara reached over, squeezing her sister's hand.

CHAPTER 80

The next morning dawned bright and soft over Muxley.

Birdsong filled the air, and a gentle breeze stirred the leaves as the town began to cautiously return to its rhythms. But on the edge of the Fowler property, things were anything but ordinary.

Mr. Mason stood in the blackened remains of the garage and home, hands on his hips, studying the scorched beams and twisted metal with a craftsman's eye.

Eli arrived beside him, portable terminal in hand, Lucy's soft voice crackling through the earpiece.

"Mason, Lucy's got the site scanned. She's compiling the materials list now."

Mr. Mason nodded, his Scottish lilt warm but brisk.

"Good. Tell her to send word to the crew—aye, we'll be needin' them here by sundown."

He paused, glancing toward the ruins with a glimmer of something deeper in his gaze.

"And tell 'em to bring the *Heartstone Brace*. We'll need it to restore the red door connection when the structure's sound again."

Eli gave a thumbs up.

Later that afternoon, under the shadow of the ancient oak tree, family and friends gathered.

They buried Aunt Janice beneath the old oak on her family land, just beyond where the garage once stood.

475

It was a quiet, intimate gathering. Jo and Sara stood shoulder to shoulder. Jo stepped forward, her hands shaking slightly, a folded piece of paper clenched in her grip.

She cleared her throat, blinking against the sunlight filtering through the oak's branches.

"Most of you knew Janice Fowler as a neighbor. A friend. A woman who ran the old house on the hill with a strict hand and a kind heart."

She glanced down.

"To me and Sara . . . she was Aunt Janice. The woman who showed up when we were too young to understand what we'd lost, and who never—*not once*—let us feel like we were alone."

Her voice tightened.

"She took two scared girls and made sure they were fed, made sure they had shoes on their feet, made sure they made it to school, made sure they learned how to fight back when life pushed too hard."

Jo's voice softened. "Every day, every moment, even when we fought, even when we didn't say thank you, even when we thought we knew better . . . she loved us. She fought for us. She *sacrificed* for us."

Jo drew in a trembling breath, glancing briefly at Sara, then back to the small crowd.

"And now . . . it's our turn to remember her."

She folded the paper in her hands.

"I don't know if there's a right way to say goodbye. But I do know this: Aunt Janice, you saved us more times than we can count. You were our home when the world fell apart. You fought for this town in the face of great evil. And we'll miss you, every single day."

Jo stepped back, her eyes shining, her voice quiet. "Thank you for everything."

She reached down, gently laid a small sprig of flowers at the grave, and turned to rejoin Sara—who pulled her sister into a tight, silent hug.

CHAPTER 81

Weeks later, under a bright sky, Janice's house stood whole again.

Fresh paint gleamed on the walls, the garden had been lovingly replanted, and the new garage doors bore delicate carvings worked into the wood by Mr. Mason's careful hands.

Sara stood near the edge of the property, talking softly with Devin.

"You know Thalion's words weren't just ceremony," she said gently, tucking her hair behind her ear. "Your people's time is coming, Devin. And you . . . you're not just part of it. You *are* it."

Devin let out a slow breath.

"Feels like a lot, but I know in my heart this is where I am headed."

Sara smiled faintly. "It is. And you won't be alone."

From across the yard, Mr. Mason and Eli approached, dusting their hands off from the last of the work.

"Well," Mr. Mason said, his Scottish lilt wrapping warmly through the air, "the red door's link is reset, the Heartstone Brace is anchored and sealed, and the rest o' the crew's headin' home."

Eli grinned, tucking his tablet under his arm. "And Lucy says we're already being pinged for another project. Somewhere across the sea, apparently."

Thariel stood nearby, arms folded, quiet but present.

Mr. Mason clapped a hand to Thariel's arm.

"You stayin' on for this one, old friend?"

Thariel gave a faint, knowing smile. "For now. I have one more journey to make."

Sara and Jo exchanged glances.

"You're leaving?" Jo asked softly.

Mr. Mason gave a small, fond smile.

"Aye, lass. To another realm. The work never stops."

Eli added with a playful wink, "Besides, you three are the new stars around here."

Sara hugged Mr. Mason tightly, then Eli, her eyes glistening.

"Thank you," she whispered. "For everything."

Mr. Mason ruffled her hair gently. "Och, you're a light all your own now. Don't forget that."

With final handshakes, hugs, and quiet smiles, Mr. Mason and Eli turned toward the road, their figures growing smaller as they suddenly disappeared.

The afternoon sun cast shadows across the yard.

Jo, Sara, and Devin sat quietly on the back steps, gazing out over the newly restored fields.

Sara glanced toward the horizon, a far-off look softening her features.

Jo nudged her lightly.

"You've been quiet."

Sara's smiled as she turned to Devin, her gaze gentle.

"Your people—the Draegorans—the time of their restoration is at hand. There's much to rebuild . . . and much to reclaim. As Thalion said, the enemy has been set aside for now, but not forever."

Then, slowly, she turned to Jo—her sister, her anchor.

"And you . . ." Sara murmured, "Thalion said Valoria may one day call on you too."

She reached out and gently touched Jo's shoulder.

In that instant, a flash sparked in Jo's mind—an image, fleeting but powerful: the girl from the painting above Smith's fireplace, but now riding fiercely across a mural landscape. The image was there . . . and gone.

She nodded softly, quietly, in confirmation.

Sara smiled.

"In the meantime," she added, "Thalion said your job is here: to make sure Muxley remembers what happened. To honor those who fought for this town, for this world. So that no one forgets."

Jo lifted her chin.

"I'll remember."

CHAPTER 82

As Sara finished speaking, Thariel approached quietly, his shadow stretching alongside hers.

He rested a gentle hand on her shoulder, then turned to Jo.

"Jolene," he said softly, "you'll need this."

From his belt, Thariel pulled a small ring of intricate silver keys. With careful fingers, he unhooked a single key and placed it in Jo's hand.

"This will let you enter Aunt Janice's protected space," he explained. "Insert it, turn left, and when you open the door, you'll step into the shielded realm she built. From the outside, it will just look like an ordinary garage."

Jo turned the key over in her hand, half-smiling.

"Yeah . . . still trying to get used to that."

Thariel's eyes glinted with a hint of humor.

Together, the small group moved toward the newly rebuilt garage.

Jo slid the key into the lock, turning it carefully to the left.

With a faint shimmer, the outline of the door pulsed once—then the handle clicked.

Jo opened it slowly.

As they stepped across the threshold, the space shifted.

A cool, pine-laced breeze stirred, mingling with the faint scent of old parchment.

The walls fell away.

Suddenly, they were inside a space vast beyond reason—towering shelves reached into shadows above, filled with strange artifacts, glowing crystals, and books too large for any normal shelf. Golden light flickered faintly from tucked-away corners, casting shifting patterns on the polished wooden floors.

Devin nodded, remembering his encounter with Janice and Halbridge in this place.

They moved deeper into the space, passing through a long hallway where faint echoes of past moments seemed to linger—Smith's library, the Healing Hallow, the vault, the orbs. All pieces of a greater puzzle.

At last, they stepped out onto a broad wooden terrace overlooking a lush, moonlit garden below. Soft waterfall sounds trickled nearby, and delicate flowers shimmered under pale silver light.

Set at the center of the garden stood three tall murals.

Thariel stepped forward, his tall form calm and steady. He raised a hand slightly and motioned the others to follow.

Together, they descended the broad wooden staircase, its railings carved with delicate Valorian symbols, the steps opening onto the moonlit garden below.

Jo slowed as they approached the three murals standing tall at the garden's heart.

She stared at them, eyes wide.

"Did . . . you make these?" she asked softly, glancing at Sara.

Sara nodded.

Jo moved closer, running her fingers lightly along

the edge of one of the painted surfaces. The mural shimmered faintly under her touch.

She paused at the one on the left.

Draegoran symbols lined its borders—mountains, banners, a crown, and an ancient throne.

Her gaze shifted to the mural on the right.

And there, captured mid-stride, was the image of a girl on horseback—the same girl Jo had seen in flashes, and in the painting above Smith's fireplace.

Devin approached the Draegora mural slowly, his boots crunching softly over the garden path.

He paused, staring up at the storm-lit mountains, the fierce banners, the carved symbols of a kingdom he barely understood but somehow already belonged to.

He let out a shaky breath, shoulders tensing.

Sara stepped quietly beside him, her voice warm and steady.

"This is where you begin, Devin. Where your people begin again."

He turned, eyes glinting faintly.

"And what if I'm not ready?" he whispered.

Sara smiled softly. "You are. Even if you don't believe it yet."

Jo came forward slowly, her hands fidgeting at her sides.

For a moment, she just stood there, searching his face.

"Devin . . ." she began, her voice rough.

He smiled faintly. "Don't tell me you're going soft on me, Jolene Sweeney."

Jo gave a watery laugh, stepping closer.

"You've been part of this from the beginning, Dev.

Part of *us*." Her voice faltered. She reached up, lightly touching his arm. "You matter. You always have."

Devin swallowed hard. "Jo . . ."

She drew in a breath, fighting back the wave rising in her chest.

"Come back, okay?" she whispered. "Promise me you'll come back."

He reached up, brushing a thumb gently across her cheek. "I promise."

Jo's breath shuddered, and before she could think twice, she surged forward, pulling him into a tight, fierce embrace.

For a heartbeat, Devin just froze. Then he closed his arms around her, holding her like he didn't want to let go.

Sara stood a few steps away, quiet, her eyes soft as she watched.

Finally, after a long, trembling moment, Jo stepped back, wiping quickly at her eyes.

Devin turned—and walked over to Sara. For a moment, they just looked at each other.

Sara gave him a small, trembling smile. "So . . . I guess this is it, huh?"

Devin nodded. He gave her a crooked smile. "You've saved me more times than I can count."

Sara blinked hard, her throat tightening. "No . . . you were the one who stood up for me," she whispered. "Back in the park . . . when this all started."

Devin's smile softened, his eyes shimmering faintly. "Well," he murmured, "looks like we're even, huh?"

Sara smiled.

Without another word, he reached out and pulled her

into a quick, tight hug, one hand cradling the back of her head like an older brother.

Sara pressed her face briefly against his shoulder, swallowing the lump in her throat. "Come back to us," she whispered.

Devin pulled back just enough to meet her eyes. "I will." His voice was steady now, his gaze clear. "I've got too many reasons to."

He then turned to Thariel.

For a moment, no one spoke.

Then Devin stepped forward and extended his hand.

"Thank you," Devin said quietly. "For everything."

Thariel grasped his hand firmly, his expression gentle but strong.

"You carry your people's future, Devin. Walk well."

He held Devin's gaze a moment longer.

"And remember—you will not walk alone. There are those waiting to stand with you. Use the strength you've been given . . . and the help you will find."

Devin drew in a steadying breath, his eyes flickering with the faintest spark of hope.

With one last, lingering look at them all, he turned.

He touched the mural's surface.

It rippled, parted.

And Devin of Draegora stepped through, vanishing into the next chapter of his destiny.

The garden grew still after Devin disappeared.

Sara stood quietly, her fingers glowing faintly at her sides, gazing at the mural Devin had just gone through. After a long, still moment, she slowly turned.

Across the garden, on the far side, another blank wall stood—untouched, empty, shimmering faintly under the moonlight.

Sara looked at Thariel.

He met her gaze, his expression calm, steady, knowing.

Sara gave a small, quiet nod.

Together, they crossed the garden.

Sara lifted her hands, and blue energy swirled up her arms like living light, wrapping around her fingers as she raised them toward the wall.

Jo watched as Sara began to paint—not with brushes, but with motion, weaving arcs of glowing power across the stone. Each stroke left behind a line of delicate, radiant color, shaping a shimmering doorway.

Thariel stood beside her, calm and watchful.

When the final brushstroke hung glowing in the air, Thariel lifted his hand.

A brilliant blue orb materialized in his palm, pulsing softly.

He stepped forward and touched it gently to the mural.

The wall came alive.

It rippled, the surface folding inward, until the mural glowed with depth, no longer just an image but a portal, a path, a way forward.

Jo froze. Her heart pounded as the realization struck her.

"Sara . . . you're leaving, aren't you?"

Sara hesitated.

Then—reluctantly, heartbreakingly—she turned, eyes shimmering, and gave a small, solemn nod.

Jo's face crumpled.

In an instant, she crossed the space between them and threw her arms around her sister, clutching her tightly.

Both sisters broke into tears, their shoulders shaking as they held each other hard, neither wanting to let go.

Sara buried her face in Jo's hair, whispering softly, "I love you so much."

Jo's voice cracked, her fingers gripping tighter. "I love you too. Please come back someday."

Sara pulled back just enough to meet her sister's gaze. "I will. I promise."

As Sara gently released her sister, she stepped back toward Thariel, wiping the tears from her cheeks.

But Jo lingered.

She turned, facing Thariel—this tall, ageless warrior, once hidden behind the name Smith, who had stood by their side through every battle.

They locked eyes.

For a moment, neither spoke.

Then Jo gave a small, wry smile.

"Sorry I was so hard on you at first," she said, her voice tinged with humor. "You know . . . when I thought you were just some weird guy hanging out with my sister.

Thariel chuckled softly.

"And I thought you were just a fierce, sharp-tongued girl who didn't trust anyone."

Jo smirked, shaking her head.

"Guess we both turned out more complicated than that, huh?"

Thariel's expression softened.

"You have become someone remarkable, Jolene. Strong. Loyal. Braver than you know."

Jo gave a quick, playful brush at the corner of her eye.

"Well . . . don't go soft on me now, Thariel."

He smiled, bowing his head lightly in respect.

"The Healing Hallows changed us both, Jo. And when the time comes, Valoria will rise to meet you once more."

Jo drew in a breath, feeling the weight of his words settle deep.

Sara turned back, her hand brushing lightly against Thariel's arm.

He gave her a nod—quiet, steady.

Together, they faced the glowing mural.

Sara looked over her shoulder one last time, her eyes meeting Jo's.

No words were needed.

With a final, shimmering pulse, Sara and Thariel stepped forward.

The mural rippled, light folding around them—and they were gone.

CHAPTER 83

Halbridge sat alone at his desk, pen in hand, the faint scratch of ink filling the room as the sun slipped below the hills.

His journal lay open before him—pages filled with hurried notes, sketched symbols, names, dates, half-finished thoughts.

He stared at the last line he'd written:

"It began with a mural."

Halbridge leaned back slowly, exhaling.

"And it ends, for now, with memory."

In the weeks that followed, Jo became the voice of the story.

She spoke in the town square. She shared in quiet interviews. She told the tale over coffee at Crowley's Coffee Shop, where she used to sit with Sara, watching the world pass by.

She spoke of the battle, of the heroes, of the realms beyond.

At first, the town listened—awed, wide-eyed.

For a time, the streets of Muxley buzzed with the wonder of what they had witnessed. The FBI cleaned out the corruption, the murals stood tall, and the whispers of magic and valor filled every corner café and newspaper column.

But slowly . . . as time passed . . .

Doubt crept in.

Whispers began to change.

The stories became embellished, then questioned, then dismissed.

People began to wonder if it had all been exaggerated. A strange night, blown out of proportion. Tales twisted by fear and excitement.

And eventually, as they always do, the stories faded.

They became legend.

Then myth.

And the town of Muxley, once shaken by forces beyond its understanding, slowly settled back into the quiet, sleepy place it had always been.

But not for Jo.

She never stopped telling the truth.

Whenever she passed a young artist at the Savor Street Market, paintbrush in hand, lost in creation, her heart would ache softly.

She would think of Sara.

She would think of Devin.

Of Thariel, Mr. Mason, Eli. Aunt Janice.

And she would remember.

Always.

CHAPTER 84

YEARS LATER

Click. The light turned on, illuminating the dust floating in the air. The garage was packed with boxes stacked from floor to ceiling, filled with years of memories, old belongings, and forgotten keepsakes. The loft at one end was crammed with storage containers, so full it seemed it might collapse under the weight. Beneath the loft, a small worktable was cluttered with some tools, artwork leaning against the wall, a palette, and a smock. For two young children, the overcrowded space with barely any room to walk was intimidating, especially since they were on a mission to find one specific item.

"How are we ever going to find it?" the girl asked, her voice tinged with doubt.

"Let's start looking in the boxes," the boy replied with determination.

They were hoping to find a game they wanted to play that afternoon and were told it was "in the garage," which didn't help much. "Let's move this one," said the girl, pointing to a heavy box. The boy joined her, and they both grunted and pushed. The packing tape on the box underneath had come loose, and the lid popped up slightly. Curiosity piqued, they opened the box and found old photo albums on top. The girl picked one up and started thumbing through

491

the photos. Both of them smiled and giggled at some of the pictures.

One box led to another. Time passed as they opened box after box. They found old dresses and costumes, which they promptly tried on, pretending to be kings and queens, military soldiers, and princes and princesses. Hours slipped by, and they forgot about their original quest. They were engrossed in new adventures.

After conquering kingdoms and slaying dragons, they stumbled upon a large leather-bound binder in one of the boxes. It was tied shut with a leather string. The children exchanged looks of excitement as if they had discovered a hidden treasure. The girl lifted it out and set it on top of a nearby box. She pulled one end of the string, and the knot gave way. Inside was a sketchpad.

They began to flip through the dazzling drawings of waterfalls, cabins in the woods, mystical creatures, and ordinary people. Each new page elicited gasps and exclamations of "Wow," "Look at that," and "I wish I could draw like that." The pictures stirred their imaginations.

"Let's pretend we are at the waterfall in the picture," suggested the boy. "We have to cross over without falling."

"In a minute," said the girl, smiling. She kept turning the pages, entranced by the magical drawings.

Midway through the sketchpad, the binder slipped from her lap and hit the floor. A different compartment in the binder opened, and something slid across the floor. The children exchanged wide-eyed glances, their eyes getting big as if they had just discovered the most amazing thing. They walked over to it, curiosity piqued.

It was a key with an ornate leaf symbol on it with an emerald in the center of the leaf.

They both sat there staring at it in silence for several minutes, mesmerized by its intricate design and the sense of mystery it evoked.

"What's that?" asked the boy, his eyes wide with curiosity.

"I don't know," said the girl. She bent over to pick it up. The key was old-fashioned, almost like something out of a fairytale.

"Can I see it?" the boy asked eagerly.

"Let's bring it over to the table and look at it," replied the girl. They examined the key closely, marveling at its craftsmanship, but they had no idea what it might unlock.

They placed the key aside and returned to the binder. Inside was another leather folder with a peculiar drawing on it—a stick figure of a man throwing a boomerang.

The girl rubbed her finger over the drawing. "You gonna open it?" asked the boy.

"You do it," said the girl.

"All right," the boy agreed. He took the folder and began to open the seal, releasing a small cloud of dust. Inside was a large stack of paper with a cover letter on top. A tiny envelope was paper-clipped to the corner. They set the small envelope aside, looked at the cover letter, and were going to begin to read.

Just as they were about to start reading the letter, a woman entered the garage, startling the kids. They quickly hid the letter and the key, adopting innocent looks while their costumes and dresses gave them away.

The woman grinned and said, "You guys having fun

in here? It's time to eat. Put everything away and come out back to the deck."

"Okay, Grandma Jolene," they replied in unison.

Grandma Jolene, with a twinkle of curiosity in her eyes, asked, "What did you guys find in here?"

"Oh . . . nothing," they answered, trying to sound nonchalant.

Grandma Jolene smiled knowingly and walked away. The kids looked at each other and started to giggle.

"Let's keep the key a secret," said the girl.

The boy nodded in agreement. "Deal."

The children straightened up the garage as best they could, putting boxes back in place and tidying up their makeshift adventure playground. The boy left the garage first, eager to join the others. The girl paused for a moment, her heart pounding with excitement and curiosity. She reached into her pocket and pulled out the key with the leaf symbol and the letter.

She unfolded the letter and read it aloud in a whisper, the words resonating with a strange, magical cadence:

> *"Like the leaf of new spring*
> *Or the first fall of snow*
> *The change is upon you*
> *This you must know*
>
> *Turn the key to the left,*
> *though it seems odd*
> *Trust the magic*
> *to give its nod*
> *Then with a deep breath*

and prayers ascending
Walk through the door
without pretending

What will you find
When you step through
Who can say
The adventure's for you

Step out, be brave,
As fear starts to swarm
Like the Eagle who flies
In the eye of the storm."

The girl stood there for a moment, the weight of the poem sinking in. She traced the outline of the key with her fingers, feeling a mix of anticipation and fear. What could it mean? What door did the key open, and what awaited her on the other side?

Alexa held the key tightly as she left the garage, the cool metal warm from her grip. She closed the red door behind her. Once closed, she noticed that the lock looked different from others she had seen—more intricate and ancient. She glanced toward the deck, where her family was gathered by the lake, preparing dinner. The sounds of laughter and clinking utensils floated over to her.

"Alexa, come on! Time to eat!" Grandma Jolene called out.

"Coming!" Alexa replied. She paused, looking back to make sure no one was watching. Holding her breath, she moved the key toward the keyhole. It fit perfectly. Her eyes widened in surprise and excitement. "To the left, though it seems odd," she murmured to herself, recalling the poem. She turned the key left, and it clicked. She pulled the key out and waited. Nothing happened.

Alexa shrugged her shoulders, a mix of disappointment and relief washing over her. She turned to leave, heading back to join her family. As she walked away, she suddenly remembered the game they had originally come to find. She turned back toward the garage, determined to retrieve it.

Approaching the red door again, she reached for the handle. Just as her fingers touched it, Grandma Jolene's voice rang out from the deck. "Wait, Alexa!"

But it was too late. Alexa opened the door and stepped inside, closing it behind her.

A Personal Request from the Author

Dear Reader,

If this book moved you, taught you something new,
or simply kept you turning the pages,
would you take a moment to leave a review on Amazon?

Your feedback helps other readers discover the book—
and it means the world to me as an author.

Thank you for being part of this journey.

Serves new and emerging authors
to help them write, publish, and promote their books.
Are you ready to share your story?

Visit us!
www.silversmithpress.com

www.ingramcontent.com/pod-product-compliance
Lightning Source LLC
Chambersburg PA
CBHW011400010726
47495CB00009B/2706